contents

Praise for Carrie Adams and *The Godmother*

"Book clubs rejoice! We've got a winner! Carrie Adams has written a debut novel as brilliant, funny, and human as her protagonist Tessa King. I fell into Tessa's world from page one and did not want to let her go as she goes on the emotional journey of a lifetime. This is a book full of real people, flawed and glorious and occasionally unnerving, but what comes to pass is a great lesson in perseverance and hope. I loved it."

—Adriana Trigiani, *New York Times* bestselling author of the
Big Stone Gap series and *Lucia, Lucia*

"First-time novelist Carrie Adams brings her British sass and wit to the endearing story of Tessa and her travails, but ultimately the lessons learned are of love and friendship with realistic heartbreak thrown in . . . the story will sweep you off your feet." —*USA Today*

"The first-time author bucks chick-lit convention with a clever, unpredictable novel about a smart, glamorous but perpetually single London lawyer's belated coming-of-age."   —*Washington Post*

"Adams keeps the story fresh and gratifyingly untidy."
—*Entertainment Weekly*

"A perky debut considers whether a Londoner's life of drinking, clubbing and one-night stands is more enviable than her friends' bumpy marriages and parenting woes . . . engaging."
—*Kirkus Reviews*

"[A] look into the fears, doubts, and desires that make and break marriages, this debut novel from Londoner Adams is notches up from the usual chick and mom lit fare."   —*Publishers Weekly*

"A poignant, surprisingly insightful first novel."
—*Parenting* magazine

"Adams' savvy debut explores modern womanhood through a hip 30-something godmother's musings."   —*OK!* magazine

the
godmother

a novel

CARRIE ADAMS

AVON

An Imprint of HarperCollinsPublishers

To Tiffany and Jokey
I owe a great deal to your buffer zone

the
godmother

a sinking feeling

I knew my luck had changed when I was upgraded to business class on my return journey. My curious gold-encrusted traveling companion made the long flight pass too quickly. He turned towards the transit lounge with the unforgettable words, "If you're ever passing through Vladivostok . . ." I waved him off, set my wheelie bag on the ground and, after five wound-licking, soul-searching weeks away, headed for home.

This was it. My moment to start again. I had dealt with what had been a hideous year and I'd put it behind me. OK, it was only September, but I had decided to return to the academic timetable. Anything to be able to punctuate what had been and now. New year. New start. New me. Tessa King was back. I smiled at everyone. Sharing the love and our good fortune at being alive. The Customs official eyed me warily and promptly took my bag apart. I didn't mind. Nothing was going to ruin my return. Having found nothing but festering clothes and gifts for my godchildren, he let me go. I was almost jogging by the time I reached the sliding glass doors. An expectant smile quivered at the side of my mouth, ready to burst forth the moment I saw my welcome-home party. The doors opened. I stepped through and yelled "Hi" at a woman I'd never met before.

"Sorry," I said. "You look just like my friend."

Francesca would have been mortally offended. The woman was older, shorter and wearing velour. I looked around me to check I was where I thought I was. I was. But she wasn't.

I must be mistaken. Francesca and I had made this plan on the day of my tearful departure. My greatest friend from university had promised to escape the clutches of domesticity to spend a lost afternoon drinking wine and catching up. It was only imagining this moment that had got me through the previous five weeks. I looked around again. Double-checking the faces of people who averted their eyes, and the placard-holding drivers who didn't. My smile wouldn't accept there was no friendly face waiting for me and kept grinning at people who didn't want to be grinned at. Maybe I was early? I checked my watch, knowing full well I wasn't. Eventually my smile accepted its fate and retracted. I sat down on my suitcase while all around me travelers ran into the open arms of their loved ones. I chose not to notice the many others who hurried on alone to the trains and buses. I only saw what I feared. I had gone to India hoping I could downward dog my way out of trouble and I was sure I had succeeded. A peppery heat prickled my eyes. Damn it, how many uddiyana bandhas would it take?

"Tessa, over here. Tessa!"

I stared at my phone, wondering whether I could be bothered to go through a month's worth of messages to get to the one Francesca may have left if she hadn't forgotten completely.

"TESSA!"

It was my name, but a man's voice, so I didn't register it.

"TESSA, you deaf old cow, it's Nick!"

I looked up. Francesca's husband, red-faced, was waving frantically at me. Nick and Francesca had been together since our first year at university. A staggering eighteen years. I knew him as well as I knew Fran and immediately my spirits rose.

"Welcome home. So sorry we're late, traffic. Anyway, you don't want to know about that. How are you? You look terrific."

We? Was Francesca here? Who was with the kids? And then I saw Caspar, my fifteen-year-old godson. The fact that I had a godson who was beginning to resemble a man was alarming, but he had arrived early to our party and I still marvel at Nick and Francesca's brave decision to keep the baby and make a go of it. These days Caspar reminds me of how far I have failed to come. He sloped towards me. We are very close, my godson and I. Throwing down my bag, I opened my arms wide. Not so long ago he would have run the length of the airport and buried himself under my neck. But he was about to turn sixteen; times were changing. I didn't realize then, how much.

"Hey, handsome, you are getting so big . . ." I saw the smile in his eyes, but nothing else in his body language changed. He was bristling with awareness. I know a defensive position when I see it. I'd been carrying myself around like that for months. I lowered my arms.

"You might like to know that my plane had a four-hour stopover in Dubai."

"Huh?"

"United Arab Emirates." There was no register on Caspar's face. "The Middle East? Ever heard of it?"

"Yeah," mumbled Caspar.

"Caspar, don't mumble," said Nick.

"Well," I interrupted, not wanting there to be a teenage scene, "it's the shopping capital of the world. Tax-free. Very iPod friendly."

That got his attention. Caspar has wanted an iPod Nano since they came out. But Nick doesn't earn that sort of money and Francesca doesn't work. Which is where I, the fairy godmother, often come in. No wonder he loves me . . . I'd love me.

"Isn't it your birthday next weekend?"

"Yeah."

"Well, let's just say I got so friendly with the sales assistant he gave me a photo of his kids. Who, by the way, live in a different country and only get to see their father every two years—just in case you were feeling a little hard done by today."

"I get enough of the Third World shit at home, thanks." Caspar sloped away. I turned to Nick with an open mouth. Sloping? Backchat? This wasn't my godson.

Nick shook his head, exhaled long and hard, then lowered his voice. "He's being a nightmare, I'm so sorry. Fran was desperate to come today, I mean desperate, but someone at school has swapped birthdays around, and she's got to bring Katie's party forward three weeks to tomorrow."

"Swapped birthdays?"

"Don't ask. We got gazumped."

"On a house?" I asked, not following.

"EuroDisney."

"Are you OK, Nick?"

He screwed up his face. Reminding me of Caspar. Reminding me of the Nick I met in the library, a spotty nineteen-year-old, a smitten Francesca standing goggle-eyed next to him. Didn't see the attraction myself at first, which is probably a good thing. They were inseparable from that moment onwards. They just fit, those two, always had. Two weeks into our third year, Francesca appeared on my doorstep in tears. She was two months pregnant. I look at the photos now, and though we thought we were grown up at the time, we were children. It was an awesome responsibility to take on.

"I'm fine," said Nick. "Birthday parties just don't seem to be what they used to be. You know how it is . . ."

That's one of the strange things about my friends. They all assume I know what it's like. But how could I? I have no kids. I don't even have the responsibility of a goldfish. What I do know is that family comes first, always. Lost in Legoland, I call it. Five weeks away, after everything that had happened, and still Francesca couldn't escape for one day. It wasn't like she was a novice, it wasn't like she didn't have a willing partner, it wasn't like she didn't have five weeks' warning . . .

"It doesn't matter," I lied. "Do you mind if I pick up a coffee before we get in the car?" I needed a pick-me-up. Look at me—not been on British soil for an hour and already I was back to my old toxic ways.

"Course. My shout," said Nick.

I walked over to where Caspar had thrown himself on to some seats and handed my bags to him. "Look after these for me while your dad and I get some drinks." I left him before he had a chance to protest.

I rejoined Nick. "Sorry about your welcome-home party," he said, glancing over at his bolshy son.

I couldn't think of anything nice to say. It was only later that I realized Caspar had thrown himself a little welcome-home party of his own. In my wallet.

Sitting in Nick's beaten-up old Volvo, it felt like I'd never been away. Was that a new banana skin wedged under the hand-break or the same one that had been there on the day I left to cleanse my soul? I counted seven squashed mini-cartons of juice in the footwell, a drawing, a reminder from British Telecom and a ruler. Domestic detritus. Something I thought I left to others. But now, well, I'd had a long time on my own to think about what it was I really wanted. The mess in the footwell was beginning to look less like rubbish and more like the collage of a happy, fulfilling life.

It became clear very quickly that father and son were not speaking to one another. But I, who had been in contemplative silence for weeks, was now high on caffeine and had verbal diarrhea. I told them about the other people on the yoga retreat and the many embarrassing positions I had found myself in. Caspar, who normally shared all his secrets and those of his classmates with me, didn't say a word and pretended not to be listening. His stubborn little face made me want to be all the more outrageous.

"The worst moment was when I farted in the middle of a tricky balancing position, burst into giggles and came tumbling down to the ground with an unladylike thud." I watched Caspar carefully in the wing mirror. He smiled at that one. I found his secret smile reassuring. Encouraged, I went further and told them about the unreciprocated advances of a short Swiss woman who took rather a shine to me.

"At first I was grateful to have a friend. I should have pretended to be a recovering trust-fund junky with two kids called Zebedee and Dewdrop, but I blew it. Lawyers and hippies don't mix. Anyway, this Swiss woman got friendly over a bowl of tofu in the second week and I was desperate by then. I believed her when she told me she was studying to be a masseuse and needed the practice. I didn't even flinch when she told me to remove all my clothes as it made it easier to get to the hips."

That broke the deadlock.

"Did you?" asked Caspar, unable to hold out any longer.

"Oh yes I did."

"What happened?" asked Nick.

"She said my sexual chakra was blocked and she wanted to work deeper."

"Oh no," laughed Caspar.

"Oh yes."

"What? What happened?" asked Nick, sounding worried.

"What do you think happened, Dad?"

Nick looked perplexed. "I don't know."

"I don't think we should tell him," I said, looking back at Caspar. "He's not ready."

"He may never recover. Just tell me, though, did she . . . ?" Caspar let the question hang in the air.

"Oh yes."

"Did what?" shouted Nick.

"Bloody hell, what did you do?" asked Caspar, streaks ahead of his father.

"What do you think I did?"

"Stood up and decked her?"

"No, I lay there like an English prude, then said thank you very much, yes, that was interesting, and spent the rest of the week in hiding."

Caspar laughed. "You wimp."

We drove on as Caspar continued to laugh intermittently in the back of the car until Nick suddenly piped up.

"Oh my God! Deeper, as in deeper."

I looked at Caspar and we laughed again. Nick had finally worked it out. Then another thought came to him.

"How do you know about this stuff, young man?" It always made me laugh, when Nick tried to be a grown-up. "In my mind, what a fifteen-year-old boy doesn't know about girl-on-girl action isn't worth knowing," I answered for Caspar.

For that I got his full-blown, toothy grin and I felt happy again. That was a smile worth coming home for.

Nick pulled up outside my building. It's a modern block full of vastly superior flats to my own, but thanks to a government initiative, I have one of the two studio apartments that property developers have to put in or they don't get planning permission these days. I am a professional with a view of the river and I tell you now, although small, it is my pride and joy.

The doorman peered at the arriving battered brown Volvo, saw me grinning through the window and waved with two hands.

"I'm so happy to be home," I exclaimed.

Nick and Caspar ferried my bags into the open-plan hallway while I allowed myself to be fussed over by Roman. Roman is the man, after my oldest male friend Ben, who knows more about me than anyone at this moment in my life. This Georgian émigré, in his late fifties, with an arthritic knee, was the one who called the police when my ex-boss came calling at all hours of the night. Roman blocked the door when he tried to get in. Roman learnt to recognize his handwriting and siphoned off the tortured prose that the postman delivered on a regular basis and warned me in advance. But he is equally good at turning a blind eye to men of all sizes, shapes and colors who have come and gone in the night. He has occasionally pressed the button on the lift when I couldn't see straight, and in emergencies let me into my own apartment.

"Welcome home, Mizz King." He took my hand in his hand and shook it vigorously.

"Hello, Roman."

"I've been counting the days," he said. "So much to tell . . ."

Roman and I often swapped gossip about my fellow residents.

"Can't wait to hear."

Nick and Caspar took their cue. "Then we'll leave you in this gentleman's capable care. It's great to have you back."

"Thanks, Nick," I replied. "And thanks for picking me up, you really didn't have to."

"I know. But if I hadn't got Caspar out of the house, Francesca would have killed him. Heathrow was as good as anywhere."

I smiled and wondered whether he knew how belittling he'd just been. Of course he didn't. It was Nick, the softest man I knew. Still, I didn't want to be anyone's last resort any more.

Nick reached the door. "Francesca won't be happy unless I can tell her you're better. Are you? Have you recovered?"

Did he mean had I recovered from being sidelined by my friend's children? Or being stalked by my boss? Or from just being single? Barren? Alone?

"Yes." I smiled. "Absolutely."

"Good. I'll tell her." He went off happy. Taking me at my word.

I put my arm around Caspar. "I know you're cross with your parents for some reason, but please try and remember that I am not the enemy. And if that isn't a reason to be nice to me, remember the iPod."

For a second he leaned into my shoulder. I kissed his head.

"See you Saturday," I mumbled into his curly hair. "Be nice to your mum, even though she stood me up and, like the selfish harridan that she is, once again put her children before my alcoholic needs. And remember, just because your father doesn't watch porn, it doesn't make him a bad person."

I was joking. But in retrospect, perhaps that wasn't obvious enough to Caspar.

As soon as the door closed, Roman put his "Back in five minutes" sign on the desk and picked up my bag.

"Mrs. B in five finally got wind of what her husband was up to while she was away in the country."

Mrs. B is a portly woman who always has the faint aroma of Labrador about her. Even though she's terrifying and has a vast bust, that didn't mean I enjoyed my weekly journeys in the lift with her weekly skinnier, younger stand-in.

"It was terrible. She turned up unexpected, found the other woman here and fell to pieces. Begged him not to leave. She ended up in my kitchen talking for hours and hours about her marriage, their absolutely hopeless children, and him. Such emotion, you'd never know it."

We were in the lift now. I pressed 11 and felt the excitement of coming home bubble inside me. "She's probably never spoken like that to anyone," I said, realizing as I said it that I may well have been talking about myself.

He knitted his Newt Gingrich eyebrows. "She won't look at me now, though."

I put a reassuring hand on Roman's arm. "She's English. Don't take it personally."

Roman helped me to the door of my flat then looked at me seriously over his moustache.

"No sign of him," said Roman, my own private security guard. "Not once. I've been keeping an eye out."

I swallowed.

"He's gone for good this time, yes?"

I sincerely hoped so. I held up two crossed fingers.

"Do you need some milk?" he asked. "I have spare."

"No, thanks. I'll go shopping in a minute. But thank you, Roman. It's really nice to see you."

He carried my bags over the threshold, then left me. I was home.

My apartment is basically a box, divided into four areas. The first, immediately on the left, is the bathroom. That has the only full-height wall in the place. I allocated a quarter of the space to the bathroom; the builder thought I was mad, but I told him I loved baths. Which I do, but actually I had designed the room with sex in mind. I'd even had stone slabs gritted under the shower—I didn't want to slip at a crucial moment. There is under-floor heating, a bath embedded into the wall and the whole thing is tiled in slate, except for a panel of mirrored cupboards above the basin. It is a "wet room," with all the Benny Hill, double entendre humor. Sadly, though, it has yet to be christened.

A lot of thought went into the rest of my flat too. For a while I became queen of the swatches. Of course, I ended up painting everything white. Anyhow, where the wall ends my kitchen begins. Delineated by a bar. I like bars too. The rest is everything else. Living space and bedroom. Not a room as such, but a bed hidden behind a chest-high wall which doubles up as a bookshelf. I love books too. Can never throw them away, even the crap ones. It would seem cramped but it's on the south-east corner of the building and one side of the box is floor-to-ceiling glass. The view is spectacular.

I walked straight to the window and stared at the swirling mass of brown river water a hundred feet below me. So different from the cool waterways of Kerala, but, in its own way, just as beautiful. Yes, I was glad to be back. Yes, I was recovered. Sabbaticals were all very well and good, but life could not be lived running away. I knew I should unpack, sort out my washing and get some food but instead I threw myself on the sofa and got straight on the phone.

Mum and Dad live in a small cottage in Buckinghamshire. They moved there when Dad retired. Which was years ago now. He's well into his eighties, though I swear you wouldn't know it. He has drunk from the spring of eternal youth. Mum, on the other hand, wasn't so lucky. She was diagnosed with MS twelve years ago and is only well because she takes such good care of herself. Everyone said my mother was mad to marry a man twenty years her senior because she'd spend her life caring for an incontinent old cripple. That's life for you, always throwing you a curve ball. My parents have taught me a lot of things; one of them is that life can't be planned because you never know what's round the corner.

"My darling girl, so glad you're home safe and sound," said Dad. "How are you? Did you get my letters?"

"They were wonderful, I was almost there myself. I've always said you can write beautifully."

I can do everything beautifully. I'm his only daughter. Only child. I once asked them why they hadn't had any more, thinking there was some dark secret. But it turned out they only wanted one. People ask me whether I missed having siblings. How can you miss something you've never had? All I ever saw of my friends' siblings when I was a kid was the constant fighting. So, no, I didn't. I probably would now, but I have a small group of friends who replace them. They are my siblings. We all mean a great deal to one another. I chatted on with Dad for a few more minutes only to discover that my poor mum was already in the car waiting to go and see some friends. Rather than get her back in the house, I said I'd ring in the morning. I said goodbye to my father, bolstered by the pride I always hear in his voice, and started to dial another number.

Billy is the mother of my second godchild. An incredibly special little girl called Cora. Billy's real name is something unpronounce-able in Polish. I can't even remember why the name Billy stuck, but it did. We rented flats across the hall from each other in our twenties and became such good mates that when a cheaper two-bedroom flat became available, we moved in together. That all changed when Christoph arrived on the scene, stole Billy's heart, then slowly began to mutilate it.

Across town the phone in Billy's tiny flat in Kensal Rise started to ring. Cora, the wisest seven-year-old I know, picked up the phone.

"Hello, Billy and Cora Tarrenot's rezi dents."

"Hi, Cora, it's Godmummy T."

"Hiiiiiiii, where have you been?"

"In India."

"Did that man at work chase you there?"

"In a way."

"On foot?"

"Not exactly. Have you been cleaning your teeth?" Cora was tenacious, you had to change the subject to something she's more interested in. It happened to be hygiene.

"By bike then? Or did he swim across the Indian Ocean with the
migrating whales?"

Obviously the curiosity with hygiene had been replaced. Five
weeks is a long time in a seven-year-old's life. So I went for the one
that always worked.

"I brought you a present from India."

"An elephant with small ears?"

"How did you know?"

"I'm weird like that," said Cora.

Cora always made me smile. She couldn't help it. "Yes, you are
and I love you for it. Is your mum around?"

"She's out, but you can talk to Magda if you like."

Magda was the au pair. "That's OK. Just tell your mum I called."

"I will," said Cora, and promptly put the phone down on me. Billy
was trying to refine her telephone skills. I hoped she'd fail in this
task. I didn't want her growing up any faster than she was already.

Helen, the mother of my most recent additions to the godchild pile,
was up to her neck in it with five-month-old twins. I glanced at my
watch. There was no point calling now. It was bath-time. Helen had
constant help, but the twins still consumed her every waking hour.
When I left for India she was still breastfeeding them. I hadn't seen
much of her. It wasn't that I hadn't tried, but she had very particular
views about how she fed the twins. She liked to do it alone, in the
nursery, with Mozart playing. I'm not joking. Finding a time to see
her between feeds was nearly impossible. She didn't like leaving the

house, and she took a lot of naps. One of the sad things I realized in India was that if I had just met her for the first time, we would not have become friends. Way, way too neurotic, she doesn't work and she's obsessed with her boys. But I had met her a long time ago on a beach in Vietnam, swinging from a hammock, laughing like a train, high on acid. I will never forget it. Two of my three best mates from school and I had gone to Vietnam after our A levels. We had visited every burial site, every temple, every battle ground in the country. Then we met Helen. Half-Chinese, half-Swiss, she was the most beautiful creature we'd ever seen. A concoction of Lucy Liu and Kate Moss, her limbs stretched on for miles. She is more graceful now but back then she jerked awkwardly like a newborn foal; perhaps that was just the drugs. Her long, arrow-straight dark hair spilled down her back like ink. She was the only backpacker I met who traveled with a hairdryer. She was the only backpacker I met who traveled without a backpack.

Helen is what you'd call privileged. Her father was a very success-ful Hong Kong businessman who'd always looked East for opportu-nities. When he died unexpectedly young, Helen had inherited her father's businesses but not his business acumen. She was a child of the universe—or so she told us. She quoted excerpts from the "De-siderata" endlessly. With little in the way of parental guidance, Helen took her bearings from a piece of writing. We were mesmerized by her and soon just as intoxicated as her. Many a happy evening passed after that day, getting stoned on China Beach with Helen reciting the poem to us until we too knew it by heart. Now she has it framed up on the wall alongside the dressing table in her enormous Notting Hill Gate house. I think it is about the only thing that reminds Helen of the girl she used to be.

Things are very different now. Why are we still friends? Because Helen is the only person in the world who knows all my secrets, and

I, in turn, understand all her extenuating circumstances, so I perse-
vere. Sometimes I even have to recite excerpts of the "Desiderata" to
myself to quell the desire to throttle her. But I've got to be honest, it
had been getting harder.

Changing tack, I dialed Claudia's number. We've been friends since
we were seven. She hasn't got kids. She has Al, though. Tall, bald,
reliable Al. It was Al and Claudia whom I'd traveled around Vietnam
with. He'd joined our school when we were in our early teens. Halfway through our twenties, their long-standing friendship metamor-
phosed into something else. They did that fairy-tale, romantic thing
of accidentally falling in love with each other. Any doubts over the
wisdom of such a high-risk coupling had been eroded by watching
them withstand more heartache in the last decade than most couples
experience in a lifetime. Claudia and Al have been trying to have
children for nine years. Their life is lived in limbo while another
kind of madness rules their household. One that lasts long into the
night. The answerphone picked up my call, which I knew didn't
necessarily mean that they weren't in.

In the same way I leave all the pineapple in a fruit salad to the end, I
called Ben last. Ben makes up the fourth in our self-contained gang
of friends from school. He is without doubt my most special friend.
Married but with no kids, I can almost always rely on him for a
pint or two and a chat. His was the voice I savored the most. He
was the person I shared all my details with. When bad things happened to me, funny-bad, I mean, like disastrous dates, or hideous
court sessions, I found that they were almost worth it just for the
joy of recounting the story to Ben. He'd love the one about the Swiss
masseuse.

   "Tess, my darling! Thank God you're back, it's been years."

"Don't be ridiculous," I said, grinning to myself. "I've been away five minutes. That's what it feels like now, anyway."

"Did you have an amazing time? Are you fit and did you shag anyone?"

"Yes, yes, no."

"No teepee action?"

"Trust me, if you'd seen what was on offer, you'd understand. A couple of scrawny Germans were the best thing going. I got offers from a Swiss woman, but I'll tell you about that over a drink. Are you busy?"

"Now? God, I'd love to, but we've got to go out to some boring dinner."

"I heard that!" shouted Sasha from the background. Sasha is Ben's wife. She's the woman who took my friend away. Hating her should have been easy but she made it impossible. Thankfully, because she worked so hard, she also loaned him back to me on a regular basis.

"You're too good for him," I shouted back.

Sasha came to the phone. "That I know. Welcome home, Tessa. Was it amazing?"

"Amazing," I replied. "But I'm glad to be back."

"Good. We were afraid you might disappear into an ashram, never to be seen again," said Sasha.

"Not Tessa 'homing pigeon' King."

"Well, this past year has been a tough one. No one knows how they are going to react after that kind of stress. But you sound well and I bet you look great."

"Thanks." Sasha always got to the heart of things; there was no namby-pamby nonsense with her. Ben reclaimed the phone.

"She is a wise woman, your wife," I said.

"I know. Annoying, isn't it? I'm glad you're back and fully recovered."

"Go dine," I replied. "I'll talk to you tomorrow."

"Absolutely. We'll make a plan."

I put down the receiver. Lay the phone on my stomach and stared at the sky. My ex-boss didn't bother me any more; to be honest, I was happy to be on paid leave. Lying on the beach in India after another morning of hardcore yoga, it had hit me: I hadn't had a proper break since Vietnam. When other people took a year off, I was doing articles. I had taken some form of major exam every year for nearly ten years, and since then I'd been working, working, working. My weekends weren't exactly periods of quiet contemplation either, and holidays were about packing in as much of the other stuff I never had time for. I was exhausted. So in a way it had all turned out for the best. I had had a chance to regroup. I had had a chance to get healthy. Yes, I had recovered. I had definitely recovered. So what was this sinking feeling I had?

I did what I always do in times like this. I called Samira.

Samira was a relatively new friend of mine. She's a professional party girl, which is convenient because I always have someone to play with but frightening because I thought I was an amateur. Of course, her life is different to mine in one major way: she is filthy rich, which buys a lot of love and lie-ins. Samira was rarely lonely. I didn't like her for her money. You might find that hard to believe, but actually her absurd wealth was the hardest part of being her friend. She was very used to getting her own way. What I did like about her was that she was always up for a drink on a Saturday night, and any other night of the week. The curse of the well-funded. The way she partied she should have resembled Teddy Kennedy, but she had more personal trainers than private bar memberships, and worked very hard at being able to play the way she did. Her mobile rang until it went on to answerphone. I left an urgent message.

*   *   *

I stared at my dirty laundry and decided I couldn't face it. Instead, I stripped out of my traveling clothes, added them to the pile and stepped into my wet room. The showerhead is as big as a frying pan; it was probably the most expensive item I bought for the flat. I saved on soft furnishings. I still didn't have curtains, for instance. But my God, it's worth it. The water cascades down you, which is wonderful but completely impractical if you have hair as frizzy as mine. I still didn't care. I now have a grand collection of shower caps. Shower caps and eye-masks. Oh, the joy of single living.

After my shower, I dug out some real clothes and put on an outfit to go to the shops. Jeans. Knee-high boots. Skinny-fit, long-sleeved white T-shirt to show off the tan. Who I was dressing for remained a mystery. Why I was dressing up, the same.

My flat is on the border of Pimlico and Westminster, a stone's throw from Tate Britain, and still has little shops tucked away down side-streets if you know where to look. The only trouble is, you have to cross a motorway to get there. Not very good for the lungs, that particular death walk. I stocked up on essentials—milk, bread, wine, light beer, limes, hummus, carrot batons and loo paper—and set off home. Then the pub caught my eye. Samira hadn't called, and though I loved pottering around my flat, it isn't very big and there is only so much pottering a girl can do. So I ducked into the pub for a quick one. The landlord wasn't there unfortunately—he's become a bit of a mate—so after my quick half, I decided to go home. I rang Samira a few more times. Three hours later she called me back. As soon as I heard her voice I knew she was in full swing. "Darling, you're back. What are you doing?"

"What are you doing?" I had a bad habit of hedging my bets. Even when I was desperate.

"I am at a friend's house. We're having some drinks and then going to a club, a new one. A friend of Nikki's has organized the guest list. Come, come, you must."

I looked at my watch. It was already nine and now I had her on the phone, I was starting to flag. "Oh, I don't know. Where are you?"

"Richmond for the moment, but we won't be here long so get your arse down here."

"It's a bit late . . ."

"Don't go all hippy-shit on me, will you? I'm dying to see you."

I could hear voices in the background.

"Who are you with?"

"People, friends, you know most of them."

I doubted it. There was no point schlepping all the way to Richmond if they were coming back into town. "Call me when you're on your way and I'll meet you."

"Perfect. We'll be half an hour at the most." Samira ended the call. I knew at once I'd made a mistake. Samira's hours were not the same hours everyone else kept. I could be waiting, all dolled up, for another three. Maybe I should just go to Richmond. I already had some catching up to do. But you could never catch up, not properly. Evenings that started disjointed, stayed disjointed. The best thing to do would be to have a glass of wine and wait for the call. Then again . . . Stop it, Tessa—you're going round in circles.

Half an hour came and went three times over, by which time I had got myself into a state. I didn't want to stay at home alone on my first night back watching my tan fade, but I couldn't face getting dressed up either. I'd been traveling since 5:00 a.m. and was knackered. And anyway, they hadn't called. Which meant I wanted to go. Even though I didn't. Eventually the phone rang.

"Where the hell are you?" I burst out angrily.

"At home. Sorry—I assumed you'd be out. I was just going to leave a message."

"Oh hi, Fran."

"Tessa, I'm so sorry about today. I really fucked up."

"Don't worry about it."

"You're pissed off, I can hear it in your voice."

Yoga was all about releasing the anxiety, letting go of grievances, moving on. "Well, I was looking forward to it." That was an understatement. The thought of coming home was the only reason I'd survived all those lonely evenings in my single-occupancy hut.

"I'm sorry, you know what it's like."

NO, I DON'T.

"Nick says you look fantastic: brown, blonde and beautiful," Francesca added, to appease me. "I'll make it up to you, I promise, but right now I really need your help."

Francesca never asked for help. So I sat up and put my bad mood behind me. "I have a problem," she said. "Caspar is being a nightmare."

"I'd noticed."

"It's so out of character. I've tried everything. Talking to him, ignoring him, spoiling him, punishing him, it makes no difference."

"Francesca, he's about to turn sixteen. He's supposed to be a nightmare."

"No, it's worse than that," she said. "I know his friends, they're not as bad as he is."

"Isn't it normal for kids to behave in other people's houses and be utter shits at home?"

"He barely speaks to me, Tessa, and he won't look me in the eye."

"What does Nick say?"

"He wants to thump him."

"Nick. Hippy, Green Party, university activist Nick?"

"Exactly."

"Must be bad," I said.

"It is. Look, I hate to ask you this, but would you mind talking to him? He thinks the world of you, as you know. He won't help at Katie's party tomorrow and now he's refusing to come to his own birthday lunch next Saturday."

"He'd better come. I planned my flipping retreat around his desire to go to Sticky Fingers to eat expensive chips."

"I know. You've never missed a birthday. You are the best god-mother in the world. Will you do this? Will you come over tomorrow and talk to him?"

There were two catches. One meant going to a children's party, which I detested but stomached for the sake of good godmothering. The second was more complicated, but was a good way to get out of going. I put on a stern voice. "I'm not going to report back to you about what Caspar says."

There was a long pause from Francesca. "Unless it's really bad," she said.

"When Claudia, Al, Ben and I went through it, Mum said it was like watching us enter a glass tunnel—she could see us, she could wave at us, but she couldn't talk to us. He'll come out the other side. It's his hormones, Francesca."

"I think you're confused. That's motherhood you're describing. Inside no one can hear you scream."

I laughed.

"Please, Tessa, he'll talk to you."

I hesitated. I found children's parties less appealing than the Victoria line at 8:15 in the morning. I would rather face a panel of judges than a huddle of yummy fucking mummies looking down their noses at me. "I sort of promised myself that I wouldn't put myself through any more Bob the Builder balloon artists . . ."

"I'm begging you. I've tried everything else."

"You calling me a last resort?"

"No. I'm admitting maternal defeat."

I gave in. This was unlike Francesca. She was an extremely proficient mother. That's not to say cold and calculating; more that she managed to see everything a moment ahead of time. In the same way she could spot a spilt drink before it tipped, she could head off sibling rivalry before it came to fruition. "All right, all right, I'll come to Katie's party."

"And if it isn't just hormones—and I really think it isn't—you'll tell me?"

"If it is serious," I said, having considered the request a moment, "I will get him to tell you himself."

"Deal," she said. I could hear the relief in her voice. "Sorry to disturb you on your first night back—I really thought you'd be out."

"I was just leaving," I lied.

"Lucky you. Have fun."

Samira had not called while I was on the phone to Francesca, so I tried again. For the fourth time. Again there was no answer. So much for dying to see me. Offended, I switched off the phone and retired hurt to my bathroom. It didn't matter that I was clean, I wanted to lie in expensive oil and sip decadently from a large wine glass. I ran the bath, put my iPod on its speakers, lit candles and cradled myself in the hot water. The room I had designed for sex had become the place I locked myself away in. The place I didn't need a brave face to walk into. There is a narrow slit window in the bathroom that doubles up as a ledge. Through it the river can be seen; it's one of the things I love best about the flat. I lay in the bath for twenty minutes, watching London's cauldron boil and bubble below me like liquid chocolate orange, pretending that I didn't know why I was crying. But that was a lie.

Having a break like the one I'd had was a double-edged sword. I'd read books, I'd slept, I'd got fit, but I'd also had a great deal of time to think and I'd started to feel increasingly uncomfortable about where those thoughts were taking me. I'd hoped that as soon as I was back, my busy life would take over again and I'd leave these thoughts behind. But no one else had time to spare for the prodigal child's return. What had taunted me on the beach was the thought that maybe it was all too hard to go back. Maybe the greasy pole was too greasy. I certainly felt I'd slipped a long way down it. Did I really have the energy to claw my way back up? Getting married and having kids was beginning to look a darn sight easier. I had always wanted to go down that path at some point, I just hadn't met anyone to go down it with. Which begged another question: why hadn't I? What was wrong with me? Oh yes, I knew exactly what I was crying about. It was the fear of being a last resort. Of missing out. And not just on one Saturday night of partying with people I didn't know. On life. The life that everyone else seemed to find so easy to have.

I sunk lower in the bath. I was beginning to feel that I might finally have arrived at the right bus stop just after the last bus had left. I could see its tail lights, but even if I ran, I could never catch it. I wrapped my hand around the stem of the wine glass, took a sip and closed my eyes.

I knew what that sinking feeling was.

It was never going to happen to me.

It was never going to happen to me.

It was never, ever going to happen to me.

suicide watch

If a child's first taste of anarchy is in the playground, then children's parties are their first taste of revolution. Teachers can do what parents cannot. Crowd control. Not even the clown was up to the job. The adults were outnumbered ten to one. I should have run for the hills. I should not have worn white. And, according to the other mothers, I should not have been there. This was about the only thing that I agreed with them on, but I was there on official duty and it had nothing to do with the princesses that ran amok in flammable outfits.

I stood like a misfit on the outskirts watching for a while, a smile fixed to my face, but no one appeared keen to welcome me into the fold. I had met criminals with less trepidation. I tried smiling directly at a couple of the other women when I caught them eyeing me suspiciously, but they looked away. Obviously, since they hadn't seen me at the school gate, I didn't count. I hate how these people make me feel. I hate that I let them. I want to jump up and down and stamp my feet screaming, "No, I don't have kids. But I am still a person in my own right you bastards!," since that sort of behavior seems to be the only kind that gets their loving attention. In fact, I have noticed that the worse the behavior in the child, the more mollycoddling and affirmation it receives from its mother. Maybe this is why I am excluded; maybe I haven't been whining loudly enough. Then again, maybe it's because I refer to the little darlings as "its."

There is only so much gore one can handle, so I'll keep this short. Katie, THE birthday girl, pushed a little boy of unknown parentage off the slide. She claimed it was down the slide, she just missed. But I knew Katie. Nick and Francesca's eight-year-old is an excruciatingly confident child who likes to get exactly what she wants. There was blood. A woman rushed past, treading on another child, who screamed, scaring a third so much that she careered into a table, upsetting the preservative-laden paper plates that were supposed to remain out of reach until the little darlings had eaten their vegetable sticks. I saw an insipid-looking boy make a dive for a rolling Whopper. His mother grabbed him by the foot and pulled him back, his outstretched hands creating a sweaty squeak along the laminated floor. The mother eyed every single slowly rolling chocolate as fearfully as if it were a miniature grenade. The boy managed to catch one and throw it into his mouth. I gave him a silent hurrah before watching him being returned to his home-made picnic of tofu and green beans.

Nick passed, a child under each arm. "She wouldn't even give him raisins," he whispered. "Poor kid."

This woman was one of the reasons why I didn't accept dinner party invitations any more. Too many mothers like this one discussing the delights of finding handipacks of antiseptic wipes and the evils of inoculation. Like smallpox was a good thing? I watched the kid reach breaking point. He'd had enough and threw the tofu at his mother. She yanked him up by the arm and headed for the door.

"He doesn't like parties," she hissed as she passed.

And who could blame him? The packet of Whoppers was winking at me from the counter. I couldn't help myself. While the mother said effusive goodbyes to Francesca, which she clearly didn't mean, I bent down to the miserable little boy and slipped the sweets into his Spiderman backpack. I put my finger to my lips and winked. When he smiled I felt vindicated. God, are you watching? I'm a natural.

I downed my warm white wine and stepped into the fray. Two women were deep in conversation about the devil's juice, Kool-Aid, so I veered around them and found another woman sitting on the sofa, staring out into the middle distance.

"Hi," I said.

"Hi," she managed.

So far so good.

"So which one is yours?"

"None," I replied, forcing an even, light-hearted tone into my voice. She looked at me. A "wrong answer" buzzer resounded round my head. "I'm Caspar's godmother."

"Oh. You have older children?" In other words, was I a slut who got herself knocked up in her teens?

"No. I have no children."

The woman suddenly stood up. "So sorry. Ben! No! Put that down! I've just got to . . ." She moved away from me in a hurry. Was it catching? Or was her child's life really being threatened by the balloon she took off it? Him, I mean, him.

I tried a few more times. They all started the same: "Which one is yours?" swiftly followed by "Excuse me one moment, I must (a) remove a plastic item from my child's mouth, (b) stop my child biting another child, (c) stop another child pinching mine, (d) go and talk to my wife because she is summoning me over because we are having too much fun out in the garden, (e) get away from you because you are a childless potential husband-stealing woman who cannot talk about MMR or the school run, which means I have fuck-all to say to you . . ." Perhaps it was jet lag, or too much apple juice, but I had a terrible urge to jump on the table and show everyone my panties. But I did not want to embarrass Francesca more than she was already doing herself.

The seventh time I was asked which one was mine and was met with the same curious suspicion when I said none of them, I grabbed a pizza and ventured upstairs. Since Caspar was clearly not going to come down, I would have to enter into the terrifying world of the teenage boy's bedroom. I didn't much enjoy it when I was a teenager; I was bound to find it even more disturbing now.

The first thing to hit you is the smell. Man, it smelled bad in there. Do boys ever wash? Or open a window? I have to be honest, I instantly recognized the smell. Sweat. Spunk. And cannabis. Nothing changes, except my boy was growing up.

Poor sod.

"Hello? Smeeeeeeeegal? Anyone at home?"

I heard a panicked clutter from the tiny en-suite shower room. Nick had built it for him in the corner of the room to save his son from Barbie bubble bath. I listened with a smile on my face to the telltale spray of deodorant. Teenagers, bless 'em. They always think they're the first.

"I bring pizza."

Caspar emerged fully dressed and told me he'd been having a shower.

"About to have a shower?" I ventured.

"Yeah."

"How much of that stuff are you smoking?"

"I don't smoke," Caspar insisted.

"Right. And I don't have one-night stands."

"Tessserrrrr."

"Casparrrrr. The least you could do is share the spliff that you're not smoking."

"It's not called spliff any more."

"Oh, sorry. What is it called?" I felt a bit put out. I wasn't that old, was I? "What about puff?"

"God no, that's even worse."

"Enlighten me," I said.

"Zoot. Draw. Weed."

"Weed, then," I concluded.

"What about Mum and Dad?"

"They won't even know we're missing. Come on, hand it over."

"You got that right," said Caspar, opening up a tin and passing over the half-smoked "zoot."

"I never thought I'd be dunning draw with a grown-up." Dunning? A grown-up? The words reminded me how very young he was, and that was why the glimpse I caught inside his tin should have alarmed me. The fact that Caspar was smoking at four in the afternoon in a house full of people should also have warned me. But I chose to ignore everything in the quest for more information. I, the grown-up, settled down on a beanbag and lit up. One inhalation and I knew that it was strong stuff. After the initial booming head rush, I decided to fake it. So, in the presence of my fifteen-year-old godson, I bum-sucked, held the smoke in my mouth, then forced it out of my nose. Caspar, on the other hand, sucked away long and hard and didn't seem any more affected than me.

Liberated by drugs, Caspar told me about the girls he'd failed to snog. The boys who always got the girls. And the girls who liked him whom he didn't like. Nothing ever changes. We giggled stupidly about nonsense and then attacked the cold pizza as if it were cordon bleu. I started to think Francesca and Nick were being a little harsh. The cannabis aside, Caspar seemed back to his lovely normal self to me. We were still snuggled up on the beanbag when Francesca walked in.

"Jesus, what's that smell?" she said, wafting her hand in front of her face.

I have to admit it, I panicked. But Caspar was as slick as they come. "Tessa brought me joss sticks from India."

"Oh. Thanks, Tessa."

Little rat. But I didn't deny it. I didn't want to get into trouble with Francesca. Or burn my bridges with my boy.

"I brought you some masala tea," I said. Truthfully.

"How long have you two been hiding up here?" There was a slight edge to her voice that I couldn't place.

"I did try," I pleaded. "But those women talk of nothing but children, so I found myself talking to the dads, which was more of a laugh because they didn't talk about their children, but the women kept coming over and reclaiming their husbands by sending them off on some bogus Kool-Aid run, so I came and found Caspar."

"What do you expect, turning up in designer white, all flat stomach and blond hair? Women who have had children don't have stomachs like yours. Not normal women, anyway. You make them nervous, Tessa. You make them feel dowdy."

"They are dowdy," said Caspar.

"He speaks," said Fran. Which I thought was quite annoying, so it didn't surprise me when Caspar rolled his eyes.

"I thought you hated them too," I added, unhelpfully.

"I'm just trying to explain it from their perspective. Anyway, they've all gone."

"What time is it?"

"It's seven o'clock."

Caspar and I looked guiltily at each other. How the hell did that happen?

"We've had a lot of catching up to do. I haven't seen him for ages."

"Well, you look all caught up now."

I got to my feet and followed Francesca out into the corridor. Caspar would have no idea I'd been spying on him after that little scene.

"As the coast is clear, I'll come down and make you some masala tea," I said.

"I'd prefer a big fat spliff, actually. Or a mallet."

Was that Fran's subconscious playing tricks on her, or was she telling me that she'd not fallen for the joss-stick story? I decided to bluff it out as I walked behind her.

"It's not called spliff any more," I said.

"Really?"

"These days it's zoot, draw, or good old-fashioned weed."

"Zoot? How the hell do you spell that?"

"Z-o-o-t—I think. I'll check with one of my friends."

Francesca stopped walking, turned on the worn carpet and, in the narrow hallway, studied me. "It must be so easy being you," she said.

"What?"

"No wonder Caspar adores you. Look at you. Stylish. Relaxed. Free . . ."

"Fran," I said, a note of incredulity in my voice, "you were the one who asked me over to talk to him. I'm just doing what you asked me to do."

"I know. I'm sorry. It's just this is . . . Oh, I don't know." She shook her head. "What do you think?"

"I think he's fine, Fran. Just a fraction on the rebellious side, but Caspar underneath."

"Are you sure I don't have anything to worry about?"

"Pretty sure."

"He hates me."

"He doesn't hate you, you silly girl. You are a great mother and if Caspar doesn't know that, then he is a fool. Please don't take this personally; it's just hormones. Repeat after me: it's just hormones."

But she wouldn't. She felt she knew him better. Turned out she was right.

Nick was at the bottom of the stairs, waiting for Francesca with a glass of wine in his hand. He handed it over to Fran.

"To survival," he said, then kissed her on her head. They walked arm in arm to the sofa and collapsed together into a heap. As I said, they just fit, those two. Always have. Could Francesca not see how jealous I was of what she had? Not that it had always been that way. In the beginning I'd felt sorry for her.

That day Francesca appeared on my doorstep in tears was when our paths irreversibly split. Still clutching the pregnancy test in her sweaty hand, she pulled it out of her cheap blue anorak pocket, and showed me the way a child shows their friend a half-sucked gobstopper: two innocuous blue lines that signified so much more than we could ever have imagined.

Nick was as worthy back then as he is now. He marched and protested then. Now he works for a non-profit organization, ensuring large corporations like Nike and Gap don't use child labor during manufacturing. But Francesca was brighter than both of us put together. She wasn't only top of her school, she got a letter in the post about being top of the region in three subjects. Her place at the best law firm was affirmed even though we hadn't done our finals. When she decided to keep the baby they said they'd hold open the place, but she never went back and eventually the offer of articles dried up as new waves of talent swept even her special mark away. They had been so careful, they didn't know how it happened. And in the end that was what swung it. If a child can be so determined to be born that they can overcome condoms, withdrawal and the rhythm method, then perhaps that child had a right to live. It is a testament to Francesca's mind that she got a first in her degree because eight days after her last exam she went into labor. Caspar was born a healthy eight and a half pounds. Even that was done with top marks. Ten out of ten in the APGAR test.

Nick and Fran married when Caspar was nine months old. The same day he was christened. I was godmother and maid of honor rolled into one horrendous late-eighties puffball skirt. It was a great day. I crossed my fingers behind my back when the vicar asked me to renounce evil. At twenty I was not ready to make that deal. I was having too much fun. When the bouquet sailed through the air, I abstained again, letting it fall at my feet. Marriage would come later, that I knew; I didn't want to rush things. I wasn't going to go catching roses to cement the deal. I was so sure that I would get married and have children that I never even questioned it. I now know a tiny fraction of what I thought I knew then, which is just about enough to realize that I knew nothing.

When Caspar was eight years old, his first sister Katie was born; three years later, another daughter, Poppy, arrived on the scene. Francesca may have given up the law but what she had achieved was far more impressive—a genuinely happy, successful family—and to think I'd felt sorry for her that day I crossed my fingers and ignored the tumbling flowers. I looked over to her, cuddling with Nick on the sofa, watching Katie rip open birthday presents. You are wrong, Francesca. Being me isn't easy, because all I want is to be you.

I collected my coat and said my farewells. I cast a backward glance at their small terrace house and saw smoke slipping out of the Velux window in the roof. For a moment I saw the lit end of a spliff, or whatever it was called, glowing in the dark and knew Caspar was hard at his new-found hobby. Before starting the car, I sent Caspar a quick text about his birthday. It was subtle. Erudite. Poetic. *b at ur bday lunch or the iPod gets it.* I drove back through the city with the roof on, playing soppy Sunday night music which I loathe but never switch off. I nearly drove to Claudia's house, but there was only so much domestic bliss I could take in a day, so I turned the Mini homeward, to face the first Sunday night alone, with no work to focus on for the following day.

As I kicked the door of the studio behind me my phone started to ring. To my surprise it was Samira. Samira didn't do Sundays. I rolled over the edge of the sofa arm and awaited my apology for the previous night, but not a bit of it. I should know Samira better by now. I think her family motto is "It is better to die than to apologize," which would explain why none of them speak to each other.

"Suicide watch for single Sunday-nighters," she said.

Naturally, I was offended.

"Not just you, you daft cat; my single friends and appendages who are in London are coming over for supper. It's a new thing I invented while you were away. I can't stand Sunday nights any more. I was about to throw myself off the building, so I'm starting a movement. Are you coming? It's very casual."

For a moment I was too disoriented to respond. Being social on a Sunday night was a big ask. On top of which, self-pity had crawled back in and snuggled up in my chest and I was a beat away from singing "On My Own" from *Les Mis*.

"Come on, Tessa. Crying on your own in the dark is not the way an adult woman should spend her Sunday night."

That is what I loved about Samira; she never minces her words and she tells you how it is. Of course, if you did it back to her, she wouldn't speak to you for weeks. But as I have learned over the years, your friends don't change; you just learn to ignore or embrace the bad bits. So I got up and started the unfamiliar experience of having a clothes crisis on a Sunday evening. I know Samira's friends. They do casual like George W. Bush does vocabulary.

An hour later I pulled up to Samira's flat, feeling pretty groovy. The roof was back down on my Mini; I had opted for denim miniskirt, cut low on the hips to show off my two main attributes: a flat stomach and good legs, even better when brown. I had taken the car to keep the goose bumps and men out cruising at bay. It was Sunday night—how raucous could it be? I was wearing a disgusting flesh-colored bra with three-inch straps which looked hideous off but worked wonders under a white T-shirt which in turn showed off my tan and hid my back spots when I had them. Which I didn't at that moment, thanks to the sun.

I was wrong about Sunday-night abstinence. Samira's casual Sunday supper turned out to be a boisterous curry for thirty. There was something of the Blitz mentality to it. What did we on suicide watch have to lose?

A couple of waiters from the Indian had been bribed away from their busy Sunday-night delivery shift to feed and water us. That was a nice touch, I thought. Who had curry on Sunday night? Couples. It was a smart middle finger from Samira to the "cozees." I told her this but she frowned at me.

"My uncle owns the place."

Oh well, so much for irony.

It was fun because so many singles had brought their single friends, so it wasn't cliquey or over-bearing. If they had children, they weren't telling. No one mentioned schools. I drank Tiger Beers happily and chatted to whoever was in my eye line and it was great. In the hours that I was there, no one asked me what I did, which is the sign of a great evening. Small talk evaporated in the presence of big chat. No one wanted to talk about daily lives; they wanted to talk about places and people, books and great hidden-away bars in other cities.

I met a guy called Sebastian. He was tall, with receding hair and bow legs, but handsome. He made me laugh and fetched me more Tiger Beer. When he went to the loo, Samira sidled up to me and told me he was an adviser to the government, a bit of an operator. I thought that was kind of sexy. I'd never been out with a civil servant before. He gave me his card. Modern unmarrieds do that. I glanced down. It was official, he worked for the Department of Trade and Industry. He said he had to go, and I felt quite bereft when he said goodbye. Twenty minutes later, I saw the big and little hand converge on twelve and knew it was well past my bedtime. I thanked Samira, then took the plush lift down to the ground floor. Outside on the pavement Sebastian was talking to a group of people I hadn't met. He smiled at me as they all waved goodbye.

"I thought you were going," I said, standing alone on the pavement with him.

"My goodbyes took a little longer than expected." He smiled. "How are you getting home?"

I waggled my car keys at him. He frowned.

"What?"

"You've drunk too much."

"I haven't really. I've eaten masses."

"You have and I should know, because I was trying to get you pissed. Where do you live?"

"The Embankment."

"Fine. It's on the way. I'm driving you home, then I'll get a cab," he said. Which is what he did, except between the driving me home and getting that cab, he ended up in bed with me.

vanishing act

It happened like this. He parked my car in my underground parking space, we went to the lift and got in. Instinctively, I pressed 11. My floor. One below penthouse. Before we got to the fourth floor he had taken my hand and pulled me towards him. Maybe he thought by pressing 11 I was giving him the green light, and I didn't have the heart to say it was a mistake. So I kissed him back and it was nice. Really nice. He did all those things that men are supposed to do but, despite all the books, magazine articles and prominent comediennes out there trying to redirect them, they still don't. He brushed a strand of hair off my face. He held my hand, then wrapped us up in our entwined arms. Courtesy of five weeks of the pigeon pose, this caused me no actual bodily harm. He ran the back of his hand down my face so lovingly that when the lift door pinged open I followed him out of the lift, opened my front door and let him in.

I didn't even get to go through the pretence of making coffee as things moved pretty fast from that point onwards. What startled me was how much my body betrayed me and obeyed him. I didn't care that my bra was enormous, or that my knickers were not matching. I wanted skin-on-skin action and clearly I didn't care whose skin it was. My passion fueled his, which in turn threw jet fuel on mine, and I pressed myself against his body. At one point it was as if we were having sex though we were still fully clothed. I could feel his hard-on through his trousers as he pushed against me.

We tumbled onto the bed, I lifted my bottom and together we pulled off my knickers. I kicked off my boots and used my feet like a monkey to work his trousers down over his hips. Perhaps it was his bow legs, but the jeans never got further than his knees. I didn't care. Hands, mouth, hair, neck, chest, everything was everywhere, and then boom, he slipped inside me and my whole body shuddered. I knew then that this didn't happen very often. That something could fit so well. We pushed and heaved, squeezed and clawed and for a few mind-blowing minutes I was free of all thought, my whole being existed for this sensation and this sensation only. It was glorious. Magnificent. And then as quickly as it had begun, it was over.

"Oh no!" he shouted. Which I thought was kind. I don't think he wanted it to end quite then either, but I didn't blame him—if I'd been a boy, I would have come in the lift. So I thought he'd done pretty well to last as long as he did. He shuddered to a halt. My body took a while to catch on that it was over and went on arching, longing, but the pressure was gone and there was nothing to push against. We lay there for a moment just recovering. Letting the animal leave and the civilized person return. My animal was being stubborn. It wanted more. You couldn't invite a wolf in and ask it to leave without feeding it. Untrained animals didn't behave like that.

Sebastian rolled off, stood up and pulled his trousers back up. Once he had done his fly up he was fully dressed. It was as if it hadn't happened. I tried to smile. But couldn't. He walked towards the bathroom. I heard the shower go on, which I thought strange, but then I heard the loo flush and I guessed he'd wanted a little privacy to pee and fart simultaneously. I lay there thinking about the story of Marilyn Monroe and Arthur Miller. The story goes, he took his new girl to meet his parents. They had a cozy little supper in the

Millers' small house. After dinner Marilyn got up to go to the loo. Embarrassed by the proximity of the bathroom, she ran a tap while she peed to protect her modesty. Later the playwright asked his parents what they thought of his new girlfriend, to which his mother replied, "She's a sweet girl, Arthur, but she pisses like a horse."

I must have been smiling when Sebastian peered over the bookcase.

"Don't pretend you're so easily satisfied. You're scowling underneath."

I'd pulled the sheet over me because in the dim light I didn't want to go rooting around for my pants, but suddenly he whisked it off me and pulled me up out of bed. Taking my hand, he led me to the steam-filled bathroom. The lights were really dim. Thank the Lord for dimmer switches and the fact that my extractor fan was currently not working. In the dim, steamy room, Sebastian started to undress me properly. The T-shirt came up over my head. The bra released its load. My skirt fell to the floor and I stood naked in front of him. He undressed quickly and pulled me under the flow of water. At last I was going to christen my wet room.

"Let's do that again," he said, "and this time I'll try to take a little more time about it."

He poured shower gel into the palm of his hand and slowly started to work the suds all over my body. It was a high-quality valet job, inside and out. I returned the favor by ruining a good blow-dry for a blow job. But it was worth it. Sebastian's bow legs were perfect for standing-up sex; they provided a nice sturdy A-frame with the added benefit of a ledge. Once it all started again, though it never reached the peak of those first few moments in the bedroom, it was good. Really, really good. A shag to remember. We ended up having sex twice more during the night until I begged him to stop and passed out with a smile on my face as a misty pink dawn crept up the river.

*   *   *

In the morning he was still there. I had to look twice at the profile of a body in my bed before believing it. For a moment I thought he might be dead, because he was so still. When Cora came to stay as a baby, I used to get up in the night four or five times just to check she was breathing. I would gently put my hand on her chest and, with my own breath held, wait for her next inhalation. Despite trying to eat this man the night before, I was now afraid of any physical contact. I rustled the sheets instead and watched with relief as he stirred. He turned over sleepily.

"Hello," he said.

"Hello."

"My name is Sebastian, I believe we've met."

"Once," I replied. "Very fleetingly. How are you?"

"Exceedingly well," he said. "I had the most amazing dream. There was this girl with fantastic legs, I've not come across inner thigh muscles like it. She wrapped her legs around me like they do in the movies. Incredible."

All the time he was speaking, he was running his fingers up and down my arm. I didn't think it was possible to feel like having more sex, but from nowhere a familiar and not completely unwanted burning sensation eked its way into my conscience. I hadn't even brushed my teeth. Last night or this morning. But in true Muppet style, this man brought out the animal in me and this time, very slowly, we rubbed ourselves into oblivion. He used his hand and my fingers to get me there, but get me there we did, as did he, neck on neck, right up to the end. If it had been a race, there would have been a photo finish. I lay back and laughed. I couldn't take the stupid look of satisfaction off my face.

"Your work here is done," I said. Then regretted it. In case he took me at my word. He glanced at the clock by my bed. "Shit, it's late. I'd better get going."

"And me," I said, before I realized it wasn't true.

"Will you join me for a shower?" He was smiling again.

"Absolutely not. I don't trust myself. I will shower alone." I jumped out of bed and walked to the bathroom, not caring that he was probably looking at my bottom. I sent him in after me with a Virgin Upper Class traveling set, complete with virgin toothbrush. He emerged, buffed and clean-smelling, with slicked-back wet hair, a few minutes later.

"You're going to work in jeans?" I asked as he finished tucking his shirt in.

"I keep a suit in the office for emergencies."

I smiled but there was a little voice in the back of my head wondering if I was the emergency.

We walked to the tube station, stopping for coffee and croissants on the way, which we ate out of paper bags. A stay-over is a big thing. Sex in the morning doesn't mean much—once they are there they might as well—but a conversation? This was unusual. Now coffee and croissants—could this be . . . ? I tried really hard to stop myself imagining the gorgeous little bow-legged children. But I failed. They were there, alive and kicking and making me nervous. We went as far as Westminster together, laughing all the way, and then he left, kissing me on the mouth.

"You were incredible," he said, then the doors closed and Sebastian was gone.

There was silence from Helen as she turned a miniature bottle of Perrier around in her fingers. I stared at my friend from across her sleek modern dining table. Finally I had got her without the babies, but she still wasn't all mine.

"Weren't you listening?" I said, sipping my wine. "He said, 'You were incredible,' and left."

Helen looked up and frowned at me. "I can't believe you pretended to go to work. What were you wearing?"

"My suit."

"You put on your suit?"

"It sort of happened by accident. I was on Monday morning autopilot."

"This was on Monday?"

"Yes. I told you. Weren't you listening?"

"Sorry."

"What's wrong with you? Why are you being so vague?"

"Sorry," she said again, twisting her long hair around her finger. "The twins kept me up again last night."

"Aren't the nannies supposed to do that?"

"Only I can feed them and at the moment, they're hungry. Growth spurt, I think . . . It's very boring. Why haven't you told me about this bloke before?"

Not my fault. Blame the bloodsuckers you've got attached to your nipples. Sorry. Think warm positive things and try not to sound too vinegary. "I've only been back six days."

"I feel like I'm completely out of the loop."

I stretched my hand across to hers. "Don't worry, Helen. There's nothing in the loop anyway."

"Easy for you to say. You're in it."

Didn't feel like that to me. "I have tried calling a few times. Didn't the nanny tell you?"

She frowned, clearly pretending that she was trying to remember, when I knew perfectly well that all my messages would have been passed on.

"Anyway, I'm telling you now and you're missing the point. He said, 'You *were* incredible.' It's brilliantly delivered. I was being complimented and cut loose in one go."

"What if he'd been going all the way to Canary Wharf?"

"He works for the government. Westminster. It couldn't have been easier. I just doubled back on myself and changed when I got home."

"Sounds as if he liked you—he bought you a croissant. Are you going to pretend to go to work next time you see him?"

It is very irritating talking to someone who doesn't listen. "No, Helen. If he'd said, 'You *are* incredible,' I may have been in line to receive more croissants. Because 'You are incredible' means let's have a drink, do it all over again tonight, and tomorrow night, and see where this thing goes. 'You were incredible' means thank you and goodnight. A genius vanishing act. Especially considering I don't have a moral leg to stand on. I shagged him after a forty-minute conversation over sag aloo. I consumed him. I took my fill, he took his; it was a short-lived contract."

"I think he'll call."

"You would," I said. "Your life is perfect. So in your world he'd call. Not in mine. And don't give me any of that 'Desiderata' bollocks about love being as perennial as the grass, because I've hit an extended bald patch."

Helen stood up, grabbed a sponge and began to wipe at a perfectly clean surface. I know it was a big house, but Helen had plenty of help. A cleaning lady came every day. A nanny came during the weekdays to help with the babies. And they had a wonderful woman who lived with them. Rose is her name. I'd known Rose almost as long as I'd known Helen. Originally she came from the Philippines; she'd been Helen's father's housekeeper in Hong Kong and had looked after Helen since she was a baby. Helen's parents' marriage hadn't lasted long, so she had spent her school holidays back in Hong Kong with Rose and her father. In reality, of course, it was Rose. Tycoons don't become tycoons by being home every night reading bedtime

stories. Rose used to fly back and forth to Hong Kong accompany-
ing Helen on those trips, but Marguerite, Helen's mother, was not
a hands-on parent either. She was busy jetting around Europe as a
newly divorced wealthy woman. The nannies she hired never lasted
very long. Helen had an incredible knack for making their lives a
misery. So in the end Rose simply stayed with Helen wherever she
was. I suppose Rose is responsible for Helen's upbringing. No, not
responsible. Her parents are responsible for that. But she put in all
the legwork. Her hair was plaited, her teeth were cleaned, she was
dressed, fed and watered by Rose. The only constants in Helen's life
were Rose, Marguerite's absence and her father's wealth.

Marguerite and I do not get on. Her open criticism of her daughter
has left me gaping in the past. If I was brought up in a greenhouse,
Helen was like one of those tiny plants that manages to grow out of
a rock face. I came to the conclusion a long time ago that Marguerite
only went through the disruption of pregnancy in order to cement
alimony. I'm not saying her father didn't pay Helen any attention. He
did. He worshipped her. But that's not the same thing. I guess Hel-
en's childhood was that destructive combination of being spoilt and
neglected at the same time. When her father died unexpectedly, Rose
came to join Helen in London permanently. She'd been here ever
since. I think Rose was supposed to be retired now, but she never sat
down, she couldn't. Needless to say, with Rose, the nanny and the
daily, there was never any mess in Helen's house. In fact, there was
barely any evidence of life and certainly none of the twins.

"I'm jealous," said Helen.

"Like hell you are. I got dumped on the tube."

"Sounds to me like you experienced one spectacular shag. Something I would offer Bobby and Tommy's school fees for right now."

"Ah, still no action in that department?"

Helen shook her head. "Neil can't go anywhere near me."

Personally, I would have thought that was a blessed relief, but then I would rather be single for the rest of my days than have sex with Neil. I liked to think that I would be more gracious towards him if I was sure he made my friend happy, but I wasn't sure that he did. Off the record, watching her marry him was one of the hardest things I've done. He was a struggling comic back then, and I have to admit I doubted his motives. Helen is what you'd call an heiress, I suppose. So yes, I wasn't sure about Neil right from the beginning. But she always had faith in him, and she was right. He was on the cusp of stardom and, boy, he never let you forget it. The years she'd carried him had somehow been wiped from memory. If you didn't know it, you'd think he'd bought their huge house himself, when I knew he hadn't contributed a penny.

"Have you heard from your boss?"

"Ex-boss," I insisted. "No. I've been meaning to call the office but I can't even bring myself to punch in the number." I still felt as though some people thought I should have kept my head down and waited until the man got bored of his failed advances. I did try. But he didn't get bored and the more I ignored him, the worse it got. First I got nervous when he was in the vicinity, then his advances got scarier and more insistent, until finally I was afraid all the time. It was no way to live. I hated going to work, I hated coming home. I started to fear the telephone, I started to fear my own reflection. Calling the office would be re-engaging with something I wanted to leave to decompose on its own accord. My colleagues at work were like my family; I'd worked there for ten years, so naturally we spent absurd amounts of hours in one another's companies. Losing them was a high price to pay in order to regain my freedom. I looked at Helen. Now I had to do something with that freedom.

The door to the enormous kitchen opened. Helen jumped. I grimaced. That was the end of our girly chat. Helen would shut up now as her dazzling, famous husband took over. Neil went over and kissed his wife hello. Then he turned to me.

"Wow, Tessa, look at you," he said. I stood and fixed my obligatory smile on my face.

"Hi, Neil. How's the new show?"

"Bloody hard work."

Personally I'd never seen the humor in Neil. He had a talent for misogynistic, hateful, racist, blue snooker hall humor which shocked. How he'd been picked up by Channel 4 amazed me. He always kissed me just on the mouth, both sides. I found it extremely invasive and had to stop myself from wiping my lips afterwards.

"Doesn't she look incredible, Helen?" he said, letting go of my arm.

"Incredible," said Helen.

"Looking at Tessa makes me think you could do with a holiday," said Neil. He poked his wife in the ribs and got a beer out of the fridge. "Get a bit of color back in your cheeks. Now that filming is finished, how about it?"

I thought that was a bit uncalled for. And if I'd liked him more I would have said so. I would have said, "Fuck you, you bastard, you haven't just had twins." But you can't talk to people like that unless you love them. So I moved away from him instead.

"Helen looks amazing, as always. I can't believe you had those giant boys only a few months ago. Could that jumper get any tighter? I love it, by the way."

"Consider it yours," she said. "I'll get it cleaned and give it to you. It's more your color."

"I didn't mean it like that," I stated. "I was just saying that you look great."

"Course she does," said Neil. "Still, a holiday would be nice. I've been working like a dog."

Trouble was, Neil was right; Helen did look withdrawn and though always slim, she now looked spindly. Concave. But wasn't it a husband's job to see beyond those things and always, only ever, compliment? Especially after childbirth. I looked again at Helen. She had big dark bags under her eyes and her once enviable cheekbones looked like what they were: a skull. A hollow, empty skull. Thanks to her Chinese bloodline, Helen never looked pale and pasty like the rest of us mere mortals, but even her complexion was looking papery and dull. Studying her now, I realized she didn't look amazing, she didn't even look OK and nothing like the lithe eighteen-year-old girl I'd met on the beach.

Neil ruffled Helen's hair. "She knows I love her just the way she is."

Helen smiled gratefully. I had to leave. Neil made me nauseous because I knew what he was really like but I could never tell Helen. The effect he had on his wife made me want to cry, but what could I do? Breaking up marriages, even ones I didn't have any faith in, wasn't my style.

"I thought we'd go out for sushi round the corner," said Neil. "Why don't you come?"

Helen may have been aware that I didn't like her husband, but Neil seemingly didn't have a clue. Ego and elephant skin are close traveling companions.

"I'm going out, otherwise I'd love to."

"Come on—it will be more fun with you," said Neil. "Honestly, left to our own devices we discuss the twins' poo for hours. It's not good for us."

"Thank you for trying to sound convincing," I replied. Not convinced. "But Ben is taking me out to dinner." That was wishful thinking on my part. I had no plans, but I couldn't face an evening with Neil and Helen. When I saw Helen, it was on her own.

"Ah well, we couldn't possibly compete with Ben," said Neil.

"Ignore him," said Helen. "He's just jealous."

"Course I am. Every time his incredibly successful wife goes away on business, he gets to take another incredibly successful woman out to dinner."

I saw Helen sigh. It was the "incredibly successful" that did it. It sounded like Neil was complimenting me and Sasha, but what he was really doing was attacking Helen. Helen had never worked. Never. She had no real qualifications though she'd started a fair few courses. Helen didn't need to work. But not doing so hadn't helped her confidence—what confidence her mother had left her with, that is.

After the divorce, Marguerite had worked her way up through a newspaper to become the editor. She was no shrinking violet and the looks Helen was blessed with were from her mother. We used to joke that Marguerite had slept her way to the top, but the truth is, Marguerite ain't stupid; in fact, she's formidable. Perhaps Helen was a disappointment to her, but jeez, a little encouragement might have helped. I don't know whether the bar was simply set too high, or never raised off the floor. I didn't meet Helen until we were eighteen and I guess the damage had been done by then. Seeing Neil do what Marguerite had always done broke my heart because I knew that somewhere in that emaciated shell was a girl with great chutzpah. The girl I'd met. The girl who'd been with me through my twenties, whom I'd done wildly irresponsible things with, the girl I missed. I tried to come to that girl's subtle defense.

"So successful that I'm currently out of work," I said.

"Not for long, I bet. So are you and Ben dining alone, à deux? Something we should know?"

He can't help himself, he always gets smutty.

"If you mean are we going to catch up over some food, yes." I shouldn't rise.

"And his wife doesn't mind?"

"Because there is nothing to mind. Can we change the subject, please?" I don't like being teased about Ben. Especially not in front of Helen.

"Defensive . . ." said Neil.

"No. Bored. I thought you were going out for sushi."

Neil put his arm around Helen. "Come on, Tessa. You know we're just digging for dirt."

Why did married people do that? Lick their lips over other people's sex lives? I felt like a specimen.

The nanny appeared with two powdered babies, pink from their bath, and ready for more food. They weren't very attractive. Sadly they resembled their rather squat, mean-looking father rather than my beautiful friend. All they had were her dark eyes. Her oriental bloodline had been milked out by his white man's overbite.

"Why don't you feed down here?" said Neil. "Helen can do them in tandem now."

Ew . . . "Are you still feeding?" I asked, surprised.

"They recommend a year," said Neil. "Improves the brain."

"Who recommends a year?" I asked. "Not people with twins, I bet."

"Not doing them any harm," said Neil proudly. "Look at the size of them."

They were fat, it was true, but I wasn't thinking about them.

"Neil has allergies," said Helen. I looked at her. Had the woman's spine gone for ever? The girl I used to know wouldn't think twice about dancing on bars, thumbing rides, flying to European cities to gatecrash a party, skinny-dipping in winter. Most of my craziest behavior was in some way related to her. Now . . . well, it had all changed.

"Helen is coping brilliantly, most of the time. Go on, show Tessa."

I really didn't need to see, but Helen dutifully pulled up her jumper and unhooked her nursing bra. I wasn't exactly repulsed, but I wasn't very comfortable either. Nor, it seemed, was Bobby; as soon as he was brought over to Helen he started fussing, kicking and arching his back. We all watched as she tried to force her nipple into the baby's mouth. I pretended I needed something from my bag.

"What's wrong with him?" asked Neil.

Bobby's crying set off Tommy. I couldn't actually tell them apart, but all their matching clothes had been scrupulously monogrammed, which made life easier. I had been so involved with Caspar, and incredibly hands-on with Cora, it worried me that I felt almost nothing for these little boys except a constant nagging irritation. They hadn't taken Helen away, they hadn't made her sell herself short, they weren't responsible for the vanishing act my friend had performed, she'd done that all by herself.

The fussing increased to a grating level.

"It's the lights and people," said Helen. "I usually do this upstairs in a dim room to get them off to sleep. Sorry, Tessa, the last two hours of the day always seem longer than the previous ten."

I smiled sympathetically, but inside I was thinking, Try it without the brace of nannies, like most people, then complain. "I was going anyway," I said, picking up my bag, desperate to leave before I gave myself away.

"Stay and have a drink with me," said Neil.

"I've really got to go."

Helen handed the baby back to the nanny, who took him without a word. She balanced them both expertly on her hips, and began the long journey back upstairs. Helen came over to me and hugged me. It was a deep hug and for a second I felt concerned for her; people only hold on tight when they're afraid of being washed away.

"I think the nanny could do with some help," said Neil, watching her go up the stairs with his bawling beefy sons.

Well, you've got a pair of fucking hands, you help, was my immediate reaction. No wonder I wasn't married. Helen did not express my thoughts. She didn't even appear to share them; instead she released me from the embrace, turned away with no conspiratorial look and smiled. "Coming," she said sweetly and joined her husband on the stairs. Hand in hand, they followed their children up to the nursery.

I hadn't paid much attention to Helen's pregnancy. I was having troubles of my own. It was during that period that my ex-boss stopped being a bore, and started frightening me. Despite carrying twins, Helen stayed small for longer than most mothers I know who are having one. So sometimes I simply forgot she was pregnant. Practically everyone I knew was breeding and all the millions of other women whom I didn't know. It was a pandemic. There were pregnant women wherever I looked. Or so it seemed to my tainted eyes. I, on the other hand, was being followed home by a married man. My friends and acquaintances were discussing fetal development and the pros and cons of taking omega-6 supplements; I was talking to ADT about putting in a panic button at home. So yes, Helen's pregnancy did not win much of my attention. The birth was an elective Caesarean at the Portland Hospital, which did not engender much sympathy from me either, since I feared Neil's influence on Helen's decision to have the babies there began on the pages of *Hello!* magazine. Rather than cooing over newborns, I was spending my time in court, getting an injunction on a man who controlled my career. I didn't even send flowers to the hospital.

I got my coat from where Rose had hung it. I quickly went to the loo and washed my hands. I could hear the bawling continue

upstairs. It was getting worse. Neil was putting his oar in; it didn't
sound particularly helpful. I still hadn't heard a word from the nanny.
I pulled my hat down over my head, looked briefly at my reflection
in the hall mirror and felt genuinely glad I was leaving. I pulled the
wide heavy door behind me and breathed a sigh of relief. The setting
sun picked out the newly auburn autumn leaves and made the trees
vibrate with color. The air felt cool and clean. There was a French
café nearby, and a bookshop. I could pick up a paperback and settle
in with a glass of wine, maybe have an early dinner on my own . . .
Why not? I was free to do as I pleased and for a brief moment I remembered what it was that I'd always loved about my life.

At the gate I heard the door behind me open again. Helen stepped
out. I turned.

"Don't leave me here," she pleaded.

Then Neil came out, grabbed her around the waist playfully and
dragged her back in, laughing. I stared at the closed door and felt
my whole body slump. Had I become so bitter that I couldn't be
happy for my friend? Wasn't that affectionate, jocular moment between them proof that the only person poisoning this relationship
was me? My relief slid away. I am ashamed to say it was quickly
replaced by self-pity. It was no longer a cool evening. It was cold.
The air wasn't clean. It was full of carbon-monoxide. An evening
alone, eating cheap food I could make better at home, reading a
worthy book short on laughs, just seemed desperate and contrived
now. I stood on the pavement until the cold seeped through the
thin soles of my shoes and made me shudder. Was it better to be
part of something than nothing? Helen had a huge house, staff, a
husband, two sons—what did I have? Perhaps she wasn't the one
selling herself short.

I have gone over that moment in my mind a thousand times since
and I swear I saw her laughing. Now I realize that I was seeing only

what I expected to see. Even though I was distrustful of it at the time and would have loved to have seen something else, I couldn't. I was programmed not to. And that is why, even now, knowing what I know, my memory can only recall her laughing as Neil pulled her back inside the house.

a suspicious high

I put in an SOS call to Ben. Dinner with him was exactly what I needed. Sasha picked up his phone. I asked her whether they could join me in a decompression tank of vodka somewhere. The excuse I gave was that I'd been with babies all day and needed to talk to a grown-up.

"I'm going out. Ben's not doing anything, but I'm not sure he fulfils the criteria."

"I don't get it."

"You said you needed to talk to a grown-up."

"Yes. Oh . . ." I walked back up to the tube station against the tide of commuters heading home. "Everything all right?"

"Don't ask."

"OK."

"Men are babies. I've been away on business for four days and get back to no food in the fridge, though he did remember to restock the beer; he hasn't thought to take out the rubbish or put on a wash, or make the bloody bed, or put a new loo-paper roll on. So yes, you can borrow my husband and no, I'm not sure I want him back."

Normally I ask to borrow him, normally Sasha says, "Only if you give him back," to which I normally reply with a jaunty, "Don't I always?," but Sasha sounded exasperated.

"Anything I can do?"

"Can you reprogram the male species?"

"No." I stopped outside the tube station. My travel plans were affected by the outcome of this conversation.

"Then I doubt it. Don't worry, Tessa, we're fine really. All I need is to go out with my girlfriend and slag him off for a couple of hours."

"Come out with me," I said, getting in the way of people hurrying up the stairs. "Either Harding will do." I felt the uncomfortable tweak that comes with a lie and quickly slathered it with something else more truthful. "I love our girly catch-ups."

"You won't do, Tessa. You always defend him."

"How annoying."

"No, it's very admirable, but this evening I need to spit some venom and get pissed. As some wise woman once said to me, 'Just because you have a husband, doesn't mean you can't have boyfriend troubles.'"

"Who said that?"

"You did, you daft cow."

"Did I?" I was amazed. That sounded far too intelligent for me.

"You underestimate yourself, Tessa. I'll get Ben for you."

"Thanks. You sure everything's OK?"

"Course. Ups and downs, that's what it's all about. The trick is trying to remember that on the down bits. By the time I get home I'll love him again and no doubt rip his clothes off and—"

"Thanks, you can save me the details."

"Anyway, he's always nicer to me when he's seen you. You're a good influence on him. So yeah, borrow him for the evening, but however reluctant he is to return, please send him back when you're done."

"Don't I always?" I said. We'd been having these sorts of exchanges for seven years now, usually without the spitting venom bit, but fundamentally the same.

*   *   *

I'd been home just long enough to phone my parents when Ben called me from the car and said he was outside my building. I told him I'd be straight down, which I was. That's what I like. Being busy. Keeping moving. The smile that spread across Ben's face when he saw me was the perfect tonic to Neil's insalubrious wit, the yelping twins and Helen's nipples. In fact, Ben is the perfect antidote to almost anything. He is tall, broad and though slightly thicker around his middle these days, still as handsome as he's always been. Dark hair, blue eyes . . . Need I say more?

"No sprucing up for me then?"

"Sorry, you get the dog-end. I've been with my godsons and I need a drink. Now."

Ben opened the car door for me. "What are you talking about? You look great. Sasha said you would."

"What's going on with you and Sasha?"

"Nothing. She just went off on one because I'd forgotten to buy some milk. She does this sometimes when she's been away on a long trip. Far too used to hotel-living and having men bow and scrape to her. Once I folded the loo paper into a little triangle to piss her off when she was being so finicky."

"That must have smoothed things over," I said sarcastically.

"We get there in the end. You know what they say about arguments . . ."

"All right, all right, no need to rub my nose in it." He closed the door and walked around the car. When he got in he looked at me again, more carefully.

"You really do look terrific, Tess," said Ben. "A million times better than when you left. I hated it, but it was obviously the right thing to do. You're glowing."

"The benefits of a diet of dried apricots."

"I bet your tepee hummed."

"And vibrated."

"I'll open the window," he said.

He put on his seat belt and started the engine. "So, you been busy on your first week back?"

I smiled at him.

"What? I don't believe it! Already?"

I nodded. I can't keep anything from Ben.

"Actually, I do believe it—look at you. God, I'm jealous. Was it a good one?"

"Don't be mean," I said. "I love your wife."

"So do I. I'm not going to get into a who-loves-my-wife-more competition, but you know, occasionally I miss the excitement, the frisson of it. It's not as if I'm doing anything or even thinking about doing anything, I'm just remembering."

"As long as it's not too wistfully."

"I'm allowed to miss it, aren't I?" he asked.

"You're asking the wrong person. I don't know the rules."

"Was it one of those can't-get-the-clothes-off-quick-enough?"

I had to smile. "Exactly. Though my pants came off."

"Naturally," he concurred.

"His trousers too, but only as far as his knees."

We were both laughing when we pulled out into the traffic and still laughing when we entered the bar. This was why we were such good friends, because we can talk about this sort of stuff. In fact, we can talk about anything. Unless it's ourselves.

We went to a bar that was within Ben's parking permit. He planned to leave the car there and pick it up in the morning. This was why I was borderline alcoholic. When anyone wanted to escape from their domestic bliss for a moment they called me, because I flew solo. I didn't have to phone home and ask anyone permission to go out with my friends. I didn't have to book a babysitter a month in advance. I didn't have to "do diaries." When my single mates felt like a blast, they called me, because they knew I was entrenched in singleton and could always be persuaded to go out and drop some coin in a hotel bar. Even my eighty-four-year-old father calls me when he fancies a night out in the big smoke, which is indecently often for a man his age. I suppose I could say no to all the offers of drink. But why would I? Anyway, there are some people you never tire of seeing. And Ben was one of them.

"So what about a bottle of champagne to welcome my old mucker home?"

"Are you paying?"

"Only for the first two bottles," he said. "Then the cocktails are on you."

See. I watched him walk to the bar. I watched other women watch him walk to the bar. I watched other woman watch him turn back to me and smile, and then I watched them fail in their best attempts to get noticed by him. I'd been experiencing that sort of devotion from him all my life and it warmed the cockles of my heart.

Ben leaned against the bar and winked at me. He had laughter lines around his eyes that had crept up on me over the years, but he was still essentially the same blue-eyed boy with the aquiline face who'd walked into our classroom a million drinks ago. It was halfway through the summer term, we were eleven. I remember his ridiculous long hair. Hair his gloriously unkempt hippy mother had been proudly growing his entire nomadic life, hair that Claudia and I chopped off a week later, at his behest, with a stolen pair of nail scissors. His mother had taken him wherever the mood suited her, or as we learned later, where the men suited her. The constant uprooting canceled out the vastly wider life experiences he'd had, and

it was quickly apparent to Claudia and me that he was both naive
and in need of some mothering. There was nothing Claudia and I
liked more than a good project to get stuck into. We got him when
he was weak and didn't know his own potential. Our friendship survived puberty. Nothing could break it now. If there was ever a child
of the universe, it was Ben.

My phone vibrated. It was Helen's home number. Talking of former
children of the universe . . . I put it on to answerphone. I'd had
enough of Helen's happy little home for one day. Ben returned with
an ice bucket. He poured out two glasses. We drank to health and
happiness, as always. It was an old habit; only the content of the
glasses had changed. To health and happiness. God knows, it's a big
ask.

I told him about my depressing visit to Helen and Neil's house.
Ben knew Neil through work. Because he worked for a media PR
company their paths occasionally crossed. Usually late at night, in
private drinking clubs. That was how I knew certain things about
Neil that I wished I didn't.

"So you're still not feeling the love for the twins?"

Ben knew me far too well.

"For the whole lot of them, frankly. He makes my skin crawl and
she's just so damn grateful. I don't know what's happened to her. You
didn't get married and become an arsehole."

"That's coz I've always been an arsehole."

"How dare you. I won't have a bad word said against you."

"Actually, I saw Neil the other night . . ." Ben grimaced at me. "Up
to his old antics."

"Not again."

"'Fraid so."

I blocked my ears. "I don't want to know."

"I'm just saying, you know, maybe you shouldn't be too hard on her."

"It's amazing, isn't it? They both decided to have kids; her life changes irreversibly, while he continues, unchecked, doing exactly what he did before."

"Now you know why Sasha doesn't want kids."

"You wouldn't be like that."

Ben shrugged. "Maybe not disappearing down corridors with drunk actresses, but . . ." He shrugged again. "I like my life as it is, playing football in the evenings, tennis in the mornings, going out with you and getting pissed. I don't want to have to change all that for equality's sake. Then we're both sitting in, bored out of our minds."

"But what about having children?" I stressed. Feeling he was missing the point.

"For once I am in complete agreement with my wife."

"Really? You really don't want children?"

"No. Do you?"

"Yes. Of course I do."

"Why?" asked Ben.

"Don't be daft. Because I do."

"But why? Look at the grief they cause."

"You are just being selfish. A typical selfish male."

"Actually, I think I'm being selfless."

I laughed. "You'll have to explain that one."

"Sasha travels a lot, she doesn't want to end her job, and children do that unless you're happy to have full-time care, which she doesn't."

"You could become a house-spouse."

"House-spouse? What *Daily Mail* article did you get that from?"

I was deeply offended. "I don't read the *Daily Mail*. I made it up."

"I'm not the type to be a house-spouse. Rule number one, know yourself. Sasha and I are not good parenting material. Better we know that than have children we don't really want, don't really know and therefore can't really love."

Ben had a point, I thought. After all, parenting skills didn't run high in the Harding household. Why continue the misery? Still, he really was a lovely man, and they were a rare breed. It seemed a shame to me that there would be no more Ben Wards of this world.

"For what it's worth, I think you'd be a great dad. Considerate and charming and generous, all the things that you are and more."

"You're just biased."

"Horribly, it's true."

"My children would love you more than they love me, like everyone else I know. Even my wife. It would be annoying."

"You're right. And anyway, I can't afford any more bloody godchildren."

Ben refilled the glasses. "How do you know you want kids?" he asked, after clinking glasses again. "I mean, other than just social programming? Coz from where I'm standing, your life looks pretty perfect to me. You know that, right?"

Good-time girl. Little Miss Positive. Happy. Happy. Happy. That's me. "I got to thinking," I started tentatively. "You know. In India—"

Ben put his head in his hands, mocking me. "Oh no, you are going to go all hippy on me and join an ashram and have a brood of sniveling, knotty-haired children with a bearded fellow called Tree."

"Falling Tree. And not an ashram, a Native American Gambling Reserve. I'll be the one in the fake nails, diamonds and excessive leopard print."

Ben let out a bellowed laugh. "I can just see it. You'll smoke cigarettes and have a boob job and think nothing of feeding your children popcorn for dinner."

"How dare you. I don't need a boob job!"

Ben threw his arm around me and kissed me on the cheek.

"Oh, Tessie-babe, can't we just keep on doing this, getting pissed together and having a laugh?"

"You'll leave me eventually for a younger drinking partner. Someone with more liver capacity, and fewer broken blood vessels."

"I'd never leave you," said Ben.

"That's what they all say, until the liver spots appear."

"No amount of healthy hemoglobin can take the place of history."

"And boy, do we have history," I said. It came out before I'd had time to rethink my words.

Ben's arm tightened around my shoulder. "Don't we just."

I pulled away. "Are you drunk?"

"Yes."

"Good." I smiled.

"Are you?" he asked.

"Definitely."

"Excellent," said Ben. "More booze."

As I said, there are some subjects best avoided.

Awash in champagne, we finally called it a night. At my building Ben jumped out of the cab and opened my door. As he always has done. He asked the driver to wait a few moments so he could walk me to the door. He needn't have worried about my safety, Roman was on duty, but Ben has always walked me to my door. He hugged me.

"I missed you," he said. "Please don't go off navel-gazing again. My life deteriorates."

I smiled into his shirt. That cottony smell I knew so well. "Didn't you get the postcard of my long deserted beach?"

"You put a cross under a palm tree and wrote, 'Send more

supplies'—three words, Tessa King, three words in a month. Not impressed."

"But funny."

"Always that." He kissed me on the lips. "Night, gorgeous," he said.

"Night, Ben." The door closed. I turned and walked to the lift, feeling an early comedown. Suddenly I remembered the Channel 4 party. I turned back. Ben was walking slowly to the cab. I yanked open the door.

"Hey, piss-head, you going to the launch of Neil's new comedy series?"

He turned around. A deep frown fading as he did so. "The party? Wasn't going to, but if you are . . ."

I nodded. "Helen has asked me. I think she wants someone to hold her hand. You know what Neil can be like."

"Great, let's make a night of it," he said, now smiling. "I'll see you there."

I kept on nodding. "Will do. And Ben, thanks for my welcome-home party."

He put his hand to his heart, bowed his head and climbed into the cab. My second walk to the lift wasn't so gloomy. I went to bed happy.

The next day I walked into Sticky Fingers restaurant on High Street Kensington at one o'clock. There was Caspar, slouched low in his chair, but present and correct. I felt the iPod box in my bag, glad that I'd had faith enough to wrap it. Sixteen is a big age for a boy. I think it marks the birth of a man. I wouldn't like to be in his shoes for all the banoffi pie in the world.

There was another boy sitting next to him, taller and slimmer than Caspar. His name was Zac. He stood to shake my hand. His jeans hung so low I could see his boxers. I wanted to yank them up and tuck in his shirt. Shit, I was getting old. Caspar, on the other hand, mumbled something that could have been anything from a greeting to a veiled mafia death threat. I winked at Francesca to stop her laying into her son. I didn't think that would help matters. Caspar's two sisters, Poppy and Katie, were there, sucking on milkshakes that were bigger than them, and Nick and Francesca, and Nick's unmarried brother Paul, whom I liked but didn't fancy. This set-up has been going on for fourteen years; luckily, Paul and I have been in cahoots since the third attempt, so, it doesn't matter. To us, anyway. I think Francesca and Nick are still holding out, though.

"Would you like a glass of wine, Miss King?" said a sultry male voice to my right. "Or a Bloody Mary?"

"Please call me Tessa. In my head I'm your age; try to remember that when you talk to me."

He smiled. "Coca-Cola, then?"

I smiled back. "Perhaps not that young."

Zac leaned closer to me, his leg touched mine. "You're as young as the person you feel," he said quietly.

Surely I had heard that wrong. This boy, this child, was flirting with me? I looked at him again; he lowered his eyelashes coyly. Well, I never . . . Was I set to become the Joan Collins of my friends? I saw an image of myself in a few years' time: convertible car, a jewelry-wearing, snake-hipped youth lounging in the passenger seat who looked uncannily like a young Robert Downey Jr. (he often pops up in my fantasies). I was beginning to enjoy the scene playing out in my head until I took a closer look and saw that the young stud in my passenger seat was filling out his college application. I quickly ordered a medium-rare cheeseburger with chips and onion rings and, as a nod to health, some coleslaw. But firstly, a bottle of Mexican beer with a lime in the top. Bliss. I was in a good mood. If there were family tensions, I bulldozed my way through them, resolutely cheerful.

"I'm glad you got my message," I said, smiling, to Caspar while the rest of the table busied itself with a milkshake spill. Then I lowered my tone and leaned closer. "But perhaps you didn't read the subtext. Turning up was one thing, but a smile clinches the deal. And while we're on the subject, I'm adding another clause. Sit up straight right now or I'll return the iPod and buy myself the pair of shoes which your birthday gift just barely beat out." It is what my mother did with me when I was a baby, apparently. She said it was all in the tone. Tone and expression, the words didn't mean a thing. It must have worked with Caspar because for a moment he looked afraid and sat up. Francesca looked over just as I moved away and her son joined his party.

As far as conversation went, it felt like I was in sole charge of the ball. I dribbled and sashayed, passed and quickly retrieved, but if I dropped the ball, the table went quiet again. By the end of lunch I was exhausted. The monkey was all performed out. The only reward for my dazzling verbal dexterity was the attention I received from Zac, who, it turned out, was unquestionably flirting with me— terrifyingly successfully, at that. He was good with Francesca too, polite and charming, but always deferring to Nick. But I had no Nick to defer to, so he could let rip on me. The sly innuendoes were always delivered solely in my earshot, the personal questions disguised as polite conversation—it was impressive, to say the least. I thought it best to return to "batty aunt"–style conversation before I crossed a line, so I put a questionnaire to the table, hoping that the family bond I knew so well would return.

"To the table, in no particular order: who was the last person you kissed?" I looked at Nick.

He turned to Francesca and kissed her on the mouth. "My wife," he said.

"Quick thinking," I replied.

"Caspar?"

"This is a stupid game."

"Oh dear, I don't think Caspar has kissed anyone," said Nick.

The girls giggled. I pointed at the youngest. "Snoopy," Poppy replied, without a moment's hesitation.

"Francesca?"

"The gardener, but don't tell Nick."

"We haven't got a gardener," said Poppy.

"Dad is the gardener," said her elder sister. "Derr."

"Zac?"

"In real life, or in my imagination?"

I had a horrible feeling I was blushing. "Real life."

"Jen Packer."

Caspar sat up. "You said you hadn't."

Zac shrugged. "What can I do, mate? She threw herself at me."

"Paul?" I asked quickly. "What about you?"

He took a deep breath. We waited. "Gary."

Nick and Francesca swung round to face him. Paul shrugged. There was a nervous silence.

"Ice cream anybody?" I asked and winked at Paul.

As we walked down High Street Kensington, Zac caught up with me. "You didn't answer your own question." Although only sixteen years old, he was taller than me, and I'm not short. His legs were so long and his jeans hung loose over jutting hipbones. I had a crazy desire to clench his belt hooks between my teeth and rip the jeans off. I couldn't think of anything appropriate to say. So I said nothing.

"I know who I'd like it to be."

"And who would that be?" I asked before I got control of my tongue.

"I think you know, Mizz King."

The laughter exploded out of me. "Sorry," I said, and held my breath. It didn't help. The laughter erupted again. I couldn't speak. He looked so crestfallen, but I had terrible schoolgirl giggles and they would not stop. I tried to apologize, but the earnest look on the boy's face kept returning to me, the lick of his lips. I imagined him practicing in front of the mirror in the privacy of his own home, working on his lines, his long, languid looks, and the laughter would not stop. I tried to take his arm to offer some sort of physical apology, but he shook it off. I was in trouble now, and that made it even funnier. Just when I thought I'd got control of myself, the explosion came again, sending spittle flying into the pedestrian in front of me. Zac stopped walking. I continued, absorbed in my own mirth. Perhaps that was why I never had a boyfriend when I was that age. Perhaps that was the reason I still didn't. I guffawed all the way home, intermittently over the afternoon and many times in front of the mirror as I got ready to go out that night.

I opened a bottle of wine and treated myself to a long bath. Every person needs a constant in their lives, this was mine: lying in hot, oily water with wine.

I rang Billy. "Hey, Billy, it's me."

"At last. How are you? When am I going to see you? Was it great?"

"Seems like years ago already. What about one evening next week? Are you busy?"

"Ha, ha."

Billy was a single mother with no money to go out with and even less inclination. I should have known.

"I've got a movie out if you want to come over tonight?" asked Billy.

"Thanks but I'm . . ."

"Course you are, being stupid. Um . . ." Billy paused. "So, was it great?"

"You could come if you want, tonight?"

"Thanks but I can't. Madga is out, so . . . But have a good time."

I knew the answer would be no. It always is. Probably a good thing in this case since I didn't think Billy and Samira were a good mix. Billy wasn't robust enough for the likes of Samira and, if I was being truly honest with myself, I didn't feel like carrying Billy that night. I had a hard enough time holding my own against Samira's exceedingly forceful gravitational pull.

"How's my baby girl?" I asked.

"Wonderful." Billy's voice softened as it always did when she was talking about her child. We chatted about Cora, how school was, her health, her latest favorite teacher.

"I'm sorry," said Billy. "This is boring. You've got a party to go to."

"Nonsense," I replied in jest. "Knowing this stuff makes me feel part of the human race." I didn't realize the accidental truth of my words. "But I am beginning to wrinkle, which will not help my ever-diminishing ability to pull."

"You're gorgeous—stop it."

"I'll see you next week."

"Love to. Bye, Tessa. Thank you so much for calling."

I made a real effort with my clothes and make-up for one reason and one reason only: I imagined there was a slim chance Sebastian would be at the party. One friend of Samira's was likely to know another, right? The hair was straight, the boobs were out, the legs were on show. Normally I don't do legs and boobs, it's a little over the top and I'm the wrong side of thirty-five, but I was feeling daring. No, not daring. Hopeful. I would not use the word desperate. Earlier in the week, I had sat in front of my laptop and flicked at Sebastian's card. The one he gave me before we shagged. The one he probably wouldn't have given me after we shagged. But I wasn't thinking like that. I was hopeful. He'd reawakened my taste for lust. Fuel for the soul, which I feared I would never have an appetite for again.

I don't want to go over and over what happened with my boss. I'm bored of it. But there were times when I thought I was wholly responsible, just for being the way I was. It was noted that I had been out to drinks with him. I had, that was true, but only ever with the rest of our department. It was said that I sometimes dressed provocatively in the office. Every working girl has an outfit that transforms itself into evening attire. The hours I kept didn't make room for time to go home and change. With a different top and fabulous shoes I often tottered out of the ladies to meet friends. I knew I had not done anything to lead the man on, but sometimes I doubted myself.

In the fallout of the whole debacle, there was rage. Pity. Sadness. Guilt. Disbelief. Meeting anyone during that time was not going to be successful because I wouldn't have let it. But then that thing with Sebastian had happened. And now my taste buds were alive again, I wanted more. One sweet wasn't enough. I wanted the whole damn factory. I had "recovered" so well that I could even see the fuzzy outline of a fairy-tale ending to a story that hadn't yet made it to print.

Eventually I had succumbed and typed in his email address and started writing a jaunty "don't worry I'm not crackers, I'm a perfectly well-adjusted, independent (but not aggressively so) woman." It didn't work. Even the "Hi" looked suspicious. I deleted it and threw the card in the bin. It was not a particularly rash act as I knew I could get his number from Samira at any time. But perhaps I wouldn't have to. Perhaps he'd see me, looking fabulous, at the party, come marching up to me and tell me he couldn't get me out of his mind, and how did I feel about the suburbs, since his salary wouldn't be able to buy a place big enough for the kids . . .

The taxi pulled up outside the address given to me by Samira. I glanced up at the illuminated five-storey house in Belgravia, and wondered if the driver had got it right. Excited, I opened up my wallet to pay when I remembered I had completely forgotten to get cash out. It didn't matter. I always had a £50 note stashed away for emergencies. And for times when I forget to go to the ATM. It had been there for ages. I looked but the fifty quid wasn't there. I checked again in case I'd missed it the first time, but it was not there. Was I going mad? Had I spent it and forgotten?

I offered the driver a card; he told me his machine was broken, and drove around for another £3.80, locating a machine. The red lights on the way back put on another couple of quid, and when I paid I noticed that the light on the card machine was on. I think someone was taking the piss. Did I complain? Make a fuss? No. I handed over the fee, and because I am an idiot who wants to be liked, I tipped him too. As the taxi pulled off I wanted to run after it and demand my hard-earned money back, but, as if by magic, all the lights went green, and anyway, I was in heels. I had hoped that India would stop these silly setbacks affecting me so; that I would see them for the city-life trifles they were and not take them as proof that the world was conspiring against me. But watching the tail lights fade into the night, like watching Helen being pulled back home by her loving husband, just made me feel alone.

I walked into an amazing house, which promised to hold an amazing party, but saw nothing except that Sebastian was not there. All the glitter of potential faded. The party spirit in me vanished. I had to admit to myself then, my first night home had not been a blip: all that brown rice had counted for nothing. No amount of downward dogs was going to change how I felt. All the immaculate miniature food and vats of champagne weren't enough any more. A tall, dark, handsome (young) waiter approached me with a frosted glass of champagne. I took it. It was delicious. Well, maybe champagne would have to do for the time being, I thought, taking another large sip.

Despite my initial grouchiness, it turned out to be a fun party. There were people there I hadn't seen for a long time who were from different aspects of my life. Old colleagues. People from college. Even an old boyfriend, which was satisfying, because I knew I was looking good, and I could tell he thought so. When he later asked me why we'd split up, I caught myself putting an imaginary red line through that chapter and scrawling "Finished business" on it. What he'd done many moons ago was tell me over a pint that he didn't fancy me. He liked me a lot, he had insisted, just didn't fancy me. That was no longer the case. I made my excuses and moved towards Samira. I looked better now than I had when I was twenty. Perhaps that was something to celebrate. More champagne, please.

We were flying when we left the house in Belgravia. There was a plan to go to a private members bar in Soho. There was a nice-looking man with salt-and-pepper hair who asked if he could come in the same taxi as Samira and me. He was on his own. Then two silly girls made a fuss about being split up and wanted him to go in another. He looked so sad standing on the pavement that I got out too and said I'd wait with him for another taxi, at which point someone else shouted there was a space in another cab and pulled me in. So salt-and-pepper man had to get back in my original cab. It all happened in a matter of minutes. But it is quite crucial for later, so I am giving disproportionate amount of attention to that merry little taxi dance.

Salt-and-pepper man was waiting in the medley of people outside a nondescript door. Apparently, there was a private party on and even the private members couldn't get in. We would have to cross Soho to go elsewhere. Remember—I was in pretty impressive shoes. Walking was not pleasurable. I was beginning to wonder whether gallivanting around town was a good idea. I'd had a great night, it was late. Did I really have to go on somewhere? I certainly didn't need another drink. But the wavering ended when salt-and-pepper man offered me his arm. Of course I needed another drink. I am a weak, weak woman.

Halfway across Piccadilly Circus, my evening took a dramatic turn. We'd actually been discussing the sorry state of modern life which saw kids, boys and girls no older than sixteen, sleeping rough. There was a scary-looking posse of hooded lads sitting around the base of the Statue of Eros. The boys carried cans of lager, the girls sucked on bottles of Bacardi Breezer. And over them all hung a pall of dope. That's when I saw Caspar. A can of Red Stripe in one hand. A spliff in the other. Suddenly nomenclature didn't matter so much as that it was in Caspar's hand, in the early hours of Sunday morning.

I stopped walking and swore quietly beneath my breath.

"What is it?" asked salt-and-pepper man, looking concerned.

"That's my godson over there, and I am pretty sure he's not sup-posed to be." Caspar was easy to pick out because of what he wasn't doing. He wasn't chewing some girl's face off with his hand up her skirt. He wasn't crashed out on the ground. He wasn't in any leery group of tracksuited boys challenging tourists to fights. He was sit-ting on his own, looking glazed, taking intermittent swigs of lager and long tokes of spliff. It didn't look right to me.

"I'll catch you up," I said, pulling my arm away and heading into the throng.

I sat down on the cold stone. He didn't respond until I spoke.

"Happy birthday, Caspar."

He jumped, scrambled to his feet and threw away the nearly burnt-out spliff.

"Settle down, I'm not the police."

"What are you doing here? Did Mum send you?"

"Charming! Do I look like I'd go trawling the streets for wayward teenagers in these shoes? Have a little fashion respect."

He stared at me nonplussed, swaying gently, like a poplar tree in the summer breeze.

"I'm with friends," I explained slowly. "In fact, there's a bloke with salt-and-pepper hair who seems quite nice, so please don't puke up on me, it may put him off."

He tried to fight it, but the smile escaped.

"Then again, I've probably had enough. Maybe it's time to go home. Do you want to come with me?"

He shook his head.

"You'd be doing me a favor. I've promised myself no more one-night stands. You'd be a perfect contraception."

"That's disgusting."

"What?" I eyed the nearest couple to us; they were getting steamy right there on the pavement. "Am I too old to have sex?"

"Shut up, Tessa."

"Don't speak to your elders like that."

He laughed at the hypocrisy of my statement. I was pleased. I wanted him on my side. I wanted the amusing, clever little boy back, the one that took the piss out of me and got away with it.

"Sure you won't come with me?"

"Sure."

"Where are your mates?"

"Around," he said, getting defensive again.

"Do Francesca and Nick know where you are?"

He shrugged. I didn't want to lose what ground I'd won, so I passed him my card with my mobile number on it, and held my nagging tongue.

"Don't tear that up for roaches," I said as he slipped it into his back pocket. "And don't give it to Zac either."

Caspar smiled again. I had obviously scored highly with Caspar for not falling for Zac's charms. Having a very good-looking friend can be difficult and I wondered if that was the cause of his moodiness. Caspar had a sweet face, but he wasn't very tall, and he had curly hair. He was more cherub than sex-god, but I knew his looks would catch up with him again, and he'd be fine in the end. His father was the same, and now he was a very handsome man. But I don't suppose that mattered to Caspar; what mattered was now. What mattered was that Zac was probably somewhere surrounded by girls and Caspar was sitting here all alone.

"Have you got money to get home?"

"No," he said straightaway. I opened my wallet. That was when I remembered the missing £50 note and the day I'd asked Caspar to watch my bag, but I put the unbelievable thought aside and handed him a twenty. He practically snatched it out of my hand.

"That ain't a gift, boyo. You have to clean my car for that. Inside and out. Twice."

"Whatever," he mumbled. And I knew I'd lost him again.

I found the club eventually, but not salt-and-pepper man. Every time I was about to leave, someone brought me another drink. And just another fifteen minutes turned into another hour. I finally found salt-and-pepper man but the way the group had gathered it was difficult to get near him. It didn't matter; I was having a grand time without him, but it was nice to occasionally catch his eye and share a smile.

I was having a nice little fantasy about him when he appeared before me and asked me to dance. I must have been really pissed, because I thought that was a great idea. To the dance floor we went where some pretty steamy dirty dancing followed. He was very tall and nimble and could do all those spinning around moves that only work if you're a professional or drunk enough to go floppy. I fell into the second category. God only knows how I managed to stay upright. At one point I remember walking backwards over the dance floor, beckoning salt-and-pepper man to follow me. I'm not sure who I thought I was—but I fear it might have been Cyndi Lauper. Even so, it was fun and when I wasn't pouting suggestively, I was grinning like an Olympian.

Only trouble was, I didn't know his name and was too embarrassed to ask. He somehow knew mine, which made it worse, and made reference to a time we'd met before. I had no recollection of this whatsoever, but because I'd pretended to remember, I was now buggered. My one piece of luck was that he knew Neil, so I stopped asking investigative questions, hoping I could get the low-down on him through Helen. Perfect. Back to dirty dancing.

Eventually we ran out of fuel, and sort of fell into a slow dance that I would not normally do, but it was dark, and I didn't think anyone was watching, and actually it was nice. I knew a second before it happened that he was going to kiss me. I wasn't going to stop it. Unfortunately the Lord had other plans.

"Tessa! Your phone is ringing off the hook, do you want me to answer it?"

Samira was standing on the edge of the dance floor, holding my phone.

"Honestly, it's rung four times in the last few minutes. Whoever is ringing isn't leaving a message, they're just trying again and again."

It was three o'clock in the morning; phones don't ring off the hook for any good reason. I pulled away from salt-and-pepper man. It was Caspar's number.

"Caspar? Are you all right?"

"Tessa?"

"Who is this?"

"It's Zac."

Dear God. "Isn't it a little past your bedtime?"

"Don't flatter yourself. I thought someone ought to know that Caspar is puking his guts up, but fuck it, I was just trying to help."

"Where is he?"

"Oh, so now you want to talk to me?"

Children. These boys were children and men were babies. I was rapidly going off the idea of conjoining myself to one.

"Where are you?"

"Corner of Wardour Street and Old Compton Street, there's a club, we're going in."

"Don't leave him, I'm coming now."

"I'm not fucking babysitting him again."

Again? "Don't be ridiculous. He's your friend. I'll be there in five minutes."

"He's covered in puke."

"Just stay with him."

"Whatever."

Bloody idiot. Salt-and-pepper man found me at the coat check. I rapidly explained the situation and ran.

I decided against calling Nick and Francesca as I assumed some cover-up story had already been concocted. I'm staying with mates, my mates are staying with me; the sort of thing parents fall for again and again. So there was no need to alarm them in the middle of the night. But I was alarmed. I should have made him come with me. Sixteen years old for all of one day, and I had left him alone, already under the influence, in Piccadilly Circus. Easy pickings. I knew in my heart how he'd gone from stoned to passed out and covered in puke. My twenty-quid note. Why had I given him that? He was never going to use it on a cab. The sly little toad probably had a bus pass anyway. I had given him that note because I wanted to be popular. For the first time in my life I understood why my mother said parents had to be prepared to be hated by their children. I felt guilty as I ran through the deserted streets of London. Guilty as a parent. It was not a comfortable feeling.

I was angry with myself and right up until the moment I saw him, furious with Caspar. Soporific, he'd collapsed into a dark, dank, urine-stained corner. He was drunk and stoned, that was obvious; he was also alone. Zac was nowhere to be seen. Then I noticed the female officer. She was standing some way off from Caspar, but she was looking at him and talking into the radio on her shoulder. I ran, in those bloody heels, I ran.

"Hello? Hello?"

She turned to me.

"He's mine. I'm so sorry. I'm taking him home."

She looked at me. "How exactly? He's passed out."

Shit.

"Taxi?"

"As long as he doesn't get hypothermia before you find one that will take you."

I looked at Caspar. She had a point.

"Is he all right?"

"He's been very sick, so I shouldn't think pumping his stomach will help."

Oh hell. "What shall I do?"

"Well, you can't leave him here. Frankly, he looks a little too young to be here in the first place. Did you know he was here?"

"He turned sixteen today, yesterday."

"Sixteen?"

I knew immediately I'd said the wrong thing. He could have sex, he couldn't drink. Was she going to arrest him now?

"He must have got his hands on some beer from home . . ."

"And where were you?" She didn't have to wait for an answer, she just looked at my get-up. I was about to protest but then I realized if I did, she wouldn't let me take him home, so I took the disapproving looks and the sanctimonious tone.

"Do you have someone who can come and get you?"

She was just punishing me now. Would I be staggering around Soho in killer heels in the freezing cold wearing next to nothing if I had someone to come and get me! No. I'd have been in bed since eleven with a good book and maybe, if I was lucky, I would have had easy, uncomplicated sex before switching off the light. I would have had someone to hold me in the dark and chat until sleep took hold of me. I would have woken to find a cup of tea on my bedside table—

"Are you all right, madam?"

I snapped out of my reverie.

"I'll be fine," I said. I'll cope. I do that. I called the taxi firm I used to use with work. I still knew the account number which meant they couldn't refuse. I knelt down in front of Caspar and tried to get his head up off his knees.

"I wouldn't do that," said the WPC, a fraction too late. The movement set Caspar's retching off; he vomited all down my front. He didn't even have the politeness to apologize. He didn't even open his eyes. That alarmed me more than the stinking streak of his stomach's contents on my dress.

"Is he unconscious?" I asked.

I think that was when the audience's sympathy turned in my favor. The officer checked him over for me. His eyes didn't respond when we shone a torch in them. He was catatonic. A dead weight. She helped me lower him on to the ground, then put him in the recovery position. People stared at us as they walked past. The jeering would have been worse if it had not been for the presence of the policewoman.

"I could call an ambulance," she said.

"An ambulance? I wouldn't want to take up their time."

"He might have taken something."

"*Taken?*"

"You could search his pockets."

I must have looked terrified because she became much more reassuring. "Let's ignore the legal side of this for a moment. And worry about his health."

I thought for a second and then decided to take the woman at her word. She'd know more about this than any parent. She must have seen kids in this state all the time.

"We've been having a bit of a problem with cannabis recently." The imaginary "we."

"Do you know how much?"

I shook my head.

"Is he experimenting with anything else?"

"Like?"

"Amphetamines, cocaine . . ."

"He doesn't have access to that sort of money," I said, then swore loudly.

"What?"

"I don't believe it." I looked at Caspar, my sweet, cherubic boy, lying in his own vomit and other people's urine. "The little bastard stole fifty quid off me." I went through his pockets at that point and quickly found the tin I'd seen during his sister's birthday party. I'd been fooled by the beanbag, the teen posters on the wall, the remnants of childhood on the shelves, but here, against the backdrop of cold, hard cement, the tin didn't look quite so innocuous as it had before. I opened it up. It was nearly empty, but the accoutrements were all present and correct. Rizla papers. Torn cardboard. A pouch of tobacco. And a smattering of grass. The policewoman took it from me. She sniffed the tin.

"Skunk," she said. "I think you need to talk to your son."

My son . . . My son . . . I couldn't tell her now.

"This is a very high-strength variant of cannabis which could be responsible for the increase in psychotic episodes among adolescents. The anecdotal evidence is fairly damning. It's expensive too, which may explain the fifty quid."

"Psychotic episodes?"

"Have you noticed any changes in his behavior?"

Francesca had. "I thought it was just puberty."

"It could be. But skunk is a bad sign. I think that statistics are something like of all the children referred to doctors with mental problems, 85 per cent of them are smoking skunk."

"Jesus Christ."

"The government is considering a rethink."

"I read about it, but didn't think it related to me."

"No one ever does."

She was right, of course. It wasn't that I hadn't noticed the change in Caspar, but that I had chosen to ignore it. Francesca and Nick were having an impossible time with him and I had disregarded them both. Some godmother I was. Caspar started retching again. This time nothing came out.

"Keep him in the recovery position so he doesn't swallow his tongue," said the policewoman.

Nice.

Finally the cab arrived. It took all my legal powers of persuasion to cajole the driver into accepting the fare. It took the three of us to get Caspar into the taxi and lie him down, on his side, on the floor.

That was when I saw the small rectangle of folded paper peeking out from his back pocket. I looked at the policewoman; she'd seen it too. I bent down and pulled it out. I passed it straight to her.

"Are we still forgetting the legality of things?"

She didn't answer. I didn't blame her. I'd already asked enough of her. We watched as she unwrapped the paper. She shone her torch on its contents, put her finger in it and rubbed it between her fingers. I saw the white powder and felt my heart break. Grass was one thing, even strong grass which turned children into schizophrenics, but this—this was worse.

"Looks like I won't be taking you home after all," said the cab driver.

"Yes, you will," said the policewoman.

"He will?"

She held open the packet.

"Talcum powder," she said.

"Damn," said the driver, under his breath.

I peered at it more closely. "Are you sure?"

"Absolutely. The young ones often get duped like this."

"Thank God," I said.

"I wouldn't be too relieved," she said, holding open the taxi door. "Your son didn't set out to buy talcum powder this evening."

Roman had seen me come and go in many states with numerous people, but until now he hadn't seen me drag my prey across the lobby floor. The taxi driver had taken his enormous tip and scarpered.

"Good grief, who is this?" asked Roman, taking an arm.

"My godson."

"Young Caspar? No!"

Yes, my doorman knew the name of my godchildren. At the time I thought there was nothing wrong in that.

"He turned sixteen today."

"Well, he's learned now. Yes?" Roman nodded encouragingly. I was not encouraged.

Roman helped me get Caspar all the way to my bedroom, then left me. I stripped him and lay him on an old towel on my bed. He'd soiled himself and was sick again. I cleaned him up, wiped his bum, squeezed his nostrils free of debris, wrapped him in a clean white towel and put him back in the fetal position to await the next projectile vomit, terrified he would choke or swallow his own tongue. I was up all night. As dawn broke I felt as though I'd given birth to a teenager.

butterflies dancing

I heard the knock at the door, but it didn't register through my sleepy fog. Then I heard my mobile ring. When that went unanswered, my landline rang. I patted around the vicinity of the sofa where I had crashed out an hour after Caspar had finally stopped retching. I knew the phone was down there somewhere because I'd used it to call NHS Direct. Caspar had felt so cold, no matter how many blankets I put on him, that, befuddled by lack of sleep, I had been convinced that he was dying of hypothermia.

"Open the door, it's me."

"Errrrrrrrr."

"I've got fresh coffee."

I opened an eye and spoke to the phone. "Claudia?"

"Who did you think it was?"

"I don't know. I was dreaming."

"I'm outside your flat. It's nearly twelve—get up."

I crossed to the door.

"Oh God," said Claudia, handing me a coffee. "Have you just come in?" I was still wearing my top-totty outfit. Though now, of course, I looked psychotic.

"Long night?"

I took a sip of the milky, sugary coffee and nearly wept with gratitude. I nodded and swallowed. She followed me down the partial passageway to the kitchen bar.

"Hmm," said Claudia, eyeing the strewn clothes around my living area. She kicked at the jeans. Toed the battered Converse. "Either you're shagging a rock star, or your conquests are getting younger."

I held a finger up in an unladylike gesture.

"Is he still here, or did he run out semi-naked?" Claudia continued, not in the slightest bit offended. I still couldn't speak so I pointed to the bookshelf. Claudia peered over. There, lying on his back, his arms spread wide, all tangled up in my sheets, was Caspar. He looked angelic, the bastard. Whereas I looked like something an owl coughs up. I needed more caffeine and some decent foundation before I could be ready to give him the moral lecture of his lifetime, and mine. Claudia was staring at me with a look of horror on her face.

"I know," I said, nodding. "I've been up all night with him. It's terrible. I'm exhausted, I don't have the stamina any more."

Claudia blocked her ears. "Jesus, Tessa. I don't want to know."

"Know what?"

"He's fifteen, are you mad?"

"Sixteen, since yesterday."

"That doesn't make it any better, Tessa."

"I know. It meant they could have charged him with public intoxication or worse."

"Public intoxication?"

"Horribly, disgustingly drunk. I didn't want to freak out Fran, so I brought him here."

"Oh."

"What did you think I was talking about?" Then the horror of what she'd thought struck me with the unpalatable force of elephant dung. "Claudia!"

"He's naked."

"I'm old enough to be his mother. I almost am his mother. That's disgusting. You're gross."

Claudia started laughing.

"You are a filthy-minded cow, dressed up in a pretty Laura Ashley dress," I said accusingly. "How could you?"

"I don't wear Laura Ashley."

"Liar."

"OK, but only in the summer."

This time we both laughed. "I can't believe you thought I'd slept with Caspar. What sort of desperate witch do you take me for?"

"Sorry, Tessa, it's the hormones. I'm all over the place."

The mention of hormones is Claudia's ultimate trump card. All irritation, horror, boredom, jealousy—whatever one sporadically feels towards one's friends—vanishes. I couldn't feel any anger towards her after that.

"I didn't realize you'd started another round, sorry."

"Yeah. I just had to drop a charming urine sample into the Lister— it's so much easier on a Sunday because I can park. Then I thought maybe I'd get to see you too. So here I am. Sorry I didn't call."

I hadn't really listened beyond the word Lister. It had so many connotations: the Lister, a hospital that performed IVF. I didn't know how to react. It had been the kernel of so many hopes, created then dashed, created then dashed, created then . . .

"Are you starting the injections again?"

"We're going down another track actually," said Claudia, who'd sniffed and injected more hormones than the U.S. beef industry.

"Is that good or bad?"

"Good. Sit down, Tess. I've got something to ask you."

This was it. I wished she'd chosen a better time to ask, one where I was less weakened by exhaustion, one where all my rehearsed ar-

guments against her request that I be a surrogate mother to their
baby flowed convincingly from within. Now I was going to cry and I
promised I wouldn't when the time came, because the poor girl had
been through enough and this wasn't about me, it was about her and
Al, and God, why was I such a selfish cow . . .

"Would you consider . . ."

AAAAAAAAhhhhhhhhhhhhhhhhhhhhhhhhhhh

". . . being godmother to our child?"

"I've thought about this and I'm afraid . . . Sorry, what did you
say?"

"Would you consider being godmother to our child?"

I could feel the puzzled expression on my face cracking through
last night's foundation. "You don't want me to have your baby for
you?"

"Jesus, Tessa, I wouldn't put you through that," said Claudia.

"I'd do it."

"Liar."

"You're right. Sorry. I've thought about it, though."

"So have I, and it isn't an option. But being a godmother is, so
will you?"

"Of course. You don't even have to ask, I'd be delighted, but there
is one small observation I feel inclined to make . . ."

"What child?" Claudia finished for me.

"Exactly."

Claudia opened her bag and for a moment I thought that she was
literally going to pull a baby out of the bag. This isn't as stupid as it
sounds. It was a big bag. A Mary Poppins sort of bag. Excuse me, I
was operating on limited sleep.

"Our daughter," said Claudia, passing over a grainy black and
white ultrasound image of perfection. A clenched hand floated over a
pouting mouth, a tiny thumb extended to the ready. Above it perched

a ski-jump nose and a bowling ball head which tapered into a softly curved nape. I stared and stared at it. Look, I've seen these things before and they've all looked the same to me. I've often wondered if it wasn't a great con—different women go into the scanning rooms but only one picture comes out. But this little lady looked as complete and unique as if she were swaddled on my lap.

"I'm three months' pregnant," said Claudia. "I haven't told anyone, just in case. There is only so much sympathy a person can take, but she's still here and the doctors tell me I'm as safe as any other woman at this stage."

I nodded because I couldn't speak. Then she pulled me towards her and I sobbed in the same way that Claudia had done as time and time again they had failed to make a baby. She held me, like I'd held her. I hadn't realized until that moment what a huge strain it had been watching my dear friend go through something that I couldn't help her with. I sobbed and sobbed with relief, fear and joy.

"I know, I have a long way to go, but right now I'm pregnant, Tessa, I'm pregnant. I'm not going to fear this miracle. I'm going to be like any other expectant mum. The doctors say I'm playing on an even field, and I'm determined to enjoy it."

I cried again. So much for bravery.

Claudia made me tea and toast. I think I was in shock. While Caspar slept on, she filled me in on the previous three months. "And then yesterday I could have sworn I felt it move," said Claudia. "It was like someone was blowing bubbles inside me. It was amazing." She was radiating happiness.

"Fran said it was like butterflies dancing," I said, as always, falling back on my friends' experiences in all things domestic and familial as if they were my own. Actually, Fran had said that about Caspar, the first one. She hadn't been so complimentary about the girls' first signals. Katie wasn't butterflies fluttering, she was six extra pounds overnight and the sure knowledge that the scales were only moving in one direction.

"How is Al?" I asked.

"Cautious, but ecstatic," said Claudia, taking a seat on my cream sofa. "God, this view is incredible," she said, changing the subject and staring out over the river. "It never fails to amaze me."

"I'm very proud of you," I said, taking Claudia's hand. "You and Al are amazing. Most couples fold after being subjected to one tenth of what you've been subjected to. This little girl is very lucky to have you as parents," I said.

"Luckier still to have the best godmother in the world."

"Hardly."

"You let your godson puke up all over your 100 percent Egyptian cotton bed sheets. If that was all I knew about you it would be enough."

"Royal sateen percale cotton bed sheets, with a thread count of 250," I said.

"Well, there you go."

We sat on my sofa, our hands held over her little belly that contained a seven-centimeter miracle and stared out at the diamond-freckled river below us. She was right, it was an amazing view. I felt blessed.

A little while after Claudia had taken her prize possession home, Caspar walked unsteadily into the living room. As a lawyer, I'd seen the products of broken homes and abuse; Caspar was not one of these. I knew that everything in life was relative and I couldn't ask him to compare himself to a starving child in Sudan. That "Third World shit," as he described it, was beyond his comprehension and sometimes mine, if I were honest. But was the softly, softly approach the way to go? Should I just drive him home and dump him in it? Was parental fury going to get to the bottom of this or make it worse? Why didn't children come with a manual? Maybe this was my chance to prove that I meant what I said when I took on the role of godmother. That I would step up to the plate. That I would be more than a donator of gifts and treats. In spirit I believed myself more akin to Caspar and his generation than I did to his parents. I had not stepped over the fence. I had not said goodbye to irresponsibility. After all, I was young enough to be Caspar's friend with the added advantage of age. I could step into the role of mother. Not despite being childless, but because of it. Thinking about it, it had to be me. Who else was there?

I ran a bath for him, I made more tea and bacon sandwiches, I found some Gatorade and a couple of Aleve, and when he had relaxed, and all the defensiveness had left his body, I changed tack. It's another legal trick.

"I'm worried about you."

"I'm fine," he grunted.

"What I saw didn't look like 'fine.'"

He gave me a sort of "Fuck off, Mum" face, before remembering he wasn't at home.

"Is that the thanks I get for scraping you off the pavement?"

"Sorry."

"So tell me. I'm here for you."

"Drank too much, I guess."

"Kind of worked that one out for myself since the contents of your stomach are still in my shoes."

He pulled a face.

"And it's not really the booze I'm worried about. How long have you been smoking this stuff for?"

He shrugged.

"Caspar, either you talk to me or we go home and you can tell Nick and Fran. You decide."

He pulled a cushion up under his chin. "You wouldn't understand."

"Try me."

"I don't need to tell you anything," he said, his voice taut with petulance.

"Oh yes you do. You'd be waking up in hospital if it wasn't for me. Or worse, not waking up at all, ever, since you were unconscious and still vomiting. Do you know how many people die a year choking on their own puke?"

At least he looked a little embarrassed.

"Not only that, if it wasn't for me you'd have the police to deal with," I said. "Because while you were unconscious you were searched. And they found this." I held out the tin.

"It's not illegal to have it on you."

"You're right. But it is illegal to have this!" I opened my other hand. The one holding the talcum powder. I was taking a gamble here, hoping he didn't know he'd been duped.

"So I'll ask you again. What the hell is going on?"

"You don't know what it's like."

"What? Tell me. Are you being bullied?"

"No."

"Someone broken your heart?"

"No."

"Are you gay?"

"No!"

"Then what is it?"

I waited. He twiddled the cord of my dressing gown around his finger. He looked very small. I softened.

"Caspar, tell me. Whatever it is, we can sort it."

"You'll think I'm being stupid."

Probably. "I'll try very hard not to."

That seemed to be an acceptable answer.

"Home," he said.

"Home?"

He nodded. I could see that it hurt his head because he winced.

"What's going on at home?"

The fact that he wouldn't tell me made me worried at first; I let my imagination take me to places I shouldn't. Then it made me furious, because it was worse than I'd imagined—turned out it was nothing. Nothing. He felt left out. Left out. It seemed that Katie and Poppy took up too much of Nick and Francesca's time. I frowned, disappointed. "Let me get this straight. You're pissed off because you don't have exclusive rights over your parents?"

"I've never had exclusive rights. Nick and Francesca only have exclusive rights for themselves and the girls."

The use of their first names annoyed me. "Don't disrespect your parents in my presence, you ungrateful little toad."

He moved to get up. "Here we go."

"Sit. Down." Something in my voice worked. He sat back down. I leaned forward. "In four years' time you will give birth to a son. You won't be able to celebrate your twentieth birthday because your girlfriend has just struggled through her finals and soon after went into labor. While all your friends are partying hard, you and she are up all night with a baby you know nothing about. It's fun at first. Quite romantic, actually. But six months down the road your son still isn't sleeping through the night and you and she are exhausted. You are doing three jobs you hate in order to pay the rent and have enough money for milk and nappies. Remember, you are twenty years old. Four years from now. All your friends tell you to run, that you were trapped, that social workers will take care of your girlfriend and baby. It is mighty tempting because your girlfriend is too exhausted to talk to you as every last piece of her energy goes into keeping this tiny, dependent creature alive. Instead of bolting, you propose marriage, you take responsibility and spend the next sixteen years making your little family work. Can you imagine that? You, four years' time, a father for life."

"It's not my fault Mum got pregnant."

"No. Has she ever made you feel as if it were?"

Caspar shook his head.

"I didn't catch that."

"No."

"So what's this all about, then?"

"Tessa, you don't know what it's like. Mum and Dad are always so involved with each other."

"And this is your problem?"

"You make me sound like a spoilt brat."

"You said it."

"I thought you understood. I thought you weren't angry with me."

"I'm not. I'm fucking furious."

After that the conversation took a turn for worse.

"They've done bloody everything for you. Do you have any idea what they missed out on?" I wasn't even talking about all the big things they missed out on, like holidays, a dishwasher, a car, Fran's career; I was talking about nipping down to the pub for a quick pint. I was talking about attending their graduation party. Having a twenty-first. Friends.

"Your mum was the smartest girl I knew, have ever known." Not so easy to tell these days, I had to admit, but she was far smarter than me. I'd always had to work twice as hard to stay level with her. I sat next to her in the first lecture, I was sitting next to her at the

last; the only difference between her and me on that last lecture was
that she had a huge stomach and I had a hangover. In the months
that followed graduation, we were both up all night but for different
reasons. While I was at law school, she was at playschool. By the
time I was doing the rounds of regional courthouses, Francesca was
on the school run.

"She had big dreams, Caspar. She wanted to work for the UN,
travel all over the world, make things better. All it would have taken
was twenty minutes under general anesthetic."

Caspar winced. But it was true, one abortion, the abortion I told
her to have, and Francesca could have been running the UN by
now.

"When it came to it, she couldn't do it and her reasons, it turned
out, were sound. Don't repay them with this shoddy behavior, Caspar,
please. For her and you. Because I tell you, you'll regret it eventually
and you'll never be able to make it up to her. And then you might
really need this shit." I held out the packet of talcum powder again.

"It was only a bit of speed."

Speed. OK, I figured that was better than coke or crack. "'Only'?
And what about all this skunk you're smoking. Do you know it can
make you paranoid? Antisocial? Irrational? Angry? I wonder whom
I'm describing . . ."

"It's only weed."

"It's not *only* weed or *only* speed, these are drugs, Caspar. I don't
care what you think, but I don't know many heroin addicts who
went from Kool-Aid to heroin—you know what I mean? There is a
process that sucks you in. And it starts with this. Honestly, I thought
you were more intelligent than this."

It was about this point that we both started to tire of the fight.

We went to the kitchen and I put the kettle on. Caspar dragged
his sorry arse on to a stool and put his chin into his hands. My

cherubic, number one godson, all curls and pink cheeks—taking speed. It was a horrendous thought. He'd been so well loved; what more could any parent do than love their child? What did they want, these kids?

"Would you prefer it if your parents hated each other?"

"No, but it's embarrassing."

"It embarrasses you because they are in love with each other?"

He grimaced.

"You have no idea how lucky you are. You think happy marriages are the norm? Think about it. Fran's parents aren't together, Ben's parents were never married, Billy is divorced, I'm alone—"

"You're not married. It doesn't count."

"I might be if one of my relationships had worked."

"You need a boyfriend first, Tessa," said Caspar. Out of the mouths of babes.

"Oi, you're in the doghouse, don't be cheeky. If your mum and dad reward themselves with a private joke that you are not part of, or a cuddle on the sofa, or holding each other's hands rather than yours, you should thank your lucky stars. It's why you have the foundation you do. It's why you have a home."

He picked at a digestive biscuit. "I feel left out."

"So you think it's your turn to embarrass them?"

"Maybe."

"But the only person you're embarrassing is yourself."

Caspar couldn't grasp the reasons for his behavior or how he felt because he didn't understand them himself. He was a boy. Having a childish reaction. Throwing his toys out of his pram. The trouble was, at sixteen, he had access to more adult toys. He rubbed his hands over his face. When he looked up he had tears in his eyes.

"You're right. I've lost all my friends. Zac's an arsehole, I don't know why I listen to him; I've put Mum and Dad through hell . . ."

I walked round the bar and put my arm around him. He leaned against me like he used to do when he was a child. I could feel my heart surge with love for him and nearly burst into tears myself with relief.

"Tessa?" he said quietly after a few minutes.

"Yes?"

"I stole £50 from your wallet," he said.

If I thought I couldn't love him more, I was wrong. I kissed his head. "I know," I said.

"You didn't say anything."

"I was waiting for you to tell me."

"I'm sorry, Tessa—for that, for last night, for my behavior when you came home . . ."

"Ssh. No more sorries. Not to me, anyway." I held him, feeling the full force of unconditional love.

"Have I got a record?"

"No," I said. "But it was close and trust me, a drug record is a very hard thing to shake." I knew what I was talking about, not just from a legal point of view, but from a personal one. Claudia and Al had wanted to adopt after their third attempt at IVF failed. They had a horrendous time. Al had a record. He was caught bringing half an ounce of cannabis resin into the country from Vietnam. It was a mistake, of course. He'd thought he'd lost the stuff but it had fallen through a tear in the lining of his bag. The adoption agency could only read in black and white; Al's grey story couldn't be heard. Ironically, Claudia was told that she'd be more likely to get a child if she wasn't married to Al, but Claudia wouldn't listen to his idea of divorce, even if it was only on paper. We all thought his insignificant record would not play a part in his adult life. We were very wrong.

"Thank you for bailing me out."

"It wasn't me. The officer gave you the benefit of the doubt."

"I should thank her for that."

"Well, you can. I know where she's stationed."

"I'll write a note . . ." He sighed heavily. "It's over, Tessa," he said into my shoulder. "I've been an arsehole."

That was when I felt the little boy I loved was gone, and a fine man would emerge, though not all at once, in his place. So much for my maternal instinct.

ticktock

Why is it that when I know I have to be suited and booted and on parade I fall in through my flat door at four in the morning, having popped out for a quick drink nine hours earlier? It was innocent enough. I'd spent the week effectively ignoring all the things I had to do while spending hours on the things I didn't. Despite having long chats with my parents about my next move, I managed to forget to make any of the calls I had to until I was in the middle of a yoga class, in the cinema, or it was three o'clock in the morning. I'd lie awake having lengthy rehearsals of what I would say when I called the recruitment agency but in the morning I'd have a boiled egg, make some coffee and spend a happy four hours listening to music and clearing out my wardrobe. Procrastination is an art I have clearly mastered.

But then on Friday evening a girl I used to work with sent me a text message saying she was in the area. We agreed to meet up in my local pub for a speedy catch up. I would have ducked it, although I liked the girl very much, because she was closer to the work drama than I cared to go at present. However, she told me she was meeting friends for dinner, which meant we couldn't get stuck into a long debate about my ex-boss, and also, she had moved to another chambers. It was to be one quick drink before going home to think pure thoughts about renouncing the devil at the twins' christening the following morning. I had a shandy, for heaven's sake. What trouble could a shandy get me into? Less and less lemonade, that's what. I am a weak-willed woman with a terrible desire to flout responsibility—except, of course, that's only half the story. Because I long for responsibility too. I long to say, "Sorry, can't find a babysitter. See you in seventeen years."

I should have never left my flat because after a few more pints, and a great deal of gossip, it seemed like a good idea to make my ex-colleague's friends come to where we were. Then it seemed like crisps were as good as anything for dinner. And then the bell tolled and someone suggested a sweaty disco club round the corner that I didn't even know existed. And then, of course, tequila . . .

Most civilized christenings are at three o'clock in the afternoon. Thus the replete and fully rested child is more likely to reflect the success of their exceptionally natural, gifted parents and gurgle perfectly through the service. It also gives the godparents, who tend to be a breed apart, time to recover from their night out. But Helen and Neil opted for the eleven o'clock service, followed by a fully catered-for champagne brunch back at their enormous house. I woke the morning after my "quick drink," pulled the eyepatch off one eye and squinted at the clock through caked-on mascara. I pressed "snooze" one more time, knowing I was getting dangerously close to cutting down even my own speedy personal record for scrubbing up to an unacceptable panic. I went over my outfit in my head. My hair reeked of tobacco, but I didn't have time to wash and dry it. I wondered whether Febreze might work. Maybe a heavily scented hat was a better option. I possessed a particularly fetching trilby that I purchased off eBay which would hold the odor in nicely, but it meant a quick rethink on the part of the wardrobe. Trouser suit.

High boots. Airy, fairy, floaty godmother look was out, gangsta-rap, hip-hop queen was in. The alarm buzzed again. Surely twenty minutes hadn't passed already?

Full-fat Coke and tinted extra moisturizing cream with an SPF of twenty-five were the first items I lined up for my repair kit. I took the Coke into the shower and coated my boozy skin with extract of grapefruit, wearing a plastic shower cap so watertight that it left unsightly indentations along my hairline, like my own personal stigmata. More scented body cream, hairbrush, no make-up—make-up, more scent, fabulous boots, bag and hat and I was ready to walk into the hallowed portals of St. John's Church perched on top of the hill that Ladbroke Road climbs. Claudia could be the good godmother. I would be the godmother that made the grandmothers' eyes roll and the grandfathers revert to their twenty-five-year-old selves. I would be the ying to Claudia's yang. I didn't know who the godfathers were. Friends of Neil's, I presumed, so I had already dismissed them.

My taxi arrived outside the church just as Neil's ochre-colored Range Rover Sport pulled up behind. I paid, then turned to see Helen, looking incredibly glamorous, emerge from the back. She was wearing a very tailored white suit with a tight pencil skirt and staggeringly high "nude" heels. Her dark skin glowed, her hair was pulled back and hung in one long thick furling strand down her back. Her bold make-up accentuated the tapering of her wide eyes. The only jewelry she wore was a diamond cross and her diamond wedding ring. The haggard creature I'd seen was gone. She looked incredibly beautiful. The transformation was hard to take in. She smiled at me as someone handed her a bundle of lace that I took to be one of her sons. Neil took the other bundle. He looked fit to burst and it reminded me sharply that despite my own prejudices towards the man, no one really knows what goes on in the privacy of a marriage. It was a secret society that boasted only two members.

It should not be judged on the snippets of information that landed at the feet of the non-members, or second-guessed by the uninitiated. Neil and Helen smiled at each other and I stepped proudly into line behind them, ready to become godmother once more. Twice more. Four times more. Tick. Tock.

Claudia was already inside the church, chatting to a portly woman clutching a stack of hymn books. I could see Al's bald pate hiding behind a rather unwieldy, old-fashioned video recorder, taping it all for posterity. I waved at some people I recognized, and then realized seconds later that I was waving at the cast of a sitcom that Neil had been in, and lowered my hand. I looked away and smiled at a pillar. I was trying so hard not to feel awkward or out of place. Maybe I shouldn't have dressed like Michael Jackson.

"You look fabulous," said Claudia, grabbing my arm.

"No, I don't," I replied. "But I appreciate the lie."

"You do," she insisted. "Why is it so hard to get you to accept a compliment?"

"I only got to bed a few hours ago."

"Now you mention it, there is a vague whiff of the brewery about you."

"Compliment, you say . . . I hoped I'd covered most of it with grapefruit."

"Don't worry, I'm pregnant. I have the nose of a hound. No one else will notice. Was it a fun night?"

"Very. I met a girl from work—"

Claudia grabbed me aside. "Oh my God. And . . . ?"

I exhaled. "He's gone. In fact, he went mad after I left. He's been committed!"

Claudia's mouth dropped open.

"I know. Complete breakdown. It wasn't really anything to do with me." I felt an odd sensation saying that. Relief. Disbelief. And a terrible sadness and anger because if it hadn't been anything to do with me, why had he chosen to follow me home? To call me during the night; stand over my desk and watch me work; ostracize me from my colleagues by favoring everything I did. Then throw an enormous boulder in the middle of my career path. If it had nothing to do with me, why was my life upended, on hold? "Turns out he's got some mad compulsive thing going on; it could have manifested itself as pencil shavings collection or avoiding cracks in the pavement. My friend didn't really know the details. They're trying to keep it hush-hush, but according to someone else in another chambers, the wife had him committed."

"Something many wives might envy."

"Not you."

Claudia smiled but carried on patting my arm reassuringly. "Seriously, you must be so relieved."

"I'm relieved because it proves that I didn't invent all of this."

"Come on, why would you?"

To make my life more interesting, I wanted to say. I paused, "Because I was bored at work?"

Claudia ran her hand up and down my arm. "No, hon, that was real." If there was a silent subliminal message in her reply, I chose to ignore it and my first answer. Just in case.

Al came up and put his arm around his wife's waist. Claudia beamed up at him. Al was slimmer in build than Ben. And obviously had much less hair. But there were similarities too. They both had an easy charm, and were men of the deepest integrity. Al spoke softly and listened to others, which was why Helen adored him as well. Hell, we all adored Al. He was fundamentally a kind man, and they seemed hard to come by. He smiled back at his glowing wife and held the smile until she was distracted by the organist, pumping up the pedals, then I saw his expression change. The look we exchanged was enough. He knew I knew, I now knew he knew I knew, and we were both terrified. Claudia's attention returned to us and the moment passed.

"So, Tessa, are you ready to welcome Jesus into your heart?" Al said, leaning over for a kiss.

"Unmarried, skilled and willing to provide food—you bet," I said.

"I thought he was married, wore dresses and had a penchant for prostitutes," Al replied, before being poked in the ribs by his wife. "Or was he married to a prostitute?"

"Al, we are in a church!" said Claudia, raising her eyes to the heavens.

"The dress thing I could probably overlook, but married men are out."

"Do you think monogamy and monotheism are part of the same package?" asked Al, tilting his head to one side.

"Alexander Ward, are you suggesting Jesus could have taken a second wife?"

"Shh," said Claudia.

I giggled. "I think Claudia thinks we are getting dangerously close to blaspheming."

"No," said Claudia, beaming broadly. "You are blaspheming. Ah, Reverend Larkin, may I introduce you to Tessa King, the other godmother."

I turned to see a handsome man in a dog collar smiling at me. "Of course, the one who couldn't make it to our little pre-christening chat."

I searched my brain for a reason why I hadn't wanted to have a tête-à-tête with this man. Oh yes. I am not a Christian and currently see organized religion as an impediment to social inclusion and world peace. I don't have a problem with God, you understand. I have a problem with what is done in His name. Any of His names. Is it hypocritical of me to accept the role of godmother, therefore? I have had this debate with myself numerous times and the answer I've conveniently come up with is no. Slight of word, an extra vowel here and there, and religious declarations are easily transformed into sensible moral codes of conduct that I've been happy to verbalize. God becomes Good, and I'm happy to welcome good into my heart. Renouncing evil is a skill I'm honing. At Caspar's christening I opted for sneezes instead of Jesus, which didn't work so well because I got the giggles; I don't think Fran and Nick minded. The day they were married and christened their son was a day of incessant laughter. We were playing at being grown-ups. Well, I was.

"Claudia tells me you are a bit of a pro at the godmother thing, so you've probably heard it all before."

I smiled at the vicar. He was being nice, but his words had a familiar sting about them that I was keen to ignore.

"A refresher course over a pint would probably be useful," I replied.

The vicar laughed.

Claudia laughed.

"You're terrible, Muriel," she whispered into my ear, as we watched him go.

She was wrong, I wasn't terrible. I felt terrible. I didn't want to be a vamp, a predator, a woman with loose morals. I wasn't really like that—couldn't they see? I was simply reverting to type, putting on a show, being what they expected me to be. I didn't want to be a professional godmother. I wanted to be me. But who was that? Just as I got a handle on her, she seemed to change.

I must have frowned because Claudia looked concerned.

"You all right with this?" she asked.

I nodded like Churchill. Not the statesman. The nodding dog.

"Remember," said Claudia, "I know how you feel."

That was true. We had both done a fair few christenings; this was only the first time she'd done one pregnant.

I kissed her cheek. "Right," I said. "Let's do it."

Claudia took my arm and together we walked up the aisle to take our place in the second pew.

A lot of my single friends find weddings hard. Another brazen reminder of what they have failed to achieve: to find someone to love them. I don't. I actually love a good wedding so long as you know the people getting married really well. The trick is avoiding the weddings of people you don't know that well but are invited to unexpectedly. I went to a few of those, thinking that venturing into new pastures may yield alternative and exciting crops. It was not to be. My dining companions were either gay, prepubescent, or sat to the right of Genghis Khan. So I stopped accepting those invitations. They are also cripplingly expensive.

Weddings of friends I find easy. I go with no expectations other than to have fun with my mates. Christenings, however, are different. At weddings you are only one step behind. Something that could be rectified by the end of the evening.

Failing that, possibly by the end of the month because no one ever knows when they are going to meet "the one" or "someone," at any rate. At christenings it is all too clear that you are two steps behind, and suddenly the one in the white dress getting all the attention is toothless and dribbling and reminding you that babies take time to cook, time to make and you still haven't found someone to make them with and the one thing you don't have is time. I lowered my head and pretended to pray, which felt largely like praying. Keep my mother strong. My father alive. My friends safe. My godchildren happy. And me? What did I pray for me? I squeezed my eyes shut. I wanted children, God, not more godchildren.

"Hey, Tessa, shift it." It was Neil. "This is David and Michael." I looked up at the godfathers. We all shook hands. David did not have a ring on his finger, but there was a chalky watermark on the left shoulder of his jacket that looked distinctly like dried spittle to me. Sure enough, moments later, a small child ran up to him and passed him a plastic train, then ran away again to a woman holding a baby. She smiled at me. I smiled back. Michael, I recognized from the world of comedy but couldn't quite place.

"Congratulations on *The Pen,* I loved it," said Claudia gushing at Michael. Ah yes, it was all coming back to me. *The Pen* was a very successful series that Neil had had a bit part on. Michael wrote it. I think it won lots of awards. "The world is yours for the taking now, I should think," said Claudia. "It was absolutely brilliant."

"My girlfriend is away filming," he replied. "Otherwise she'd be here."

Claudia looked perplexed. "Right," she said, and looked at me to see whether she'd misheard. She hadn't.

"But yes, things are going well for us," he continued, then turned back to David, the other godfather. The organ began to play.

"Welcome to my world," I whispered in her ear.

"I don't understand."

"You're not wearing your wedding ring."

Claudia glanced down at her hand. "So? It's at the jeweler's."

"He needed to mention that he was attached, just to make sure there were no misunderstandings."

Claudia frowned again. Bless her, she'd been out of the game for a long time. "Misunderstandings about what?"

"About marrying you and siring your child."

"But I was only complimenting him on the show," she whispered furiously over the Mozart.

"You are a woman of a certain age, with no ring on your finger, and he is male and therefore in your sights as a potential sperm donor. He was simply marking out the battle lines."

Claudia sat back against the pew. From time to time I saw her shake her head a fraction as she digested my words and his.

"But I wasn't being remotely flirty."

I shrugged. "You spoke." Claudia went back to shaking her head. At one point she gave my hand a quick squeeze.

"You are very brave, Tessa," she said, staring straight ahead.

I squeezed her hand back before letting go. Coming from the bravest woman I know that was a compliment I would take.

There are a million little reasons why you love the friends you have. When Al came to join us in the pew, he slid in next to me so I was sandwiched between him and his wife. He flung his arm over my shoulder, leaned forward and shook hands with the other two men. Claudia slid a fraction away from me so that even Al's fingers weren't touching her. Al wouldn't even have noticed, but I did. And so did the comedian with the girlfriend because when we all started talking again, he happily engaged with me; he looked me in the eye, he looked at Al, but he never once glanced Claudia's way. She lent me her buffer. It wasn't for long. Who belonged to whom would materialize quickly enough, but for the moment I was not the social pariah, something to be feared, I was just a reasonably good-looking woman with enough social skills to make a professional comedian laugh. I did not care one bit that he graced me with his attentions, but I observed wryly how he ignored my friend. The whole episode lasted a few minutes but I learned a lot.

We sang hymns, listened to readings, heard from the Gospel. It was a major production. Then we processed back up the aisle to the stone font where water was rather unceremoniously poured from a couple of two-liter Sainsbury's bottles into a glass bowl. The vicar went down in my estimation at that point. It's hard to imagine that the waters of the River Jordan are flowing out of green plastic bottles, though he asked us to. The twins did not make a sound. They slept through the whole thing. Neither even grimaced when the cold water was ladled over their scalps. Since I had barely seen those boys do anything other than cry, it was amazing how easy it was to adore them when they were asleep and I felt a warm outpouring of love for them which, I am ashamed to say, I hadn't experienced before.

Helen stood before the assorted throng as ravishing as she'd looked the day Claudia, Al and I had met her in Vietnam. I thought again what extraordinary potential Helen had had back then. Potential that was still untapped. Maybe the twins would be the making of her. Maybe she needed something to love to make her whole. Maybe Neil was a means to an end and the means were worth it.

"Do you turn to Christ as Savior?" The vicar was looking directly at me. Taken aback, I mumbled my response, conscious that if I did not believe one iota of this then I would be able to hold the vicar's stare and stand mute.

"Do you submit to Christ?" he asked, still looking at me.

Is it just me, or are these questions getting harder? "Submit" is not a word that forms easily on my lips.

"I submit to life," I quickly replied, swallowing the fourth word. I should have swotted up on these questions.

"Do you come to Christ, the way, the truth and the life?"

Oh dear, I could feel the rumblings of schoolgirl giggles. The involuntary flicker of muscles at the side of my mouth. Claudia knew me well enough not to look at me, but I saw Al smirk behind his video camera. I think we were fourteen when we were thrown out of the school carol concert for exploding with laughter during "Oh Come All Ye Faithful," *Oh come ye, oh come ye to Bethlehem . . .* Absurd,

I know, but it was impossible to stop laughing. I pretended to cough. The vicar looked away. He'd probably seen enough.

The catatonic babies were passed in front of the four godparents and we all made a sign of the cross over their untroubled brows. Mine was more a kiss than a cross, but the love I felt for them was beginning to feel real. After that it was easier as the service became more of a group affair and the attention was no longer on us four. We took our seats for one final hymn and the Lord's Prayer. I had always liked the Lord's Prayer; it made sense to me and I used to say it with gusto. But then they changed the words which I was gutted about because I'd believed them when they said it was in the words that the Lord had taught us. Well, how could it be if they'd changed them? I may have only been thirteen, but I knew when I'd been conned. I started to wonder what other liberties my religion had been taking in the name of the Lord. I'd been meaning to ask a priest for years. Maybe today would be the day.

Suddenly four trumpeters appeared. Claudia, Al and I stifled more giggles, silently agreeing that the pudding was now definitely being over-egged. One more "Thanks be to God" and, to the tune of "Oh When the Saints," we heirs of the promise of the spirit of peace were free to go and get drunk.

Outside in the sunshine, everyone was smiling. There was a lot of milling about and calls for photos. We lined up along the cemetery wall and smiled into a dozen lenses. Still the twins slept, even through the trumpeting, which I thought was odd. Everyone said how incredibly good they were being. I watched Marguerite, Helen's mother, approach the newly baptized twins and noticed that even Helen's nemesis could not dim my friend's dazzling smile. Helen was protected by layers of christening gowns, delicious baby smells and the love of her friends. Yes, I thought, giving Neil a kiss on the cheek. Maybe the means was worth it. Not for me, but for Helen. I was happy for her. I was happy for Al and Claudia who were now entwined in each other. I glanced at my watch. Yes, I was happy, happy, happy—now, surely, it was time for a drink?

No one was making any obvious moves towards the gate, so I loitered and smiled some more.

"Tessa King," said an accented voice I knew too well. "Are you alone?"

No, I'm standing here with my imaginary friend, what does it look like? But then Marguerite knew that. She is brutally aware of the power of words. It is her forte.

"Marguerite," I said, smiling as I turned. "You must be very proud of your daughter today. She looks absolutely ravishing. Honestly, I think she gets more and more stunning as she gets older, and to think she only just gave birth."

Marguerite matched my smile but I knew the scoreboard read one-all. Marguerite never appeared to pride herself in her daughter's beauty. She never prided herself in anything Helen did. We all knew the interior design course Helen had started would come to nothing, but at least she had tried to turn her hand at something. Helen was fantastically cultured. Jetting between her warring parents, she had had the chance to visit every major art gallery in the world, most historical sites of both the modern and ancient world, and had picked up an amazing eye for beautiful things. Her house in Notting Hill was a testament to that taste. But Marguerite had slammed interior design as the playground for dizzy, rich blondes. Helen never recovered and left the course halfway through.

I studied my friend's mother, so different from my own. Her long grey hair was plaited down her back. She wore Nicole Farhi grey cashmere trousers and matching wrap secured in place by a hunk of amber. The collar of a crisp white shirt framed her long neck. She was and always had been the epitome of elegance. Marguerite wore Farhi. It was like a signature thing with her, along with the short, rouge-noir-coated nails. She also wore heavy, dark eye make-up and could still get away with it. She was Helen, without the Chinese gene. There were many things I knew about this woman—she was vain, she was selfish, she could type 110 words a minute, she liquidized most of her food and she should never, ever have bred.

"I don't really understand the need for all of this," said Marguerite, her accent still carried a hint of her Alpine youth. "Of course, it's wonderful that she has managed to have children, but did we really need the trumpeters?" She smiled conspiratorially.

I resisted the urge for a little bitch. "Nothing wrong in wanting to show off your achievements," I said, looking over at the bundles of lace.

"Tessa, do you really think having a baby is an achievement? Anyone can do that."

I looked over at Al and Claudia. He was standing behind her, his chin resting gently on her head, his arms wrapped around her, their four hands resting on her belly.

"Not everyone."

Marguerite was watching Neil take slaps on the back from other small white men in dodgy suits. "You know what I'm saying. The baby bit is easy for most people. Let's see how they do as parents. Perhaps it's not as easy as she thinks."

That was probably the first time I'd heard Marguerite refer to her own mothering skills, however obliquely.

"She has Rose to help her," I replied, not letting her off that easily.

"Rose. Of course. But you know, having too much help is something she should be wary of." She looked back at me. "You have to learn to cope by yourself in the early days or you may never be able to.

I was surrounded by my ex-husband's family, jabbering away at me in Chinese, grabbing Helen all the time; I had no idea what to do."

Was I supposed to feel sorry for her now? No way. Not after all the years of mental torture I'd witnessed. "I think twins are a bit different. I barely see her as it is, and that's with help. She's completely ensconced in babyville."

"She wanted a girl, you know. Can you imagine why?" Marguerite sucked in her cheeks. I didn't reply. I didn't want to go there.

"Poor girl got twin boys instead. What are we going to do with boys? They are so primeval. They have to be exercised like dogs."

"She loves those boys," I said.

"Are you sure about that?"

"Of course," I replied, without even thinking about the question. "Don't you? They're your grandsons."

She scowled. "Why do you always make everything so personal. It's very dull."

"Oh dear, Marguerite." I smiled jovially, teasingly, but I was trying to claw back some ground. "Finding the notion of granny a little hard to take on board?"

"Tessa, you know you are more intelligent than that, please don't play dumb for me. My point, which you are choosing to miss, is that maybe you only see what you want to see, what you expect to see. Helen has a husband and children, ergo she must be happy. Am I right?"

I wanted to stick my tongue out at her, but that would make it three-one to her. She looked over at her grandsons. "I don't think life is really as simple as that," she said. "Of course, I am pleased to have grandsons. But you are asking me to jump for joy because my daughter has managed to do what women are programmed to do. These are babies we are talking about. Babies are not very interesting, as I'm sure you're aware."

"Except to their mothers," I said, digging again.

"There are no guarantees for that, Tessa."

Clearly.

Marguerite went on. "What if you discover you have a child but you don't possess the martyr gene required to enable you to give up most of yourself to the upbringing of your child at exactly the point in your life when you are in position to take the benefits of your own upbringing and do something of note? Are we lemmings? Can we not break the pre-programming? Are we not allowed to be individuals? It's absolutely ridiculous."

Marguerite was right about one thing. I did make it personal. I wished I didn't, because then I could enjoy some of these debates, but I knew she was just justifying her abysmal mothering, when what she should really be saying was sorry. I think that's all it would have taken. I don't think Helen asked for much more.

"Great women and good mothering don't go hand in hand," stated Marguerite.

So that's your excuse, I thought to myself. But I'm not as brave as I look, so kept mum.

"You and I both know that Helen didn't have many other options left to her. What else was she going to do?"

Actually, your daughter had a great deal of potential, if only she'd been better directed.

"It figures," I said.

"What figures?" she replied.

"All the mothers of my friends with children have told me that they love their grandchildren as much as they did their own, if not more." I paused. "Obviously it works the other way around."

"I know that there is a part of you that agrees with me, Tessa, whether you care to admit it or not, otherwise you wouldn't still be single. Unless you're another of those desperate women waiting for a man to come and take care of them?"

She thought she'd cornered me, but she was wrong.

"I think it's more about taking care of each other."

"Christ, Tessa, if you want something to care for, buy a pot plant. But whatever you do, don't be a lemming. It would be such a waste."

Marguerite left me strangely fascinated in the moss-covered stone wall. I picked at the soft green plant until she was safely back with the congregation. I knew she was mean, but sometimes I forgot that what made her such a dangerous opponent was her intelligence. With that final unwanted compliment, she'd taken the round. Now I definitely knew that I needed a drink.

The basement of Helen and Neil's house resembled Carluccio's deli by the time we arrived, and I was quickly soothed by fabulous char-grilled vegetables, streaks of Parma ham and a fishbowl of Gavi di Gavi. I hadn't moved away from the buffet table when I was joined by David, my co-godparent, the one with the spittle on his jacket and the plastic train in his pocket.

"It's Tessa, right?" he asked. I had a mouthful, so I nodded the affirmative.

"So how do you know Helen and Neil?" he asked, helping himself to food and putting it straight in his mouth. I quickly swallowed. I wanted to make this absolutely clear. "Helen is my friend, I've known her since I was eighteen," I replied.

"Neil?"

"Only met him after they got engaged."

"It was quite quick, wasn't it?"

Four months. You're telling me. "When you know, you know, or so they say."

David shrugged. "So you and Helen were at school together?"

"Actually, we met in Vietnam."

"Vietnam? I thought Helen was half-Chinese."

"She is. We were all backpacking."

"Helen backpacked?"

"Well, not exactly, but it wasn't Louis Vuitton either." He still looked unconvinced. If only they knew what she'd been like. Was still like. Underneath all the gilding. "Don't be fooled by the Gaggenhau kitchen and Manolos. Helen was the original wild child."

Since Helen was busy doing a convincing impersonation of Bree from *Desperate Housewives,* my fellow godparent did not believe me, but I really wanted him to know the Helen I knew.

"Honestly, when I first met her she was trapped in a hammock, laughing her head off because she couldn't get out. Lysergic acid had a lot to do with it." David smiled. I went on. "Needless to say, we all developed a mammoth crush on her, and spent the rest of the trip a happy foursome, mesmerized by the sunsets, and sampling much of the local produce."

"By which you mean, that not sold in the market."

"You didn't hear this from me."

"Sounds like fun."

"It was one of the best times of my life," I said, truthfully. I looked over at Helen and felt a pang of nostalgia. One of, or *the* best time, I wondered. Was that it? Was that what I was forever trying to recreate? China Beach. LSD. Freedom. All underlined by the raw pain of a broken heart that made me feel so alive? I looked around the room. Helen had moved on. That was clear enough. So had Al and Claudia. Friends once, so much more now. Just me, then. Standing alone on China Beach, always waiting for the sun to set? I looked up, lost in my own thoughts, to see Helen standing next to us.

"What are you two looking so conspiratorial about?" she said with a smile.

"Tessa here is filling me in on a few missing details about you."

"Oh?" Helen looked at me.

"He's exaggerating," I said, obviously poking David in the ribs.

"What was she telling you about? Because I can top any story about me with one about her . . ."

"Well, there's a challenge," said David. "China Beach."

I thought Helen might lose her cool, but to my relief her smile broke into a laugh.

"That's probably all true, the bits Tessa can remember, anyway," said Helen. "But ask old innocent here about hitching a lift on the back of a Honda Eagle in the red-light district of Aix-en-Provence and driving topless through the countryside with a saxophone player . . ."

I pointed at Helen. "I wasn't alone."

"Nor was I on China Beach."

She turned to David. "Or when I got stuck in a mountain bar drinking schnapps and had to ski home with the pisteurs by torch-light . . ."

She rubbed her chin. "Or when I got chatting to a pilot and hitched a ride in his plane . . ."

Helen put her finger on her temple. "Or when I was in transit in Bali, on my way home from backpacking around Australia, and decided to stay after seeing a certain world-champion surfer walk towards Customs . . .

"Or when I—"

"All right," I laughed. "You win. I'm a reprobate too."

"They say youth is wasted on the young," said Helen. She shook her head. "But not in our case, hey, Tessa?" She kissed me lightly on the cheek.

"Sounds like you two had a bloody riot."

"The benefits of being an heiress and a perennial student." Helen winked at me.

"What have you studied?" David asked Helen.

"Not me. Brains over here." Helen linked her arm through mine. "Tessa was at university, then law school. It was great for me because she got lots of holidays."

"Lots of bloody work," I retorted.

"That's the amazing thing about you, you've always managed to do both so convincingly." Helen turned to David. "So, David, have you ever been to Vietnam?"

He shook his head, smiling dumbly. I recognized the expression. I'd come across it a million times over. My fellow godparent had just developed a crush on the mother of his charges.

She touched him on the arm. "Well, you must. Take the kids, it's so easy over there. And the food . . ." She closed her eyes a moment, reminiscing again. "We had the best time."

I smiled too. Because we had.

"When I die, I think I'd like my ashes to be scattered on China Beach."

"Helen! A wholly inappropriate topic of conversation at your sons' christening!"

"It's important," she insisted, her expression quite serious. "You never know what's around the corner."

I shook my head. "China Beach will probably be like the Gold Coast by the time you pop your clogs, all casinos and girly bars."

"OK then, any beach would do."

"My wife comes from ridiculous aristocratic stock," said David. "The family all hate each other, but when they die they're all put in this huge vault whether they want to be interred or not. Personally, I like the idea of being scattered on a beach. Will I be able to? Not unless I get divorced, which I'm not planning on doing, or our kids don't get their slice of the pie."

"You're joking?"

He laughed. "Some old madman made it a stipulation of the money."

"That's weird," I said.

Helen smiled and made her excuses like the professional hostess that she was. We watched her flow effortlessly into another group of guests and work her magic on them. "That's the first time I've really chatted to Helen," said David. "She's so different from what I expected."

"Told you."

"You just wouldn't know it," said David, staring after her.

"That's because you're a friend of Neil's." It came out sounding more detrimental than it was meant to. "I mean, you know, there are some things you don't tell your husband, I guess . . ."

David looked back at me.

"You're not his mystery brother, are you? God, I'm always doing things like this."

"I didn't know Neil had a brother."

"No one does, that's why he's a mystery."

Neil walked past with a bottle of champagne in his hand. I tried to silence David, but it was too late. I knew why Neil didn't see his family, Helen had told me. He was embarrassed by them.

"Hey, Neil," said David. "Is your brother here?"

"God, no," said Neil, without stopping, though I swear I saw him bristle. "He and I are not alike. Trust me, you wouldn't like him."

But I'd love him. My thoughts obviously registered on my face because David smiled at me again.

"What?"

"You don't approve of your friend's choice of husband, do you?"

I grimaced. "No, I mean, yes . . . Of course I do. She's really happy . . ."

"Oh, don't worry, your secret is safe with me. To be honest, I don't really know the bloke that well."

"Huh?"

He leaned a bit closer. "I work at the BBC. We've done some things together a few times but I wouldn't describe us as proper mates."

"Why did he ask you to be godfather, then?" I asked, probably being a bit slow on the uptake.

David looked a little uncomfortable. "Well, we're not doing too badly. We think they're hoping for good gifts."

I shook my head. "They're pretty well off themselves, I don't think that's it. What do you do at the BBC?"

"Head of comedy."

"Ah," I said.

"Ah, indeed."

"Why did you say yes?"

"How can you say no?"

"I don't know," I replied. Just when I was beginning to feel warm, happy feelings for Neil, I was reminded just how awful he was. Of all the men in the world Helen could have married, why on earth did she marry him?

"Don't worry," said David. "My wife is great, Al and Claudia seem really nice; we'll just have to stick together and get horribly drunk at all their birthday parties and take it in turns to forget Christmas."

"What about godfather number two—are we not going to be getting pissed with him?" I whispered.

"Not unless you want to spend all day talking about Michael Kramer."

"I suspected as much."

A woman leaned over David's shoulder. "Hello. I don't need to ask who you're bitching about, do I?"

"Tessa, my wife, Ann."

I took an involuntary step back. I didn't want this woman to think that I was after her husband. "It's all right," said David. "Tessa thinks Neil is a pig too."

I hid my face in my hands.

"David, you're supposed to be shining the light of Jesus on the world, not slagging off your host."

"As you can tell, Ann is a much nicer person than me," said David.

"So nice that I came all the way over here to tell you that Sam has crapped everywhere."

This was the moment that wife reminded husband of his familial duties and cut him from my web.

"Nice," said David. "Excuse me, Tessa, it's my turn."

"Oh no you don't. I'd prefer to get elbow-deep in baby crap than have to listen to Michael Kramer wang on about himself because he thinks I'm going to repeat everything to you and therefore you'll give him a job."

"Sorry." David looked genuinely apologetic.

"I'm used to it, I just get bored when they think they're hood-winking me." She turned to me. "Sorry, don't mean to sound like a sour spare part, but it is very annoying when people only talk to you because of what your husband does." She squared her shoulders. I liked her. "Right, I'm off."

David said, "Where's Luke?" He turned back to me. "Our three-year-old."

"Trying to peel open the twins' eyelids. I figure there are enough staff in the house to stop anything disastrous happening." Ann took a glass of champagne from the bar. "More booze, I think. See you later," she said, smiling at me. "I'll be the one smelling of poo. Maybe that will ward off all ambitious comics."

"It will definitely work on Neil," I said.

"Not a nappy-changer?"

I shook my head.

"Well then, I hope he's hot shit in the sack," she said as she walked off, thankfully leaving me no need to respond. Neil was not a fantas-tic father and, from what Helen had told me, he was not a fantastic lover. Was he a good husband? Well, I couldn't prove anything, but . . . I didn't want to think about that. Think happy thoughts. I excused myself from David and went in search of my godsons.

I found Claudia with the twins.

"Is it normal for babies to sleep this long?" she asked me as I approached. "Shouldn't they be fed at some point?"

"Presumably they were well fed before the service." I glanced at my watch. It was nearly three o'clock. "Helen probably cheated and gave them meat and two veg for the first time in their lives. I remember when Billy weaned Cora, the first time she had chicken I think she slept for six hours. Her body simply shut down in order to digest the stuff."

"You are going to be invaluable when our baby is born," said Claudia. I sat down next to her and lifted a sleeping baby on to my lap. We had one each.

"Any idea which one is which?" I asked.

"None," said Claudia.

The baby on my lap stretched. "It's real," I exclaimed, leaning over him. Sleepily, the baby opened one eye and looked at me.

"Hello, little one," I said. "You've missed all the excitement."

He yawned with one eye open, then slowly opened the other. He was still very floppy from his deep sleep but managed a gummy grin when I smiled at him. As if by magic the baby on Claudia's lap also started to come to life. Claudia and I purred and stroked our little parcels and were rewarded with more sleepy smiles by our captive audience. I caught Helen looking over at us. She looked worried. I wanted to put her mind at rest that her little boys were fine.

"They've just woken up," I mouthed, so as not to scare the babies. Helen broke away from the people she'd been talking to and hurried over. She was not smiling.

"They're fine," I reassured her. "The drugs have just worn off, that's all."

She stopped dead in her tracks. "What?"

"I'm not being serious," I said quickly. I was just continuing the fun.

"That is a bloody stupid thing to say, Tessa." Helen took the baby I was holding and called to the nanny to take the other. It felt to me like the child was being removed from me. He arched his back and started fussing like he had the day I'd been at their house the previous week.

"They were fine," I said, trying to reassure Helen and make the awkwardness of the situation disappear. It didn't work. I made it worse.

"And now they're not," she said. Implying it was my fault, or was I being paranoid? People had started to notice that the stars of the show, who had hitherto been largely absent, were awake. A crowd started to gather. I watched Helen's entire physical presence change as people approached, asking to hold them. The twins started to fuss more and the one in the nanny's arm started crying.

"Hungry," said Helen loudly, backing away from everyone. "Won't be long." I watched her bolt from the room. I knew of women who got psychotically protective over their newborns, but this was ridiculous. Did Helen think I was going to contaminate her children in some way?

The following evening, back at home, in my wonderfully disgusting tracksuit, with my aching feet and liver being soothed by a pot of chamomile tea and some homemade brownies (yes, I bake), I rang Ben. I told him about my run-in with the Wicked Witch of the West, the dishy vicar and the fact that the godfather barely knew Neil and Helen.

". . . then she just switched. I was holding the baby and when she saw, she just swept down and snatched it off me."

"I'm sure you're just exaggerating."

"I'm not," I insisted. "I was kinda hoping you'd be there."

"We got the stiff invite, but Sasha's mate was down for the weekend, you know, Carmen and her husband . . ."

I did and I didn't. That was sort of "their world" and I didn't really belong. Except for me, all of Ben and Sasha's friends are married. Sasha used to throw big dinners for them all; she'd ask me and a random banker from the City, but she got busier and said I didn't appreciate her efforts, so she gave up.

"It was good until Sash and I made arses of ourselves singing a duet. Oh my God, you'll never guess who we ran into. Guess, you'll never guess—"

"Give me a clue," I said.

"Blew his finger off trying to make a bomb."

"No. That nutter, Kevin, Trevor—"

"Keith."

I screamed. "Keith Jackson, of course! Where were you? Is he still missing a finger?"

"He's a serious hot shot."

"At karaoke?"

"I didn't hear him sing."

"Idiot. I meant did you meet him at the karaoke bar?"

"No. He's the bloody head of ICI or something, I don't think people like that go to karaoke bars."

"Wow, Keith Jackson."

"We went to a new hip restaurant first and frittered away money on expensive water. He was there too with a foxy blonde."

"Keith Jackson and a foxy blonde?"

"I'm telling you, he's done well for himself. He came up to our table because he recognized me. Couldn't believe we were all still friends. He wants to meet up. I think he quite liked the idea of seeing you again."

"Perleease. Does he still look the same?"

"Exactly."

"Thanks. I'm not coming . . ." We chatted on, through the *Antiques Roadshow,* and the news. Eventually my ear got too hot and itchy to continue talking, so I called it a night.

"Don't worry about Helen," said Ben. "She's just hormonal, remember that, and don't take it personally."

"See you at the launch."

"Love ya," said Ben and ended the call.

I should have heeded Ben's words. Instead, I lay in bed and rolled the Helen thing over and over in my head. We were fine going over old ground, but when it came to her husband and children I made her defensive and nervy. She had snatched the child out of my arms— couldn't get more personal than that. Finally I came to the sad conclusion that she had gone through the portal and wasn't coming back. Her children were more important than our friendship, naturally, but did that mean there was no room for our friendship at all? And if that was the case with Helen, would it be the case with Claudia and Al? Would I lose them all? I punched my pillow a couple of times; for some reason I simply couldn't get comfortable. Normally on a Sunday night I panicked if my dry-cleaning wasn't hanging in the wardrobe and I wasn't in bed by nine-thirty, but I suddenly remembered that I wouldn't be in my clean pressed suit on the tube at eight the following morning; I could sleep all day if I wished. So I pushed myself out of bed, went to the kitchen, made myself some food and lay on the sofa channel-surfing until I found a stupid movie to watch. It was two-thirty when I finally fell asleep.

baby bunting

I always relished the opportunity of going to Claudia's house. Her staircase held a permanent exhibition of my life. Every time I saw those seven-by-ten-inch photos, I was amazed all over again at how fresh the memories are, how open the wounds, and what fun we had. They go up the stairs in chronological order. I first appear on the third step. I was seven years old. Claudia reckoned she'd run out of stairs at forty. She'll run out of wall space entirely if the baby is born. When, I mean. I meant when. Her collection of photographs is almost identical to mine, except mine are in a huge sports bag under my bed.

In fact, Claudia's house was a testament of the time she'd had while trying to have a baby and the courses she'd taken while trying not to obsess about it. None of them worked. Her drawings were of children, her sculpture was fetal, her cushion covers were pastel and her knitting only came in one size. What it did mean was that her small cottage south of the river had a very cozy, bric-a-brac feel. The only thing missing was a baby. Since I had nothing to do that week, I had happily agreed to help Claudia finally decorate the nursery in a non-toxic paint. Al was on his way to Singapore to look at building a new hotel. Claudia had drawn the outline of bunting three-quarters up the wall. All I had to do was follow her color scheme.

I waited for her on the third step, staring at our seven-year-old selves, earnestly holding hands and frowning at the sun. I swear we hadn't changed much. She still had shiny dark hair, I still had frizzy blond hair (though now much assisted since I had started going grey). She still had blue eyes; I still had brown, except when I cheated and wore colored contact lenses. We were still physically diametrically opposed. I was always considerably taller than her. I'm straight. She's curvy. Her skin is like porcelain; mine is pock-marked (that's an exaggeration, of course—I have two small scars from the personality-defining spots I had during my teens, but they feel like pockmarks to me). Her nose is like a button; mine is like a beak. My legs are long; hers still go down to the ground without changing shape. Many times we've swapped body parts and reckoned that, between us, we could achieve perfection. Although I always thought there should be more of her and she always thought the opposite. We had a drunken fight about it once. Girls are silly sometimes.

The picture a couple of steps up was of us lined up with our uniformed classmates at school in Camden. Ben and Al were in it too. It was a historical picture, because it was the term that Al joined our threesome. Ben and Al had met when Ben's mother had briefly lived in North Yorkshire. Some quirk of fate meant that, for completely different reasons, Al's family upped and moved south. One day there was lanky Al, sitting at his desk looking nervous. He didn't stay the new boy for very long: Ben remembered him immediately, their friendship took off where it had been left, with Ben's sudden departure, and our threesome became four. Al brought the countryside into our urban world. In Regent's Park we ploughed fields and herded cows. Our games were as real to us as the zoo was. We were a very happy foursome.

*   *   *

Claudia came up the stairs behind me with coffee for me and something herbal for her.

"That's my favorite," said Claudia, pointing to the only one that I too have framed. It was taken after our O levels and we were about to be ripped apart by evil parents with differing views on further education. We took a train and buckets of cider to the south coast. We were huddled on a pebble beach, the sun setting, drunk, happy and free. A passer-by took the photo. Ben and Al have their arms wrapped around me and Claudia. We are all laughing at something Al said, and not paying the photographer any attention. It is a great shot; the pebbles have turned magenta and the sky behind us is a deep purple. I envy our youth and often wish I was back on that beach. It was all so platonic, so innocent, untroubled. Al and Claudia didn't become a "real" couple until nearly a decade later. She always teased me that if anything were to happen it would be between Ben and me. Man, did she get that one wrong.

"What was it that Al said, to make us laugh like that?"

"I can't remember," Claudia replied.

Ben didn't do his A levels. His mother needed him to start earning money so she wouldn't have to rely on lovers any more. At sixteen he was still bewitched by her carefree ways. Only later did he realize they'd been neither caring nor free. So he got a job in a post-production company as a runner. It was there that he met Mary. Mary was two years older than us and worked on reception. It was a ridiculously serious relationship. On the weekends, when Claudia, Al and I were reconvening to puke up on Southern Comfort and lemonade, Ben was playing house. He and Mary had dinner parties with avocado vinaigrette to start with. Mary was nice enough, but she was old even for her older years. I think it happened because Ben didn't have a normal family. There was never any food in Ben's house. In Mary's there was every foodstuff you could imagine, as well as a mother, a father, a friendly sibling and a dog. They even had sex once a week like an old married couple. Ben was only seventeen; we all thought it was hilarious. Well, Al and Claudia did. I was a bit pissed off.

"I lost him during the Mary years," I said, looking at another photo of me, Al and Claudia in Camden market, without Ben.

"We all did," said Claudia.

"That's what I meant."

My parents had a bit of money by then—two incomes, one child, and so they thought it was time to go private. I didn't want to go but I have to admit that I got better A levels than if I'd stayed. I needed to be forced to focus because we were messing about too much. Being a new girl in a new school, costing my folks an arm and a leg, did that. I worked hard during the week, then met up with Claudia and Al during the weekends. (And Ben, when he was allowed off the leash.) I found the richer kids hard to understand—they took the piss in class, some barely turned up; they didn't seem to care one iota about the exams, or anything else for that matter. It was quite an eye-opener for me and I ran back to where I felt comfortable. With my old mates. It wasn't that I was intimidated, though I think my parents thought that; it was that I was disappointed. These were bright kids, brighter than me, and so advantaged, but they mocked education, I guess because it was a tool they thought they didn't need. It is a testament to that time that I walked away from college with straight As but no friends. I know my parents were right to split us up—my career, my independence, my gorgeous flat are basically thanks to those As—but I sometimes wish they hadn't. "What about this one?" said Claudia, pointing to one of Ben in hospital with his leg in traction. Al was leaning affectionately across him. I nodded. What about that one? It was the summer after our A levels.

The summer we were supposed to go to Vietnam, the four of us. Ben had wangled time off because he'd got himself a better job starting the following September. Things were waning with Mary by that time, thank God, and we all hoped their relationship wouldn't stand up to the time apart. But there was no time apart. Ben broke his leg a week before we were due to fly. I was with him when it happened. I stared back at Ben's leg and his unsmiling face. A lot of my life lies in that break. But that's another story.

Claudia pulled on my sleeve. I followed her upstairs where she presented me with one of Al's old shirts. I dutifully put it on. I'd half expected a smock with my name on it.

I started on the green flags. Claudia went for pillar-box red. We tuned into Magic FM on the radio, opened the window and sang into our paintbrushes when any favorites came on.

"How long is Al going to be in Singapore?" I asked over the din of Claudia getting carried away with Shakespeare's Sisters' "Stay."

"Months. Typical, isn't it? But it's a huge building project and we'll be needing the extra money. The plan is he works on this contract while I'm pregnant, then can take a bit of time out after the baby is born." Claudia smiled. I felt the fear in my chest tighten.

"Do you remember how Ben used to sneak away from Mary and meet us in Ed's Easy Diner?"

Claudia put down her paintbrush. "Please, Tessa, let me talk about it," she said softly. "Nothing bad is going to happen."

"Sorry." She was right, of course, but I felt so afraid for her. I think that part of the reason why I had been so happy carrying on my life as I had was because I knew that I didn't feel the same desperate need to have a child that Claudia did. Although that was changing, I still wanted it more for Claudia than for myself.

"I do remember Ed's. Mostly the cheesy fries—what I wouldn't do for some of those now," said Claudia. There was a look of longing on her face. I put an arm around her. "You really are pregnant, aren't you?"

She smiled at me. She was so happy. "I'm inventing cravings, just so I can have them. I'm wearing maternity clothes even though I don't need to. I'm pathetic. Al went out and bought me ice cream before he went this morning."

"You be very careful, Claudia Ward. The extra calories required to fuel a pregnancy equates to one yoghurt a day. Not a tub of Ben and Jerry's."

Claudia dipped her brush into the paint pot and moved back to the wall. "How do you know this stuff?"

"Osmosis," I replied.

"It's weird."

"Not really. Everyone I know has had, or is having, babies. I'm a walking encyclopedia of this stuff. Cracked nipples? Use Kamillosan—also a very good lip gloss. Cradle cap? Olive oil. Talcum powder is now a no-no, the fine particles get on to their lungs. Pacifiers are now encouraged. I don't want to know any of this stuff, I certainly don't need it, but, bless 'em, they tell me anyway, and, for some reason that I will never understand, think that what they're telling me is gripping."

"I'm doing it too, aren't I?"

"I don't mind it from you," I said. "Maybe I'm being a tad defensive. I guess I file it away in the hope that it will become gripping some day."

"Oh Tessa, it will. You've just got to meet somebody."

"Haven't you heard? It's not about meeting somebody any more."

"Huh?"

"No, it's that I've put my career ahead of my biological clock. Apparently there is now some machine that all career women like me can pee on to find out how many eggs we have left. Just in case I go to a meeting one day and miss my opportunity to have a baby."

"I'm lost."

I leaned against a dry piece of wall. I was lost too, to be honest. The article had enraged me. "All this time, I thought I was working to pay off my mortgage, the bills, feed and water myself, since no one else is going to do it for me. Turns out I've been selfishly pursuing a career instead. I *have* to work. I'm not not having kids because of my job, I'm not having kids because I haven't met anyone to have kids with. Now if they invent a machine that I can pee on and a blue telephone number of my ideal partner appears on a stick, then I'll purchase."

"You don't need a machine, you'll meet someone soon. No one knows what's round the corner."

"How many corners, Claudia? Because I feel like I've turned them all." This conversation depressed me. I was better at not thinking about all of this. "I meet people all the time. It never works out. I don't know why."

"Hmm," said Claudia.

"Why, what do you think I'm doing wrong?"

"Do you really want to have this conversation?" she asked, a more serious tone creeping into her voice.

"Yes. I need all the help I can get. Claudia, I want this to be me soon. I really do. Tell me, what am I doing wrong?"

Claudia put her brush down. I did the same.

"I don't think you're doing anything wrong," said Claudia, turning the radio down.

"But . . . ?"

"But, then again, you don't really let anyone close enough to you for you to have to do something wrong. You don't blow it. But you don't grab hold of it either. I've seen boys drift away from you because you give them nothing to hold on to."

I picked up my paintbrush again.

"That's yellow," said Claudia.

"Sorry." I put it down again.

"Do you disagree?"

I exhaled loudly. "I feel like I'm out there grabbing at things. I know last year wasn't great, but that was understandable. I shagged a guy two weeks ago, if that helps."

"That doesn't count, you're never going to see him again."

"It's not my fault I like the bad ones."

"Whose fault is it then? And anyway, that's bollocks because you don't just like the bad ones."

I ducked the question. "I met a nice bloke last weekend. It got quite heated on the dance floor but then I had to go and make sure Caspar didn't drown in his own vomit."

"But you didn't really need to look after Caspar, you could have called Fran."

"I couldn't."

"Yes, you could have. You chose not to."

"He needed my help—trust me, dobbing Caspar in to his parents would have been worse, and anyway, he didn't ask for my number."

"You should have given him yours."

"Not possible. Remember how that bloke was with you at the christening?" Claudia nodded. "He snubbed you just for saying hello. You just can't go around looking like you're interested these days. People write you off as a stalker if you so much as mention a number . . ." I paused for dramatic effect. But thinking about it, what I was saying was real. It was tough out there. Whether it was being done to me, or I was doing it to myself, I couldn't tell, but I was beginning to feel like a failure just for thinking that maybe I wanted a husband and some kids. Was it so bad to want what everyone else had? Why did I have to do everything for myself when everyone else was getting help? When was someone going to look after me? I picked up a stick and stirred some paint absent-mindedly. I didn't like these conversations. "I've been hurt. I guess I've got more barriers up now."

"Don't pull out that stock answer. Everyone has been hurt; it's not a good enough reason to barricade yourself in. And it's not about your boss either."

"Ex-boss."

"Whatever. Tessa, I'm talking about something that has been going on for a long, long time, and you know it."

"Since when?"

"Tessa . . ."

"I don't know what you're talking about. Tell me."

Claudia looked at me intently. I played dumb. An act I'd perfected so well I convinced myself most of the time that I had no idea what she was insinuating.

"You're gay."

There was a second of silence before we both burst out laughing.

"You silly old tart," I spluttered.

"Had you." She laughed again.

"What if I was? This could have been a very difficult thing for me."

Claudia laughed again. The woman had a heart of stone. "Bollocks. I've often wished you were. I know some great gay women who'd be perfect for you."

"And this I'm supposed to thank you for? Mind you, I did snog a girl once, and it wasn't bad."

"Maybe you could go to see an acupuncturist and ask her to bring out your feminine side."

"Masculine side, you idiot."

"Depending on whether you wanted to be the bloke or the girl in the relationship."

"The girl. No, the bloke. No, the girl. I'm not doing away with my girly products and I don't really want a blokey girl shaving in the bath, so she'd have to be a live-out lover. So I'm the girl, I'd still earn—must have my own money—live on my own, and just call in my bitch, who's a bloke in disguise, for the occasional shag. Hang on, isn't that my life?"

Claudia laughed again. "Stop, I'm going to pee in my pants."

She left the room. I heard her laughing up the stairs to the little bathroom on the landing. Silly old cow. I sighed with relief. Claudia was a wise woman. She knew better than to open that old can of worms. But for a second there, I thought she was calling my bluff—and I don't know if I could lie as easily to Claudia as I frequently did to myself.

I turned up the radio and moved on to the pot of biro-top blue. The bunting was beginning to look real. It was during my A level year that I realized I was in trouble. Perhaps it was Mary, talking about the plans she and Ben were making, or perhaps I was a late starter and my hormones only kicked in at seventeen, or perhaps I had always liked him more than I should have. It wouldn't have been hard. At fourteen, Ben opened the door for girls. He wasn't a bully and he knew how to talk to women, and though he went through the girls, he always let them down gently. Everyone, even teachers, had a crush on him, but it was me that he chose to be his friend. Me. Nothing ever happened between us, but a lot of people imagined it had. I got grief from girls who liked him and saw me as a threat. And I suppose I was the greatest threat of all. I was his best friend and that gave me the edge. It terrified me when I realized I wanted to be more than friends. Not only did I risk losing our friendship, I had become just like everyone else and I knew exactly how he felt about all of them.

I never told anyone I liked him. Not even Claudia, though I suspect she and Al have discussed the possibility of "us" at great length. It would make a neat ending, wouldn't it? But they don't know what happened the day Ben broke his leg. The only person who knows is Helen. And I only told her because when we met on a beach in Vietnam, I never thought I'd see her again.

I heard another song end. That made it four since Claudia had gone to the loo. "Claudia? Are you coming back, or what?"

There was no answer. I put down my brush and wiped my hands on Al's shirt. I opened the door. "Oi, you lazy cow, you can't get me over here to work while you have a little nap."

Still there was no reply. Have I mentioned this wasn't a large house? You could hear the cat-flap flap from the top landing.

The bathroom was only half a staircase in front of me. The door was a fraction ajar.

"Claud, are you in there?"

She didn't reply. But I knew she was there. I could feel the density of her behind the door. I carefully pushed the door open and stepped inside. I would rather be blind than have seen what I saw that day. Claudia sat on the loo with her pregnancy jeans around her ankles. Her knees were parted wide open. I couldn't see her face because she was staring into the toilet bowl, but her arm was stretched up towards me. In the palm of her hand was tissue sodden with blood. It had seeped through her fingers, and dropped on to the white wooden floor boards around her feet. Floating in the palm of her hand was . . . I still to this day don't know what it was. It looked like an old grey piece of rotten sponge. The fact that it wasn't red scared me, it was the color of a tombstone.

The smell of blood coming off Claudia was intense—earthy, sweet and thick. I could hear dripping sounds. One was rapid, high-pitched, as if a metronome had been set with the weight at the base.

The other was set to a slower, heavier beat. It wasn't until Claudia looked up at me through the trestles of her long, dark hair that I realized what it was. Bright red blood was spilling out of her. Intermittently her body hacked up viscous-blackened globules and spat them into the toilet. They sank through the red water and congealed on the base of the bowl.

"I can't get the red paint off," she said, staring at her hand.

"OK, sweetheart." I took the thing out of her hand and physically shuddered as I felt it slip like raw liver through my fingers. I threw it into the bath. "I need you to lie down, honey, OK? Can you do that?"

"I can't get the red paint off," she said again.

"It's OK, we'll clear it up later. You lean on me. Lean on me." The moment she was standing I realized I should have taken her jeans off. But it was too late, I couldn't stop. I saw a rivulet of blood run down her inside leg. I wrapped a towel around her waist, held on to her and it, and we shuffled like geriatrics to her room. I didn't give a second thought to her hand-embroidered sheets. I pulled them back, lay her down and covered up that awful, awful mess between her legs. Then I left her, because I had to talk to her doctor and I didn't want her to hear. I would have called 999 but I didn't want her being carted off to the nearest hospital. She had specialists, people who'd understand what she was really losing.

"118 118, this is Craig speak—"

"The Lister Hospital, London."

"Sorry, what was that?"

"The Lister Hospital. Please, this is an emergency."

"What town is that?"

"London. Jesus, please—"

"I cannot get you a number if I don't know—"

"I'm sorry." I wasn't sorry. I wanted to punch him.

"Would you like to be put through directly?"

"Yes."

"There will be an addit—"

"I don't fucking care."

There was silence, and for a terrible moment, I thought he'd cut me off. Then the phone started ringing. I don't know what I said to the woman who answered the phone, but very quickly I was talking to someone who knew Claudia and said her name softly. He wanted to know what I'd seen, how much blood she was losing and what color it was. I told him.

"She's losing the baby," said the voice.

"I fucking know that," I screamed. "Tell me how to stop it, just tell me, tell me how to stop it, please, please tell me how to stop it . . ." My voice had cracked the first time I asked him, but I couldn't stop repeating the words because I knew that when I stopped asking I would have to come to terms with the fact that there was no answer. Claudia was losing her baby girl and there was nothing I could do to stop it. The bunting was coming down.

pretending to forget

I ran back upstairs to Claudia's room. She hadn't moved. I told her what the doctor had told me. "An ambulance is coming. They'll get you to the hospital and run some tests. Even a dramatic amount of blood loss doesn't mean a person is losing their baby."

She didn't seem to understand what I was saying. She just looked at me. Her hair still sticking to her face. I lifted the sheets off her. The towel had slipped. There was blood everywhere. Too much, I knew that, but I kept the reassuring smile stapled to my face. I peeled her trousers off, wiped her down as best I could, then put her into a clean pair of underpants. I'd found large sanitary pads in the bathroom, a half-empty pack. Too much blood had been soaked up in this household over the last nine years. I put two pads into her underpants, and pulled them up her legs. I got a flannel and wiped up what I could on her hands and legs. Everything was going pink. I eased her up, put a skirt over her head and got it down around her waist. I wanted to hide as much as I could, but I couldn't hide the truth.

Claudia didn't say anything, she just kept shaking her head from side to side. It was a small movement, with enormous meaning. I got her to her feet. She cried out, cramped over, and fell back down on the bed with her head between her knees, her breath coming in short, staccato pants. We waited for the pain to pass. Slowly I watched her face loosen from its contorted position. Then she retched. She was sick all over the floor.

"I think it just came out," she said, looking back up at me.

"OK. It's OK." It's not fucking OK, stop saying it's OK. I peeled her underpants down again. I felt sick and had to screw up my face to stop myself from retching. I tried not to look.

"Is it my baby?" asked Claudia. I took the sodden underwear away and threw it in the bath. It was more of the same. Grey sponge. Like placenta with no blood. Dead.

"No, honey," I called back, "just more blood." Like that was OK? I walked back into the bedroom. Claudia was staring at me.

"Too much blood?" she asked.

"I don't know," I said. But I did. I repeated the process with the pads and the underwear and got Claudia downstairs. The ambulance was fast. I went with her. She lay down on the gurney and let a medic pull up her top. She was still wearing Al's shirt. We both were. I'm used to bargaining with a God I don't know if I believe in; when my mother's MS rears its ugly head, I start hedging my bets and offering deals to any God who'll listen. But while I watched the technician squirt clear jelly on to Claudia's stomach, I prayed harder than I'd ever prayed in my life. The inside of the ambulance went very quiet. I didn't breathe as the medic rolled the ultrasound through the jelly, over her belly. We waited for the sound of life to come out of the amplifier. A hectic heartbeat, racing to grow. There was nothing but static. I saw the medic's shoulders droop. I reached over and took Claudia's hand.

"There are more advanced machines in the hospital," he said. "The baby may be in a strange position. How many weeks are you?"

"Fourteen," I said.

"We'll get you there as soon as we can. It's possible I'm not picking up the heartbeat."

Claudia smiled weakly. The medic radioed through to the driver, the ambulance lurched forward and sirens filled the air. I couldn't get the image of that grey, sponge-like matter from my mind. My tiny, perfect, thumb-sucking goddaughter was dead. I knew it.

The bleeding eased up when we got to hospital, almost stopped, and we were suddenly hopeful. Claudia was rushed through to the scanning room where she was given more jelly. More false hope. They turned the sound off the machine, and turned it away from Claudia. Only I saw the baby's outline. Floating in the dark. Still. There'd been more vitality in the picture that Claudia had given me than there was on the screen. At one moment the technician moved the device and it looked like the baby moved. I gasped, but the technician rapidly shook her head. She removed the stick, wiped off the jelly, pulled Claudia's top down then wheeled her chair to Claudia's side.

"I am so sorry, Mrs. Harding. The fetus is dead."

Jesus, did she have to be so brutal? I saw Claudia bite down on her lip. Maybe she did. Maybe that was the only way to get a mother to believe that the invisible life force she'd been carrying around inside her had gone. She hadn't even been feeling ill.

"We'll get you cleaned up and then your consultant will come and talk to you about your options."

I took Claudia's hand. We both nodded numbly.

They tried to put Claudia in a wheelchair, but she refused. She climbed off the bed, stood up tall and walked out of the room.

There was nothing to say. After a while, Claudia looked at me.

"Al," she said.

I let go of her hand. "I'll leave a message."

"Don't tell him."

"I won't. I'll just tell him to call. Claudia, I am so sorry."

"I know," she said, then went back to staring at her lap. When I returned she was talking to the consultant. He offered her two options: let the miscarriage continue naturally, or have a D and C, which involved a general anesthetic during which time her uterus would be cleared out. I couldn't imagine anything worse than more of what I'd witnessed back at Claudia's house.

"How long would it take to happen without the D and C?"

"Anything up to ten days."

I looked at Claudia. "Don't put yourself through that."

"Are there any risks?" she asked.

"As far as conceiving again, a D and C is probably better; there is less risk of matter being left behind. It is often done as a precursor to IVF treatment, creates a nice clean environment, but it is invasive, and you've had a lot of invasive treatment." Claudia once told me she'd had a film crew up her vagina. But at least she'd be out cold for this one.

I don't think Claudia was listening to the consultant, so I tried to think what Al would do if he were here. He'd want her to suffer as little as possible; he'd want it to be over. For the blood and gore to end. He wouldn't want Claudia to feel chunks of herself falling out and for ever wonder what it was she'd held in her hand, which bit.

"Can you do the D and C today?"

"I can do it now."

Claudia looked at me again. I nodded. She turned back to the consultant. "Let's get this over and done with," she said. It was a futile comment. Things like this were never over and done with.

I was with her right up to the time she counted backwards from ten. I watched the anesthetist open up the valve in her wrist and pour the opiate in. She didn't make it past seven. I looked at the consultant. "Make sure you get it all. No complications. No infections. No more bleeding. And please come and get me when she comes round."

I was shown through to a small green waiting room. When I was sure I was alone, I opened my wallet and pulled out the twelve-week scan that Claudia had given me when she'd crossed the three-month line. I stared at the little head, the little thumb, the perfect lips and baby profile. I traced them all with my finger. When I started crying it was for Claudia, for that tiny baby I'd never meet, and I couldn't stop. I wailed silently into my hands. I thought about the nine years, the previous failures, the innocent hope she'd had, who we'd been before all this, where we thought we'd be by now, where we were, where I was, my own childlessness, my own loneliness, and a fresh wave of tears overran me. I couldn't be brave any more. Not for Claudia, not for myself. And that made me cry even more. How could I feel sorry for myself when I wasn't the one losing a baby? A nurse came in, took in the scene and jumped to the wrong conclusions. I was a grieving mother. She put her arm around me and offered me a tissue. I don't know why I didn't correct her. But I didn't. It felt nice to have someone's arm around me for a change.

My phone vibrated in my pocket. I looked at the number. I turned to the nurse.

"It's the father," I said.

She took her leave. I waited until the door closed then I answered the phone.

"Tessa? Is Claudia OK?"

"Yes. But—"

"The baby."

"I'm so sorry, Al. She's had a miscarriage."

"Can I talk to her?"

"She's in theatre. They're operating now."

"Jesus . . ."

"It was very quick."

"Tell her I'm on the next plane back. Tell her I love her. Don't forget."

"I won't."

The phone went silent. I imagined Al running through Singapore Airport, trying to find someone who'd help him get home. Not wanting to explain why, but being forced to by people who wouldn't otherwise take him seriously. He may even have to exaggerate it, as if what was happening wasn't bad enough. One in three women had miscarriages, what was the big deal, right? It wasn't one, until it was your turn. There was a gentle knock on the door. Another nurse came through. "She's back."

It had taken twenty-seven minutes to take out what had taken nine years and ninety-eight days to build.

Claudia was just opening her eyes when I came into the recovery room. She was bleary-eyed and slurring her words. She smiled up at the consultant. Then me.

"I spoke to Al. He's on his way home."

"Tell him not to feel sorry for me," said Claudia. "I have a beautiful daughter at home."

The consultant and I exchanged glances.

"He wants you to know he loves you with all his heart," I said.

"He'll leave me now."

"No. He'd never do that."

"Don't let him leave me. Where's my baby? Tessa, what have you done with my baby?"

"It's all right, Mrs. Harding," the consultant stepped up. "You're a little confused. You're at the hospital, remember? We've had to operate. You've lost the baby. But there will be more."

"No more," said Claudia. "Don't make me do it again. Don't make

me do it again. Please, Tessa, don't make me . . ." Her voice trailed
off. She fell asleep. I was alarmed.

"It's just the effects of the drugs," said the consultant, reassuring
me. "Let her sleep. You'll be able to take her home at about six."

I left her to the hospital staff. Hailed a taxi and returned to Claudia and Al's house.

It was very still inside the house. I walked up past the photos without looking at them, and into the nursery. Our red and green flags
stood out against the white wall. Our paintbrushes were stiff. I carried on up the stairs. The bathroom was a mess. I pulled on the
washing-up gloves and picked up the items in the bath and put them
into a plastic bag. I threw Claudia's jeans and pants in with them. I
flushed the loo without looking into it. When the water had stopped
gurgling I checked everything had gone. It hadn't. The thick, black,
liver-like substance stuck to the bottom. I reached for the loo brush,
pushed it around until the water went red, then flushed again. I did
it three times before the sticky stuff went completely. I threw the loo
brush into the bin liner, along with everything else. I stripped the
bed and carried the blood-sodden sheets down to the laundry room.
I put them all into a hot wash then went back upstairs to deal with
the mattress and the vomit. I sponged down where the blood had
soaked through and then tipped the mattress on to its side. I picked
the contents of Claudia's stomach out of the carpet and sponged that
down too. Then I went back downstairs and watched the sheets spin
inside the drum. I looked at my watch. I needed help.

Twenty minutes later I opened the door to Ben. He was in his suit.
He'd come out of a meeting to take my call and never gone back in.
As soon as I'd told him what had happened he'd left the office. "I
don't know what to do, Ben, I don't know whether to paint over it or

not. But I can't leave it and the white won't hide it. I don't want to use red, and pink has too many connotations . . ."

He held his arms out wide. I simply fell forward into them. For a while I let him hold me. I had help now. Somehow we'd manage.

"Ssh," he said, stroking my hair.

"I feel so awful for Claudia, Ben. It was horrific—one minute we're painting away, laughing about stupid things, the next, she's hemorrhaging. Blood everywhere. We've got to get that room re-painted. She can come home tonight."

"Orange." Ben let go of me and picked up two cans of paint from the doorstep. "It's bright, but dark enough to cover what you've al-ready put on the wall. I picked these up on the way."

"You're amazing. Thank you."

"Don't be silly. This is Al and Claudia we're talking about. How long have we got?"

"The hospital will ring me when they're sure she's stopped bleed-ing. But hopefully no more than two hours."

"Let's get cracking."

We didn't talk much while we painted. I was concentrating so much on slapping on the paint that I didn't think about anything else. We covered the wall with most of the flags on first. Then I put down the paintbrush and went downstairs to put another load of sheets on. I pulled the first set out of the machine. There was a pink stain, with a darker red outline. I swore loudly. I had no choice but to throw them away. I stuffed them into another bin liner then went back upstairs. Ben was making good progress with the second wall.

"You all right in here? I've just got to make the bed up."

"Need help?"

"No. You keep painting. You've got it in your hair, by the way."

"Sasha will think I'm having a mid-life crisis, and have taken to dyeing my hair."

"How many mid-life crises would that be now?" I said, trying to smile.

"One too many," he said, turning back to the wall.

I pulled the mattress over on to its other side, found some fresh bed linen and started making the bed. When I'd finished I noticed a drop of blood on the carpet. I went down to the bathroom to wet a sponge when I saw the blood still in the bath. Suddenly it felt like there was blood everywhere. I could still see the faint echo of pink on the bottom of the toilet bowl. I couldn't get rid of it. I felt very queasy all of a sudden and toppled over. I hit my head on the door handle as I fell forward and cried out in pain. I felt my head, it was slick with sweat. This was not the time to get flu. I tried to stand up, but I wobbled and fell back down with a thump.

"Tess, you OK?" I heard Ben run up the stairs, push open the bathroom door and gasp at the sight of me on the floor, a bloody sponge in my hand.

"I can't get the blood out," I cried. I thought I was going to be sick, but Ben grabbed me, pulled me up, put the lid of the loo down and sat me on it. He opened a window and told me to stay put. A few minutes later he returned with orange juice and a banana.

"Eat, you're having one of your funny turns."

I felt like an idiot. I am mildly hypoglycemic. Sometimes, if I'm stressed, tired or don't eat, my blood sugar level drops through the floor. Or my insulin goes through the roof. That day, I was all three. I practically swallowed the banana whole and drank half the carton in a couple of glugs. I handed back the carton to Ben.

"Come here," he said and pulled me into his chest again. Tears overwhelmed me. I must stop crying like this, none of this is happening to me. He stroked my hair. "Hey, you, ssh. They'll be all right. They've got each other, those two, they'll be all right."

I mumbled into Ben's chest. "When Claudia came round, she said Al would leave her now."

He held me away from him and looked at me. "Al would never leave Claudia. What they have is real. Based on a lifetime. I promise you, he would never leave her."

I sniffed. Ben offered his sleeve. Then he tucked my hair behind my ear. "Come on, funny face, we've got some painting to do."

I nodded. As we walked back down the stairs, I asked him how he knew Al would never leave.

"Because I asked him once, after one of the IVF treatments had failed. Told him he could consider, you know, another route."

"You suggested he leave Claudia?" I asked, suddenly cross.

"We were just discussing it. He jumped down my throat too. Said he'd never even considered it. I guess I was having a bad time with Sasha and was feeling disillusioned about marriage. Anyway, he was right. Women like you and Claud don't come around very often." He looked back up the stairs to me. "Actually, they don't come around more than once."

I looked away, because he didn't. There was the photo on the wall. The one of Ben in traction. His leg smashed to smithereens. Ben followed my gaze. We looked back at each other. He stood two steps below me, our eyes were level. Everything went very still. It made me think about Claudia's baby.

"The stain in the carpet," I spluttered, and ran back upstairs.

Ben was still painting the last wall when I left to get Claudia from the hospital. When we returned, not only was it finished, the paint pots had vanished, there was fresh soup and bread on the kitchen table, and a bottle of soft red that Claudia likes. Ben hugged her. In the absence of Al, he was the next best thing. Ben had spoken to Al just as he was about to board his plane home. Al hadn't said any of the things that Ben said he had. Al was in total shock, he could barely speak, but Ben knew Al well enough to know what he would have wanted to say, and he did it perfectly.

I heated the soup up for us all as I listened to Ben talk to Claudia. He didn't try and make it better. He didn't tell her it was for the best. He told her to mourn. He told her to think about having a small service. He told her to frame the picture of the scan if she wanted to. He held her when she sobbed and didn't tell her to try and stop. I waited in the kitchen, stirring the soup until the crying had ended of its own accord. Afterwards, when we had tucked Claudia into bed, I kissed Ben on the cheek.

"Thank you," I said. "I couldn't have done this without you."

"You don't have to," he said. We sat in the kitchen and finished the bottle of wine. We talked in circles about what Al and Claudia would do now. Would they go for it again? Would they go abroad to adopt? Russia? Sri Lanka? China? Would they travel? Move away? Collapse? Survive?

"They'll survive," said Ben.

I nodded.

"They will, Tess." Ben stood up and stretched. "Do you need a lift home?"

"No. I'm going to stay here until Al gets back."

"Where are you going to sleep?"

"On the sofa."

"Do you want me to stay with you?" asked Ben.

"No. I'm OK. There's no room, anyway."

"We've slept on that sofa before."

"Only when we've drunk so much I don't register your snoring."

"And I don't feel your bony elbows."

"I haven't got bony elbows."

He kissed me on the forehead. "Yes, you have. And you fart in your sleep."

I pushed him away and followed him to the front door. For a long time we hugged again. It had been that sort of day. He tucked my hair behind my ear again.

"You are a great friend, Tess. It's us who couldn't do without you."

I was too tired to speak. Too tired to trust myself to speak. I just stared up at him through emotionally drained eyes. He held my face in his hand and gently stroked my cheek with his thumb.

"Thank God you were here. Thank God you were back," said Ben. Then he leaned closer and kissed me on my lips. It wasn't that it was a fraction longer than usual that made the bolt of electricity shoot through me. It was because he still had his hand cupped over my cheek. I felt his fingers move around the side of my head and spread through my hair. Our faces were still inches from one another. Neither of us moved. All I could feel was the gentle massage of his thumb in my hair.

"I missed you more than I should have, Tessa," said Ben.

I put my hand up to his cheek, expecting to move it away, but instead my hand glued to his and I found myself being pulled into his gravity. We moved closer so slowly that when our lips touched again it was like someone had burnt me with a flame. There was no salve but pressure. The kiss spread to every part of our lips. My heart was pounding in my chest as we stood there, stuck to one another, not daring to move. And then the dam burst and without any warning signal both our lips parted, our heads angled away from each other, our arms snaked around each other's bodies and for a split second an invisible line was crossed and the kiss changed shape completely.

"Al? Al? Help me!"

The retraction was instant. We stood facing one another, breathing hard, for another second or two. I shook my head, I don't know why—in disbelief, in warning, in shame? Claudia cried out again; I turned away and ran up the stairs.

When I came back down, Ben had gone. I sat at the top of the stairs, staring out between my fingers, feeling foolish and confused. What had happened? Had anything happened? A kiss on the lips was no big deal; Ben always hugged me when things were bad. Surely my mind was playing tricks on me. That was all. Nothing had happened. Nothing was going to happen. Ben was married, Ben was my friend; he would remain my friend. End of story. Eventually, my eyes rested on the photo of him with his leg in traction. I walked up to it and took it off the wall. I carried it through to the sitting room, lay on the sofa with the rest of my glass of wine and stared at the picture until my eyes watered.

I never indulged myself with this old, locked away memory, but the day had been no ordinary day, and life seemed more magnified because of it. It was the summer. I had just got my A level results. They were better than expected and I had got into law school. Ben and I were in Camden alone. Al had gone up to Cheshire to see family, Claudia was doing work experience in Reading, Mary was away with her parents and Ben, for once, had decided not to go. His mother was in the west country celebrating the summer solstice and my parents were completely relaxed when I told them I was going to stay at Ben's for a week. Why wouldn't they be relaxed? It had happened so many times before. I don't know whether I told them Ben's mum was away, but as they didn't have her down as the responsible type I don't think it played a large part in their decision-making process. I'd worked hard and stuck to the rules. This was my reward.

We didn't see or speak to anyone else for four days. We watched *Halloween 1* and *2* in bed together and freaked ourselves out. We cooked and drank wine in the sunshine and chatted constantly about our adult lives ahead. We spent a lot of time in the pub. I started to ache with longing on the second day. I would put myself in his path just to feel his hand on me as he maneuvered me out of the way. I would tickle him, punch him, put my arm through his, poke him in the ribs. I was addicted. I delighted in watching him go about doing normal things. Ordering a pint, picking out a T-shirt, making me a cup of tea. There was a cheap Italian near his house where you could eat spaghetti bolognaise for £1.99; we had dinner there on the third night. I must have drunk too much cheap red wine because I started making suggestive comments that had always been out of bounds in our friendship. He thought I was taking the piss.

That night I lay awake next to him, consumed by lust and fear in equal measures. The brush of his skin along mine made the hairs on my arm bristle. I had to breathe with my mouth open, so suffocating was the sensation of being so close yet not able to touch him. At about four o'clock in the morning I reached out and took his hand. He squeezed it. I squeezed back. Neither of us let go. The squeeze got harder and harder, the blood in my fingers pulsated as my breath shortened. Sounds absurd now that holding someone's hand could be so erotic, but it was. Every thought I'd had about him, every moment I'd nearly told him what I was feeling, every time I'd thought I'd caught him looking at me and dismissed it, raced through my hand to his. More was communicated in that tightening grip than I could have said, anyway. It was a physical declaration of desire. I think I reached orgasm during that clench; as the muscles in my hand burned with the exertion of holding on so hard, so did all the other muscles in my body. Perhaps it wasn't a physical orgasm, perhaps it was more in my mind. Not that I imagined it, but that it happened at a deeper level than my simple flesh and blood could measure. I loved him. I loved him with all the energy I could muster, and all I could do was hold on. Not a word was spoken. We fell asleep holding hands. In the morning neither of us referred to what had happened and I began to wonder if it had all been in my imagination.

The next day Ben suddenly had things to do that did not include me. I felt deserted. Cut loose. Confused. It made me panic. I called some friends up from college and met them in the park. I went through the motions of a picnic, Frisbee, warm wine and cold sausages, but all the while I was thinking about his hand in mine and whether I'd been the only one experiencing the lightning. I went home that night. Rather than back to Ben's house. I had to force my feet to get there, though, step by step, in the opposite direction to where I wanted to run. My mother was awake. She called me into their room.

"Everything all right?"

"Yes. Why?"

"Ben's called. I thought you were with him."

"He had things to do, so I saw some mates from college."

"Well, he's rung, I think he was worried."

I played dumb. "I'll give him a call now." I've been playing dumb ever since.

We didn't have mobiles then. I dialed his home number. What did he expect? That I'd wait home for him all day?

"Where are you?"

"At home."

"Oh."

And? Oh and what?

"I didn't know how long you were going to be."

"I was only signing some papers for the new job, I told you that."

Had he? Was I being completely over-sensitive? Irrational? Why had two hours out of the house felt like a betrayal? "Sorry. I misunderstood. I thought you had things to do all day."

"As long as you're all right."

"Fine."

"You sure?"

"Yes. Are you?"

"Yeah."

"OK. We'll speak tomorrow then."

"OK," he said. I put down the phone and groaned.

*   *   *

The following night Ben arranged to meet me for dinner at a more up-market restaurant than we'd ever been to before. We talked around the subject of us. How spending this time together had been so great; that he'd missed me when I hadn't been there last night; that he had no real inclination to talk to Mary. I didn't know if he was leading on to something or referring to our "friendship" in order to remind me of the boundaries. Everything could be taken either way. He told me he adored me. But I knew that. What I didn't know was in what way. Or how much.

On the walk back from dinner we cut down a narrow passageway. There was one street lamp at the end. Our footsteps echoed off the high walls as we walked in silence towards the puddle of yellow light. Something caused us to stop walking. A noise? Intuition? Who knows, but we both turned towards each other. It was the tunnel that did it. It made it feel as if the world no longer existed. There was no Mary. No foursome of friends. No expectations. Just Ben and me. Our world. Brought on by four days alone together.

"What's happening?" he asked.

"I don't know."

"This is driving me mad."

"Me too," was all I managed to say.

"What are we going to do about it?"

About what? We couldn't even say out loud what it was we were talking about. I didn't dare speak. I wanted to. But I was terrified of ruining everything we had. He stepped towards me . . . What would one kiss do? Lead to another. Then more. How long would that last? We were eighteen. It wouldn't last for life. We'd split up in the end, and we'd ruin our friendship in doing so. I panicked. Instead of pulling him towards me, I took hold of his hand.

"Let's go home," I said and pushed him towards the end of the passageway. I needed time to think. Because once we'd kissed, there would be no going back.

If only I'd had the courage of my convictions. If only I could have followed my heart, not my head, and spent a little more time lost in that passageway, the cyclist would have sailed by and I wouldn't know the name Elizabeth Collins. If only I had answered him with a question. Or poked him in the ribs and laughed at him as I had countless times before. Or just kissed him, like I wanted to—would it have been so bad? But I didn't. I chickened out. I said, "Let's go home"—put it off, sleep on it, think about it, delay it, run from it, anything other than face it.

What we had to face instead was a cyclist, lying twisted on the ground, sixteen feet from where we'd stepped out of the passageway. She'd been racing downhill on the pavement; she had no lights and no helmet. We hadn't even stopped to look for pedestrians, let alone cyclists. She hit Ben at full pelt, smashing his leg to pieces. I watched her jettison off the bike and fly over Ben's body as he crumpled to the ground. I watched her head miss a lamppost by a millimeter. She skidded across the cement, shearing off the skin on her face, then rolled into the gutter. Ben let go of my hand and started to rock with pain. Whatever moment there had been evaporated. The real world had come back to remind me that there is nothing so brutal as life and you mess with it at your peril.

The girl was so concussed she didn't know her name, so I stayed with her. Ben was taken away in another ambulance. By the time I got to him, Mary and her family were lodged alongside him in the hospital room. I couldn't get near him, and when I did, it was awkward and uncomfortable. I couldn't get rid of the image of the cyclist's head streaking past the lamppost. Any closer and she'd have been dead; I would have killed her. It was a stark warning to leave

Ben well alone. Two weeks later our plane landed in Hanoi and I
spent the next few months learning how to pretend to forget.

As I said, a lot of my life lies in that break.

At six o'clock the next morning I heard a key in the door. I sat up as
Al walked into the sitting room. He didn't look like he'd slept much
either. I hugged him. I told him Claudia was still asleep, that the
doctor had given her some sleeping pills, but that she'd been crying
out in her dreams. Then I left and drove home through London. It
wasn't until I got home that I realized the photo of Ben in traction
was still in my pocket. I slipped it into my bedside drawer, pulled
back the covers and climbed into bed. Curled in a ball, with the
duvet pulled high over my head, I fell asleep sucking my thumb,
wishing that none of this was happening.

comfort blanket

I didn't know what Claudia would feel like eating, if anything at all, so I brought everything: bacon, eggs, yogurt, organic muesli, fresh bread, kiwis, juice, almond croissants, green tea and caffe mochas for all. I rang the doorbell and listened to Al's heavy footfalls as he made his way downstairs. He opened the door a fraction with a fierce expression. I watched his brain recognize that standing on his doorstep was friend not foe; his face softened, his body relaxed and finally the door opened wider. Instinctively, he took the bags from me. Ben and Al are cut from the same cloth in that respect.

"I don't know how to ever thank you," said Al, wrapping the plastic bags around me in a bear hug. "Thank God you were here. Come in. She's sleeping."

I followed him down the hallway into the kitchen. On the staircase wall was the faint grimy outline of a missing photograph. I swore silently in my head. The photograph was still back at home, though that was not what I was swearing about. I stared at the step and watched again, as I had a thousand times during the night, a kiss that had come nearly twenty years too late. I put my fingers to my lips and the memory made me giddy with yearning.

Al poured the coffee into mugs, put them in the microwave to reheat and pulled out a croissant each. Neither he nor I had slept a great deal and what we craved was a hefty dose of sugar. I'd make something sensible and slow-burning in a while, but what we needed right then was a hit. I dunked the croissant into the caffe mocha and sucked. Al did the same.

"You think of everything, don't you, Tessa? I couldn't believe it when I saw you'd repainted the . . ." Nursery. Spare room. Constant reminder of their infertility.

"I couldn't have done it without Ben. He chose the paint."

"You are the best team of friends anyone could wish for."

I kissed Ben on the steps. I used your personal tragedy to cross a boundary. What kind of friend does that really make me? If Claudia hadn't cried out . . . Once again, my face registered my thoughts because Al looked concerned.

"I'm so sorry, it must have been horrible," he said.

I dismissed his concern. "What are you going to do?"

"Get out of here," said Al immediately. "It's all organized. I just haven't told Claudia yet."

"Move house?"

"No. I mean get out of the country. I still have a job in Singapore. We've been put up in a sister hotel of the one we're working on. It's stunning. Claudia can rest, spend her days in the spa, swim, recover at whatever pace she can. The work isn't taxing. We'll be able to have lunch most days, travel around the area on the weekends, go island hopping. My bosses know the situation and are happy to be flexible, not for ever, but for a little while."

"How long would you be away?"

"A couple of months. Don't you think it's a good idea?"

"I think it's a great idea, I just don't want you to go. But you should absolutely, definitely go."

"I'm going to try and sell the house too. I booked an agent to come and see it tomorrow while Claud is at the doctor's. I know this is a bit cheeky, but I thought maybe you might oversee the sale."

"Of course I will," I said. "Consider it done."

He reached over and placed his hand on mine. "Thanks, Tessa, I knew I could rely on you."

The feeling of satisfaction rose up inside me faster than the dampening reminder of why Al was asking me to sell his house for him. I couldn't help it. I had always done a great deal for my friends, they were my family, so it was reaffirming for me that Al and Claudia felt they could rely on me. Although this was happening to them, we were, as I'd always suspected, in this together.

"You really have got it all organized," I said, when Al retracted his hand.

He stirred his coffee. "I've learned to fear the worst." He rubbed his eyes. It was an involuntary movement but it reminded me of the incredible strain Al had been under all these years. You can't be the strong one indefinitely. Somewhere, something has to give.

"You are an exceptional man, Al. Claudia is lucky to have you."

"You think? She'd probably get pregnant like that"—he clicked his fingers to demonstrate—"with somebody else. She'd certainly have been able to adopt."

"Don't think things like that. It's you, only you, and it will always be you," I said.

"But we all know that's not true. People lose husbands and wives and find new people and are just as happy, sometimes happier. People are heartbroken and go on to find new people to love. There isn't just one person. Claudia would find someone else."

He was scaring me. "Al, is this about you, or her?"

"Her. She's the one upstairs, drugged up with opiates so she doesn't feel the pain that I'm causing her."

"You didn't do this to Claudia, in the same way that Claudia didn't do this to you, or herself," I said. "This is just some terrible shitty thing that has happened to you both. I know Claudia wants children, but not without you. That would be too high a price."

"This is already too high a price, Tessa," said Al. "I can't watch her do this again."

"I'm sure she doesn't want to go through this again. What about going back to adopting again?"

"We can't. My record."

"Not here, abroad, where papers aren't so strictly adhered to. China, Africa, Estonia, Russia. There are orphanages everywhere, Al. Countless children who need a home."

"Maybe it is time to look into that," said Al. Frankly I was surprised they hadn't looked into it before.

"It could be exciting," I said, trying to sound positive.

"Maybe. But Claudia has to accept that the IVF has failed and she will never be a mother to our child."

"And you?"

"If Claudia is happy again, I can live without children. But her survival mechanism throughout all of this has been that ultimate failure was not an option. She had to believe that it would work. If not this time, then the next. She had to believe that or else she wouldn't have been able to get up in the morning. How do you undo that steadfast faith? It's like telling someone not to believe in God any more."

"So you would consider it?"

"We went for adoption before we went for IVF because they told us our chances were so slim. We went for adoption first and they screwed us. I screwed myself. I screwed us."

"Stop it. Let's not go back to that. The drugs had fallen through the lining of your bag, it could have happened to any of us. We were all guilty."

"But I knew it was missing. I could have looked harder. How is it possible that one second in time, almost twenty years ago, can still make my stomach clench into a knot and leave me unable to breathe?"

Let's go home. "I don't know," I said, feeling the familiar sensation of my heart pounding in my chest and my airway contract. But it could.

I sat on the side of Claudia's bed. The bed I had stripped and remade the day before. I glanced at the carpet. I could still see the faint trace of pink from the single drop of blood. I wondered if I always would. *Out, out, damn spot.* Maybe Al was right. This house had too many sad memories. Al and Claudia needed a change. Singapore was as good a place to start as any. Claudia moved her head on the pillow. Very slowly she opened one eye and looked at me. She smiled and closed it again. It opened again as she yawned and I watched her force her other eyelid, prising it open; she blinked a few times in a battle to keep her eyes from closing again. It was like watching her come round from the anesthetic all over again. It was like watching the twins wake up after the christening.

"Hey, you," I said softly.

"Hey," Claudia croaked.

"I brought you some fresh juice and some green tea."

She smiled and started to prop herself up in bed. Within seconds she'd slumped back down on the pillow. "Where's Al?"

"Downstairs. Do you want me to get him?"

"Is he all right?"

I stroked a strand of her hair away. "He's worried about you. How are you feeling?"

"Numb. No, not numb. Empty."

I took her hand.

"Did they tell you why?" she asked me.

I nodded. This was hard. "The placenta had come away from the uterus wall."

"My baby starved to death."

"No, Claudia. You can't think like that." I moved round the bed and lay next to her. "Once the oxygen supply was lost it would have been very quick. She would not have felt a thing."

"I thought I felt her move while we were painting. How could I not have sensed that something was wrong? Shouldn't I have felt something? What sort of mother would I make?"

"Stop it. This isn't going to help you or change what has happened. You have suffered a medical problem, one that isn't even that uncommon. The doctor said there is no reason to think that the IVF won't take again and this time they will monitor you and keep you in bed. He will explain it all at your visit tomorrow."

Claudia let out a long breath. We lay there in silence for a while as I stroked her hair and waited for some words of comfort to come to mind. None did. Al found us there some minutes later. Claudia's tea had gone cold. She propelled herself off the pillow and fell into her husband's chest. He wrapped her up like the precious parcel she was and rocked her gently side to side. I could hear Claudia was crying and I could see that Al was too.

It was time for me to go. There are some things that friends are for. There are others when only husbands will do.

I was halfway down the stairs when I heard Al. He ran down after me, held me for a moment in a tight embrace, then kissed me quickly on the lips.

"From both of us," he said. "We love you."

He hugged me again for a split second then returned to his wife. I stood on the step. It was unnecessary to thank me but I was grateful, except for one thing: any notion that what had passed between Ben and me on the same steps, in the same circumstances, the previous evening was purely platonic was ludicrous. What had just happened with Al was platonic. More than that, it was familial, brotherly, fatherly. What had happened between Ben and me was something else entirely and I had no idea what to do about it. I pulled the front door behind me quietly and walked to my car, heavy with sadness and guilt. Whatever terrible outcome kissing Ben at eighteen may have had, it could not be worse than this.

My phone vibrated in my pocket. It was Ben's home number. I looked at it. If I ducked his call it would be tantamount to admitting something was really wrong. I had never ducked a call from Ben in my life. If I answered it, was I going to make it worse? Could I pretend nothing had happened? I stared at the phone . . . Who was I kidding? I'd been pretending for years.

"Hi," I said gently.

"Hey, Tessa, I thought you might need scooping up."

It wasn't Ben. Of course it wasn't Ben, he always called me from his mobile. Not home. "Sorry?"

"Ben told me what happened."

No. No. No. "What?"

"You're not all right, are you? Ben said you were there all night. Al is back, right?"

"Yes."

"Are you still with them?"

"I'm just leaving."

"Right, I'm not taking no for an answer. Meet me at that organic café in Battersea. I'm leaving now."

"Oh Sasha, thanks but I'll be—"

"No, Tessa. I'm taking you out for lunch, plying you with lentils and organic wine then I'm taking you home. It's time someone looked after you. Twenty minutes. I'll be there."

"Really, Sasha, I'll—"

"Tessa, you can't carry everyone else's shit all the time. You just can't. You've got to leave a little bit of room for you. I'm already getting into the car."

She ended the call, leaving me with no choice. Why does she have to be so fucking nice? The same reason she has always been so nice. She just is. This is why in normal circumstances consuming alfalfa beans and wine with Sasha, then lying on a sofa chatting and farting, would be a great way to spend a Saturday. But ordinarily I hadn't just kissed her husband.

The café is tiny but we were early and Sasha had a table in the window overlooking a little triangle of shops. Sasha is a striking lady with Annie Lennox hair and figure. She wears narrow rectangular glasses which make her look trendy and intelligent all at the same time. In truth, she is more intelligent and less trendy than her glasses. Her somewhat sloppy dress sense is probably a good thing—if she were too finely turned out she'd be terrifying and when she's in a suit, I can't help but imagine a whip in her hand.

She has always come across as smooth to me; I don't mean smooth as in smarmy, I mean as in the absence of sharp corners. She is opinionated, as most of us are, but you won't find yourself impaled on her arguments; she doesn't charge at you as some people do. What Sasha does is walk slowly and steadily into conversational battle, somehow managing to deflect all incoming targets until she is standing in your corner with her flag dug firmly into the ground. I think it comes from the deep-seated confidence she possesses in her core. I don't know Sasha's family that well, but I have met her parents and her two younger brothers and they all possess it. I think it is the powerful combination of encouraged individualism and a strong family unit. She possesses every quality Ben needs. For this reason I could only ever rejoice in my friend's choice of wife.

Sasha gave me a big hug and passed me something green and

zingy to drink. I drank it thirstily. Turned out something green and zingy was exactly what I needed. Sasha knew me well. I wanted to be the woman she knew. I didn't want to be the nervy, distracted, guilty woman who sat before her.

"Tell me what happened," said Sasha. I presumed, since she was offering to buy me lunch, she was talking about Claudia losing her baby and not me kissing her husband. I enveloped myself in the memory. It wasn't hard to obliterate all other thoughts that way.

"It was awful," I said. "We were painting the nursery, giggling about the dire state of my love life—I think Claudia was suggesting I become a lesbian or that I am a lesbian and somehow don't know it yet; she simply put down her paintbrush and went off to the loo laughing at her own phenomenal sense of humor. No warning, nothing. I just went on painting, I didn't even realize she hadn't come back. She didn't make a sound when it happened. She just sat on the loo and that was where I found her."

While food came and went I told Sasha about the blood, the cramps, trying to clean everything up. I told her about the hospital and how I had cried into the arms of a nurse and hadn't put her right when she thought I had lost a baby. I told her about the strange globules of blood that stuck to the bottom of the toilet bowl. I told her about the thick, industrial-sized sanitary pads and watching Claudia's eyes roll into the back of her head as the anesthetist counted down from ten. I told her everything, in excruciating detail, until it came to tucking Claudia into bed. Then I skipped a bit.

"Ben left, I sort of slept on the sofa until Al came home at six and then I went home."

"And how was she today?"

"Blaming herself and very drugged. Al doesn't want her to go through it again."

"I'm surprised they've gone through it as many times as they have."

I've thought much the same myself. But every time they thought about giving up there would be a new technique, a new man with a new method, better statistics. Medically, IVF is an incredible growth area; a lot of the cutting-edge treatments come out of genuine clinics with good intentions, but not all of them. Claudia spent hours on the Internet; somebody else's miracle story would grab her and off she'd go down another fertility worm hole.

"She isn't even the gullible type," said Sasha.

"But she wants it to be true so much. Talk about a soft target."

"Why don't they just adopt? I don't understand."

"They tried," I said. "It didn't work."

"Years ago."

"I think they're considered too old to adopt now."

"Maybe in this country, but not in China."

"I've had this conversation with Al. He says they'll look into it."

Sasha pulled a disbelieving face. "Now, after nine years they are going to look into it?"

I held out my hands. Sasha was repeating my very thoughts. "I guess it is very hard to go through IVF several times—all that invasive treatment, the complete eradication of sex for sex's sake—without believing 100 percent that it will work, and if you can convince yourself it will work, then you do it again and adoption seems second best. I don't know. It doesn't make sense to me."

"You and Ben don't feel particularly strongly about kids, so it wouldn't."

Sasha pulled a strange, disapproving face, but she didn't deny it. "Do you want children?"

"Of course I do." If I were absolutely honest I would tell her that the single thing that terrified me the most was the thought that I wouldn't have any children. I didn't want it to, but it did, it terrified me. How could I tell Sasha that? How could I tell her that my desire

for children had begun to affect how I behaved? How it was eschew-
ing my judgments. How it made me look at her husband with a
longing I didn't know what to do with. I couldn't tell her that. "I was
crying in the hospital yesterday because of this fear I have started
to feel."

"Fear of?"

"Not having kids. Sasha, I cried because of the imaginary children I might never have while Claud was having a real baby cut out
of her. I'm despicable." I was despicable, but not necessarily for that
reason.

"No, you're not, Tessa, come on. I think being single at your age
must be hard sometimes, but you know, having kids isn't necessarily
the answer."

"That's because you don't feel like this. I envy you. It's a horrible
feeling and it makes me feel desperate. I never thought I was desperate, the very word makes me . . ." I rubbed my eyes. "I don't know."

"You're wrong. I do feel desperate about having children, Tessa."

I glanced up from the food I'd been fiddling with and stared at
Sasha. "Huh?"

"I feel very strongly that people have children too often for the
wrong reasons."

I was confused. "How could wanting to have a baby be a wrong
reason?"

"Because there is a huge difference between wanting to have a
baby, and wanting to be a parent. I think the baby thing gets in the
way. The perfect Pampers baby that we're all supposed to have."

"It's maternal instinct."

"No, it isn't. It's a desire to procreate."

"Sasha, come on. I don't want a mini-me, I want a baby, a child, a
person, to love. An individual."

"Then go to China and get one."

"It's not as simple as that."

"Because . . ." Sasha let the question hang in the air.

Because I do want a child of my own? Because I do want a mini-me? Because I do want a husband who adores me, a picket fence, a baby with his eyes and my legs? Because I want what everyone else has? "I can't even manage the boyfriend bit." It was a pathetic duck and Sasha knew it, but she didn't pull me up. Instead she ordered decaf soya latte and carrot cake. I was feeling defensive and angry with her. I felt Claudia and Al needed our support, not an intense examination of their motives. I overlooked the fact that Sasha was saying almost exactly what I had said to Al myself. But I was still angry with her.

She was right, of course. There was a huge difference between wanting to have a baby and wanting to be a parent. One was selfish, the other selfless. If they happened to come together, wonderful. But they often didn't, because if they did, there would be no such thing as a bad parent. And as Ben, Helen, even my own mother, could testify, there were plenty of bad parents out there. I was angry with Sasha because I wanted to be. I was angry with Sasha because in the middle of the night I imagined she was married to the father of my unborn children. I was angry with Sasha because I adored her and knew she was married to the right man and I would never have those children.

The waitress put the cake and coffees down.

"I'm sorry, Sash, I'm all over the place."

"Don't ever apologize to me. You have nothing to apologize for."

For some reason the bite of carrot cake I put in my mouth didn't taste nearly as good as it should have. I watched Sasha as she stirred brown sugar into her coffee, slowly and methodically.

"I'm the one who should apologize," she said. "It is a subject I get too involved with, too personal. What Claudia puts herself through is her own business."

"She just wants to be a mother."

There was that same strange, disapproving look. "That's exactly what I'm talking about."

"I don't understand," I said.

"If all women thought like Claudia, I wouldn't have a mother."

I frowned. "But you have a wonderful mother who would do anything for you and your brothers."

"Yes, I do. But as you know perfectly well, she didn't give birth to me."

I sat back in my chair. Of course . . . Sasha's biological mother ran off when she was still a baby. Her father remarried when Sasha was about six. She was the person Sasha called mum. I'd completely forgotten that she wasn't Sasha's "real" mother. Clearly, that was her point.

"Stop thinking about having a baby, Tessa, and start thinking about whether you really want to be a parent. Not the fantasy— bouncing baby, adoring husband, picket-fence stuff—the real nitty-gritty, life-altering, mind-blowing responsibility that is being a parent with all the risks it involves, and if the answer is yes, then you can. These days there is nothing stopping you. If you really want to."

That morning I had woken with a head full of desperate, self-piteous, downright treacherous thoughts but I walked back into my flat lighter for having had lunch with the one person I could have sworn I didn't want to see. Even my mercy mission to the shops to buy things for Claudia and Al was merely a dressed-up good intention. I couldn't bear my own company since the only thing I could think about since my eyes had opened was Ben. It was easier to throw myself back into Al and Claudia's drama because it meant I didn't have to think about Ben any more. A scary fantasy had begun, with alarming detail and repetition, to play over and over in my head. Ben announcing his undying love. Sasha and Ben amicably agreeing to go their separate ways and Ben and I dancing off into the sunset to have several little Bens and Tessas. It was hideous. It was delicious. It was enticing. It was revolting. It was perfect. It was utterly stupid.

I kicked my shoes off and sat down on the sofa. First things first. Yes, we had crossed a boundary. But only for a split second. It was a need born of dire circumstances. And by that I meant the dire circumstances that were taking place in our oldest friends' lives. Not the current state of my life.

We had both run the moment we heard Claudia's voice. If we were true charlatans we could have ignored Claudia's delirious mumblings and gone at it like hammer and tongs. After all, she was heavily sedated and would not have known about me coming in and rearranging her pillows, pulling up her sheet, fussing with the window. She was not aware of the procrastination taking place in the disguise of good nursing. Ben left. He did not wait to acknowledge, discuss or reignite what had happened. The spell had been broken. There was no cyclist careering towards a lamppost. No damage had been done. Nothing was broken. Nothing had been done that couldn't be undone. It had been a moment and the moment had passed. I lay very low for the rest of the weekend.

The best thing to do, the only thing to do, was to forget about it and concentrate on the future. My future. There were headhunters I needed to call. There were hours and hours of research to do about where else my legal training could take me, if not directly back into law. Irony of ironies, Sasha had inspired me. It was time to think about what I really wanted out of life and then go and get it. Did I want to be a parent? That was too big a question to start with. That was jumping the gun. What I needed to do was work out what I wanted to do and how I was going to do it. How and why—not who and when. At nine o'clock sharp on Monday morning I was ready. I took a deep breath and picked up the phone.

"Hello, this is Tessa King, I'd like to talk to your legal recruitment department . . ."

"Just putting you through."

I waited. The reason why I'd been putting this off was because I couldn't face explaining why I was currently out of work. But I had to move on. I had to put an end to the halt that man had caused to my life. By that I meant my ex-boss, but thinking about it . . .

"Tessa King, I'm Daniel Bosley, head of legal. I've been hoping you'd call."

"Oh?"

"Yes, you've been on my radar some time, but I didn't think we'd ever prise you out of your chambers."

"Well . . ." I took another deep breath.

"Don't need to say a thing. I know all about it. Don't worry about that, draw a line, we can move right on . . ."

The conversation went on nicely from that point. I was to send in my CV, which was good, there were no sordid details on my CV. In fact, my CV put me in my best light. Consistent. Conscientious. Untroubled by the world of chicken pox and sports days. I could come to work early and I could leave late and the risk of maternity leave was rapidly diminishing. I'd employ me.

Emboldened, I carried on and called another. Why are these sorts of calls rarely as bad as you imagine them to be, yet you always imagine the worst? I worked away the rest of the day. I printed off forms and filled them in, I ticked boxes, I printed off my CV several times on smart, stiff paper then realized everybody did everything by email. Times had changed since I was in the market for a job.

When my phone rang I was so engrossed in work mode that I didn't recognize the voice at first.

"Hello," said a deep male voice.

"Hello," I replied.

"Tessa, is that you?"

My lungs suddenly constricted. "Who's this?" I asked.

"Caspar," said Caspar.

I exhaled loudly. I slowly unclenched my fist from around the phone and exhaled again. My palms had gone all sweaty. When did Caspar's voice get so deep?

"Tessa, are you there?"

Not as breezy as I thought. One step forward. Three steps backwards. Damn it. Damn it. Damn it. "Sorry, sweetheart, what can I do for you?"

"Just ringing to say hi."

Oh, really? "Bullshit, my darling boy. What is it?"

"Really, I just wanted to say thanks for bailing me out last weekend."

"Caspar, I love you, you know that, but in sixteen years you've never called me unless you wanted something. It's all right, I don't mind, that's what I'm here for."

"I love the iPod."

He was tenacious, I'd give him that. "Good. Got music on it yet?"

"Yeah. I went to this kicking place where you can download 800 tunes in . . ." I phased out about here. Caspar is a bit of a techno-geek. Always got great marks in maths and physics and IT. He was a genius with computers. Without the IT guy at work to come and sort out my laptop problems I was hopeless. I did that girly thing of rebooting at the first sign of trouble.

". . . I can come and update yours if you want. Surely you're getting bored of Abba by now."

"Oi, I'd like to have you know that I'm listening to Eminem right now."

"Ooh—a white rapper. Very cutting edge, Tessa. What will she do next?"

"Caspar, you are a gruesome child. Anyone told you that?"

"Constantly. Have you spoken to Mum and Dad recently?"

"Why, what's happened?" This was the reason for the call, then.

"Well, Mum is really on my case again. I was wondering if you could have a word with her."

"What have you done?"

"Nothing, I swear."

I bet. I stepped away from my desk and walked to the window. A police boat putted slowly up river. "Well, what's this about then?"

"There was a party, I took some beer, but—"

"Caspar!"

"What? Four fucking cans of beer. Cheap stuff too. Shitty own-brand."

"Hey, language."

"Yeah, right, I've heard you turn the air blue with swear words before now." That was a problem. Was I a mate, a bad example, or a good excuse, I wondered. Whichever it was, I was beginning to think that perhaps I wasn't the ideal person to rein Caspar in; he certainly didn't sound like he was going to be taking instruction from me any time soon. "I thought about what you said, Tessa, and I think they're being like this with me because of what you said. You're right, you got it, it's spot on, isn't it? Right, so now I know, I'm not taking it, for no reason, see?"

And in human speak that would mean what exactly? "Huh?"

"Missing out, they missed out; they don't know what's going on, what's normal, right? They're like stuck in a time warp. Need a Tardis. Four beers, man. Zac nicks vodka all the time from his old man and no one notices."

How many bottles of vodka did a kid have to nick before he got noticed, I wondered, but Zac wasn't my problem. "Well, that's OK then."

"Nice."

"No. I was being sarcastic."

"I've given up the ganja, but she can't keep me in all the time."

Why not? One morning your lovely son goes out and that afternoon comes back all f-ing and blinding and confounding you with middle-class "street" talk.

"Just coz she never went out."

Manipulative little bugger. I didn't mind letting Caspar think he was getting one over on me when it came to treats and extracting extra pocket money but I wasn't going to be complicit in his plans to get one over on his parents. Not knowingly, anyway.

"Don't twist my words. They were much older than you are."

"Come on, T-bird, you know the score. It's all relative. Please. They'll listen to you."

T-bird? I had no idea what he was talking about. "I'll talk to your mum, but get one thing straight, she's the boss."

He laughed.

"I'm being serious," I insisted, trying to sound like a real grown-up.

After the call, Caspar's laugh came back to me. We'd laughed a lot over the years—it was the basis of our peculiar friendship—but that wasn't the jolly, heart-warming laugh I'd heard before. That had been a thinner, meaner laugh, and it repeated on me like cheap meat.

If teenagers were advertised in nappies on the telly all the time, perhaps I wouldn't feel the pinch of my ovaries so much. My sympathy for Francesca and Nick was on the increase. Looking after babies was tough, no doubt, but *kidulthood*, now there was a challenge. I know Fran got a great deal of backchat from Katie and Poppy, especially

Katie, who seemed to have an answer for everything, but they could still be sent to their room, or made to sit on the naughty step. What did you do when they were bigger than you? What did you do when they laughed at you?

I returned to the desk and closed my laptop. I felt a huge sense of achievement as I tidied my papers away, put the laptop back in its case and slid the printer back under the small Ikea desk that inhabits a little corner of the room. It was no good worrying about everyone else all the time, I had to get on with my own life. I washed up the cafetière and mug I'd been using. My flat is too small to leave anything lying about so it has taught me to be tidy. Naturally I'm very messy, so it took a huge amount of energy to locate and train my tidy gene. Now I'm like a reformed smoker, I detest mess. Probably because I know that my whole life is only one dirty coffee cup away from chaos.

That Monday, however, despite everything that had happened I felt under control. I'd made a huge first step to reclaiming my life and decided to reward myself with an outing to the video store. I could order movies over the Internet—I used to—but I worried that it closed off another avenue to the outside world, so since leaving work I'd stopped doing it. Organizing food, laundry, books, CDs and gifts on the Internet meant my field of contact had vastly diminished, which meant I often nipped into the pub to make up for it. Now that I had more time I realized this wasn't necessarily a good thing, so I put on a better pair of jeans and walked to the video store. I always enjoy chatting to the dweeby film boffins behind the counter, though, like everyone else, they seem to be getting younger. They advised *Guess Who's Coming to Dinner*—the original, naturally; it has been a mission of mine to watch all the great films. I've barely scratched the surface.

At eight I watched the film. At ten I ran a bath. At ten-thirty I went to bed. At half past one in the morning I was still staring at the ceiling. My resolve to forget about Ben had crumbled. Suddenly I got it. I could deal with teenagers. I could deal with the whole damn lot. I wanted stretch marks. Bring on the piles, collapse my uterus and make me incontinent if that's what it would take to make me whole. I wanted children, God, not godchildren, and I knew who with and where he was. I propped myself up on one elbow, opened the bedside-table drawer and pulled out the photograph of Ben with his leg in traction. I placed the cool glass against my cheek and lay back down on the pillow. I felt the same now as I had then. No, I felt more. And it really, really hurt. The photo was a strange sort of comfort blanket, but I was at a strange sort of age. I needed reassurance now more than I ever had at any time in my life.

walking on eggshells

The following morning I packed a small case and fled to my mum and dad's cottage near Marlow. I had that bloody photograph in my case until the last minute, but just before leaving the flat I managed to yank it out and hide it among the books in my bookshelf. Twice, I nearly went back.

I said goodbye to Roman, telling him I was going away for a night or two, but a week later I was still in Buckinghamshire. My parents' constant warm embrace was hard to leave. More than that, I didn't trust myself to be in London without a chaperone. It was nice to be cooked for, put in front of a fire with a book, handed a glass of wine at six whether asked for or not, sent to bed. It was nice to tell them about my trip in minute detail and know that they were genuinely interested. It was nice to be able to switch off my phone. It was nice to be able to set off along the bridleway and think of him for hours in peace. It was easy to explain my lengthy stay if they questioned it. I hadn't seen them since I'd returned from India and as I wasn't working it was nice to hang out with them for more than a hurried weekend. Normally, Sunday night arrived just as the stress cogs in my system had stopped spinning.

As it happened, I didn't have to explain myself, since they didn't ask. A week had nearly passed and I thought I'd got away with it, but then Mum and I went scavenging for the last of the blackberries.

I was stretched precariously over a thorny branch when she got me.

"Tessa?" she asked in a concerned voice.

"Yes?"

"Is there anything you'd like to talk about?"

I threw the berries in the old ice-cream container she held. "Well, I've been thinking a lot about the state of the union."

"Seriously," she pleaded. "Dad and I are a bit worried about you."

"Don't be."

"Well, you say that, but you seem a bit . . ." She struggled to find the appropriate words.

I couldn't fill in the gap either. Lost at sea . . . In a trance . . . Dazed and confused . . . Desperate and alone . . . Going insane . . .

"Are you OK?"

"Yup."

"Are you sure—"

"Mum, I'm fine."

We carried on picking berries. The easy silence between us had gone. The air prickled with expectation. I waited for Mum to pluck up the courage to come at me again. I can be horribly obtuse when I want to be. I wasn't going to make it easy.

"You've been here a week now . . ."

Ah-ha. Just the trap I wanted her to fall into. "I thought it would be nice. We never do this, I'm always rushing off somewhere."

"Don't choose to misunderstand me, Tessa. You're very good at that."

"Mum, I'll be back at work any minute, then it will be back to the occasional Saturday nights again."

"Will you be back at work?"

"Course."

"You are trying to get another job, then?"

I was indignant. "I told you. Weren't you listening? The head-hunter I spoke to was really positive about getting me another job."

My mother blew her nose into a hanky.

"You're getting cold, Mum," I said, immediately concerned. "We should go home."

"I'm absolutely fine. We haven't got enough yet," she said, shaking the blackberries. And I wonder where I get my obtuseness from?

"You didn't tell me about the job thing," she went on. "You told us about Caspar and tracking down Billy's ex Christoph in Dubai, and the christening but—"

"I'm sorry, I thought I'd told you," I said.

"That's what I'm trying to say . . ." I waited. My mother's hand hovered over the brambles. "I mean, you do seem to be spending quite a lot of time focusing on your friends . . ."

"I know I've been on the phone a lot to Claudia, but she lost a baby."

"It's not just that."

"What do you want me to do, tell her to get over it?"

My mother finally stopped pretending to look for blackberries and turned to face me. "Darling, you've always been there for your friends, it's one of your best attributes. Please don't misunderstand me, but . . ."

"But what, Mum? Al was away."

"This isn't about Claudia. I worry that, well, while you're busy helping everybody else, your life is somehow . . ." She faltered.

I stepped in, before she had time to voice her fears. "Mum, come on, I had a shitty year, I took a bit of time off, but considering everything that happened, I think I'm doing pretty well."

"Of course you are. I just wanted to check that everything else is all right."

My mother was being brave. I usually put her off the scent much more easily than this. But then I'd never been in a position like this before. I mean, I had been—for years—but I hadn't realized it. I loved a man I couldn't have and instead had settled for the crumbs off Sasha's table. The less you eat the less you need to eat, or so you think, until you're so weak your vital organs start to fail. I was beginning to think that was what had happened to me. I'd been malnourished for so long I no longer recognized hunger pangs. I suppose in the beginning I was young enough for an ill-fated, imagined love affair not to affect my life too much. Everyone else was out having fun, not taking life too seriously, we were in it together. But bit by bit, the ones became twos, then threes and fours, while I was still wasting away on crumbs.

"Are you sure you're OK, darling?"

I turned my back on her and stared at the tiny thorns that kept me from getting to the thing I wanted most. No, I wasn't OK. I wasn't in the slightest bit OK. I felt tears well up behind my eyelids. I closed my eyes purposefully, urging them to behave.

"Tessa?"

I didn't want to worry her. I didn't want to be a burden. I didn't want to add to the deep-seated fear she must carry around with her at all times. My job was to augment, to add, to be a source of pride. But she was my mum and, God, I needed to tell someone . . .

I turned. Walking up the track in mustard-colored corduroys was Dad. He waved at me enthusiastically.

"Hellooo," he bellowed.

Mum still watched me.

I stepped away from the hedgerow.

She grabbed my hand. "Tessa?"

Glancing at her fleetingly, I squeezed her hand and pulled away. "Everything's great. I'd tell you if it wasn't, I promise." That was the biggest lie of all, of course. Mum had MS lingering dormant in her system, like a terrorist sleeper cell, able to rear up and strike anything at any time. My father was in his eighties. They had enough on their plate without having to add me to their worries. I bounded down the track to my father.

"Perfect timing," I said. "The nice ones are getting harder to find."

He smiled at me. I noticed that his teeth were beginning to look old. I averted my eyes. Dad placed my arm through his and we walked back to Mum. He peered inside the ice-cream carton. Picking out a couple of blackberries and throwing them back into the hedgerow, he said, "Well, you can't go picking any old manky ones, it's not worth it; you'll get the jam but it won't taste nearly as good as it should."

I looked at my father, then back at the blackberries and finally at my mother.

"Very true," she said nodding. Looking straight back at me. "Very true indeed."

That afternoon we made jam and thankfully the subject of my life didn't come up again. Their friends came over for dinner. They like to show me off, though I am keenly aware they have less news to tell than they'd like. We went into the nearest town one afternoon and I forced my mother to buy some inappropriate accessories. Dad and I had a mammoth chess battle. It was fun because I won. That didn't happen very often; I swear the man never let me win at anything, not even running races when I was a kid. I once overheard Mum imploring him to give me a break, since I was only six, but he wouldn't budge. Said it was no good thinking life was a pushover. I longed to beat him. I do now, of course, and wish I didn't.

It wasn't like that in Claudia's house. She was another only child and if she did a poo, her parents clapped. Although it's true that she hasn't achieved a great deal, she has an intrinsic belief in herself that has held her in good stead. Watching my father potter around the garden, I thought to myself that actually his way was a good way. Because deep down, below all the doubt and nonsense, I too have an intrinsic belief in my self. It's just that sometimes I forget.

By the second week my visit to my parents' house had worked its magic on me. I was feeling much more positive. Just watching them go about their strange daily routine, they reminded me to take things both not too seriously and very seriously all at the same time. It's a difficult mix to get right. I had almost, almost stopped thinking about why I had fled there.

But then Claudia had called the house and told me she was leaving the country. I'd been expecting it, but not that fast. As ever, Al had done what he'd said he was going to do. They were leaving for Singapore on Sunday.

It was Claudia's idea to have a leaving lunch for her close friends the day before they left. She said she didn't want to sneak out of the back door. She didn't want to pretend that nothing had happened; neither did she want to make her miscarriage a taboo subject, nor did she want anyone to feel bad. She had lost the baby, she was devastated, but she would, in time, she said, get over the worst. More than that, she wanted lunch to be fun. I was dreading it. The day she called me she asked me to telephone "the others" and let them know where and when. She said she didn't want to phone as she was conscious that no one knew what to say to her. She thought it would be easier for everyone if I did it. She gave me the list. It would be her and Al, Helen and Neil, Ben and Sasha and me. Seven. I am always the odd number.

I did the easy jobs first. I booked a table at a bustling Italian

restaurant where I knew the food was fairly priced and the waiters exceptional. Nothing like a good Italian waiter to set the mood.
None of this surly French stuff. Then I rang Helen. Neil answered. I
explained the reason for my call.

"Sounds like a barrel of laughs," said Neil.

Well, it won't be if you're there, I thought meanly. "Actually, Claudia is doing really well. She just wants to have a laugh with her mates
before they go."

"All right for them, two months in the Far East. Wish I could send
my moody wife away."

This is why I detested the man. I didn't think I was being
unreasonable.

"She won't get out of bed," said Neil.

"Is she OK?"

"Course she's OK. She just sleeps all day."

"Probably because she's up all night."

"The boys sleep fine. She's just neurotic about cot death or something. She checks them all the time. What's the point of having Rose
live here if she can't do the odd night?"

I'd seen the way Neil spoke to Rose, and it wasn't pleasant view-
ing. It was a subject I didn't want to linger on, it made me too venom-
ous. "Why don't you tell her to give up the breastfeeding? Honestly, I
think it's reeking havoc on her. She doesn't seem herself."

"Then what would she do? We've got two nannies as it is, it's not
like she's run off her feet."

"Yes, but producing that amount of milk every day is like running a mini-marathon. It just knackers you out."

"I've read the stuff—immunity, asthma, breast is best, as they
say," he said. "Course, it means I don't get my hands on them."

I didn't think he meant the twins. I would have changed the subject, but I wanted Neil to think about what feeding those giant babies
was costing his wife. So I continued to talk breasts.

"Well then, at least tell her to pump it off and give someone else"—meaning you, you lazy bum—"the job of feeding. They are really slow eaters."

"She's been moaning to you?"

"No." I didn't want to get Helen into trouble. "She spends hours locked away in the nursery at the top of the house. I don't think it's good for her."

"How would you know, Tessa? You don't have kids."

And I'd thought this was going to be the easy call to make.

"Will you be able to make it to the lunch?" I said, forcing a softer tone into my voice. "It would mean a lot to Claudia and Al."

"No probs."

"Great. Shall I leave you the number at my Mum and Dad's house in case Helen wants to call?"

"No, she'll be fine. See you Saturday."

Goody, goody. I replaced the phone. Round two. I cheated and rang Sasha's mobile. There was a long tone. Sasha was abroad again.

"Sasha Harding."

"Hey, it's me, can you talk?"

"Sorry, hon, not really."

"It's about a goodbye lunch for Al and—"

"When?"

"Saturday."

"Great. I'm back on Friday. Just call Ben. Give him the details. Gotta go."

Just call Ben. Just call Ben. Simple. Just call him the way I'd called him a million times before. I took a deep breath and pressed the numbers of Ben's mobile into the handset. I stared at them. Naturally, I knew the number by heart. I must have dialed it ten times while I'd been in Buckinghamshire, but I had never actually pressed the little green call button. I wanted to. I wanted to hear his voice. I wanted to keep this sensation alive. I wanted to live in my dreams. I could still feel his lips burn mine. I could recall perfectly the moment our mouths opened wider and the soft inside of his mouth met mine. It made me shudder with longing and shame. I had to find a way out of this mess.

The phone jangled in my hand.

"Anyone there?" shouted my father.

I pressed the green button and watched Ben's number disappear.

"Hello?" I said.

"Hello?" replied a woman.

"Hello," said a man, followed by confused silence.

"Tess?"

"Mum?"

"Hello, Mrs. King."

"Who's that?"

I knew who it was.

"It's Ben, Mrs. King."

"Ben, for God's sake, stop calling me Mrs. King. You're pushing forty, aren't you? It's indecent."

"Old habits," said Ben.

"How are you, anyway? We haven't seen you for ages."

"Very well. How about you?"

"Keeping out of trouble, just. Campaigned to get a twenty-mile-an-hour limit set outside the school gates, then forgot myself and got three points on my license."

Ben laughed. This was all true. It may have seemed like an odd response to an enquiry about her health but I know my mother well and what her story meant. It was intended to convey that her MS was still at bay, she was still driving, still living independently, still part of life. During those occasional bad episodes she usually says something like, "Doing a lot of puzzles" or, "Catching up with my photo albums."

Ben and Mum chatted on. I was quite happy to let them, since I couldn't seem to open my mouth.

"Tessa told me how wonderful you were the other night," said my mother. I grimaced silently into the other phone. "Thank God you all have each other. Anyway, love to Sasha. I'll leave you two to chat, though please remember dinner is at seven."

Another of my mother's jokes. Since it was only three in the afternoon. Ben and I have been known to chat for hours. I didn't think this would be one of those occasions. I heard the second phone in the house go click. We were alone.

"Hello, Tess."

"Hello, Ben."

Silence. A strange silence, since it wasn't in the slightest bit uncomfortable.

"I thought I'd lost you," he said.

"Sorry. Didn't I tell you I was coming down here?"

"No."

"Sorry," I said again.

That was followed by another silence. A slightly more uncomfortable one.

"I had lunch with Sasha," I said.

"She told me." I waited. "She said it was great to see you," he said.

In other words, you didn't rock the boat.

"It was great to see her, actually. She was very helpful. Gave me some good advice." I wondered if he was going to ask me about what, but he didn't. I'd opened the door a crack. Ben had closed it again. Even though I wanted to kick the door down, I had to leave it closed.

"She's a wise woman," said Ben.

"Yes, she is," I said.

"Anyway, I just wanted to check that you were all right. I know this is about Claudia, but it was horrible for you too."

I remembered staring into the toilet bowl, then banished the memory. "I feel desperate for them. I think it's good they're going away."

"Is that it, then? No more IVF?"

"Claudia hasn't said so, and the doctor assured me that next time would be different, so, who knows . . ."

"Different, but not necessarily successful."

"They are clever, those doctors, they pick their words carefully."

"Well, it's a business, I suppose," said Ben. "Anyway, she was lucky to have you there. Did the orange paint work?"

"Yes. Thank you so much for coming to help me."

"Don't be silly. You know I'd always drop anything if you needed me."

But not your wife. My stomach lurched. Banish that evil thought. Banish it! "I know. Thanks."

"Al rang me about lunch on Saturday, said you were organizing it."

"I was just dialing your number when you called."

"Well, the telepathy was a bit delayed; I've been urging you to call since last Monday. I thought for a horrid moment you'd buggered off back to the Swiss lady at the ashram."

And so the merry dance continued for another fifteen minutes or so. We brushed against the subject a couple of times, not that anyone listening in on our conversation would have known that. I realized then that we had perfected this skill over the years since Ben had been hit by the cyclist. It was a two-way thing—we were both complicit in it—but Ben was clearly faring better out of the deal. He had Sasha. An incredible woman who suited the very fiber of his being right down to not wanting children together. I had no one. I think it was what Marilyn Monroe in *Some Like It Hot* called getting "the fuzzy end of the lollipop." Ben was not going to leave his wife for me and, anyway, I didn't want him to. I wanted to inhabit a parallel universe that didn't exist outside the realms of my imagination. I wanted things to be different. And they were never going to be if I didn't do something about this now.

I had to make a decision. I had to change the pattern of my life. I had to leave an imaginary twenty-year relationship. I had to get divorced from a man I had never married. I had to move on. For survival's sake, I had to accept that the man I had somehow considered mine was not, never had been and never would be. I had to say goodbye and yet he'd never know I had.

"I've got to go, Ben," I said, more firmly than I felt.

"All right, sweetie. See you Saturday."

Well, now it was Saturday and I felt sick. I pushed the door to the Italian restaurant open and inhaled the aroma of garlic and olive oil. Al, Claudia, Ben and Sasha were already at the table. That left three empty seats between Sasha and Ben. I kissed everyone hello. Ben first, which was probably normal. Then I sat down next to Sasha, which was not. I had done it. I had made the first break. Ben was the person I always sat next to. I wouldn't have even thought about it; it would have been an automatic response. Not any more. I, Tessa King, was in control of my destiny.

The waiters insisted on us ordering wine, brought bread and olives and then left us in peace to peruse the menu. I poured out the wine. Solemnly we raised our glasses.

"To health and happiness," we chorused. Our big ask was getting bigger by the day.

"Helen and Neil?" I asked.

"They haven't phoned to say they're not coming," said Claudia.

"Helen will be here," said Al.

She'd bloody better be, I thought.

The more relaxed we tried to be, the more awkward lunch became. We all knew why we were there but no one wanted to mention it. Instead, we talked about all the places around Singapore that Al and Claudia could visit. We talked about where they were going but not why. The two empty chairs between myself and Ben were distracting me from the job in hand: that of providing Claudia a happy send off. I kept glancing at my watch.

"Maybe I should call her?" I said eventually. "I didn't actually speak to Helen, I spoke to Neil. Maybe he didn't tell her."

"No, Helen called me to see if I was all right," said Claudia. "She's definitely coming. It's probably got something to do with schedules or routines."

I wanted off this subject as quickly as possible.

"Where were you this week, Sasha?" I asked, looking away from Claudia.

"Germany again. Berlin." She shook her head and smiled naughtily. "It's a wild city. I always go out far too late when I'm there."

"You be careful, Ben," said Al. "Sasha will finally realize what a terrible choice she made and run off with a broad-chested, beer-swilling Bratwurst called Bruno."

"Nice alliteration," said Ben.

"Thanks."

"I don't think Ben has to worry about me," she said, looking fondly over at her husband. There were consecutive "ahs" around the table. Not from me; I was wondering who Ben did have to worry about, if not Sasha. Or did she mean he was the one who was the cause for concern?

"Actually, I've met most of the men that Sasha travels with on a weekly basis and they are mostly small, pot-bellied types with chronic overbites and—"

"Very large brains," said Sasha, finishing for him. "Who, incidentally, control 75 percent of the European money markets."

Ben looked at the gathered crowd. "I'm fucked."

"Luckily I'm not looking for a sperm donor, so you're safe for the time being."

It was a good gag, in ordinary circumstances, but these were not ordinary circumstances. Sasha knew immediately she'd said the wrong thing. I couldn't think of anything quick enough to say to get her out of it. I couldn't even make it worse, because that would have made it worse for Claudia. Sasha put an imaginary gun to her head and pulled the trigger.

"Sorry, Claud," she said.

Claudia slapped her hands on the table. "Stop it," she said. "All of you. Stop doing a really good job of pretending we're not here because Al and I lost another baby. That is why I wanted this lunch," she said emphatically. "So we don't have to do this. I haven't got cancer. I'm not dying. We tried, we failed, maybe we'll try again. Maybe we'll even fail again. It can rule my life, it has ruled my life and Al's, I am perpetually sorry for that, but it doesn't have to govern our friendship. I want to know who you've been shagging for fun, Tessa, I want to know that having children is the last thing on your mind, Sasha, I want Ben to tell Al he wants Sasha to stop demanding sex in funny positions—"

"How do you know about that?" said Ben.

But Claudia wouldn't be deflected. "You can say 'period' without going puce. I want my friends with children to be able to moan about their children without feeling guilty. I want to tell Helen she is a brilliant mother when she arrives and the table not to choke on their vongole. Do you understand?"

We all nodded. "No more pussyfooting. No more walking on egg-shells. Understood?"

We nodded again.

"So, first things first," said Ben. "Who is Tessa shagging for fun?"

Loaded question, if I ever heard one. But I wasn't playing any more. "I came to a scary conclusion the other day," I replied. "I'm single but not sexually frustrated, which can only mean one thing."

"Good electronics," said Sasha.

"Never really been an electronics girl myself," I said.

"You should be. The only way I stay faithful on those business trips is because I take a little something with me."

"Less of the little," said Ben.

"Is that true?" asked Claudia. Sasha winked. A long, sexy wink. The woman is smooth.

"The boys have their porn. The women, their toys; we all go home happy to our husbands and wives. It's the ones not watching the porn or without the toys you've got to worry about."

"And these people control 75 percent of the European money markets?" asked Al.

"Yup."

"Honey, I think it's time to buy yen," he said.

"I think it's time we ordered. We're getting smutty and it's not yet one," said Claudia.

"Where the hell are Helen and Neil?" I said.

Claudia, who was facing the door, pointed. "Here they are." Then she frowned. I turned. Helen was standing in the doorway, strug-gling to get an enormous pram into the small restaurant. It should have come with a "wide load" sign and some outriders. Some waiters were trying to help her, with smiles and cries of "beautiful bambi-nos," which I knew were insincere: the twins were still at their James Gandolfini phase. The waiters were simply keeping up appearances.

Being Italian waiters. Earning their reputation as the best in the world, and their tip. But I wasn't really focused on that. It was one thing trying not to pussyfoot around Claudia or walk on eggshells; it was another thing to bring two screaming nearly newborns to lunch with a woman who two weeks earlier had lost her own.

Ben stood up. "She looks like she could do with a hand."

"Where's Neil?"

No one answered. Instead, we watched Helen push the ludicrously large pram through the tables, knocking people, bags and coats as she went. She must have said sorry twenty times between the door and our table at the back of the restaurant. If I had thought for one second Helen was going to bring the twins I would have chosen another place to eat, but, call me old-fashioned, I sort of assumed she'd know that it was not a good idea.

"I'm so sorry I'm late," she said.

Late? Sorry you're late? Don't you mean sorry for being so sucked in by the importance of your own offspring that you've lost all sensitivity to those around you?

"Don't worry," said Claudia. "I'm just glad you're here." Sometimes Claudia's generous spirit is very irritating. Isn't anyone going to mention how inappropriate this is?

"Where's Neil?" I asked again through a clenched smile.

"Tied up, um, called into work. Sound-editing . . ."

Another late Friday night, then. I was not feeing hugely sympathetic. Everyone moved chairs around to make way for the twins.

"I didn't realize you were going to bring the boys," I said to Helen when she sat down next to me.

"The nanny had the day off. Neil was going to cover, but then he had to work, and I so wanted to come, and . . . Any trouble and we'll leave."

"Don't be ridiculous," said Claudia. "I'm not going to see my godsons for a couple of months, I'm delighted you've brought them."

"They've been fed, so they should sleep."

I examined Helen closely. She was wearing more concealer than Marilyn Manson, but even Touche Eclat couldn't hide the lies. She was covering for her shitty husband, as usual. There were dark circles under her eyes and she was shaking. She used to tell me about the nights that Neil went AWOL, but after a while I suppose it got embarrassing for her, since he didn't appear to change and she didn't do anything to stop it. "Won't be late." "One more and I'm coming home." Or the classic, "I'm on my way home." Yet several hours would pass; Helen would go mad with worry, then finally he'd fall through the door too pissed to undress himself. I told her to lock him out when he did that, but she was too afraid he'd leave her.

I reckoned that Helen had probably been awake most of the night, either furious with Neil—I think she was over the worried stage—or with the twins, who couldn't possibly sleep as much as they did during the day, then sleep through the night too. Maybe Neil had come home, maybe he hadn't. Either way, he wouldn't have been able to look after the twins. Helen must have tanked herself up on coffee and dragged herself and the twins to the restaurant. It would have been better not to have come at all.

"What about Rose?" I asked. I could hear the daggers in my voice but couldn't seem to hold back. Helen looked at me nervously. I was making her nervous. Good.

"She's worked three weekends in a row. I couldn't ask her."

"But I'm sure she would have looked after them for a couple of hours."

"She had plans."

For some reason I didn't believe a word she was saying.

"You need a glass of wine," said Al.

"I can't. Still breastfeeding," said Helen.

"Oh, go on," I said, goading her. "One won't hurt."

"Trouble is, I don't want just one," said Helen.

Everyone laughed.

"That bad," said Al.

"They're lovely when they're asleep," said Helen. "They just set each other off all the time when they're awake."

"Sasha has got friends from university with twins," said Ben. "They said it was hellish to begin with, but once you're out of the baby bit, they're a self-contained unit and just play with each other. You get the payout later."

"Play or beat each other up?" asked Helen.

"These twins are girls," said Sasha. "Though I hate to sexually stereotype at such a young age, they do seem to color for hours."

"I'm not sure the boys will do that," said Helen, with what I thought sounded like a touch of pride. I wanted to slap her. I looked over at Claudia. She had a smile superglued on to her face. Stop, I wanted to shout. This is wrong. We shouldn't be here talking about your babies. Don't do this to Claudia. She's been through enough!

I was too riled to find a way out of the situation, but Al was thinking straight. He called over a waiter and announced we were ready to order, which, of course, we weren't since we'd barely glanced at the menu. For a while, at least, everyone's attention was elsewhere and by the time the final order had been taken Al had launched into a story about one of the building projects he'd worked on in India. It was a funny story. I half listened and half had a conversation in my head with Helen where I told her what I thought of this stunt. I was furious that Al was having to drag up old material in order to stop Helen from turning the screw on his precious wife.

I'm hopeless with anger. I'm hopeless with any extreme emotion towards another person. It bubbles up to the surface and explodes.

I cannot control my feelings of disappointment, rage or sadness. When I'm confused, I look confused. I'd be a hopeless spy. The other side of the coin is that when I'm happy I laugh my head off, I smile at strangers; when I'm content I radiate calmness. There is a third side of the coin: my brick-wall face. That is reserved only for when heady emotions are turned my way. I don't like that at all. But Helen wasn't fighting back, so my anger just got worse and worse. During that lunch I could feel myself bristle every time Helen spoke, I could hear the meanness in my own voice when I spoke to her. Eventually I went to the loo just to get out of arm's reach of Helen.

I was staring hard at my reflection when Claudia came into the ladies' loo. I smiled sympathetically at her, figuring I knew why she'd escaped too.

"Are you OK?" I asked her.

"I'll be fine as soon as you stop picking on Helen."

"What?"

Claudia leaned back against the basin. "It's not her fault that Neil had to go to work."

"If he is at work."

"Tessa, don't you think you're being a little unfair? How many times has your friend Billy messed up childcare arrangements and you've ended up dragging Cora along to something. Didn't Francesca fail to collect you from the airport for the same reason? The kids come first, that's just tough shit. If it's OK for Fran and Billy, then it's OK for Helen."

"I know that, but this is a bit different, don't you think?"

"Weren't you listening to what I said upstairs? Of course it's hard, it's been hard for years. I count babies on the street. How many I see. My record is forty-four in a day. Forty-four babies that weren't mine."

"Exactly, this is your goodbye lunch. You've been through hell."

"You are missing my point. I didn't want those forty-four mothers not to have babies. I don't want Helen not to have her twins. I want you to have children, when you want them. I want you to bore me with every burp and poo when the time comes. I'd like to bore you too, that's all. Not instead of. As well as. If Helen had not come because she thought I would prefer not to see her than see her and her children, then I will just become so isolated that I'll be doomed. I'm flattered she brought them."

"I think you give her too much credit. I think she is completely blinkered by those babies and her dreadful husband."

"I'm sure you're right, Tessa. I'm sure that when Neil was called away, she thought, Great, we'll all go to Claudia's farewell lunch which is taking place because Al and Claudia lost their baby a week ago. Ideal."

"I don't think Neil was called away."

"Irrelevant. Neil isn't my friend, Helen is. Her decision was based on establishing a normality between us. If I hadn't had a miscarriage she would have brought the twins. I need you all to be normal, so that I don't disappear into the madness that is threatening to consume me." Claudia swallowed hard, ran her fingers back through her dark bob several times, before looking at me again. I watched her closely. With her hair pulled back I noticed for the first time that her hairline was receding. Because she wore her hair in a bob, it always fell forward, but actually, on closer inspection, it looked—I peered closer—thin.

I pulled back when Claudia looked back at me. "Helen bringing the twins here forces me to be normal. You have to understand that."

"But it must be so hard." Emotionally and, by the looks of it, physically.

"Even if it was too hard, it's not too hard for you. Why are you so angry?"

I stared at her.

"Tessa, what is it?"

I shook my head.

"There is something, though, isn't there?"

This is the trouble with such old friends. No hope of reinvention.

"Are you pregnant?"

My jaw dropped. "God, no."

"If you were, you would tell me, wouldn't you?"

I pulled Claudia towards me so she couldn't see the relief on my face. "I'm not going to get pregnant, I don't have a boyfriend."

"Yeah, but you sleep around."

"Thanks."

"I'm just saying, accidents happen."

"No, accidents don't happen. People take risks and get caught. I don't take risks—"

Claudia opened her mouth to protest.

"I don't."

"That's bollocks. Did you use a condom with that bloke the other night?"

Not the first time, I grant you, or the second in the shower. "Not fair. They were exceptional circumstances."

Claudia crossed her arms. "In other words, 'No, Claudia, I didn't, because I'm an idiot.'"

"I'm on the pill," I said, defending myself.

"Ever heard of Chlamydia? Not to mention the obvious."

"Of course, but—"

"It won't happen to you."

"It was once, Claudia."

"Hmm." She wasn't convinced. "Won't it be nice that when you do finally meet someone and try to start a family, you'll discover you can't have kids because you slept around without a condom? That'll be fun."

"We're not in here to talk about me."

"Nice deflection, babe. You're good at that."

"Claudia," I said, stung. "I'm sorry I came down on Helen, but don't be mad at me."

"Sometimes you are maddening."

I was confused. Helen was the one we were mad at—spoilt, selfish Helen with her giant Bugaboo pram and matching nappy bags.

"You're holding something back from me, I know it," said Claudia, her blue eyes staring at me.

"No."

"Don't you think it's time to face a few things?"

What, like you accepting you can't have kids? I turned on the tap and washed my hands methodically. I wanted out of this conversation before I said something I regretted.

"I'm sorry I was angry with Helen for bringing the twins." I walked to the hand-dryer and waved my wet hands under it. Nothing happened. Claudia passed me some loo paper.

"Thanks. I'll rein it in, I promise. Do you think Helen noticed?"

"You've got a big personality, Tessa, and when you're cross, we all duck."

"You're no wilting flower, my friend."

"It upsets me when I see you . . ." Claudia paused. I used it to my advantage.

"I'll be nice to Helen, I promise."

Claudia put her hand on mine and looked at me long and hard. "Tessa, ever worry that we're stuck? Me and this baby thing, you and . . ." She didn't finish the sentence again, and I wasn't going to help her. I looked at her blankly. It's all about how good your poker face is. Mine is excellent. Thinking about it, I should learn how to play because I may wear my emotions on my sleeve when it's about others, but I can conjure up an unscalable blank wall and hold it for hours when it's about me. It drives my mother mad. Claudia gave up. "I know you can't stand Neil, but Helen isn't as strong as you. She needed a base. Away from her mother. At least she's achieved that."

"Out of the frying pan . . ."

"Maybe. But you should try and be more understanding. You have been loved from the moment you were born. You expect that standard of love and won't accept anything else. That's good—you should be loved. But Helen has never had that, so cut her a little slack if she is one-track-minded about those little boys. I bet it's a double-edged sword to discover the depths of her own maternal love and learn for the first time how little she's been loved herself. Throw in the hormones, which I can testify will send the sanest person off kilter, an unsupportive husband, too much money, no sleep, and, frankly, I think she's doing pretty well."

I wanted the anger in me to dissipate, but it was stubbornly clinging to my ribcage.

"She needs you, but she'll never ask," said Claudia.

That worked. I like to be needed. "I'm going to miss you," I said. "Even if you are a harridan."

"Come out to Singapore. We could go beach-hopping for a couple of weeks, let Al get his work done and give him a break from worrying about me."

That didn't sound like a bad idea. "I could."

"You could."

"I mean, I really could."

Claudia nodded enthusiastically. "In the meantime, will you stop terrifying the living daylights out of Helen?"

"Yes."

"Good." Claudia took my hand. "Now let's go and have another glass of wine. There's got to be some benefit to not being pregnant any more."

I couldn't actually apologize to Helen but I did look into the pram and make appropriate noises about how sweet the boys looked and how good they were. They were as soundly asleep as they had been at the christening and I wondered if Helen exaggerated her "nightmare" and exhaustion over the sleeplessness to hide what was really keeping her awake at night: namely, an absent husband. Helen visibly relaxed and I felt bad that I had that sort of control over her so I told her again how incredible she'd looked at the christening and how well it had all gone.

"I'm sorry I vanished like that," said Helen quietly to me. "I think I was polite conversationed out. I'm sorry I snapped at you."

"You didn't."

"And I'm sorry I've been such a grouch. I'm getting it together, I promise. We'll have that night out we keep talking about"—for a year and a half now—"not the launch thing, you and me, like we used to."

"That would be great," I said. Though I wouldn't be holding my breath.

"I could do with a girls' night out," said Sasha, joining in. "Far too many men in my life these days."

"I'll leave the boys with Neil, he can put them to bed."

"From what I hear, that'll be a shock to the system," said Ben.

I waited for Helen to bristle, look at me and tell me off for gossiping, but she didn't. "You're telling me," she said, smiling broadly. "I don't think he knows which one is which without their names on."

Everyone laughed, Helen loudest of all. The table rallied around her. I should have been pleased that Helen was exceeding my expectations of her but instead it made me feel oddly uncomfortable.

I ordered more wine and poured generously into everyone's glasses. We soon felt the effects of lunchtime drinking, except Helen, and our table got steadily rowdier. The babies were good as gold and we all wished we could sleep through all the bad jokes and old stories we somehow never tired of telling. Claudia smiled broadly at me. She had got what she wanted, against the odds: we managed to have a fun, relaxed, happy lunch, a group of old mates with no cares in the world, when, in reality, nothing could have been further from the truth.

Al and Claudia were leaving first thing the following morning. At five we finally signed the bill and left a smattering of empty limoncello glasses on the ruined white tablecloth. Helen had left earlier when the babies started to stir. We urged her to stay but she said she couldn't face feeding them in a restaurant, and they were easily distracted. I thought she was probably aware that breastfeeding in front of Claudia would be a bridge too far.

There is a difference between striving for normality and rubbing someone's nose in it and I silently appreciated the gesture.

The five of us stood on the pavement. This was it. The goodbyes. I hugged Al first and was surprised that I could feel his ribs. He'd lost yet more weight. I told him again how amazing he was. Then Sasha hugged Al and I hugged Claudia and told her I would look into flights. Then Sasha hugged Claudia and I was left standing next to Ben. Al hailed a cab. Claudia and Sasha were talking. My arm was touching Ben's; I could feel the heat through my shirt. Ben put his arm around my back and squeezed my opposite shoulder, then he let his arm fall away as he walked over to Al. We waved at Al and Claudia until they rounded the corner. And then there were three.

Sasha saw a bus. "Come on, it goes straight home."

"A bus?" said Ben.

"Don't be such a snob. Come on, run, you lazy sod."

He turned back to me.

"Come on!" Sasha was already halfway to the bus stop, waving her hand madly.

"Go," I insisted, smiling.

"I don't want to leave you here by yourself," he said.

"I'll be fine."

"Sure?"

"Go," I said again, pushing him slightly.

"See you at the launch?"

The launch?

"Neil's TV thing."

God, I'd completely forgotten he was going to that. "Absolutely."

"That's a date." He blew me a kiss, turned and ran. They waved at me from the top deck, smiling drunkenly. I waved back, swearing as I did so. My days of using Ben as my walker were supposed to be over. My days of filling Sasha's shoes had to end. This was my promise to myself. I pulled my jacket around me. *I don't want to leave you here by yourself. I don't want to leave you here by yourself. I don't want to leave you here by yourself.* I stared after the bus.

"Then don't," I said, lowering my hand. Finally, it too rounded the corner, taking the last of my friends away. And then there was only one.

pants on fire

I awoke on Monday morning feeling despondent. The week stretched ahead of me with nothing in the diary but an interview with a head-hunter on Wednesday and a meeting with my accountant on Friday. Whoop, whoop. Throw in a couple of yoga classes, some chores and food shopping and there was still a vast expanse of time to fill.

I missed Claudia and Al. Not that I saw them on a weekly basis, but I missed their presence. Sasha had told me she was away all week, which meant avoiding Ben at all costs until my mind had stopped tripping. Helen said she was taking the twins and Rose to her house in the country for the week so she was well rested and looking her best for Neil's launch on the weekend. Helen always looked so glamorous at large events, but I knew she did not find them easy. For such a beautiful woman, she was incredibly self-conscious and strangely shy. Reading between the lines I thought that Neil was probably being punished for doing an all-nighter the night before Claudia and Al's leaving lunch. Despite his resistance to getting his hands dirty with the twins, there was no doubt he loved his sons and heirs, as he referred to them. Well, if not loved them, then loved the fact of them, which would probably do until they were older and a little more rewarding as companions. I was pleased that Helen seemed to be finding a little backbone.

Outside the sky was bright autumn blue. I refused to sit on my arse and stare out at the world any longer. I watched bikes cross the bridge. That's what I'd do—I'd get my bike out of storage, and go for a ride. I quickly dialed Fran's number before I changed my mind.

"Hey, Fran, you busy?"

"Funny."

I didn't think I was being funny.

"Where are you?"

"About to cycle home from school."

"Great, do you want to meet me instead? Battersea Park, go for a cycle, then have coffee?"

"Um . . ."

"It's a beautiful day."

"Sod it, why not. The laundry can wait. It'll take me about twenty minutes to get there."

"Perfect, it'll take me twenty minutes to get the cobwebs off my bike. I'll see you at the gate, Chelsea Bridge end."

"Brilliant," said Francesca. "Just what I need."

Roman laughed at me when I appeared in my helmet and reflective strip. My bike hadn't moved since the week I'd purchased it following a decision to cycle to work every day. It would save me paying a fortune to a gym just to cycle on the spot. The craze lasted one day. Cycling to work was great; it was cycling home that was the problem. I met up with friends in the City that night and after a few drinks got lost in the backwaters of Aldgate East and ended up, I still don't know how, descending into the Limehouse Link tunnel and being forced to cycle madly in the carbon-monoxide gloom for miles before I resurfaced at Canary Wharf. Unable to face the fumes and fear again, I Zingoed a cab and spent a fortune getting myself and my bike home. I had bruised buttock bones for a week. The bike was banished to the basement, and I hadn't ventured out since. But this was a new me.

Francesca was sitting atop her old-fashioned bike, a basket full of God knows what and clips around her trouser bottoms. Her wavy brown hair was cut sensibly short, her clothes hid her figure, but her skin was still youthful and smooth. I guess that came from a life of not burning the candle at all. She did look a bit barking though, in a nice, eccentric, but homely sort of way. I was about to tease her, but she laughed at me before I had a chance to laugh at her. I guess it did look a bit sad, all that brand-new bicycle kit on a girl who didn't bicycle. We turned our bikes through the gate and pedaled off at a nice, sedate, ladylike pace. I wanted to talk to her about Caspar, but I thought I'd beat around the bush for a while first.

"How's Nick?"

"In Saigon."

"Lucky thing. I loved Saigon."

"He doesn't get to see much more than inside a hotel. He's at an international conference about child labor—you know, kids making flashing trainers. On the other side of the universe, I'm in Woolworth's doing battle with a five-year-old over those same flashing trainers."

"Is this a rhetorical discussion we're having?" I said, feeling my cheeks start to glow as I pedaled.

"Oh no. Poppy screamed and screamed and screamed when I said no. You should have seen the looks I got from the other mothers. £4.99 would have brought me peace. It's the principle of the thing. You cannot give in. If you do, you're doomed. Your word means nothing; your children will run you out of town. I only went in for a tin-opener."

I had to laugh.

"It's all right for you, you're not being forever humiliated in public by your children."

"No," I replied, speeding up a bit to chase a squirrel. I turned back to Francesca. "But then I can do that all by myself."

Fran caught up. She didn't look remotely out of breath. "She told me I was ruining her life! Five years old! I could have killed her," she said. I hid my smile. I'd be hopeless at the discipline bit. I'm sure I'd get the giggles.

"I'm turning into a sour puss. It's the summer holidays, they don't half drag."

"Summer holidays? Fran, it's October."

"Exactly. And I still haven't recovered. Nick has been away so much; Caspar, as you know, has been a bit of a challenge; the girls know exactly when to tighten the screws. I'm bored of it, bored of fighting on all fronts."

Fran had given me the perfect segue into the next topic of conversation. Caspar. I grabbed my moment. "How is my charming Caspar?"

"Full of it. He honestly thinks I don't get it. That I don't understand, that I never had a youth. It's so annoying, because it's all just repeat, repeat, repeat. Yeah, kids today probably are under more pressure than we were, but to think I don't understand." Francesca shook her head under her helmet. "It's so stupid. They're so indignant and whatever I do is wrong. Thanks again, by the way, for bailing him out the other night. He does listen to you, actually, which is one thing."

I phrased my next question carefully. "He told me you grounded him over the beer thing."

"Really? Did he?"

"He called for a chat the other day."

"A chat?" She pulled on the brakes. I stopped pedaling too and

cycled back round to face her. It was obvious that Francesca hadn't
bought his social call either.

"Did he tell you it wasn't our beer?"

"Er, no."

"I bet he didn't. He only sneaked into the neighbors' kitchen and
took it. They have kids the same age, so we have a kind of open house
policy, and we were having lunch together . . . But all the same, I was
so embarrassed. Anyway, I told him he couldn't go out. Lots of slamming doors followed. I really can't face thinking about it."

"Little toad. No, he failed to mention all of that."

"I don't know what's got into him, I really don't."

I thought about my own bad behavior as a child. It was all fairly
mild but I recalled holding a grudge against my parents for months
because they hadn't let me go to a party and, like Poppy, I thought
they'd ruined my life.

"Anything you've done that he's punishing you for?"

Francesca looked at me, horrified.

"I don't mean anything you deserve, just something he thinks
you've done?"

Francesca shook her head slowly but, without actually answering, pedaled away. She turned her bike towards the pond and picked
up speed. I followed a few paces behind. I hadn't meant to insult her.
Halfway round the pond, she slowed down and I caught up.

"That's better," she said. "Get some air in the lungs."

"Maybe you need a couple of days away, leave Nick at home
coping with all of this. We could go to a spa. They do really good
deals mid-week. In fact, I think I still have a voucher that I won at
some charity auction. I could take you! Maybe you're just knackered." Talking of knackered, I noticed I was now definitely puffing.
And she definitely wasn't.

"I need some more ginseng," she said, ignoring my spa invitation.

I didn't know whether it was because she hadn't heard me over the cacophony of geese around the pond, or that she wasn't taken in by my voucher story and hated accepting charity.

"To hell with the ginseng, you need a night out. I mean a proper night out. Get dressed up, wash your hair if that's not ruining the ozone too much, put on some heels, get your lovely legs out and come out on the razz with me."

"Prop up a bar and get chatted up?"

"I was thinking more along the lines of a proper party. One without jelly and tedious women discussing MMR."

I got a kick for that. It's good to know one's boundaries.

"Celebrities, free booze, live entertainment and enough shallow conversation to drown in. What do you think?"

"Sounds perfect."

"Great. Come to Neil's Channel 4 party on Saturday."

"Neil as in Neil and Helen?"

Francesca was a bit intimidated by Neil and Helen.

"He can't bring himself to look at me, let alone remember my name; he certainly won't be inviting me to his party."

"It's not his, and anyway, he doesn't have to. You can come as Claudia, Nick will make a fine Al, and I'll bring Billy as my date. She could do with a laugh too, I suspect."

"You're on. I'll ask Caspar to babysit."

"I thought you were against child labor."

"God, you're annoying."

I smiled and increased speed, cycling through another glut of fat pigeons pecking away at half a loaf of Hovis. Was that the whiff of an endorphin rush or something else? I was pleased.

With Fran, Nick and Billy, I would go to Neil's party armed with a buffer zone of my own.

*   *   *

When I got back to the flat I called Caspar. The poor unfortunate boy has a mobile phone of his own. I had to wait until I was thirty-two.

"Hello?" came a whispered voice.

"Hi, Caspar, it's me, can you talk?"

"No. I'm in class."

"Why are you answering your phone, then?"

"Why are you calling me during school?"

"Don't be cheeky."

"You like it really."

"Why are you in such a good mood?" I didn't mean it to sound so suspicious.

"Christ, can't win, can I?"

"Sorry, bollocks—listen, Caspar, the beer thing—"

"Here we go. Look, Tessa, you're not my mum, so please, back off."

"But—"

"What?"

"I'm trying to help. Please call me after class."

Half an hour later I stepped dripping out of the shower, threw a towel around me and answered the phone. But it wasn't Caspar, it was Billy.

"Sorry to disturb you," said Billy. Billy always apologizes for everything. "Are you busy?"

"Far from it," I replied, wrapping another towel around my hair and lying on my bed to dry.

"I have a huge favor to ask of you," Billy said.

"Fire away."

"I'm having some problems with money and—"

"How much do you need?"

"I don't need to borrow any, um, but it's Christoph, he hasn't made some of the payments he's supposed to, and I've been trying to talk to him for a while, but you know what he's like, always traveling, so . . ."

"How long has it been?"

Billy hated telling me when Christoph had been behaving badly. Her loyalty to the man who'd broken her heart, ruined her life and turned his back on one of the finest children I know was anathema to me. "Four months."

"And he's not returning your calls?"

"Well, as I said he's been away and—"

"Billy."

"I know, I know, so that's why I need your help. I've got an appointment with the solicitor tomorrow."

"Great, that's great."

"Would you mind collecting Cora from school?"

"Not at all, I'd be delighted. It will be the highlight of my week." Which was true. "Honestly, you're doing me the favor. Listen, if it's all right with you I'll take her over to play at Nick and Francesca's house. Katie and Poppy love her so much."

"Perfect. Thank you."

"That's what godmothers are for."

"You're the best, Tessa, thanks."

The following day at half past three I was outside Cora's school gates. The mixture of people milling about with prams and bikes, dogs and scooters was amazing. Cora was lucky, her school only went up to age eleven, so she didn't have to venture through throngs of older, intimidating kids who had a tendency to flex a little muscle when it came to the smaller ones. Cora was slight; although she was seven, she looked only five and I always feared she would be picked on. Since birth she'd always been below the bottom percentile on the charts. Whenever she mentioned this I told her it was better than being average.

She grinned at me and came running out, her long hair straggling behind her. She looks like a gypsy, with her pale skin, large brown eyes, missing tooth and narrow limbs. I crouched down, spread my arms wide and waited for the bundle of energy to hit me at full pelt.

"Hello, beautiful," I said.

"Hello, Godmummy T, you've gone a funny color," she said.

Ah yes. Fading tan, too much time on my hands and an old bottle of the fake stuff found while tidying out my bathroom cupboard can do that to a person.

"I was hoping it wasn't that obvious."

"It's stripy, not obvious." Cora took my hand. "Like the zebra, you can hide in the bush and not get eaten by a lion."

So, one positive to come out of this. I look like a freak but at least I won't get eaten by a lion.

"Did you bring my elephant with small ears?" Nothing gets past this kid.

"It's in the car."

She beamed.

We chatted about school and friends of hers whom I'd never met in minute detail, and had a lengthy dispute about socks that got mixed up at gym time. Cora clearly found it hilarious. I found it hard to follow what she was saying, but it didn't matter, I let her easy chit-chat wash over me and was soothed by the sound of her voice.

"And how's Mummy?" I asked her.

"Cross with Christoph." Cora had always called her father Christoph, despite being coached by Billy to do otherwise. Billy feared it would put Christoph off on the few times he deigned to grace them with his presence. As if Cora could put anyone off, ever. I think it reflected the innate wisdom that Cora was born with. Christoph wasn't worthy of that most precious of words, "Daddy." My goddaughter may look like a five-year-old but she is seven going on seventy. Sometimes she says the most extraordinary things that leave me gaping at her in wonder; I want to write them down and tuck them away into fortune cookies because they seem so worldly-wise. *Cora, says* . . . Maybe I'm just biased. Other times she gets very grown-up words mixed up and comes out with something I'd be more tempted to put in a cracker. It came from listening in on a predominantly adult world with only a seven-year-old brain to decipher it with.

Cora pointed to the local supermarket as we walked to the car. "We had to give all our shopping back to the lady in the shop, even though I'd helped pack it and everything, but she gave us our baked beans and bread, so it was all right. It's Christoph's fault, he's a liar, liar, pants on fire."

Poor Billy. I could easily lend her money. She was too proud.

"The shop lady gave me a lollipop, but told me not to tell anyone."

"Why are you telling me then?" I said, ruffling her hair.

"Because you're not a real grown-up."

I took out an imaginary pen, scrawled an imaginary note, rolled it into an imaginary scroll and inserted it into an imaginary cookie. *Cora, says* . . . You're not a real grown-up.

We arrived at Nick and Francesca's house. Katie and Poppy loved having Cora over to play as much as she loved going. Cora was the jam to their sandwich. Katie and Poppy were the siblings she missed. She was a perfect middle child, actually. She deferred to Katie and encouraged Poppy and since she spent a huge amount of time amusing herself, she didn't need to compete for attention. As a result, the girls gravitated towards Cora's calmness, a gap was bridged and three perfectly happy little girls disappeared into a world that neither I, Francesca nor Billy could follow.

Full of sausages and mash, they went off to play, leaving Francesca and me to make another vat of tea and settle down to a proper chat. One without constant interruptions. I was pretty used to having conversations peppered with, "Hang on a second, I just have to . . . get down a toy, fill up the water, turn on the telly, break up a fight, get a plaster, wipe a bottom, find a Barbie" followed by the "Where were we?" which was inevitably followed by "Hang on a second, I just have to . . ." But the three of them were at the bottom of the garden and apart from a curious request for wooden spoons and gravy granules, we were largely ignored.

"So how is the boy wonder today?" I asked.

"Bit better, actually. He made breakfast this morning."

"Oh, good." That was the answer I was hoping to hear.

"You talked to him again, didn't you?"

"Briefly," I replied. Caspar had finally called me back that evening, by which time I had decided to go for the approach that worked best with children: blackmail. I'd gently reminded him about the police record, the speed, and nearly drowning in his own vomit and then, before he had a chance to get surly on me, I'd told him any more antics like nicking someone else's beer, and I was going to reclaim the iPod. I was glad he'd taken my threats seriously.

Francesca poured more tea into our mugs. "I think not being allowed out had its effect. I think you were right, maybe we have been taking him for granted a little bit." I'd said that before he nicked the beer, though. "So we've agreed to start paying him for the jobs he does, rather than just assuming he doesn't mind babysitting or trimming the hedge or whatever. He says he thought he'd been told by Rachel, our neighbor, to help himself to drinks. It's a bit implausible, but he's been pretty contrite since talking to you, so thank you."

A bit implausible?

"You know, he wants to save up for driving lessons. It's a lot of money, but he has a year."

"That's good. That's positive."

"I think so."

"Whatever he saves by next birthday, I'll match it," I offered.

"I wasn't saying it for that reason. It might take him two years."

"But I'd like to. That's what Mum and Dad always did with me when I wanted something that cost more than 50p."

"Well, there was only one of you; it's a bit harder to do that with three kids. We'd be forking out money all the time. We do fork out money all the time. I swear it disappears. Anyway, it wouldn't be fair to the girls. Talking of which, I'd better go and see what they're up to."

I heard the front door close, a bag drop, and something heavy thump up the stairs. Fran was outside negotiating with the children over how long they had until bath-time. I pushed myself off my chair and went into the hallway and shouted up the stairwell. "Hey, Caspar, aren't you going to come and say hello?"

"Who's that?" came a surly voice.

"Tessa."

"Oh, hi, Tessa," said Caspar, from behind his door. "I didn't know you were here."

"Come down and say hello."

"Will do, give me a sec."

My handbag was slung over the end banister. I lifted the flap and looked at my wallet for a moment wondering whether to count its contents. I let the flap fall back, dismissing my thoughts. Trust is everything. If Caspar said he was done with drugs, then he was done with drugs.

Francesca returned, having agreed to a ten-minute ruling.

"Caspar is back," I said, finishing the last of the dishes. "I think he might be hiding from me."

"He's probably still a bit embarrassed. He idolizes you, so being sick out of a taxi window the night you rescued him is probably eating him alive."

I had, of course, spoken to Francesca about that fateful Saturday night and although I'd given her a much watered-down version of events, I didn't think I'd said that. What had I said? It was nearly a month ago now. That was the trouble with lies; they were much harder to remember than the truth. I had left Caspar the job of deciding how much he wanted to tell his parents. And while I hadn't expected him to tell them everything, I hadn't thought he'd lie. I wanted to know what I had rescued Caspar from, but realized it wouldn't look good asking Fran.

"Everyone has to drink themselves stupid, it's a rite of passage. One I'm still going through," I said, fishing.

"Yes, but it was wrong of Zac to lace his drinks like that."

Ah, so that was his little story. All Zac's fault. No mention of the dope, the speed, the stolen money or the brush with the law, then. Implausible wasn't the word.

"I'm just so grateful he had the good sense to call you," said Fran. Quite a feat, when you're unconscious. Ratbag. Then I remembered his forlorn expression, his solemn promise that the drugs would stop, his insistence that they had. I didn't want to be too hard on him—getting very drunk and puking up was a rite of passage. So was getting horribly stoned and paranoid. And it wouldn't be the first time that a teenager nicked booze from someone's house. OK, the speed might not have been quite so pedestrian, but I bet it wasn't that unusual either. I never told my parents about the time that Ben had to stick his fingers down my throat because I'd drunk too much rum, and I was even younger than Caspar.

I was telling Fran the story of how we'd raided Ben's mother's drinks cabinet when Caspar finally materialized. He was all washed and scrubbed, his wet hair gelled, his clothes obviously fresh. It made

me immediately suspicious. Then I smelt the toothpaste mingled
with some rather strong aftershave, and my suspicions intensified.
I looked closely into Caspar's eyes, but they didn't seem bloodshot
and he wasn't slurring his words. Perhaps I should mind my own
business. Then again, what if he hadn't stopped smoking, what if it
was getting worse?

"Hey, Caspar, I know you're all squeaky-clean, but I believe you owe
me a car wash." I glanced at my watch. The girls' ten minutes were
up. We had about an hour for bath and general messing about before
I took Cora home.

"When do you want me to do it?" he asked.

"How about now?"

"What about homework?" asked Fran.

"I'll do it later. Dad's got all the stuff under the stairs." Caspar left
the room.

"Definitely some improvement." Fran didn't even ask me why her
son owed me a car wash, so I didn't tell her. Instead, I told her I
would go and get the bath ready. I picked up Cora's pajamas and
went upstairs. I turned the taps on a fraction and let the bath begin
to slowly fill. I reckoned I had a good ten minutes before Fran got the
girls inside and upstairs.

I heard Caspar go out on to the street and then stealthily climb
the stairs to his bedroom. I looked under the beanbag. Behind the
bookshelves. I found a porn mag rolled up behind the bedhead, but
no tin of incriminating drugs. I got down on my hands and knees
and looked under the bed.

"What are you doing, Tessa?"

"Fran—wow, you were quick."

Three little girls stared accusingly at my bottom. "It's bath-time,"
said Katie.

"The ten-minute rule really works, heh?" I said, pushing myself off the floor.

"What were you looking for?"

I held up my bare wrist. "Silly, really. I lost one of the bracelets I bought in India, I thought there was a slim chance it might be in here." Liar, screamed a voice in my head.

I followed the troupe of little heads back down to the bathroom where a half-filled cold bath awaited them. They weren't impressed. I got back down on my knees to rectify the situation.

"Bubbles?"

"Yes," said Poppy.

"No," said Katie.

I turned to Cora. "Half," she said, which I thought was a daft answer until I watched them spend the next twenty minutes very happily damming the bubbles down Poppy's end of the bath to much squeals of delight as the disobedient bubbles escaped in fronds beyond the demarcation zone. Finally we had them well scrubbed, towelled off, teeth cleaned and ready for bed. I don't know if there is anything more delightful in this world than three little girls messing about in a bath together. Except, perhaps, three little girls in clean pajamas, curled and draped over every limb, listening intently while I read *Cat and Fish*. Personally, I thought the story was a bit trippy, but the girls seemed to like it.

It was a magical forty minutes and I breathed in their collective smell and committed to memory the feel of little hands absently caressing my skin. Then Poppy let off an enormous fart and everyone fell apart giggling. I decided it was time to take Cora home before we crossed the invisible line between angels and demons. You never knew quite where it was but by the time you'd crossed it, you realized you'd seen it coming. I kissed the girls goodnight and picked up Cora. She was still very easy to carry. Sometimes I worried she had hollow bones. Caspar came up the stairs. I kissed my godson as I passed, thanked him for cleaning the car and promised to take him out to lunch soon.

Francesca appeared from Katie's room as I was halfway down the stairs with my human parcel.

"I'll see you on Saturday night," she said. "Did you ask Caspar about your bracelet?"

"It doesn't matter," I said.

Fran was too organized to let that put her off. She liked to find missing puzzle pieces even if it took all day and she had to search the entire toy collection. "What does it look like?"

I was trapped. "Beads. Coral beads. Red."

"Tessa thinks she may have lost a bracelet in your room . . ." Fran turned back to me. "Where did you look?"

Damn it. "Just around the beanbag and under the bed. The clasp wasn't very good." I was as bad as Caspar and he knew it. The look on his face said it all. Liar, liar, pants on fire.

"Have you found anything like that?" his mother asked him.

He shook his head slowly, still looking at me in a really uncomfortable way. "I don't think you were wearing a red bracelet, Tessa," he said. "If you remember, you were all in white that day."

"What an extraordinary memory you have, Caspar," said Fran, kissing her son on his head. "You smell nice," she said, oblivious to the alarming look that Caspar was giving me.

"Smile, Caspar," said Cora. As I said, nothing gets past this kid. Cora climbed down and followed Francesca down the stairs. I stood and looked at Caspar.

"Caspar, I'm sorry—"

"You went sneaking through my stuff. Not even Mum and Dad would do that."

"I'm worried about you."

"I'm not a fucking kid any more."

"Yes, you are."

I knew as soon as I'd said it, it was the wrong thing to say.

"Christ, Tessa, just mind your own business, would you?"

"You rang me, remember?" Now who was being the child? "I mean, I thought you needed some support here."

"Your idea of support is rummaging through my room?"

He turned and walked away from me.

"Caspar?"

He didn't respond.

"Caspar?"

"Forget it, Tessa. I don't need you butting in all the time."

He shut the door.

On the drive back to Billy's I only half listened to Cora. My mind was on Caspar. Cora was unimpressed when I failed to give the right answer to a couple of her questions. For example, when she asked, "What makes hair curl?" I replied, "Nearly there." The second time I got it wrong, she got quite cross and told me I wasn't listening to her. She was right. However good my intentions, even Cora's constant babbling was hard to stay tuned to all the time.

I pulled up outside their narrow red-brick ground-floor flat in Kensal Rise. Billy opened the door before we'd made it all the way up the heavily weeded garden path. She looked like a dancer, Billy. She had the same long dark hair that her daughter inherited off her, although it was now streaked with grey, the same sinewy limbs and large brown eyes. Her look hadn't changed since I'd met her in the corridor between our rented bedrooms: Slavic gypsy, which was what she was, I suppose. There was always enough material in her skirts to wrap her up ten times over and her tops always clung to her muscular, narrow torso. It was a distinct look that has come and fallen from fashion approximately four times in the time we've known each other. Only during her time with Christoph did her appearance change. He preferred short skirts and heels, which made her look like an underaged gymnast from behind the Iron Curtain dressing up like a "sexetary" to please a corrupt judge. Her jewelry was a socioeconomic reflection of herself—ethnic and minimal—which meant she got away with it. Billy smiled at her daughter. "You are without doubt the best thing that ever happened to me," she exclaimed and hugged her child.

Bad news from the solicitor, then, I thought, watching Cora squash Billy's cheeks between the palms of her hands. Billy seeks solace in Cora. I wish she'd seek solace in the world around her, but she couldn't seem to find her place in it. She gave so much of herself over to Christoph, sometimes I wondered if there was anything left.

"Did you have fun?" asked Billy.

"It was great, we cooked monkey pie in the garden with magic crystals that can turn your bottom green."

Billy looked at me. I shrugged.

"You wouldn't understand," said Cora, walking into the flat that she shared with her mother and Magda, the Polish au pair. It only had two bedrooms, so it was a bit of a squash. Cora used to have her own room and Billy used to fork out for expensive childcare that left her running into the red every month. Cora, knowing that Billy was alone, would make nocturnal forays into her mother's room and Billy would wake up to find a small body curled up next to her. Everyone told her she had to get firm, and put Cora back into her own bed. Trouble was, Cora was so stealthy that Billy never woke up to put her back into her own bed. Eventually, I suggested to Billy that she turn Cora's deserted room into an asset—get someone to live in who could help in the mornings, collect Cora from school and man the gates until Billy got back from work. As well as having help when she needed it most, it would cost her a third of the price. We re-evaluated her monthly expenditure and worked out she'd be in the black. By not changing her frugal ways, she soon paid off her debt. Magda was a blessed addition to their lives. She even had a nice boyfriend, so Billy had enough evenings to herself, and was on-site to babysit whenever Billy wanted, which wasn't very often. Everyone was happy. Even Cora, who now shared her mother's bed and her wardrobe. Cora had started her life in an intensive care unit, then spent months on a ward. She could sleep anywhere, through anything, at any time. Billy came to bed, pottered around, read, did her face, and all the while this tiny curled creature breathed gently under the duvet, seemingly undisturbed. If my current security blanket was a hard-edged framed photograph that didn't even belong to me, then Billy's was her daughter.

I had the privilege of tucking Cora into bed that night in Billy's room, but the last kiss, as always, was reserved for her mother. Billy softly closed the door behind her and escorted me to the fridge. She handed me a bottle of wine, took two glasses and a corkscrew from the drawer and followed me to the sofa.

"What's happened?" I asked.

"I've got to go to court again." Her expression was neutral.

"Why?"

"He has changed how he does his accounting. I get 17 percent of what he earns."

"Which should be plenty?"

"Not if he doesn't declare it. Now he's building boats exclusively for some very rich guy abroad, the money isn't coming into England. He is claiming to earn much less, which, of course, puts an additional burden on his outgoings, which means he can apply to have his percentage dropped back to, worst case scenario, 10 percent."

"Which leaves you with?" I was trying not to get wound up. We'd been having these conversations about Christoph for most of Cora's life.

"Diddly-squat. He isn't claiming not to have earned the money, he just isn't bringing it in, so I have to put a case to the court that he needs to bring more money in. Trouble is, it's all back-handers and cash in brown envelopes. God knows . . ."

"What about his other"—I faltered slightly as I tend to do with this subject—"family?" Christoph has a new wife and two children, who both go to the best private schools and want for nothing. Except a nice dad, I suppose.

"She has money. They live off that."

"Cunning."

"I guess it's already declared and taxed."

"How very trusting of her," I said, sipping wine. "Poor woman, I almost feel sorry for her."

"That's what you do when you're married, Tessa."

I was perplexed. She expanded for me.

"You trust your other half."

"Yes, maybe Nick and Al and . . ." I suddenly saw where I was going with this, and wanted to retreat. But it was too late.

"And Ben. I know, all the marvelous men out there who are faithful and honest as the day is long. But Christoph was that to me, and he'll be that to his new wife. You don't willfully give yourself to a man you think will shag everything that glances his way, spend your cash and leave you high and dry with a couple of kids and no money."

For a second, my mind conjured up an image of Helen being evicted from her house, two kids in tow, and Neil speeding off with a blonde in a sports car. It wasn't wholly unpleasant, because after that I appeared on the horizon, like Zorro, to save the day.

"You know it goes on, you just don't think it goes on in your life. She'll probably be thinking how brilliant Christoph is and looking forward to buying a Swiss ski chalet, a Tuscan villa and a house on the fucking Palm."

I frowned again.

"It's in Dubai, where this rich bloke lives. Doesn't matter, all I'm saying is you assume your husband isn't lying to you. You have to," continued Billy.

All I could think of was Sasha kissing Ben goodbye as she went off for another week away in Germany.

"I don't want to sue him, Tessa. I don't want all that friction in my life again. He's seen Cora twice this year, things have been getting better."

"What do you mean, you don't want to go there again? You've never gone there. Billy, please, don't get me wrong, but you've rolled over every bloody time. And it's October, that's hardly regular contact."

"He travels . . ."

I'd heard it all before. "Come on, Billy. What good is living like this doing you? You think he's going to be grateful that you've been so understanding? He doesn't give a shit about anyone else apart from himself. I'm sorry, Billy, but when are you going to see it?"

"I think she makes it hard for him to come and see us."

"She?"

"His new wife."

I stood up. It was too infuriating to have this conversation sitting down. "New? Billy! New? They have two daughters!"

"He told me once she was very demanding."

I silently screamed inside my head. "Really. Poor man—a wife who expects her husband to contribute to family life. You're absolutely right, she must be a witch."

"She doesn't like the fact of us."

"I bet. Reminds her of what a shit of a man her husband is."

"Tessa!"

"What? Do you want my help or not? Because I can probably get that money for you."

"Without going to court?"

I wanted to shake her. But thinking about it, maybe there was a way to do this without going to court. In fact . . . I felt the tingling excitement of a plan. The lure of a project.

"What?" asked Billy. "You've got a strange look in your eye."

"If I can find a way of proving Christoph is earning more than he says he is . . ."

"That sounds like spying."

I dismissed her concerns. "No more than the shit deserves."

"Tessa."

Please stop being so pathetic, I wanted to say, but I didn't. I was on a roll. "I have a good friend who works in this field. I tell you, men hide money from their wives all the time, usually just before they announce their intentions to leave them. It's a dog-eat-dog world. If you're right about brown envelopes, he won't want me sniffing around." I turned to face Billy. "We could scare him into handing over more cash. The threat of court might be enough!"

For a moment a wicked little smile crossed Billy's lips.

"What do you say?" I asked.

"Go on then, but don't do anything without telling me first."

"I promise."

"A real promise. Not a Tessa King promise."

I put my hand to my heart and feigned shock. "What is that supposed to mean?"

"Fuzzy around the edges."

"I sincerely promise. Now, let's order a takeaway, I'm famished."

This was a lie. I'd eaten far too many of the children's sausages, but if I ordered and paid for a large Indian takeaway I knew Billy could live off it for a few days.

"So," said Billy, a mouth full of balti, "any bad behavior you can tell me about?"

I shook my head, and helped myself to more food that I didn't want.

"I take it that bloke didn't call?"

I wasn't sure how much I appreciated her "I take it," but I shook my head again. The fantasy of Sebastian the civil servant waiting outside my building in the pouring rain to tell me he couldn't get me out of his mind had been superseded by a far less palatable one. The one where I play the marriage-wrecker. The one in which I divide the loyalties and affections of my root friendships, the one in which that kiss did not end with Claudia calling out for Al.

"Just another notch," I said finally. "What about you?" I asked, knowing it was futile. Billy had cut the wires that sent any kind of signal to the opposite sex. It wasn't that she played hard to get. You had to do a little come-on dance first, to do that. She played nothing to get. And it worked.

"What about any of the men who come through the surgery?" I asked, trying to be encouraging. Billy worked for a nearby dentist.

"People with teeth," she said. This is what I meant by no signal. "I'm hardly what the average male wants, am I?" she continued. "Practically middle-aged myself, bogged down by a seven-year-old. Divorced. Broke." She was wrong, of course. If she could see what I could see, we could duct tape those wires back together again. She was beautiful, ethereal, considerate, caring; she was honest and faithful, dedicated and conscientious and she looked fit enough to ride in the Grand National or play Giselle. When Christoph left her, he stole a chip from inside her that rendered her inert. It was the worst kind of heartbreak. He didn't want her, but he made sure no one else would either.

"Oh, I nearly forgot," I said, trying to cheer her up. "I was wondering if you'd be my date on Saturday night. Channel 4 are hosting a grand party for the launch of the comedy series that Neil is in. Nick and Fran are coming," I added quickly, before terror got the best of Billy. "Francesca could really do with a good night out; we can get dolled up and dance around our handbags."

"I don't know, babysitters on Saturdays are—"

"Billy, Magda is supposed to sit twice a week for you and she never has to."

"No, but she covers when I'm late back from work and—"

"It's free booze. You can come round to mine beforehand and we'll get ready together. Please. It'll be like the old days . . ."

What I wanted to say was, "What are you so afraid of ?"; instead, I smiled. "Fine. Meet me there."

"I don't know . . ."

"One good turn deserves another. I'll look into this," I said tapping Billie's file on her ex-husband. "You be my date."

"You're the one who wants to go after Christoph."

I put the file back down on the table and put my hands on my hips. "So you don't want me to do it?"

She blinked a few times.

"Come on, Billy, not this again."

She waved her hand over the file. "OK, take it. But I'm sure you have hundreds of dates you could go with."

"No, Billy, I don't. I just thought it would be fun for us all to go out, that's all." It was like pulling teeth with her.

"OK. I'll come," she said.

What was that? An involuntary surrender. Sometimes I wanted to shake her, remind her she was alive, prise her out of the bog she'd got herself in. But I couldn't, because ultimately it was down to her. I watched Billy stifle another yawn so I carried the tray of half-eaten food back to the kitchen, kissed her goodnight, took the file of damning evidence against my goddaughter's father and drove myself home.

pumpkin time

I walked into the Channel 4 party alone. It is something that I pride myself on being able to do. It gives me confidence to step over the threshold of a room full of people I don't know all by myself. That extra bit of confidence fuels me as far as the bar, the rest is down to alcohol.

Channel 4 had taken over a huge restaurant in Mayfair, complete with state-of-the-art pod loos that looked like they'd come off the set of *Cocoon* and a VIP bar that if you couldn't get into, you could at least look down into from above. In fact, the toilets were above the VIP area, so actually you were defecating on the heads of those special people who were separated from us mere mortals by a length of twisted red chord. I wondered, as I waited for my drink, whether the architect had been making a point.

There was the typical jostle at the bar. The TV workers knew the drill—get in as many drinks as possible before it becomes a paying bar and don't digress from what is on offer. Vodka and cranberry "cocktail" was free, vodka and tonic would set you back seven quid. I opted for a free bottle of beer, raised it to my mouth, when an elbow appeared from nowhere and knocked it hard against my teeth.

"Ow!" I exclaimed.

"Oh my God, are you OK? So sorry."

I could taste blood.

"Oh shit, you've lost a tooth."

I put my hand up to my mouth. Toothless was not going to help me find a spawning partner.

"Perhaps that wasn't very funny."

I shook my head. I made sure I had a full set of teeth before finally turning to look at my assailant.

"Cinderella," he said.

Salt-and-pepper man. "Ow," I said, though strangely it no longer hurt.

"You'd look perfect at a vampire party."

I frowned.

"Still not funny?"

I shook my head again, but was beginning to smile.

"Good thing I chose to represent comics rather than be one."

"I'm not sure you had a choice."

"You're right. I didn't. Though I always thought I had the potential to do the hideous-until-on-stage sort of thing well." He shrugged. "Didn't work, though. I have to rely on becoming incredibly wealthy instead."

"Is that a possibility?"

"Have you heard of Ali G?"

I was impressed. "You represent Ali G?"

"No. But I could. And that's the point, as I keep telling my mother."

I smiled again.

"Can I buy you a drink?"

"It's a free bar," I said.

"I didn't mean now."

Smooth. I started to feel quite excited about the evening. Which was a far cry from sitting on my sofa at home wondering if I could possibly get out of coming at all.

I extended my hand. "Tessa King. In case you forgot."

He took it. "James Kent. In case you never knew."

How about that, I wouldn't even have to change my initials. What was I thinking? I was turning into a nutter.

"Are you all right? You're frowning. It's making me nervous. Whatever you've heard about me is untrue. OK, she was fifteen. But I was eleven, so it doesn't count."

"What are you talking about?"

"My last sexual experience. What were you thinking about?"

There was a beat in my head, a comic beat. You read them in scripts. Someone says something funny then, beat.

"My next one."

I turned back to the bar and sucked on my beer. I couldn't believe I'd said that. Filthy cow.

We walked across the room together. James seemed to know every other person at the party, which had a strange way of making him appear even sexier, and I was sober, so it wasn't a beer-goggle thing. He introduced me to almost everyone he spoke to, which I liked. I can't stand being a spare part. When he didn't, he always apologized afterwards and said it was because he couldn't remember the person's name. Then he introduced me to someone who needed no introduction. Helen's mother. What the hell she was doing there I couldn't imagine. I always forgot that she was editor in chief of a broadsheet, which meant she didn't need invites. She looked magnificent, of course.

"Tessa. How are you? Still single?"

"Actually, I'm a lesbian these days. I'm sleeping with a top female judge. Who's married. But don't tell anyone."

Marguerite smiled through her perfectly capped teeth.

"Darling, I'm so pleased you've finally accepted it. But honestly, you should tell people, it won't come as a surprise to anyone, I can assure you."

Damn it, I walked into that. Before I had a chance to reply, though the perfect one wouldn't come to me until at least twenty-four hours later, she touched James on the arm. "James, I've been meaning to call you."

"Anything I can do?" said James, smiling at her. I wanted to slam my stiletto heel into his shoe.

"I was hoping you would think about joining our media panel." Those squared off, stubby dark red nails that I knew too well jutted out of the long cuffs of a white silk shirt.

"Monthly meetings at the Groucho Club, dinner on me. We have some incredible people on it." She listed some. I had no idea who any of them were, but James was obviously impressed. "We would so like you to join. You're our first choice."

Marguerite looked good that night, clad in black leather trousers and fabulous boots, but it is amazing how ugly beauty can be on the wrong person. I noticed her hand stay a fraction too long on James's arm. I had enough competition from women in their twenties; if I had to compete with the forty- and fifty-year-olds as well, I was damned. That thought sparked off another, more terrible one: Marguerite wasn't looking to settle down and breed—in fact, for the commitment-shy male, she was perfect. I felt a terrible urge to snatch James back, but even I (misguided as I am) knew that would be unseemly.

"We could have lunch," she said. "Or meet after work for a drink."

I rolled my eyes. "I saw your grandsons the other day," I said, butting in. "They'll be talking soon—what's it going to be? Grand-mère? Grand-maman? Nan?"

"I've no idea, I really haven't thought about it," Marguerite replied. "Listen, Tessa, I have a favor to ask you."

I narrowed my eyes. Now what was she up to?

"Would you mind keeping an eye on Helen? I fear she is a little out of her depth here. Apart from friends, they've really invited the very top people. It's important for Neil."

"Come on, you've nothing to worry about," I said. "Helen doesn't have to say a word, and people fall over each other to get to talk to her."

"Exactly. I think people probably expect a little more content from her," said Marguerite. "I'm just saying she might need your support. Please think about my offer, James, and call me next week," she said before turning away. Her brutality lay in her subtlety. You can retaliate against barbed insults; it is harder when they are so veiled. We continued weaving our way through the room.

James frowned at me. "You seem to be on peculiar terms with Marguerite. You do realize she has a reputation of crushing anyone who crosses her."

"She wouldn't dare. I know too much."

"And why exactly would that be?" asked James.

I shrugged. "She's Helen's mother."

"Oh, I see." There was a pause. "Do you mind me asking, but who is Helen? It's just that it seems like a crucial detail I'm missing."

"Neil's wife," I said confused.

"Neil's married?" It came out quickly. He tried to cover it up while I tried to ignore the intonation in his voice. But I knew what that question meant. It meant Neil didn't act like a married man. He didn't tell people he was a married man. And he didn't wear a wedding ring because he said it made him look like a "poof."

"They have twins. My godsons, in fact."

"Jesus, more godchildren."

I imagined Mr. Kent mark a cross in the negative column.

Nearly five. "Four," I said. Funny how things change. Once, having a smattering of godchildren was a compliment. It meant you had good friends; you were chosen above others to care for the most important people in their lives; it meant you had staying power. Right now it felt like a sign around my neck. Leper. Outcast. Unfertilized. Pitied but could be useful some time in the future when little _____ needed a job.

"Oh, yes," said James. "I remember. Course. Stupid." He was trying to cover up his bluff. I definitely hadn't told him about my godchildren when we'd performed our own special brand of dirty dancing on the night Caspar drank himself unconscious, and it made me feel bad for him. It wasn't his fault Neil was so disrespectful of his wife.

"Come on over and meet her, she's lovely. One of my oldest friends, in fact." I didn't want to think about it. Not tonight.

"One more thing, then I'll drop the subject."

"What?" I asked, perhaps more aggressively than I should have.

"Is it Cherie Booth?"

"What?"

"The judge you're sleeping with. Is it Cherie Booth?"

I winked at him.

Helen was inside the place for special people. Her week in the country had worked: she looked phenomenal. Sleek and thin in a strappy black Dolce & Gabbana dress which showed no evidence of a bulge, let alone the sagging twin skin she claimed she had. That Helen had carried two six-pound babies inside her just over five months ago seemed impossible. A week was not long enough to have had surgery and recovered, was it? No, Helen was just born that way. She caught my eye and immediately came over to the twisted red chord. She looked so relieved to see me that I was reminded what a strange double-edged sword beauty was. She wanted to look her best, but her best made her virtually unapproachable. She hugged me hard. Heavily.

"Thank God you're here. Come on in."

"Sorry, there's a list," said an emaciated woman with a clipboard.

"I'll just get Neil," said Helen.

"Don't worry about it."

"It's fine, hang on."

Helen returned a few minutes later, looking flustered and embarrassed. I could tell that the conversation with Neil had not gone well. I had seen for myself how he had kept her waiting—he was too busy holding court. Before barely hearing her out, he had glanced over at me and then spoken rapidly into his wife's ear before turning back to his eager audience. Clearly I was not important enough. I put Helen out of her misery.

"I can't come in. I promised Billy I would loiter by the door and she'll be here any minute. We'll come and find you later."

"But—"

"It's all right. You're working tonight, meanwhile we all get to enjoy the party; it doesn't seem fair. And, by the way, you look spectacular, so go back into that hallowed place and knock 'em dead. But before I go, this is James Kent." I didn't mean it to sound like such an announcement. This is James Kent, the father of my unborn children. "He knows your mother," I said, covering my hormones.

"Poor you," said Helen.

"How are all the performing monkeys in there?" James asked.

"Vying for limelight."

"That's why they keep them cordoned off. Channel 4 knows they're better off keeping their comedians seen but not heard. They're all moody bastards in real life."

I hoped he hadn't gone overboard. Helen got defensive if she thought Neil was being attacked, but not that night. That night she needed ammunition.

"You're right about that," she replied, smiling at him.

"Very nice to meet you. Neil is a lucky man."

We turned to leave when I heard the lucky man himself. "James, James, you're on the list, mate. Come on in, let me get you a glass of champagne." He frowned at Helen and me. "Don't you two girls ever run out of things to talk about? Tessa, sorry about coming in. If it was up to me . . ." He looked at James. "But you didn't have to queue, mate."

"I wasn't," he said.

"Come in, come in."

"Thanks, but Tessa and I are going to find . . ." The pause was tiny. "Billy. But it has been a joy talking to your lovely wife." Was it my imagination, or did James put an unusual emphasis on that last word?

"Tessa is with you?" Neil couldn't take the tone of incredulity out of his voice.

"Actually, I was tagging along with her. See you later. Hope the show is a success." He put his arm across my shoulders, turned us around like a couple on a cuckoo clock, and we walked away giggling. I wasn't going to say my friend's husband was a tosser, and he wasn't going to say my friend's husband was a tosser, but I knew we were both thinking it. My only regret was not being able to take Helen with us.

James got ambushed a couple of times. On the third I saw Nick and Francesca walk through the door, so peeled off and went to see them. It wasn't until I was a foot in front of them that I realized Ben and Sasha were just behind them. I felt my stride falter and it confused me so much I felt myself begin to dither around them and, rather than risk kissing Ben hello, I kissed none of them and held back awkwardly. I don't think anyone noticed. All four of them were in a buoyant mood. I gathered they had bumped into each other in a nearby pub, which they'd both independently ducked into for a quick nerve-tightener, which turned into three. I was smiling at all of them, but trying not to look at Ben, which made me look at him, which made me feel as if I was staring. Damn it.

James followed me over. I introduced him to my friends but it didn't feel so fun any more. Feeling queasy, I deserted them by offering to do battle at the bar. My heart was racing. I had really hoped this thing had passed. I thought a couple of weeks of abstaining from clinging to the photo frame and I'd licked it. I felt a cool hand snake around my shoulders. I turned. It was Sasha.

"Thought you might need a hand."

"Thanks."

"Who's the dish?"

"I just met him at the bar."

"I met Ben at a bar."

I know. You picked him up. "Don't. You'll fuel my already overactive imagination. I'm trying not to think about what color our en suite should be."

We laughed. But the sad thing was, it was partially true. Or had been, until Ben and Sasha showed up.

"Well, he seems like a good bloke."

Most of my friends were desperate to see me paired away and impregnated, but usually not Sasha. She gave me more credit than I was due and believed I was in the situation I was because I chose to be.

"Bright, funny, articulate, good-looking."

"There must be a catch," I said.

"Perhaps he's married," said Sasha.

"Why do you say that?" I asked defensively.

"He seems quite well trained. Oh, Tessa, don't look so horrified, I was only joking. I know your rules, you don't do married men."

And why? Because since turning thirty I'd been propositioned by so bloody many. But my moral high ground was beginning to feel like quicksand. I decided it was better to change the subject. "He mentioned his mother."

"Ah," said Sasha. "That'll be the catch."

We returned to the table, carrying drinks for the eagerly inebriated. I tried to remember how I normally acted around my friends, but I couldn't. I didn't have Helen there as a foil for my anger and I couldn't turn my back on Ben and engage in deep and meaningful conversation with someone else because we were huddled around a tiny table and it wasn't a deep and meaningful sort of atmosphere. The wives were admiring the exposed buttock cheeks of the young men handing out the drinks and the husbands were trying to spot tit tape. I suspected their nerve-tighteners had been doubles or they'd been in the pub longer than they should have been. Francesca was being particularly raucous. I was delighted to see her in skintight jeans, high black boots and a ribbed black polo neck—perfect boho chic. Nick just sat and watched her adoringly. Sasha looked striking, as always, and Ben smiled at me effortlessly, chatted to me effortlessly, took the piss effortlessly. Was this whole dramatic episode taking place in my head and my head alone? I swallowed more beer and moved up to vodka. Someone grabbed my cheeks and squeezed them. It was Ben.

"Smile, honeychild," he said.

I stared at him.

"What's the matter?" He asked me quietly enough, but everyone turned to hear the answer.

"Nothing."

"You look so worried," said Ben.

I am a foolish, foolish, foolish woman. "I was just wondering where Billy's got to, she promised she'd come this evening."

"She'll be here," he said and turned back to the table.

"I think Tessa is actually wondering where that handsome James Kent got to," said Nick.

"I'm not."

"Rarely have I seen you so subdued at a party, Miss King. Has this one got under your skin?"

"I only just met him."

"At the bar," said Sasha.

"Sasha met Ben at a bar," said Francesca, giggling.

I KNOW.

"I said that."

"Could it be, yes it could," hummed Nick, clicking his fingers like a Jet. Nick was a lovely man but he didn't really drink, so it went to his head quickly.

"Oo, Tessa, let's have a drink to celebrate," said Francesca. Actually, she shouted that.

"There is nothing to celebrate," I insisted.

"Well, let's have drinks anyway."

"What's got into you?" I asked, laughing at her.

"I'm a mother on day release. Don't get in my way. Ohmygod, he's looking over here again, I think!"

Sasha leaned forward conspiratorially. "He's making sure he knows where you are. Let's do a test," she said—and she is supposed to be the grown-up of the group.

I shook my head in despair. My friends were pissed. More pissed than I was. This was not the status quo.

"What kind of test?" asked Nick, enthusiastically.

"Tessa has to get up and go somewhere; we'll see if he comes over as she is leaving."

"He has to see her go," said Nick, "otherwise it won't work."

"Yes, stand up and when Francesca gives you the sign, pretend to go to the loo."

"Pretend to go to the loo?" I repeated, bemused. I thought my tone alone would make it abundantly clear that I had no intention of playing their game.

"Wait, what's the sign?" asked Francesca, rocking slightly.

Am I this stupid when I'm pissed? I wondered. I couldn't be. I didn't feel that stupid. I always thought I was incredibly funny and held my drink particularly well.

"A wink," said Nick.

"Too obvious," said Sasha.

"You're right," he said, looking a little crestfallen.

"I'll say 'now,' but quietly," shouted Francesca.

Everyone nodded.

"Right, stand up, Tessa, but stand there until Fran says—"

"I'm not going to stand up."

"Come on, it'll be interesting," said Sasha.

"Not interesting, very silly."

"Oh, come on, Tessa, give us old marrieds something to talk about." It was Nick who said this, and I know that he didn't mean anything by it because the man hasn't got a bad bone in his body, but honestly, what was I—a performing seal? I felt an invisible red ball balancing on my nose and had an irresistible urge to throw my head back and hawk loudly in the hope of being thrown the head of a mackerel in return. I stood. I was not their live entertainment.

"That's my girl," said Nick.

"I'm leaving you because you are all ridiculous and I need several shots of something lethal before I can find any of you even vaguely amu—"

"NOW," shrieked Francesca, making everyone look around in the direction of James Kent who was, to my utter amazement, walking towards our table.

I turned back to Francesca, feeling my skin redden. "Subtle," I said.

"Sorry."

"Plan B?"

"Pretend to make a phone call and you need to get out of this noise," said Sasha, locating a few of her famous brain cells.

"I want you to know," I said, pulling my phone out of my bag, "that I hate you all." I looked at my phone. Three missed calls. All from Billy. Thank the Lord, a genuine reason to be standing here like a lemon. I started dialing frantically. I saw Fran's eyes widen so I knew that James was behind me. I turned.

"Is it pumpkin time already?" said James.

"I'm not going anywhere, I just need to make a phone call."

"The lobby is empty," he said, and took my arm. I felt four pairs of eyes glued to us as we walked away. I glanced backwards. They all smiled. Well Nick, Fran and Sasha smiled. Ben didn't. After giving me irritating thumbs-up signs they returned to their witchy huddle to congratulate themselves. Ben, however, continued to watch me. I got caught in his stare. Even as James led me through the doors to the entrance, Ben's eyes remained firmly fixed on me and mine on his.

The double doors swung back into place, swallowing the noise of the party with a ladylike burp and the sight of those deep blue eyes. The stairwell seemed like a sanctuary after the maelstrom of the party. My ears rang while they adjusted to the drop in decibels, my lungs offered themselves up in gratitude to the smoke-free air. The peace was short-lived. Up ahead on street level there was more pandemonium. Faces, ten deep, filled the pavement, rocking side to side to see whether someone on the inside could get them in.

"Shit," I said. "She'll never get in."

"I may be able to help," said James. "Find out if she's in the queue."

I rang Billy's number.

"I'm so sorry," she said immediately.

"For?"

"I was late. The queue goes round the building, I'm just going to leave you to it . . ."

"Don't you dare. Come to the entrance."

"Thing is—"

"Just come to the front of the queue. I'm here."

"It's not going to work; some bloke from the telly is behind me. There are too many people in there, that's what they said."

"That's what they always say. Now, come to the front. Stay on the phone." I looked at James. "Are you sure you can do this? I can get Neil, I don't care what he says."

"Trust me," he said. "It's fine. She's on her own, isn't she?"

I put the phone back to my ear. "You're alone, right?"

"Well, the thing is . . ."

"You brought someone?" I was delighted, despite the problems this could make.

"I didn't think plus two would be such a problem and . . ."

"It doesn't matter. It's fine."

I grimaced and held up two fingers to James, two nice fingers.

"Oh, I can see you," said Billy. I pointed Billy out to James and decided to leave him to it. Just in case it didn't work. I didn't want to embarrass him as well as Helen. I watched from afar, trying to see which of the men pressing themselves up against Billy was my date's date. Sensing a lifting of the twisted red chord, the crowd surged. I saw Billy lurch forward, I saw James's hand stretch out to hers, I watched her come through the human barrier of barrel-chested bouncers and emerge triumphant into the cool vestibule. James Kent was a magic man. Billy got lost again in a group of people waiting to check in their coats, James returned to me.

"How the hell did you do that?"

"The bouncer is a comic."

"A good one?"

"No. But he's coming to my office Monday morning."

"I owe you."

"And I shall collect."

Billy arrived from handing in her coat. She smiled sheepishly. "Sorry I'm late."

"Doesn't matter. Who did you bring?"

She was about to reply when I heard my name ring out loudly around the stone foyer. From behind Billy an apparition in green velvet sprang forward, immune to the stares and baffled silence her high-pitched voice had commanded over the other guests savoring some time away from the bedlam.

"GODMUMMY TEEEEEEEEEEEEEEEEEEEEEEEE!" Cora's run through the assortment of legs between us would have made David Beckham proud. With an involuntary but brief look of reproach at Billy, I crouched down and as usual spread out my arms and braced myself for impact. She was wearing the long green ballerina skirt and little green velvet jacket that I had given her for Christmas which made her look more elfin than normal. "What a surprise to see you here, little one," I said, inhaling her fluffy scent.

"You always come to my parties," said Cora.

This was true. I hadn't missed a single one. There was a time in

Cora's young life when we thought she may never make it to one birthday, so it seemed sacrilege to miss any of them.

"Mummy got the day wrong and booked Magda for tomorrow, Magda had tickets for a band tonight and couldn't miss it. But don't tell her I told you, because she thinks you all think she's incontinent, but it was just a mistake."

I clenched my jaw tightly shut to stop the laugh escaping. That was Cora to a T—full of wisdom and malapropisms in equal measure.

Billy appeared behind Cora, her long hair washed this time, and wafting in dark tresses behind her. When she is stressed, you can see the nervous energy tearing through her at hyper speed. When she is relaxed, she looks like she could fly. That night she was at hyper speed.

"God, I'm sorry—so late. Magda got a cold and I so wanted to see you all so Cora suggested she put her pretty dress on, and we both came."

I knew the last part of that sentence was true.

Perhaps in hindsight I had bullied Billy a fraction too much if she thought bringing a seven-year-old to a coke-fuelled, smoked-filled, over-crowded media party was a better idea than calling me and telling me she couldn't come. I smiled broadly at Cora, then Billy. "A brilliant idea. You both look lovely."

Cora beamed.

James approached. "You probably need a drink after that experience. I'm going to the bar, can I get you a drink?"

He spoke to Billy. She looked totally perplexed, so I introduced them. Billy isn't used to talking to people she doesn't know. I think she thinks she is invisible.

"What about champagne?" I said, fishing out my credit card. "To say thank you for that miracle stunt you just pulled."

"Put that away," said James so firmly that I did.

"And what can I get for you, Cora?" asked James.

Cora beamed again. "Pineapple juice, please."

"Cora, honey, they might not have—"

James interrupted me. "This is a five-star club. If they don't have pineapple juice then they don't deserve their stars."

"There is a girl in my class who gets stars she doesn't deserve," said Cora seriously. "I'm afraid it does happen."

"You're right," said James. "All too often."

Cora nodded in agreement, her brows knitted together. "Apple then, they should have apple."

"It's a bit of a bun fight in there—absolute chaos," I said to Billy.

"We won't stay long."

"I'm sorry," I said. "Did you have a nightmare getting into town?"

"Actually, it was quite fun getting ready together," she said, ducking the question of dragging Cora out on the tube on a Saturday night. "We danced around the room in our pants and sang High Five songs. The new Abba."

"Always is the best bit," I said, taking Billy's arm and clutching Cora's small hand. "Remember the hours we spent getting ready, just so we could go out looking like everyone else?"

"Drinking wine out of mugs."

"Or the bottle, if we hadn't done the washing up," I recalled.

"That was a long time ago," said Billy.

"Don't say that, it feels like yesterday to me."

"Probably was in your case."

I poked her in the ribs. We reached the double doors. "Ready?"

Billy and Cora nodded. We pushed open the doors and walked into a wall of sound. I elbowed, jostled, rumbled and tussled our way back to the table. Everyone was delighted to see Cora and she was immediately passed around like the trophy she is, until she finally settled on Ben's knee. Ben is her favorite. He would be, she knows him best. We do the surrogate parenting thing quite a lot when Billy needs a break and Sasha is away.

"Where are the buns?" asked Cora.

"What?"

"The buns for the bun fight?"

Everyone laughed. Except me. I stared at Cora, playing with Ben's ear. And I wondered how long I had been borrowing someone else's child to play with someone else's husband and kidding myself it was normal.

"Where are Helen and Neil?" asked Francesca.

James Kent arrived with two bottles of champagne and seven glasses. I jumped up. "I'll go and find her," I said. "And bring her over for a drink."

I returned to the VIP bar and approached the emaciated woman. She averted her eyes, so I made my intentions very clear.

"I don't want to come in, I was just hoping my friend Helen Zhao could come out for a while and join us for a drink."

"She isn't in there."

I frowned.

"I know for a fact," said the woman, "there was a bit of a scene."

"A scene?" I was confused.

"She has drunk a bit too much. You'll probably find her in the loo."

"Neil Williams's wife, are you sure?"

"Yes, his wife. Bit embarrassing for him, really."

I was horrified by her over-familiarity, frightened for the reason why that might be, but, more than that, I was concerned for Helen. "She has just had twins," I said, though I wasn't sure why.

The woman shrugged at me. It may have been in a noncommittal way, but to me it looked like "More fool her," or, worse, "What do you expect, then?" I suddenly felt for Helen in a way I never had before. No wonder she'd drunk too much inside that insidious space; it was protection against the anorexic dementor standing in front of me, and the rest of her kind. There is little in this world less attractive to me than when the sisterhood breaks down.

I left her standing behind the rope and went up to the pods. There were eight of them. They were unisex, had no engaged sign and offered no queuing system. It was therefore impossible to know which of the pods Helen might be in. I started circling them, my head craning backwards and forwards at the slightest sign of any movement. I plotted them like battleships in my brain and crossed them off as I watched men and women spill out of them, usually in pairs.

After about ten minutes I located two that had shown no sign of life. I had once missed an entire wedding passed out in a Portaloo, so I knew it was possible. I approached the first. I knocked gently. There was no answer. I leaned closer and was about to call Helen's name when I heard a noise that sounded like retching.

"Helen? Are you all right?" I called out, loudly enough for some people near me to look over.

The retching stopped. In my experience retching doesn't stop to command.

"Sorry," I said to the white plastic door and moved away as the retching started up again. I went and hovered out of sight until the people whose attention I'd attracted moved away. Five minutes later the retching pod door opened and a man and a woman stepped out, walked to the top of the stairs and, without exchanging a word, parted company. Was it just me, or was it getting harder out here?

I moved to the last pod that had shown no signs of activity. Luckily, it was the one that was furthest away from the stairwell, and the door faced the wall. I knocked again and again; there was no answer.

I leaned closer. I couldn't hear retching, or grunting, but I could hear something. It sounded mechanical. A pulsating, mechanical sound, like something was malfunctioning inside. I looked for an out of order sign, but there wasn't one. Then I heard a human sound. A sob. Thinking back on it, it was more of a yelp, more animal than human, but it was female.

"Helen?" I said, more urgently. "It's me, Tessa. Let me in."

There was no reply.

"Right," I said loudly. "I'm going to get someone to open the door from the outside."

"No!" came the immediate response.

"Then let me in now, there is no one about, no one can—" The door opened a fraction.

"See you." I pulled it wider, gave a last furtive glance to check no one was watching, and stepped inside the pod.

Helen stared at me from the loo seat. Her black eye makeup was smeared over her face. She had snot hanging out of her left nostril. Her lower lip hung open like a boxer's after a fight. Her bare shoulders were hunched forward. Her dress was around her waist, leaving her top half naked. On each small breast was a clear plastic cone that tugged at the unyielding flesh. The mechanical noise I'd heard was the sound of suction. At the base of each cone were two clear pipes that joined a third, like a stethoscope, near her belly button. The single pipe ran into a plastic bottle which Helen held in a white-knuckled grip. She appeared to be immune to the intermittent pull on her breasts. I prised the device out of her hand, found the switch, and turned it off. One cone fell off Helen's breast with a pop. The skin hung loose and empty over her ribcage. Her nipple was purple and swollen. I gently pulled the second cone away. It was then that I noticed the tiny specks of blood on the tip of Helen's nipple. I glanced at the bottle in my hand. Creeping down the tube into the few droplets of thin grey liquid at the bottom of the bottle were beads of blood.

There was no resistance from Helen as I pulled her dress back up and fed her skinny arms through the straps. She didn't attempt to help as I struggled to place the straps back in place on her bony shoulders but her eyes never left mine. I took her head and pulled her towards my stomach and held her there, silently, waiting for her to awaken from her trance. Finally she spoke.

"I'm going to ruin your beautiful dress," said Helen.

"Sod the dress," I replied. "What happened?"

"I just wanted to have fun, like it used to be."

"How much did you drink?"

"I didn't drink," insisted Helen.

"It doesn't matter that you had a drink, Helen, no one would blame you."

"I can't drink, I'm still breastfeeding."

"Why are you hiding in here then, with that?" I pointed at the contraption lying lifeless in the sink. Helen squinted at the electric breast pump, then back up at me.

"Tessa?"

"Yes?"

"Do you think he loves me?"

Coming from a professional blind-sider, I should have seen that coming. But I didn't. Instead, I panicked. "Come on, Helen, let's get you home."

"I can't go out there."

"It's all right, I have a plan." I sent out the SOS call by quietly texting Billy while I held Helen to me. Next, I bent down and pulled Helen's hair away from her face. Nothing wet loo paper and some professional cover up couldn't cure, and after a lifetime of spots, I was the master of cover-up. Helen had darker skin tone to me, so she was a little pale by the time I'd finished, but at least she no longer looked insane. There was a knock on the pod door. Helen jumped.

"Don't tell Neil," she said.

"Tell him what?"

Helen didn't answer. I turned the lock. Billy held our coats in her hand. She fed mine through the slit in the door. As I got Helen into my coat, she watched me anxiously. "I've tried to be a good mother and wife, why is it so hard, why can't I do it? Why is it so hard?"

I could feel the hysteria inside her build. The hysteria that had forced her into a plastic cubicle to cry her makeup into paste. The hysteria that had left her wasted, spent and exhausted. I pulled her up.

"All you have to do is get out of here. We'll deal with everything else when we're home." Who was I to make such sweeping statements? How telling it was that I really thought I could, with sheer will, make it all better for everyone. Even myself.

The party was well into its third stage by the time we left the pod. I gathered the breast pump into my hand and put my other arm around Helen. No one batted an eyelid to see two women emerging from the loo, fall into the arms of a third and stagger down the stairs. Taking one arm each, we bundled Helen out of the party like a celebrity. At the door Francesca was waiting with Cora. Cora simply slipped her hand into her mother's and the four of us moved to the exit.

"What about saying goodbye to James Kent?" whispered Fran into my ear.

I frowned at her. Not now. There were more important things to worry about.

trickery

It was a quarter to twelve when I got Helen into a cab. Since Helen and Billy lived in opposite directions, I gave Billy enough cash to get her and Cora home in another one.

A few minutes after pulling away, Helen remembered that she hadn't got her keys. I assumed that Rose would let us in, but Helen insisted we go back and I get her bag from the VIP bar. It made no sense to me, but Helen was in too fragile a state to argue with, so I asked the taxi driver to turn around and go back. If we hadn't, I wouldn't have seen Billy sitting at the bus stop, with Cora, curled like an oversized cat, already asleep on her lap. Billy didn't see us pass, and for that I was grateful.

I managed to find the handbag fairly easily, but I only just missed bumping into Neil by ducking onto the dance floor. There were Ben and Sasha doing pretty good dirty dancing for a couple of oldies. I stood stock-still among the moving mass of bodies and watched them gyrate, swing, smooch, laugh and laugh and laugh. For a brief moment Sasha looked straight at me, then Ben swung her upside-down again. She didn't look back. I had to get out of there.

By the time I'd wrestled my way back through the throng we'd ratcheted up another fiver on the clock and Billy and Cora had boarded their night bus and gone. I pulled Helen into my arms and held on to her tightly as we drove through the busy streets of London in the full swing of Saturday night. In her lap lay the dormant breast pump. She ran the empty plastic tube through her fingers like the beads on a rosary.

Having deposited Helen, fully clothed, in bed, I decided to go and check on the twins. As I reached the top floor Rose stepped out of the shadows onto the landing and gave me such a fright, I nearly fell back down the stairwell. She eyed me suspiciously, which I thought was fair enough, given I was creeping around the house in the middle of the night, in the dark.

"Bloody hell, Rose, you gave me a fright. It's me, Tessa. I just brought Helen home," I whispered.

"What happened?"

"I think she had a bit to drink, but she's obviously not used to it. She's in a real state."

"How much?"

"I don't know. She's denying it."

She nodded her head, which felt to me as if she were looking me up and down. I realized it was the middle of the night, and she'd probably been woken by the twins already, but she wasn't being very sympathetic. What I'd seen in that loo was a very distressed woman. Maybe Helen had got nervous, had too much to drink and then felt guilty about the twins and didn't want Neil to know, but then, maybe it was more serious than that.

"Are the twins all right? Are they hungry?" I asked.

"They're asleep. She shouldn't disturb them."

"I agree. We should let her sleep as long as possible. You'll have to give the boys some formula if they wake up. Have you got any formula?"

Was it my imagination, or was Rose frowning at me? Was she

a breast-is-best guru as well? Since when had formula become so vilified? Rose turned away from me and retreated into her room. I wasn't sure which room the boys slept in, since Helen always preferred to feed up there alone. It was also at the top of the house, and I had never felt sufficiently inclined to endorse the grotesquely expensive handmade cots in the perfectly decorated themed nursery from Dragons of Walton Street to brave the five storeys. Anyway, since the babies were always produced, powdered and clean in matching Moses baskets, it didn't seem necessary. Helen said running up and down to the nursery kept her fit. It tired me out just looking at them. Caspar spent the first six months of his life sleeping on a changing mat in the bath because Nick and Fran lived in a one-roomed flat. Cora was in hospital but when she moved into her room, I knew it like the back of my hand. I knew where everything was kept. The booties. The wipes. The muslins. I turned back down the stairs feeling conscious that of the four doors in front of me, I did not know behind which my godsons slept, or if they even slept together.

I went over to Neil's drinks cabinet and poured a whisky into a cut-glass crystal tumbler that was too big to get my hand around. I raised the lid on the ice bucket expecting to find nothing, but was greeted by fresh ice. So that was what having full-time, live-in staff meant— fresh ice and, if Marguerite was right, only a passing knowledge of your children. I plopped a couple of pieces into the whisky and threw myself into one of their three huge cream sofas. Just you wait till crayon time, I thought, and melting ice-lollies, and Marmite soldiers, and Play-doh . . . but I dismissed the thought. All those images were from a happy home and something about this house didn't feel very happy. I curled my feet up under me. Had I really been so involved with what was going on at work not to pay Helen any attention, or was it something else? Something less palatable, though I was beginning to be able to taste its unappetizing flavor. I was jealous. That's why I hadn't listened to Helen's complaints of piles, of breathlessness, of stretch marks and rancid indigestion. In the absence of a decent role model, Helen worried about being a good mother. I dismissed those fears with a wave of my hand. When Neil looked at her and told her she was huge, I laughed because it wasn't true. She looked amazing right up to her delivery date. But it must have felt true to Helen. I had put up an invisible force field between Helen and myself. I had repelled her advances. Why? Because she had deserted me. My fellow fun-loving, girl-about-town, devil-may-care, throw-caution-to-the-wind playmate had deserted me. And I had made her suffer for it. It was worse than pure jealousy, because I was jealous of something that I didn't even want for myself.

I couldn't stand Neil. I knew that Helen had been subjected to a loveless childhood and that the money she inherited from her father would never make amends. I knew that she was insecure, unconfident, caged by her own looks, and could be inflicted with deep wounds by people who should have had no impact on her whatsoever. So beneath the jealousy lurked anger. I thought I was angry at her for selling herself so short, but really I was angry at myself because somewhere inside me the thought of selling myself short appealed. Trouble was, I couldn't even seem to manage that. I put the empty glass down on the side table and peeled myself off the sofa. It was two in the morning. I groped my way upstairs and found a spare bedroom, stripped off, fell into the luxurious, squishy bed and fell asleep immediately.

I didn't know if I'd been woken by the smell of smoke, or the persistent thudding resonating through the floor into my ribcage. I reluctantly opened my eyes and took in my surroundings. Dawn outlined the thick curtains. I sat up, turned on the side light and squinted at

my watch. I wrapped the waffle dressing gown I found hanging on
the back of the en-suite bathroom around me and stepped into the
hall. I heard a noise above me. Rose was leaning over the banister,
glaring down the stairwell. When she saw me, she shook her head
and moved back.

I started my descent. There were two girls sitting on the bottom
step in deep conversation, waving cigarettes around.

"Excuse me," I said, stepping between them. They barely paused.
"You might want to get an ashtray," I said, pointing at the long arc of
ash that hung precariously off the cigarette. I may as well have asked
them for a kidney. I followed the sound of the bass into the drawing
room where I had wistfully sipped whisky a few hours earlier. Five
people were huddled around the glass-topped coffee table. There
were all sorts of bottles open on the table, every ashtray spilled over
with fag butts, some still burning. They must have been in residence
for a good couple of hours. Neil stood by the state-of-the-art stereo,
controls in hand, dancing furiously on the spot, shaking his head
from side to side, facing the wall.

"Do you mind turning that down?" I said to Neil. "You're going
to wake the babies."

"Jesus, you scared the shit out of me!" exclaimed Neil turning
around. "Oh God, I thought you were the nanny. Join us, have a
drink, sit down. Did you enjoy the party?"

I was standing there in a robe, but Neil didn't seem to register
that.

"Could you please turn the music down? Helen is knackered and
I really don't want her to wake up."

"Since when did you become such a bore, Sasha?" said Neil. He
looked like a cow chewing cud. His jaw never stopped moving.

"Tessa," I corrected him.

"Fuck, sorry, I always get you two mixed up. You're weirdly similar, don't you think? Have you ever thought that?" Neil didn't know what he was saying. He had verbal diarrhea. Talking shit. "Come and have a little livener. You've always been more adventurous than Helen. Always liked that spirit about you. At first I thought you were just a bit of a loser, but I admire you. You're so independent, wish my wife was more like you." I just wanted him to shut up. I peeled his heavy, sweaty arm off me.

"She really needs some proper sleep. It's six in the morning. Isn't it time everyone went home?"

I looked over at the people around the coffee table. They were a grim-looking bunch. Cocaine is not good for the complexion. They stared back at me through vast, dilated pupils.

"We've only just got here," said Neil.

The girls from the stairs came in. "Any more coke?" asked one.

Neil pulled a wrap from his pocket and threw it on to the table. Two men pounced. I knew I was fighting a losing battle; no one was going to listen to me, so I surreptitiously turned the volume down on the stereo and retreated, closing the doors behind me. I wondered, as I climbed the stairs back to my room, whether this was a one-off or not. I knew that Neil often went AWOL; I didn't realize that he'd started bringing the party home. I got back into bed. Half an hour or so later, I heard the music again. It thumped in and out of my consciousness until eight. Eventually I got up, had a bath, got dressed into my party dress and, after silently opening Helen's door just enough to check that she was still sleeping, I went upstairs to find the nursery.

Thankfully it was the first door I tried. The nursery was just as I had expected: a shrine to privileged parenting. It had everything. Hand-painted cots with rather girly canopies. Beatrix Potter character-shaped rugs on the floor. Machines that played Mozart. Machines that projected lights on the ceiling. Machines that read

the temperature and humidity of the room. There was a matching
feeding chair and stool in blue gingham, and two of everything else.
Baby bouncers. Changing-tables. Play-nests. Potties. There were
more Beatrix Potter characters stenciled above the skirting board,
complete with the words of Miss Tiggywinkle. A struggling artist
had painted a blue sky with fluffy white clouds on the ceiling, some
of which hosted round-bottomed putti smiling down from on high. I
wasn't sure the Renaissance and the Potter combination worked, but
hey, these weren't my offspring to confuse.

There were two built-in wardrobes. Behind one was a collection
of designer labels to make a grown woman weep, except not even the
thinnest of them could have squeezed into these minute ensembles.
Behind the other I found a kitchenette with a microwave, a kettle, a
fridge/freezer and every accessory I'd ever seen in the baby section
of John Lewis, and others that I hadn't. Helen wasn't taking any
chances. I opened the freezer and was confronted by row upon row
of miniature colostomy bags—a stationary army of expressed milk,
ready for the off. That was when I remembered the double-headed
monster gnawing away at Helen's once remarkable cleavage last
night. I looked around the light, airy room, amazed by the equip-
ment that could be amassed if you had the money and the inclination, and recalled once again baby Caspar's nursery. A changing-mat
in the bath. Cora's was the life-support unit at St. Mary's Hospital. In
either case, I'd never seen their mothers as distressed, disorientated
and disheveled as Helen was last night. I pulled the door behind
me. The nursery boasted everything an expectant mother's heart de-
sired. Except one thing. Where were the babies?

Behind another door I found a spare room that had once been occupied by the maternity nurse. Which left one more after the nauti-
cally themed bathroom. I knocked and heard Rose's voice. She came
to the door and, rather suspiciously, I thought, opened it a crack. She

looked me up and down and sneered with blatant disapproval. At first I was insulted but then I remembered the coke whores downstairs; I was still in my party dress and Rose had seen Helen and me after some of our own long nights. But that was all in the past. I hoped I looked better that morning than they did.

"I haven't been downstairs with Neil. I've been trying to sleep," I said to appease her. I didn't get the thawing I was expecting. She stonewalled me.

"Are you all right?"

"What do you think?"

I was cross too, but I didn't understand Rose's hostility. She was a mild-mannered woman who had loved Helen unconditionally. Perhaps that was changing. Perhaps Helen's choice of husband had been one condition she couldn't work with.

"Do you have the twins?" I asked.

"No," she said.

"Where are they, then?"

"With their father," she said furiously.

"Their father!"

"He wanted to play with them."

"Neil has them?"

"As I said, he wanted to play with them."

"But he's . . ." Coked off his face. "Been up all night."

"He is their father. I am just an ugly Filipino who is paid to do as she's told."

I immediately knew the source of that gut-wrenching sentence.

"Oh, Rose, I'm sorry." I wasn't going to make excuses for Neil, because there weren't any. I could have stood there all day and sympathized with Rose. I could have happily spent hours discussing how horrific Neil was, how racist, how puerile, how sexist, how stupid, but I was more concerned about my godsons. So I left her. I didn't operate within the same boundaries that Rose did and had no qualms about telling Neil exactly how disgusting he was.

I hope never again to see what I saw that morning. Neil was holding one of the babies above his head, dancing. The other was lying on the sofa between two girls who took turns to coo, and then take long drags on their cigarettes, while discussing their own desire to procreate. I saw one stub out a fag and then, with the same hand, stroke the baby's face. The room was thick with smoke, so what did it really matter?—the boys were already a packet down—but the proximity of her nicotine-stained fingers to that precious baby's mouth filled me with hatred. I went for him first.

"What the fuck do you think you are doing!" I shouted as I hauled the baby off the sofa. I turned on Neil. "These fucking morons clearly don't know better, but you are their father. It stinks in here. There is coke on the table. Are you insane?"

"I did say they shouldn't be in here," said some hunched bloke from an armchair. I ignored him. I took the baby I was holding out into the corridor and placed him on the carpet. When I returned, Neil was slagging me off. I heard him say "cobweb cunt," which could not have bothered me less, since I was no longer interested in him. I just wanted to get my godson off him. I went to the heavy curtains and pulled them back, and watched with some satisfaction as everyone winced like oysters in lemon juice at the bright sunlight that poured into the room. The thick grey smoke lingered around us like wisps of Dartmoor fog. I unbolted the window and threw it wide open. Then I returned for the other baby. Luckily Neil was too pissed to successfully resist, though he did try.

"You don't deserve them, and you don't deserve Helen."

"Fuck off." He took an unsure step towards me. "Give me back Tommy, you stupid cow."

"If you touch me I will call the police. I swear to God, Neil, I will call the police."

"Leave it, man," said the bloke from the armchair. "She's right. They shouldn't be in here. Come on, mate, have a drink."

I left the room, picked up the baby I now knew to be Bobby, and in my heels, started back up the stairs. By the first landing I was out of breath. These boys weighed a bit and didn't offer much help in the way of supporting themselves. My arm muscles soon started to burn. I kicked off my shoes and made it up the next four flights. I could smell the smoke on their matching baby gowns and hated their father deeper and more fervently than I ever would have thought possible. Four round conker-colored eyes stared back at me. I couldn't stop apologizing to them. I kissed them both repeatedly on their round, warm foreheads as the word "sorry" poured out of me. Finally I got them up to the immaculate nursery and closed the door behind me.

"It's all right, boys, we're going to get you out of these stinky clothes and into the fresh air. Godmummy T is in charge."

I placed Bobby on Peter Rabbit and Tommy on Jemima Puddle-duck and went back to Rose's room. I knocked again. This time she answered in her overcoat.

"I need your help," I said immediately.

She shook her head.

"You don't understand, Helen is exhausted and Neil is with these awful people and I don't have—"

"I'm sorry."

"But please, I don't know how to—"

"It is my day off."

"Again?"

Rose frowned.

"Sorry, I didn't mean that. I know you work nonstop. But please can you stay? I'm sure Helen will pay you, I'll pay you whatever you want."

Her eyes narrowed. "Money," she said in disgust.

"I didn't mean to insult you." In my panic I was messing things up. "I desperately want Helen to sleep, that's all."

"I came back because of the boys. But I cannot stay any longer." She picked up a suitcase that I had not noticed before and opened the door wider.

"Where are you going?"

Rose didn't answer me.

"Please don't go, not now. Helen needs help."

"Yes, she does. But not from me."

"But she's desperate," I pleaded.

"I know. I cannot help her while she continues in this way."

"It's not her fault. It's Neil!"

"Tessa, make all the excuses in the world, but I will not stay here and watch Helen do this to herself."

I knew what she meant. I hated watching it too. I hated what Neil did to her, but this wasn't going to help her. Rose saw the boys lying on their respective rugs through the open nursery door. I thought for a second that she started to lower her suitcase, but then she shook her head again and straightened up. When she looked back at me I thought I saw tears. I watched her descend the staircase and a few moments later heard the heavy front door close with a firm thud. I returned to the nursery, stripped the boys, peered into their nappies to check there was no poo, and, relieved, picked out new outfits that didn't match. Tommy was in something with a train motif. Bobby got the bear suit. T for Train. T for Tommy. B for Bear. B for Bobby. At least I could call them by their names now.

I had to get out of my ridiculous dress, so I crept into Helen's room and found a tracksuit and trainers that looked like my size, but were, of course, too small. I didn't dare go back in, so I squeezed into the pink velour and hoped that I didn't bump into anyone I knew. You have to be very beautiful to wear pink velour well. I carried the boys back downstairs—no mean feat—to the basement, where I knew the pram was parked. I had made three more journeys to the nursery when I remembered I should take supplies. I fetched the frozen milk but forgot the bottles. Then I needed something warm for them to wear. Then Bobby was sick, so I had to carry him back up for a whole new outfit. Luckily, there was two of everything, so another bear suit was easy to find. At least I remembered the nappies on that trip. By the time I left the house I was exhausted and Tommy had been waiting in the pram for forty minutes. He was clearly pissed off. I couldn't face another ascent, so I found something for him to amuse himself with. The jam-jar lid went straight in his mouth and he promptly fell asleep. One bonus to all of this was that Neil had vanished along with everyone else.

I left a note for Helen, telling her to call me when she woke up and that I had the twins and everything was fine. Then I set off down the street with my charges to find some fuel for me. I glanced at my watch. Was ten-thirty too early for a stiff drink? Caffeine would have to suffice. Notting Hill Gate was full of lovely little cafés to sit in and idle away a morning, but there was no way I could get the pram through the doors, let alone navigate the tables. The pram may have been state-of-the-art, but it was still preposterously large and, frankly, a little too showy to gain much sympathy. I noted that as I stood outside one café emitting enticing warm, doughy smells, and wondered whether there was any chance of getting in, those on the other side of the glass glared at me with open hostility. With little sleep and terrible clothes, I looked perfect in my role of frazzled new mother.

I walked away and headed for the one place I knew I could hang my hat and dump my load. I avoided Starbucks like the plague usually.

There was nothing that made me feel the pinch of my ovaries more than a visit to Starbucks. You were usually confronted by a mammary gland, or several if a Lamaze class was "getting together," before you reached the incomprehensible barista, and by the time it took the twenty minutes for your cup of warm milk to arrive, you'd heard several women discuss drying their nether regions with a hairdryer and could list nipple creams off by heart. But there were double doors, and women with babies to help hold them open. No one sneered at me. Instead, I got a look of pity from some and a knowing look from others that said "IVF was it, dear?" I ordered a triple-shot dry cappuccino and sat down on the scurf-covered brown velvet chair with relief. Someone had left a paper and for a few glorious moments I read it, drank coffee and thought, Hey, this isn't so bad.

Bobby woke up first and started crying. Fine, I thought. Milk. No problem. I got a large cup of hot water and plonked a bag of frozen milk in it. That was probably my first mistake. I should have got two. The milk seemed to take for ever to defrost, meanwhile Bobby got increasingly restless and soon got tired of crinkling brown sugar packets in his chubby little fingers. Personally, I thought the twins could probably do with skipping a meal or two, but clearly they didn't. Tommy woke up and went straight from sucking the jam-jar lid to full scream. I returned to the counter and asked for more hot water. One sweet girl offered to heat the milk in the microwave for me. I could have kissed her.

"I have twins," she said, which surprised me, since she only looked about twelve. She took the bags and the bottles from me and a few minutes later, which felt like hours, she returned with an apologetic look on her face. I knew immediately something was wrong.

"I am so sorry," she said, above the increasing din of Tommy's hunger. "It seems to have curdled. There wasn't a date on the bag. How old is it?"

I shrugged. "They're not mine. I'm looking after them for a friend."

She looked concerned. I felt terrified.

"What shall I do?"

"Go to Boots and buy a carton of ready-prepared baby milk."

"But they only have breast milk."

"Or find their mother."

I swore silently under my breath.

"You sure I can't give them that?" I looked at the bottles for the first time. She was right, the milk had curdled.

"It doesn't smell right," said the woman. "You go, I'll watch the babies."

I could have kissed her again. There is such goodness in the world, I thought, my spirits rocketing back up from around my ankles as I ran out of Starbucks.

There were several brands, for several stages. I didn't have time to read the tiny writing and anyway, I didn't know what the boys weighed, so I bought two of each, which set me back a bit. Then I ran back to Starbucks. The waitress was rocking the pram backwards and forwards and singing something in Spanish.

"Thank you so much. This is probably the last thing you want to do; you probably come to work to get away from the kids."

She shook her head. "They are at home in Chile with my mother."

"Wow," I said. "That must be hard."

"They are well fed," she said smiling bravely. "So how old are these boys?"

"Five months."

"Big boys. My colleague cleaned the bottles, you can start again now."

I wanted her to stay but a party of eight came in and she had to go back to work. I ripped open the carton with my teeth and noticed a woman looking at me disapprovingly. I smiled at her then poured the contents into the bottles, tightened the lids, and without remembering to warm them, offered them to the two hungry mouths. They started sucking furiously as soon as the plastic teats touched their lips, and despite some excessive dribbling, they seemed completely unfazed by this dramatic change in their young lives. As they stared up at me from inside their pram I thought about the slight girl behind the counter and her babies miles away and thought how very lucky we all were and how easy it was to forget. My confidence was soaring as the boys drained every last drop. I picked up Tommy to wind him and was rewarded with an enormous belch. I picked up Bobby and was coated in a thick slick of milky slime while he simultaneously filled his nappy. The rapturous noise was competing with the steam machine but still won. People turned to look. I smiled apologetically.

"Gee, thanks, kiddo," I said to Bobby, and placed him back in the pram alongside his brother so we could all pay a visit to the loo. There was no way the pram would get through the door, so I returned to my seat, lifted Bobby out again and asked the woman on the next-door table to keep an eye on Tommy. He was happily sucking the jam-jar lid again, so I didn't think he'd be any trouble.

"I'll only be a minute," I said, feeling pretty competent at this point, and picked up my bag of tricks. It was a disaster. As soon as I removed the odorous nappy, Bobby pooed again. Thick, squitty, sweet yellow poo. It was disgusting. I tried to wipe it up with loo paper but it ran down his legs and, more choicely than that, up his rather hairy back. The skid mark quickly soaked through two layers of clothes. I ferreted around in the bag, knowing full well that I hadn't factored in a change of clothes. The recycled loo paper came apart in my hands and only managed to smear the excrement further afield. Was this putrid-smelling stuff normal? Maybe I had poisoned him with the baby milk?

In the end, I used up a whole precious nappy wiping him up, hoping that Tommy had a firmer constitution than his brother. I finally got the last of the clean nappies under his bum, when from out of his willy shot a perfect arc of pee. Luckily, I had turned away at that moment so most of it went in my ear and trickled down my neck, rather than in my eye. By the time I had grabbed more loo paper, he and I were soaking. There was a knock on the door.

"It's occupied," I shouted rudely.

"Your child is screaming."

"Oh, sorry, can you . . ." No, she couldn't. I didn't know who this woman was. "I'll just be a minute."

"That's what you said fifteen minutes ago."

Fifteen minutes! Lying toad. I glanced at my watch. Shit. She was being generous. It was more like twenty. I unlocked the door and heard the bawling.

"I'm so sorry. Had a bit of a nightmare."

The woman glanced over my pee-soaked shoulder. A pile of poo-covered paper and nappies were piled high around a wet, poo-stained baby who lay in a messy state of undress. He was smiling, though. Bless him.

"I can see," she said.

"Would you mind just—"

"I'm terribly sorry, but I have to go."

I was in a jam. I didn't dare leave Bobby unattended on the changing-table, since I hadn't bothered harnessing him in, but I couldn't leave Tommy screaming the place down.

"Look, I'll push the pram over here."

"Thank you so much," I said, filled with gratitude. "Really, thank

you. Thank you." Shut up you, mad woman. "Thank you," I said
again. In the space of one hour and forty-nine minutes, the twins
had turned me into a gibbering wreck.

An hour later I was back at Helen's house. I'd been sitting outside her
house for half of that time before she finally called, though naturally
I didn't tell her that. I think she was a little surprised to discover that
Bobby was naked under his snowsuit, but she hid it well. I threw
the damaged goods into the laundry room and closed the door on
the sorry mess. Helen returned with a freshly dressed Bobby. I sat
while Tommy happily played under another play-nest in the "family
room."

"Was Tommy sick?" she asked.

"No, but Bobby was."

"Bobby?" Helen looked down at the play-nest.

Something was wrong. The baby lying on the play-nest had a
train on his tummy.

"Isn't that Tommy?"

"No. Hard as it is to believe, I do know the difference between
them."

You might, I thought. But your husband doesn't.

"So sorry. How do you tell them apart?"

"Tommy has darker eyes."

"What do you do when they are asleep?"

"Hope no one has swapped them around."

I smiled, thinking Helen was joking.

"Once they wake up again, I soon know. Tommy is sick all the
time. Bobby isn't. It's weird."

"What if they both take turns in being sick, and you just think
it's always Tommy."

"Tessa, please don't do my head in more than it is already."

As I said, I thought this conversation was quite jovial. Breaking the ice from the night before. Washing over it with humor. But then Helen burst into tears.

I couldn't calm her down. I couldn't make the tears stop. I couldn't. I didn't know a human being could have so much liquid inside them. Babies are strange. The twins got agitated and distressed by the noise. I knew how they felt. It was horrible seeing someone you loved in that much pain, and not being able to stop it. I was frightened they would start crying too, so I extracted myself from her and took them to another part of the room. I found their baby bouncers and put them in front of *Baby Bach*. The hypnosis was instant. Eventually, I thrust a glass of brandy in Helen's hand (and poured one for myself) and told her to drink it. She looked at me with such sorrow in her eyes that I couldn't bear to hold her gaze. I knew it was far too early in the day, but sod the babies and their pure boob juice, I couldn't think of anything else.

"Drink it," I insisted. She obediently knocked it back in one. Then she stared at the glass so I took it away.

"Don't beat yourself up about it, Helen, it's one fucking drink." I knelt at her feet and took her hands. "You've got to tell me what's going on."

She shook her head.

"I can't help you until you tell me. You are clearly depressed, that much I can see for myself. You need help."

"I've got tons of fucking help, all I have is help, help, help. I can't cope. I don't know what the hell I'm supposed to be doing."

"I don't blame you. I had them for two hours and they reduced me to tears."

I wanted her to smile, but she didn't. So I tried to think of a serious solution.

"There must be a book, something to help you know what to do . . ."

"Books. Books. There are millions of books all telling you different things; there are books about how many books there are, which promise to make it simple, but they don't. They don't. None of them can tell me why I feel like this!" She sighed heavily. "Trust me, I don't need books."

OK, not books then.

"Neil says I'm pathetic. Says it isn't right, a woman of my age having a nanny, and he's right."

"He is not! You've got to stop believing your husband."

"Don't worry, I don't. Not any more."

Was the reason for these tears Neil, and not the babies, as I had thought? "I meant about when he puts you down."

"I know that's what you meant."

"What did you mean?"

"The world is full of trickery, Tessa. You know what I mean, everyone fucking knows what I mean. Even that nice man you met at the party knows what I mean, and I've never met him before. I don't even care any more. He hurts me, but not because of that."

"What do you mean hurts you?"

I saw the tears spill over again.

"Helen?"

"He's done this, he's made me into this. I wouldn't be like this if it wasn't for him."

"What does he do? Helen, what does he do? Does he hit you?"

"He shagged someone in a corridor of the Soho House when the boys were six weeks old." She shook her head. "I confronted him. You know what he said? He said, 'What do you expect when I'm getting so little attention at home?'"

It was not a pleasant feeling having your worst fears confirmed. Gossiping about scandal, and that scandal reducing your friend to pulp, were not the same thing.

"You've got to leave."

"No. He is not running me out of my own home."

"Fuck the home, you'll get another home—"

"My mother, I could take it from my mother. It hurts more from Neil."

"Your mother?"

"You see, she never said she loved me. Do you understand? Neil said he loved me and then turns me into this. I know where I stand with Marguerite. I didn't see it coming from Neil."

"I want to get you out of here before he comes back. Who knows what sort of state he'll be in."

"Rose will be back soon."

"No, Helen, she's gone."

"She'll come back. She'd never leave me. She just does it occasionally to show me who's boss."

"What?"

"But she always comes back."

"You need to see someone, Helen, a doctor, a psychiatrist, someone who can help you. I'm sure there is something he can prescribe to help you. Postnatal depression, it's very common and that's without your pig of a husband."

She laughed. "Pills. Pills don't make it go away. I've got to save the twins. None of this is their fault. They didn't ask to be born. I should have known. I should have known I'd be like her." Suddenly she looked at me. "They'll take them away from me."

"Now you're being crazy."

"You should take them. You're their guardian."

"Stop this, Helen."

"You don't want them."

"No one is going to take your children away. You just need to sort yourself out."

"Whatever you do, don't let my mother get her hands on my boys."

"Stop it."

"Promise," said Helen.

"This is a stupid conversation."

"Promise me, Tessa."

I thought I was dealing with a woman on the verge of a break-down. I would have promised her anything.

"You've thought it yourself, though, haven't you? Helen is doing a shit job of this, I could do better than that. Don't lie to me and tell me you haven't." I felt shame creep up into my cheeks. In my most evil thoughts, while gripped by the terrible green-eyed monster, I had indeed had that thought.

"That was before I knew how very hard it is. Honestly, Helen, I had no idea. I saw the perfect Pampers baby on telly and thought it was all smiles and bubble bath, and yes, I have to admit, I thought it looked pretty easy. I didn't know babies could do this." I looked at her.

"It's not their fault. It's mine."

"You've got no support. I've been crap. Your mother hardly wins the 'good granny' award, and where the hell is Neil's family? I've never seen them at any of your parties."

"Neil doesn't like them."

"Why not?"

"Because he's an arsehole."

Frankly, hearing Helen talk like this was progress.

"In fact, if you're ever in Norwich, you should look them up. Neil is embarrassed by them, but it's them who should be embarrassed by him. If you're ever in Norwich, you should look them up."

She'd said that already. But I was still not likely to go to Norwich.

"They live off the cathedral green. It's easy to find because there is a weeping willow in the garden. It goes down to water. It's the only one with a weeping willow."

"We need to work out what you're going to do."

"They are lovely people. A real happy home."

"Right. Norwich. Cathedral. Weeping willow. Got it."

"Happy home. That's good."

Helen's eyes were beginning to close.

"Wake up."

"I'm so tired." Her head nodded forward. "So tired." She literally fell asleep sitting up. All I knew about depression was that it wiped you out so I eased Helen back on to the sofa. I looked at my watch. I would have liked to go home, get some sleep, tidy the flat, but Helen needed the sleep more and with Rose gone, someone had to look after the babies. Neil couldn't, even if he did come home. Which I actually hoped he wouldn't.

That Sunday afternoon, while Helen lay catatonic on the sofa, I played Mummy with the twins. I loved it, for an hour or so. They gurgled at my animal impressions and I enjoyed holding their attention. Their eyes followed me everywhere. Only when I left them to make a cup of tea and some toast did they start to grizz—which led me to the premature conclusion that looking after kids was a piece of cake, as long as you had nothing else to do. And that included going for a pee. I made three cups of tea over the period of that afternoon and drank none of them. I had the twins asleep in my arms when Helen finally stirred. She made some coffee, took it upstairs to have a shower, and came back down twenty minutes later. She seemed much better. Amazing what caffeine and make-up can do.

"Thank you for letting me get that off my chest."

"With all due respect," I said quietly, "I think it's going to take a little more than a chat with me to sort out your problems."

"You're right. Neil has to be dealt with and I am going to deal with him. This shouldn't have gone on as long as it has."

"I know a very good divorce lawyer," I said.

"I can't afford to get divorced," she replied. Then she laughed.

"Only joking. Don't worry, you remember my solicitor, he makes a pretty good ally. He's good at dealing with Marguerite, too."

"And what about seeing a doctor?"

Helen met my gaze. "I have a very understanding doctor," she said.

"Good. Talk to him, then."

I couldn't bear it, she looked so sad. "I will," she said.

"I think you should give up breastfeeding, too. It's wiping you out, you've lost far too much weight."

No wonder Neil wanted Helen to feed, I thought. It kept her locked up behind her pearly gates while he went out and sampled the pleasures of early stardom.

"We'll get you back on your feet, Helen, don't you worry. You're a child of the universe, remember?"

Helen looked at me then. "I've lost a bit of the magic dust, haven't I?" she said quietly.

To the point that you are barely recognizable. "It's natural. I don't know much about marriage and kids, but I guess it's hard."

Helen nodded. "I thought it would be easier than this. I thought I'd feel bigger as two. I didn't realize I'd feel smaller."

I hugged her because I had no idea how to respond. Neil had been a panic buy, but she was well over the twenty-eight-day returns policy.

"Thank you, Tessa. You have always been a great friend to me and I know I'm not that easy."

"Who is? The older I get the more I realize everyone's a bit nuts."

"You're not."

"Don't be fooled."

"I don't care what you say, I couldn't have got this far without you."

I felt a pang of guilt. I'd been so mean, so unsupportive. "I'm sorry I didn't realize what a tough time you were having. I think I was jealous."

"Jealous of Neil and me?"

"OK, well maybe not the Neil bit."

"I've really fucked up," she said. I presumed she was talking about Neil.

"Nothing you can't change."

"It's going to get really tough. He'll come after me, he'll try and get the twins, he'll ask for ludicrous amounts of money, I know it."

"He has a problem with drugs, and a problem with booze. What court in the land would give a parent like that the twins?"

"None."

"There you are, then. What have you got to worry about?" I took Helen's hand and squeezed it. She smiled at me.

"You're right," she said. "I want them to have a happy home, Tessa. I didn't and look what it's done to me. I don't want that for the twins. I'll do anything to make sure that doesn't happen."

"OK. I'll help you with the twins too. Francesca has had three kids, she'll have all the answers. I bet every new mother feels like this, in way over their heads, knackered, depressed, I bet it's all normal. We just need to get Neil out of the way." I was trying to be helpful.

"You think?"

"Yes. I know the girl from China Beach is in there somewhere, we've just got to find her again."

"I'm pathetic," said Helen.

"You're not. You've taken a beating but you'll be OK."

Helen suddenly stood. "You're right. Thank you. You must be desperate to go home, I'm so sorry for keeping you here and spoiling your evening."

"I'm OK. I've got no plans."

"Actually, I think it would be better if you went. I could do with spending some time on my own with the boys, and if Neil comes home, we should be alone. You've been here all day, you must want to get home."

"Of course, right. Well, OK then. If you're sure."

"I need to do this by myself. But thank you for everything."

"I'll go and change," I said.

"It's OK. Give the stuff back to me another time," said Helen. "Here's a bag for your dress and shoes."

Did I get the feeling I was being hurried out of the house? Absolutely. But I had no idea why.

I took the number 52 to Victoria and walked along the Embankment to the flat. I think I passed every love-struck couple in London. It was the decent weather. It brought them all out of their love nests. I trounced back in my pink velour to the sanctity of my flat, forgetting that I'd left it in a tip. Clothes crises do that to small studio apartments. My mail winked at me from the breakfast bar. I had unread emails in my in-box and a DVD to return. To hell with it, I thought, changing out of Helen's clothes. I looked up the cinema times on the Internet, put on my old flying jacket and a thick hat, took the roof off the car and drove up the King's Road in shades. I could. So I would.

I spent the next few hours smiling through blissful sobs to some ridiculous rom-com where, of course, the girl got the guy even though she was a bog-cleaner and he was a king—well, not quite that bad, but nearly. Then I sat outside in the sinking sunlight, watching the world go by, flicking through the Sunday papers and somehow, while going through the motions of enjoying my own company, I started enjoying my own company. Suicide watch for single Sunday-nighters had been temporarily axed due to a new inappropriate man in Samira's life, which was fine by me. I had enough on my plate with my old friends right now, I didn't have time for any new ones.

fairy-tale ending

On Monday morning the floor around my bed was still strewn with clothes from Saturday night. I was losing control of my life. But rather than spend the morning clearing up and preparing for my first interview, which is what I should have been doing, I pulled on some jeans, a long-sleeved white T-shirt, pink Converse and hopped into the car. I had decided that the only person who could set Helen straight was Francesca. The model mother. The woman with all the answers. It was probably a mad thing to do, but I felt I had to do something. Guilt does that. I drove to Poppy and Katie's school and arrived just in time to see two over-sized backpacks disappear between the double doors.

"I was supposed to be clearing out the garden shed today," said Francesca, kissing me on the cheek. "But I still feel so lousy from Saturday night that all I can do is eat."

"Quite the party girl you were."

"It was those Martinis that Ben got us, killer drinks. I hope we weren't too annoying."

Ben. I'd been doing very well not thinking about him. Encasing myself in my friends' lives was helping, but just hearing his name made me feel funny.

"Your silence speaks volumes."

"Planning my wedding to the man I'd just met was probably a bit much," I said.

"Well, makes a change to you meddling in our lives—we were just getting our own back for once." She punctuated this with a taut smile. I was left-footed, but she held the smile so I forged ahead regardless.

"Well, I'm on more meddling business this morning."

I thought she'd laugh, but she didn't. "I didn't think you were here for fun, not at this hour. There's a Starbucks round the corner," said Fran.

"Please, not Starbucks," I pleaded.

"Why not? Bad coffee?" she asked.

"Bad memories." I tried to take her arm, but she pulled away. I dismissed it. "Let's find a real coffee shop and I'll explain on the way." I told Fran about my hopeless attempt with the twins the previous morning and my concern for Helen's state of mind. Fran had done this three times—surely she could shed some light on the matter?

"So you came here to talk to me about Helen?"

"Yes. I was hoping you could speak to her."

"I thought Helen just drank too much on Saturday night."

"So did I at first, but things aren't good at home. She seems completely at sea with the twins. I'm worried about her."

"It's totally normal."

I shook my head. What I'd seen didn't look normal. "Are you sure? She seems really depressed. I don't think she can handle this."

"Hasn't she got huge amounts of help?" asked Francesca, with a tone that sounded tinged with disapproval.

"Not any more. She feels she's doing it all wrong."

"She probably is. Most people do. I made some terrible mistakes with Caspar. My mum tried to help but Nick and I were so proud and stubborn, and I suppose, looking back on it, we were being defensive. We'd got ourselves into this mess and we were going to cope, even if it killed us. Which it nearly did."

"I don't remember you having a bad time."

"You weren't really around that much."

I knew that was true. "Whenever we spoke on the phone you said everything was going well and how sweet Caspar was."

"He was. I adored him. He still drove us mad though. He was still sleeping in our bed at eight months. Eight months of lying in bed, convinced I was going to squash him."

"If you didn't like having him in bed, why didn't you put him in his cot?"

"Because he screamed until he was sick." She shook her head, remembering a dismal, distant time. "It was my fault. The demand-feeding was great in the beginning, he ate then slept, ate then slept. Easy. But, slowly and surely, it all went crazy. When he woke up he wanted to be fed to get back to sleep. Trouble was he was so tired he never ate enough, so he'd wake up again. It seemed to be every forty-five minutes during the night, so in the end it was easier to have him in bed with us. Once I woke up and he'd latched on by himself."

I squirmed.

"It was all my fault. Eventually my mum had to come and stay. She put him in his own bed and when he screamed she wouldn't let me go and pick him up. It was the most hideous thing in the world. I hated her, I hated myself for letting her do it, I hated Nick for not sticking up for me . . ." Francesca shook her head. "It was awful. And there was only one of him and I was much, much younger."

"And you have a nice mum," I said, thinking of Marguerite. "So what happened in the end?"

"Mum stood resolute; we had three nights of utter hell and then he slept happily through the night in his own cot, in his own room. There were the odd little yelps, but he learned to settle himself pretty quickly. In the end, I thought it was probably me who'd been keeping him awake. Any little noise and I'd stroke him, pick him up, check him. I was deranged with exhaustion. Nick was fed up with the whole thing. But no one was more tired than Caspar, poor little thing. If he could've spoken he probably would have said, 'Will you just fuck off and just leave me alone?' That's certainly what he says now, anyway."

"He doesn't."

"Yes, he does. A seminal moment in one's life when your baby towers over you and swears like a sailor. One for the baby book, I think."

"I thought things were better."

"Yes and no. Instead of disappearing off and going AWOL, he stays in his room all the time, listening to terrible music and burning joss sticks. A habit I have to thank you for."

I remained silent.

"Oh, look," said Fran. "A real coffee shop."

"He really told you to fuck off?"

"You know what," said Fran, holding open the door, "I really don't want to talk about it."

Fine by me.

The coffee came in a tall glass with a metal handle and a long spoon. I watched Fran drop hunks of brown sugar into her drink and slurp at the milky foam thirstily. I then watched as she inhaled a cinnamon and raisin swirl.

Since returning to England I had regained all the weight I'd lost in India. Not working was not good for my waistline—far too much opportunity to eat. And drink. The ten days with my parents had not helped. On top of that there had been lunches with friends. Teas with godchildren. Out most nights. I used to crawl in from work,

heat up a bowl of soup, have a bath and go to bed. Now I could usually find someone to have a drink with at six. That's a long evening of
consuming calories. I had promised myself I was going to be good,
but that was before the mention of joss sticks.

"How come you can eat anything and still stay so slim?" Sublimi-
nally I think I was trying to get Francesca on my side.

"Because I don't sit down between seven in the morning and nine
at night."

"But the kids are at school."

Francesca waved a threatening fork at me. "Don't you dare, Tessa
King."

"Dare what?"

"Make me justify my day to you. I get enough of that from
Nick."

"I didn't mean that, I promise. I thought you got a bit of time to
yourself with the kids at school, that's all."

"Time to myself to fix light bulbs, change loo rolls, pick up wet
towels, do the laundry, finish projects, take our shitty car to the
garage, unload the dishwasher, fill up the dishwasher, unload it again,
cook, shop, clear up in time to cook again . . . Shall I continue?"

"No."

"Fucking boring, isn't it?"

"Yes."

"Wait a few minutes, the sugar will hit my bloodstream and I'll
feel more reasonable."

I took a sip of my coffee and scalded my tongue. It seemed puny
to complain, so I replaced the cup and watched Francesca stab at the
rest of the pastry.

"This is what one night on the razz does to me," she said.

"I've never seen you like this, even after a night out," I said, trying
to be reassuring.

"That's because you're usually at work," said Francesca harshly.

Didn't see that left hook coming. "Nor on the weekends when I come over," I replied, with a defensive jab of my own. I'll take so much . . .

"On the weekends when people come over it's fun and I stop worrying about the minutiae."

I was confused. "What are you saying?"

"I'm not saying anything, Tessa."

What sounded like not saying anything felt like a swift low undercut to the ribs. Francesca turned away and ordered another milky coffee. I gave in and ordered one too.

"Tell me more about Helen," said Francesca. "She's too thin—is she eating?"

"She's always been thin."

"Not that thin. Though it does often happen when women give up breastfeeding, they suddenly shrink."

"She's still feeding them. She told me it made her lose weight."

"That's bollocks. What it does is give you a ferocious appetite. An appetite that is impossible to ignore. And you lay down this really pleasant layer of brown fat on all the worst bits. Tummy, bum, thighs get a nice mottled, jelly-like appearance. Charming, really."

"Francesca, I have never heard you be so negative in all my life. What's up with you?"

"I told you, I can't do late nights any more."

"Fran, you're only in your thirties, not your fifties!"

"Are you sure? I feel like I've been a grown-up for an awfully long time. I'm half tempted to buy myself an iPod, lock myself in my room, smoke dope and listen to Carole King."

"Dope?" I asked nervously.

Francesca looked at me. "Sorry, whatever they call it these days. Bung, skank, or the latest—you might not have heard it—joss sticks."

I felt uncomfortable meeting Francesca's gaze. The hostility suddenly fell into place. "Oh." I didn't know what to say.

"You should have told me that Caspar was smoking cannabis."

"He told me he'd stop."

"And you believed a sixteen-year-old boy?"

"I believed Caspar, yes." I frowned, knowing that wasn't quite right. "I mean, I wanted to believe him. I thought it was a blip."

"Well, that blip has meant he's been off school with acute conjunctivitis."

"Has he?"

"No," said Francesca, raising her voice. I watched her visibly regain control. "He hasn't been at school at all. He lied. He wrote a bloody note: God knows how he got hold of doctor's stationery."

Caspar fixed my computer when it did crazy things. He's a genius with computers. "I bet it was in IT class. There isn't a great deal your son can't do on the computer."

"It was a rhetorical question."

"Oh, sorry."

"You should have given me a heads-up."

"I didn't want to betray his confidence."

"He's my son, Tessa."

Right hook and I was down.

Francesca made me tell her about what really happened the night of Caspar's sixteenth birthday. She was shaken by the information that Caspar was already experimenting with more than just cannabis. She made me tell her what I was really looking for when I went snooping around in his room, and what, if anything, I had found. I assured her that if I had found anything I would have told her, but since I had just admitted to lying to her, my argument didn't hold much weight.

"When did you find out Caspar had been missing school?" I asked, changing tack.

"Friday."

"So you were pissed off with me on Saturday night."

"No. I had no idea you knew. I was on a mission to get obliterated. I succeeded."

"I noticed."

"Tessa, this isn't funny."

"Sorry."

"Caspar and I had a showdown yesterday and he dropped you in it, told us you'd said it was OK."

"Bollocks, I said that."

"Well, I don't think he was much impressed with your snooping. I didn't believe his version, and now I know what really happened."

"I'm sorry that I didn't tell you what I was looking for, but you said things were better so I wanted to give him the benefit of the doubt—"

"While searching his room for drugs."

"Fran, I'll take the rap for my part in this, but this isn't really all my fault."

"You should have told me about his birthday, that cock-and-bull story about Zac lacing his drink when actually it was drugs he was experimenting with and you knew."

"I told him to tell you everything, but I left it up to him to do the right thing."

"Well, he didn't. And frankly, nor did you."

I don't like being boxed into a corner. My natural instinct is to come out fighting. "Francesca, it was a complete freak of chance that I saw him that night and gave him my card."

"And enough money to get high."

"And enough money to get *home*. If I hadn't we'd all be none the wiser. Come on, Nick told me he'd been a nightmare for months, driving you mad, having rows, slamming doors. Something has been wrong for a while. I admit I didn't realize it was this serious, but then nor did you and you've been living with him."

Francesca looked deflated. It was so much easier being angry with someone else.

"How long do you think it's been going on?" she asked quietly.

"I don't know."

"Where does he get the money from?"

That I did know but didn't want to say. "Have you noticed anything going missing? The odd fiver?"

"Christ, Tessa, are you saying Caspar is stealing?!" She ran her hands through her hair. "Not my kid. No. If I've tried to do anything for my children, it is teach them morals."

"What about the beer?"

She put her head in her hands and swore again. How could I tell her that her kid lifted fifty quid from my wallet the moment my back was turned?

"That was for a party."

"What about selling things, then?"

She shook her head. "Hang on, he sold his bike to a friend. It was too small for him. He was going to buy another, but . . ." Francesca paused. "How could I not notice something as big as not buying another bike?"

"He did say that the girls took up a lot of your time."

"So this is my fault?"

"I didn't mean it like that. That is just Caspar's adolescent perspective."

"They do, though. There are two of them for a start, and they are considerably younger."

"This is not your fault. This is Caspar's fault. You have been a model parent. They don't come better than you and Nick."

Francesca just looked at me sadly.

"What does Nick say?"

"He's ready to throw him out."

"I don't think that would help."

"Nor do I. So now we're arguing too."

"Well, it's working then, isn't it? Caspar is getting your attention. Then again, he might actually have a real problem."

Francesca frowned. "Do you think he does? He's so young!"

I had to tell her what I knew. "He did steal £50 from me."

"What! When?"

"The day I came home."

Francesca stood up.

"I'm sorry, I didn't want to have to tell you."

"I've got to go." She ferreted around in her bag.

"Leave it," I said. "I'll do it."

"I can write you a check for the money Caspar stole."

"Absolutely not. Caspar will work off his debt and if you want to send him over to mine this week, I have millions of little jobs that need doing."

"None that would be horrid enough."

"The gutter on my balcony is blocked."

"No, it's gone beyond that. Way beyond."

"You know, Fran, I'm sure he didn't think of it as stealing. Not from me."

"You think your relationship is that special?"

I didn't like the edge in her voice.

"Well, you're wrong. He has been stealing from us for ages."

"But you said—"

"I didn't want to think it was true. But it is. It's been in front of my nose for months. Sorry, Tessa, I really have to go."

"OK." She turned to leave, but I foolishly grabbed her arm. "Do you mind if I get Helen to call you for a chat?"

"About what?"

"About how to stop making mistakes with her boys."

"Tell her to get used to it."

I screwed up my face. "Huh?"

"Honestly Tessa, I would have thought it fairly obvious right now that since I am still making those mistakes, I am not the ideal person to talk to."

I watched her go. On reflection, perhaps I should have waited for a better moment to mention Helen again.

I walked back to my car when my phone buzzed in my pocket. I didn't recognize the number so I left it to go on to answerphone. I never used to be so guarded. It comes from having been spied on by an obsessed man. No wonder I haven't moved on to the next stage of life. I was too busy fending off a man who, having spent the day sending me crazed emails, went home to his wife and children. Kind of puts you off the whole thing. But as I walked I knew this was another lie; like the lie of telling yourself that your son isn't stealing, when he palpably is. I told myself that love couldn't be further from my mind, when actually, it provided the background musak to my life. My phone bleeped. I called the message service.

"Hi, Tessa, it's James Kent. Last time you ran out on me, this time you disappeared into thin air. Maybe you've got this weird witching hour thing when you get all hairy and start sucking blood, so I thought daytime might be safer. Are you hungry?" He left a number. I scribbled it on the back of my hand and stared at it. If not now, then when? What the hell was I waiting for? Ben to leave Sasha? No. Ben not to leave Sasha? No. Life was passing me by. If I wanted to dip my hand in the lucky gene pool of life, I had to buy into the game. I dialed.

"You mixed your fairy tales up. Vampires aren't hairy. Werewolves are, but I don't think they suck blood, they just rip you from limb to limb. It's more a total consumption thing with werewolves."

"Hello, Tessa King."

I liked the way he said that.

"Hello, James Kent."

"So are you?"

"Not unless there is total amnesia after the change," I replied.

"I meant hungry, but we can continue with the nonsense if you like."

"I like the nonsense."

"So do I, but it doesn't get me a date, does it?"

I felt a tingle. A real one. I ought to reply. But I couldn't. I was too busy grinning.

"Starving," I finally mustered.

"I thought for a second you'd vanished again."

"Sorry. Right now, actually, I'm starving. Had a measly breakfast." I glanced at my watch. "Is 11:07 too early for lunch?"

"Not at all. Where are you?"

"At the gates of Hammond School." As I said it I knew it was a mistake.

"Not more godchildren?"

"No, but I was on godchildren business."

"Don't you work?"

"I accept charitable donations. Where shall we meet?"

"What about lunch at the Ivy?"

"I'm not dressed for the Ivy."

"Even better. The scruffier you are, the more important they think you are."

"I don't believe you."

"You're right not to, but if you are with me they'll think you're some comic genius on the cusp of international stardom."

"Does that mean I have to be funny?"

"Real comic geniuses aren't funny."

"Is the Ivy open so early?"

"No."

"So this was all a bluff?"

"Complete bluff. I couldn't get a table for love or money."

For some reason I didn't believe him. I looked at my watch again. I'd go and check on Helen afterwards. "So where do we go for lunch at 11:09?" I asked.

I followed his instructions to the letter and half an hour later parked down a dodgy-looking side street off the Edgware Road, just north of the Westway flyover. I filled the meter with coins, crossed the road and pushed open the door to an easily missed Burmese restaurant. I was greeted by the owner with overt fondness and was shown to our table. Since the restaurant was not much bigger than a card table, I thought that was a nice touch. James was already sitting at the table, a strong black coffee in front of him and a bottle of unlabelled mineral water. The cooks clattered behind an open hatch in the wall behind him and an extremely elderly Burmese woman sat next to a plastic banana plant in the corner. She was chewing betel nut. I knew that because her mouth was stained a telltale red. I'd seen women all over Vietnam do it. I decided it was a good omen.

James stood and kissed me gingerly hello on one cheek. We sat. The owner brought me a small thick black coffee, poured out some water in a mismatched glass and then asked me how hungry I really was. I told him I was ravenous. He smiled and retreated to the kitchen.

"Strange place, this."

"I know it's a little out of the way, but it is the best food in London."

"Burmese?" I asked, not completely convinced.

"Go with me on this one. You don't even order, he just brings you the food."

"So how come you can get out of work at a moment's notice?"

"Because it's my name on the letterhead."

"Impressive."

"Not really. A few quid at Prontaprint gets you fairly decent stationery."

"The clients take a little longer."

"Yeah, but I've been at it long enough."

"How long?"

"Twenty-four years."

I was quite taken aback by that. He looked my age. "Did you start work when you were three?" I thought I should be generous, since what I was really saying was, "How old are you?"

"No, after university. I'll put you out of your misery. I'm forty-six."

Wow. Four years off fifty. I was surprised. Yes, he had greying hair, but he was so sexy. Ah well, being with an older man made me feel like a spring chick, which was no mean feat these days.

"What about you?"

"Sixty-four, but the virgin's blood gives me an excellent complexion. Do you think it's too early for a beer?"

"Nice change of subject."

"What my father would call a run down the blind side."

"Do you get on well with your dad?"

"Very. I came late in life and I'm his only daughter, child, in fact, so naturally I can do no wrong."

"And you haven't found a man to match him?"

I felt Ben's lips on mine. Heat flared up my face. I'd involuntarily put my hand to my mouth. James misunderstood my expression.

Or maybe he read it perfectly because he pulled my hand down and held it.

"Sorry, that came out more intrusive than it meant to sound. Let's make a pact now, no rehashing of past love lives in any shape or form." He shook the hand he was holding. "As of now, it is a banned topic."

My first reaction was to be suspicious, ask him what he had to hide. But I had to stop finding excuses to keep people away from me, because at our age, who didn't have something to hide? So imagining a fairy-tale ending, I held his hand and shook it back. "Deal," I said with a smile.

"Tell me why you're not working at the moment," he asked.

So I did, because my ex-boss did not fall under the heading of love life, in any shape or form. For once I did not relay what had in fact been an incredibly stressful time with the jovial inserts that I usually did. I did not laugh about having my boss stand sentry under a lamppost outside my flat. I did not add how flattered I was by the pictures taken of my flat from across the river, and how the grainy effect of a long-distant lens did wonders for my complexion. I did not imitate, with an am-dram voice, the middle-of-the-night phone calls from his furious wife who called me a whore. I did not pretend that I was in two minds about sending back the Gucci hand-bag, the Hermès scarf, the invitation to a weekend at the Cipriani in Venice. He listened beautifully and I felt a great weight lift from my shoulders. I felt the guilt ease. My ex-boss had been punished with a mental breakdown. I was here, having lunch with a lovely man, and I was OK. I had not imagined it, I had not exaggerated it, I had not started it, but I had needed this break to get my head back together.

"Do you feel bitter that it was you who had to go?"

Interesting question.

"I mean, you worked there for how long?" he continued.

"Nearly ten years, but I couldn't face that battle at the time."

"And now?"

"Nothing I can do. He's gone now. Anyway, I signed an agreement, took the hush money and the letter of recommendation that my mother couldn't have written."

"Glowing?"

"Blinding," I replied.

"I've no doubt you'll be snapped up in no time."

"Hope so. All this leisure time leaves far too much time to think."

"To be avoided," said James.

"At all costs," I agreed.

The dishes came and went. We shared them all. I quickly realized I had underestimated how well lunch would go, and had to go and move the car and fill another meter up with more coins. I returned to find the table covered with new dishes. I began to feel as if our host was breaking me in gently to Burmese cuisine, though it was obvious that James had eaten there many times before. When I'd finally stopped talking about myself I asked him why he had chosen this spot above all others.

"You never see anyone you know," he replied. "Business lunches in my field mean you go to the latest, best restaurants but never get to enjoy the place and see far too many people you are supposed to know, but don't remember the name of." He scooped some spinach dish on to his fork and proffered it to me. I ate it. He'd done this two or three times already and it felt wonderfully intimate. I was really enjoying myself. "You can't do that at a business lunch. You can't say, 'Wow, this is delicious, try it,' and stick your fork in some TV producer's mouth."

"My goddaughter—"

"Cora?"

I was impressed. "Yes, Cora. Well, she was very premature and is still little for her age."

"What is she, five?"

"Seven."

"She's so slight."

"Billy has had huge trouble getting her to eat. Cora just isn't interested, which the doctors say not to worry about, but of course Billy worries about. Anyway, she realized she'd gone too far when she was holding out yet another spoonful of something nutritious saying, 'Try it, it's delicious,' and Cora, who is the only child I know who doesn't do tantrums, flung the spoon across the room and yelled, 'I HATE delicious!'"

I gave myself another mouthful of food that I didn't have room for to stop myself talking about my godchildren. It didn't augment the sex-kitten feel that I should have been exuding but kept forgetting about. James made it far too easy for me to be me, whoever that was.

"I envy you. I have a godson whom I don't like. He whines all the time and his parents always make excuses for him—he's got a cold, he's over-tired, he needs refueling—when actually he is just a whingeing little Mummy's boy. Naturally, I overcompensate horribly, and spend more money on him than anyone in my entire family."

"How old is he?"

"Fifteen."

I laughed. "Something else we have in common. I too have a sixteen-year-old godson, but he's a pickpocketing, dope-smoking truant."

"Nice."

"Children," I said, with a slight guffaw. "Who'd have 'em?"

James looked at me seriously for a second.

Oops. Don't get me wrong, I'm not the child-catcher, but, well, you didn't see my friend Francesca this morning, or my friend Helen yesterday, or my friend Billy sitting in the bus stop so she could pocket my twenty quid to buy her daughter some healthy food which will take all her imagination and powers of persuasion to get down her throat.

"You don't want kids?"

"I haven't really thought about it." Which was the moment I stopped being me and started being the person I was supposed to be.

"That's a lie," said James Kent softly.

"A great big whopping lie," I said, nodding.

"You know what?" James stood up. "Let's go for a walk and find somewhere to have coffee before we talk ourselves out of something that has barely begun."

"I like the way you said that," I said, standing up too.

"I like the way it sounded." He paid the bill and we left. The old woman was still sitting in the corner chewing betel nut.

We stopped at a little Italian deli and had espresso and some gelato standing up at the counter chatting about less intense things. Another hour passed easily by, then the place started to fill up with rather large intimidating-looking kids. We made our way on to the street.

"A sea of school children," I said, dodging a football, then a bike. James looked at his watch and swore.

"I've got to go," he said. "I'm really sorry. Can I get you a cab?" he said, hailing one down.

"No, you take it, I've got the car."

The taxi pulled up.

"Where to?" asked the driver.

"Baker Street," he replied. "Sorry to leave so unceremoniously."

"It's been really, really fun. Thank you for lunch, pudding, good chat. Go. I don't want you to be late."

"Let's do this again," he said. Without kissing me goodbye he climbed into the cab, which pulled out into the traffic and accelerated away in a rude cough of black smoke. I was a little deflated, I'd been rather hoping for a lengthy goodbye.

I walked back to my car. I had a million and one things to do, so I should have been grateful for a few hours to get my life in order, but I didn't fancy going home, and anyway, I needed to check on Helen, so I turned the car around. At the junction, my phone rang. I put the car into neutral.

"Hello?"

"Would tomorrow be too soon?"

Instant re-inflation. "No."

"Great. How about dinner tomorrow night, then?"

"Dinner sounds perfect."

"I'll book somewhere where pumpkins are welcome and get back to you."

"Which reminds me, how did you get my number?"

"Your friend Sasha gave it to me."

"She didn't tell me you'd asked for my number."

"I didn't. She just put it in my hand."

"Oh."

"Well, I'd been looking for you for two hours, so she probably felt a bit sorry for me. Or perhaps she's just desperate to get rid of you and goes around pressing your number into the palm of any bloke with a forlorn expression on his face."

"Perhaps," I repeated. *Perhaps, perhaps, perhaps.*

"Was I the only one who called?"

"Yes."

"Good. See you tomorrow, Tessa King."

I hauled back my good feeling, but it wasn't all there. "Goodbye, James Kent." I put the car back into gear, and accelerated out into Edgware Road.

The traffic was horrendous. Every cunning move I made to wiggle through the heavy afternoon traffic was thwarted by double-parked cars being loaded with children. I wasn't used to driving around the city in the mid-afternoon. If I had been, I would have known not to venture anywhere during the "school run." It was a nightmare, so forty-five minutes later, stuck somewhere in Paddington, I called Helen. She didn't answer her home phone, or her mobile, so I turned the car round and headed for home.

bombshell

Billy wanted me to get proof that Christoph was earning signifi-cantly more than he was telling the courts but she didn't want me to go any further until she was ready. I feared all my efforts would be in vain and Billy would never be ready. My friend the divorce lawyer spent his days screwing as much money out of people who at one point in their lives had stood in front of their friends and family and declared to love, honor and whatever the modern way of saying obey is. I asked him where that common ground had gone and he told me that what hadn't been eroded away by infidelity, unhappi-ness and neglect was demolished by the lawyers. I had attended his wedding a few years back, so I enquired after his own marriage. I was relieved to hear that it was going well, and asked him what his secret was. "I know how horrid divorce is, so I make it work, we make it work," he said, then added, "but just in case, my assets are well protected." I didn't think he was joking. He gave me a number of a private investigator who specialized in this field, but warned me he was expensive, although the expenses would be recouped if we won. There was no way Billy would go for that, so I had to be a bit more conniving. Christoph was clever, but he was also vain. I intended to get him on his vanity. I put a call through to Cora, who I knew would be at home with the nanny. It may be using an underhand source, but Cora knew things she didn't even know she knew.

"Hi, sweet pea, how are you?"

"Tired," said Cora.

"Long day at school?"

"Uh-huh." She coughed to make her point.

"That doesn't sound good," I said.

"I've got bogeys on my chest."

"Sounds like it. Have you been to the doctor's?"

There was silence. I guessed that Cora was shaking her head.

"Mummy at work?"

More silence. Cora nodding. Billy should have got a job in a doctor's surgery, instead of a dentist's. It would have been much more useful. Since food wasn't her thing, especially sugary things, Cora never had any trouble with her teeth.

"Just a quick question, then. Do you remember the postcard Christoph sent you with the picture of the boat on it?"

"Yes."

"Do you still have it?"

"No."

Damn it. My first lead was a dead-end.

"Mummy keeps it in her bedside table drawer inside a book."

Oh, Billy. "Great," I said, full of faux cheerfulness, "I need it. Clever Mummy for keeping it."

Cora wasn't convinced, so I didn't bother trying to convince her. I was about to ask her to get it, but she had quite a bad coughing fit, and I had to wait a minute until it calmed down.

"Have you got any cough medicine?" I asked her when the coughing had subsided.

"Magda has gone to get some lemons."

Gone to get . . . ? "Who is with you?"

"She'll only be a minute."

"OK, well, let's chat until she gets back."

"I'm too tired to chat, Godmummy T."

"OK. Take the phone, sit on the sofa and I'll tell you a story. OK?"

"OK."

I heard her walk across the room, climb on to the sofa and snuggle down.

"Ready?"

"Uh-huh."

"Once upon a time . . ." One minute turned out to be sixteen. My story waffled on, making no sense, with no obvious plot and no obvious finishing line, but it didn't matter, since Cora was asleep for most of it. I was grateful for the lungful of phlegm the poor girl had because it provided me with a reassuring backdrop to my pathetic tale. As long as I could hear her breathing, she wasn't burning to death in a house fire, or being kidnapped, or choking, or swallowing bleach, or any of the millions of life-threatening things a household presents to a well-guarded child, let alone an unaccompanied one.

"Cora! I'm back!" came a distant voice. Footsteps. A crackle as the phone was lifted from Cora's hand.

"Hello?" I said loudly.

"Fuck."

"Madga, it's me, Tessa."

"Hello, Tessa."

"You left Cora alone?"

"I had to get her something, she's been coughing and coughing. I thought hot lemon and honey would help."

"But she's been on her own!"

"Billy sometimes does go to the shop on the corner. I was as quick as I could be."

I liked Magda. She was honest and great with Cora, but it wasn't that quick.

"What's wrong with her?"

"A bug."

Cora got lots of bugs. Billy said if she kept her off school every time Cora got a bug, she'd never be at school. It worried me. It worried me that she wasn't stronger. All that personality, in such a little frame. It would probably help if she ate better food. Saw the same doctor. Got out of London occasionally. All the things that were possible with a bit of extra money.

I told Magda about the postcard in Billy's drawer and waited while she went to get it for me. I remembered when Cora received that postcard. It fell through the letter box on Cora's seventh birthday. We were all amazed—Christoph never remembered Cora's birthday. Turned out he still hadn't. It was a coincidence. It was just a quick note saying that he wasn't going to make it back for half-term since he was still in Dubai on work and his family were going to come out and join him. It was a fairly cursory note, hurtful, but cursory. On the front was a picture of an enormous yacht. Christoph didn't send pictures of other people's yachts. It wasn't his style. He was showing off to Billy, letting her know what she was missing, turning the knife while stoking the fantasy. It worked, too. She'd kept the postcard though it was addressed to Cora.

What I wanted was the name of that boat. Armed with that, I put a call through to Camper & Nicholsons, the best boat builders I knew of, and asked them how I would go about tracking down a yacht registered in the UAE. They were extremely helpful. I felt a real sense of excitement as my sleuthing started to reap results, so I rewarded myself with a glass of wine.

Halfway through pulling the cork, the phone rang. It was Francesca.

"Is this a good time to talk?"

"Hang on."

I finished opening the bottle, poured myself a large glass, slipped off my shoes, and lay on the sofa.

"It is now."

"I'm sorry about this morning."

"No, I'm sorry, Fran, I should have told you."

"You know I have always loved the relationship you and Caspar have. I wouldn't have survived if you hadn't taken him off my hands so often when he was younger. I realize that I can't have it both ways. He trusts you."

"Trusted me."

"I didn't tell him we'd spoken. He doesn't know I know about the speed, the police or the money he stole. I have given him the opportunity to tell me everything. I've put him on the train to stay with his grandparents until he's allowed back at school. I packed his bag and searched his pockets. If he had drugs on him, they were up his arse. We'll see what happens next."

"You needn't protect me. I've been thinking too. Above all, you are my friend, not your son. You come first. He needs a good shake-up. Drop me in it if you have to, but get him to see sense."

"Hopefully it won't come to that."

Personally, I thought it already had. "What has he stolen from you?"

I felt her wince. "Nothing for sure, but too many things have gone missing. Money I could have sworn I'd left for a school trip, the laundry, twenty quid here or there that I thought I had in my wallet. I think the CD collection has been dwindling. And his has disappeared completely. My pay-as-you-go mobile phone. I thought I'd been pickpocketed."

"Oh Fran, I'm so sorry."

"Why is he doing this to me?"

"I don't think he's doing it to you."

"He is." Francesca sighed heavily.

"What have I got to do to convince you, to reassure you, that you are and have always been an exceptional mother to that boy? What you gave up for him, without prejudice, is still beyond me."

"You sound like a lawyer."

"I am a lawyer."

Francesca sighed again. Or was it a sob? A quiet sob.

"Where's Nick?"

"Still in Saigon."

"Everything all right?" I'd just been talking to a divorce lawyer who was never out of work. It got my imagination running on overdrive. I could hear Helen quoting that bloody poem at me: *do not distress yourself with dark imaginings* . . . Easy to say, not so easy to do.

"Yeah, we're fine. We're good. I would like a little more support from him on this one, but Nick just isn't that kind of man. He has many other strengths, but he can't do this one."

"You are very generous to your husband."

"As he is with me. When I get wound up because things haven't been put back in their proper place, completely unimportant things that get me incensed, he just calmly brings me down off the ledge."

"You have always been an enviable team."

This comment made Francesca fall silent.

"You don't sound so good. Do you want me to come over?" I asked. I checked my glass of wine. I wasn't over the limit yet.

"No. I don't think I could tell this to your face."

"Tell me what?"

I waited. It was a legal trick.

I heard Francesca take a deep breath. "There was a time when Nick and I weren't doing so well."

I wasn't expecting that.

"That's normal, isn't it? Even great marriages can't be fantastic all the time."

"I met someone."

Bombshell. I instinctively sat up on the sofa and placed my feet squarely on the floor.

"When?"

"Caspar was twelve."

I relaxed. Many moons had waxed and waned since then and Nick and Francesca were still firmly together.

"I nearly left."

"Left Nick?"

"I can't believe it now, but Tessa, what I felt for this man felt so real. I honestly thought I had made a mistake, that I had never felt for Nick what I felt for this man. It was utterly all-consuming. I was possessed."

"But you've always been so, so happy with each other."

"It takes a lot of work to be that happy. We got lazy, I guess. Someone once said marriage is like standing in a corridor lined with doors. You go off through your door, he goes through his, but at the end of the day you have to come back to the corridor, touch base, hold hands, because through every door are more doors, and beyond them, more again, and if you both go through too many without coming back to the corridor, you may never find your way back. That's pretty much what happened; it didn't take long, either."

I hadn't really listened. I was still reeling. Fran had an affair. "Who was it?"

"Doesn't matter who it was. None of it was real. Poppy wasn't talking, Katie was being an utter madam, Caspar was hitting puberty and I was lost. I met him in the doctor's surgery. I'd had a cough for months that I couldn't shift."

"I remember that."

"I was utterly depleted. Nick was off saving the world and I was nothing. Nobody. We started meeting for coffee. I was just grateful to have a friend who wasn't another moaning mother like me. He was a lecturer, you know I've always been attracted to intelligence. I fed off him. It would have been fine if I'd told Nick right from the beginning that I'd made a friend, albeit divorced, male and supremely clever, but I didn't. The secrecy of it started to take on its own life. Finally there was something more exciting in my life than nappies, the Mr. Men books and having doors slammed in my face and washing out Caspar's skid marks. Why can't boys wipe their own arses? Why can't men, for that matter?"

"Sorry," I said, speaking at last. "Can't help you on that one."

Francesca fell silent again.

"Are you sure you don't want me to come over?" I asked.

"No. Just stay on the phone."

"OK."

"I'm so ashamed, Tessa. That's why I could never tell you."

"Fran, you don't have to tell me anything. It was a long time ago now, it's over."

"I have to tell someone."

Tell me what? Was there more?

Slowly, she went on. "I think I know why Caspar is doing this."

Did teenagers need a reason to be hateful to their parents?

"Do you remember when I asked you to have Caspar to stay for the whole weekend? Nick was away and my mum had taken the girls."

I'd had Caspar to stay quite a few weekends.

"I had gone back to college—"

"Oh yes, it was some weekend field trip or something, lecture course, I can't even remember what you were . . ." My voice trailed off. Studying, was what I was going to say. Was she going to tell me there was no weekend course?

"There was no course."

"You dropped it, halfway through. I remember thinking it wasn't like you to be so flaky."

"I mean, there was no course at all."

"Oh." That was a substantial lie to tell your friends and family.

"I wasn't thinking at the time. I got myself in way over my head."

"How long did it go on for?"

"Six weeks. It ended that weekend."

"Why?"

"I thought you'd know."

"Me? Why me?" I stood up. I needed more wine for this.

"You brought Caspar home, that Saturday afternoon."

"Did I?"

"You stayed in the car."

"Did I?"

"Caspar must have let himself in with his key."

I didn't like where this was going. "What happened, Fran?"

"I was hoping you could tell me."

I poured more than I meant to into my glass. "This is the first I've heard of any of this."

"So Caspar didn't tell you?"

"Tell me what?"

"That he'd seen me."

"No."

"He didn't behave strangely when he came back to the car?"

"No."

"Are you sure, Tessa? Think. This is important." She sounded desperate.

"What do you think he saw, Francesca?"

"I fucked up, I really fucked up. I was supposed to be ending it. I was. We'd walked around the park in the rain for hours talking, he only came in to dry off . . ."

I didn't dare speak.

"I was so lonely." Francesca was crying now. "I couldn't be in the same room with any of them. Sometimes when Katie was dawdling as she always did, I would yank her by the arm, knowing it was going to hurt, but yanking her anyway. I was angry with myself for getting into this situation and taking it out on them—"

"Francesca, what did Caspar see?"

"I don't know, all I heard was the door slam."

"What could he have seen?"

"Oh shit, I can't even say it . . ."

"Where were you?"

I heard Francesca take a deep breath. I said a silent prayer. A few of them. Not on the kitchen table. Nor the stairs. Or the floor, the sofa, up against the wall . . . There were too many prayers and I figured God wasn't particularly partial to hearing all of these rather sordid details. Adultery being one of his bugbears. The truth was there is no good position or place to catch your mother having sex with another man.

"Our bed," said Francesca finally.

Better than on all fours on the sitting-room floor, I guess. I could not pretend I wasn't shocked. Me? After my friend Samira, I was the least prudish person I knew. I was very careful with my next words, more careful even with how they sounded.

"OK, let's think about this rationally," I said brightly.

"You're horrified, aren't you?"

"No." Yes.

"Disappointed?"

"No." A little. "You would have had your reasons—"

"I felt like someone had bricked up all my fire exits. I was suffocating. I couldn't get out."

"Not a good time to go around lighting fires, then."

Francesca sighed heavily. I didn't want to sound like a school mistress. I wanted to try and be a good friend. "You would have had your reasons and you can explain all of them if you like, but it's in the past, it happened, whatever. Let's concentrate on Caspar for now. He wasn't any different from when he got out of the car to when he came back in a few minutes later."

"Are you sure?"

I thought hard. It was a long time ago, but I was fairly sure I would have noticed something. Caspar could not have witnessed what Francesca thought he had witnessed, then get back into the car as jovial as before. We went to get burgers as a treat. I remember where we went. I remember what we ate. And it was a lot. I can't imagine he'd have had much of an appetite if he'd seen anything.

"Did you hear him come in?"

"No."

"Well, then."

"We were making a lot of noise, he'd have heard something."

I felt a bit queasy. That sort of detail made it all too real. I preferred talking around the issue.

"Why had we come back?" I asked. "I can't remember."

"Some voucher for the War Museum."

Of course. After the burgers we went and looked at a lot of killing machines that Caspar was fascinated with at the time. "Good memory," I said.

"Not the sort of thing you forget. He had left them on the kitchen table. If only I'd seen them, but I hadn't—hadn't bloody clocked them sitting there."

"If they were on the kitchen table he wouldn't have come upstairs."

"Our clothes were all over the place."

"Well, you're a fucking idiot." It didn't make me feel any better, and I was pretty sure it made Francesca feel worse and I was sorry as soon as I'd said it, but the words just blurted out. We both sighed and for a little while neither of us said anything.

"That wasn't helpful," I said.

"But honest."

"At home, Francesca, why do it at home?"

"I didn't mean for it to happen. I would never have done it in our bed normally . . ."

"Like that makes it better?"

"No. I don't know. It felt like it made it better at the time. But we were at home, I was upset, I didn't want to end it. We're talking about a man with whom I risked everything I had, just to see him for half an hour. He was in my house. We were alone. I was trying to end it, I really was, but . . ."

"Don't tell me, one thing led to another."

"A paltry excuse, right?"

"Always has been. Though I've used it myself when I've slept with undesirables."

"You're allowed to sleep with undesirables," said Francesca.

"True. But they're not good for my health."

"That may be true, but that is your choice. I wasn't just going to hurt myself, I was going to break my family apart."

"And that's why you think Caspar won't listen to you."

"Lies to me, swears at me, has no respect for me. Frankly, being ignored would be easier to bear."

"It doesn't make sense—why wait four years before punishing you?"

"Maybe he didn't realize what he'd seen."

"Your son was twelve, not two."

"Maybe he just blocked it out; that was why he could get back in the car as if nothing had happened."

"Something doesn't wash. He told me about the erection he got every time his art teacher, Miss Clare, walked into the room; he'd have told me about you. Maybe he got off on the whole thing . . ."

"Tessa!"

"Sorry. Trying to introduce a little light relief."

"A Tessa King one-liner is not what I'm after here. This is serious."

"Of course it's serious, but it's not the end of the world. You and Nick are still together."

"Thank God."

"And there hasn't been anyone else?"

"God, no. Though I can see how it happens, if you don't get caught; it's a slippery slope. You think you're going to be struck down for being unfaithful, that the world will end, so it's quite weird when you discover you're not—you can walk back into your marital home, put on the fishfingers as if nothing has happened, so why not do it again? Eventually, the secret becomes as delicious as the affair itself. We'd talk for hours about our life together—a cottage on a moor, a farm in Spain—it was all wonderful while it was still fantasy. But when I thought Caspar had seen . . ." I could hear Francesca fighting to control her breathing. "That's why fantasy is so alluring, no one gets hurt."

"So what happened after Caspar left?"

"I realized what I was doing had hideous consequences. Caspar literally snapped me out of my reverie. I told my friend to leave immediately. I was beside myself. I sat by the phone waiting for you to call me to tell me Caspar had phoned his dad and it was all over, bar the shouting. My friend rang me every hour on the hour for the rest of that afternoon, most of the night and throughout the next day. I just let it ring and ring and ring. Finally, I went and dropped my phone in the river. I regretted it as soon as I'd done it and nearly followed suit, but I managed to drag myself home. I knew I would find it a darn sight harder to call him from home. Eventually, I stopped yearning for him; in fact, that was the weird thing. Here was someone I truly believed was the love of my life and within ten days I was fine."

"Lust is a very powerful thing," I said. "And being lonely can drive you to do terrible, stupid things." My place on the moral high ground wasn't so firm either. "And things got better with Nick?"

"That's the strange thing, the affair sort of saved my marriage. I know, you're right. Maybe I say that to make myself feel better but Nick kind of mended me. Maybe he thought I was ill, I certainly looked ill. My cough came back. He sent me to bed, took himself off, rented me videos and even picked the girls up from school. He saw me through my period of mourning so well that I started to look forward to him coming home to break the monotony of being depressed. Somehow we managed to find our way back to the corridor and one morning I woke up and realized it had all meant nothing. I had not loved this other man. The man I loved was Nick. What was so terrifying was that if Caspar and you hadn't come back that afternoon, I might never have had the willpower to end it, I would have broken up my family for nothing. Things with Nick and me got better. In the end, the only real casualty was Caspar. Apart from the hideous guilt I carry around with me."

"Morning," I said.

"What?"

"Caspar and I came back in the morning."

"No, it was afternoon. We'd been out in the rain all morning.

Didn't get back until, don't know, but later in the day."

"Well, it wasn't early morning, but it was before lunch."

"Couldn't have been."

"It was. I remember it. Honestly, we sat in the car when he'd got the tickets and discussed either going to the museum first and then having a late lunch, or having an early lunch and then going to the museum. In the end we went for burgers then bombs."

"I didn't see your car; I heard a car leave."

"We definitely sat there for a while. He really wasn't in a state of anxiety. Maybe you were hearing things."

"Footsteps on the stairs and a door slam? I don't think so."

"You said yourself you didn't see the tickets on the kitchen table. We'd been and gone while you were mooning about the park. I promise you, it was the morning, eleven-thirty, twelve. No later than twelve."

"We were in the park at twelve."

"Well then, it wasn't Caspar—he didn't see anything, he isn't scarred for life and he isn't punishing you. I've said this from the beginning, this isn't your fault. Caspar is being an arsehole and he needs to sort it out."

"There is no way he came back later?"

"No. We were together for the rest of the day."

"So who was on the stairs, who slammed the door?"

"The cleaning lady?"

"Tessa, I am the cleaning lady."

"Oh." I paused, thinking. "Well, who else has keys?"

"No one."

"Someone must, unless it was a burglar." No. A burglar would have assessed the situation and scarpered. Or assessed the situation and taken everything he could have got his hands on from downstairs, knowing the lady of the house was otherwise occupied upstairs and unlikely to hear a thing. And then it dawned on me. Just as it did Francesca.

"Nick," we said in unison. The only other person who had keys was Nick.

After that Francesca was inconsolable, so in the end I got in the car and drove to her house where we remained until the early hours of the morning, talking about whether a man could see his wife with another man and not only love her, but seemingly love her more. Several times I stopped her from ringing him. If it had been Nick, and we were still not absolutely sure that it had been, then he had decided, for reasons known only to himself, to keep quiet about what he'd seen, or heard. Instead of blowing up, walking out and making her pay, he had cared for his wife and helped her mend an imaginary broken heart, which had felt as real as a genuine broken heart at the time. All along he had known that it had not been the persistent cough that had floored her, but the end of an affair, and still he had taken her cups of tea in bed, run her bath, taken the kids off her hands and given her space. So my conclusion was this: Nick was a bigger man than I had ever thought him to be. He loved his wife more than I believed possible and she owed it to him to repay his silence with silence. Making a happy home would be thanks enough since that, I was beginning to learn, was a bloody hard thing to do.

Alternatively, there was a petty thief walking around with a photographic image in his head of Francesca and her mystery man going at it hammer and tongs and Nick was nothing more than another blissfully ignorant spouse. Personally, I started hoping it was the former. In all its weird complexities, I found Francesca's infidelity and Nick's subsequent forgiveness more encouraging and life-affirming than a meaningless shag that she somehow got away with.

*   *   *

Of course, what neither scenario dealt with was Caspar and why he seemed intent on blowing holes in his young brain. I had drunk too much to drive home, so crawled into bed with Francesca and took the place of her cuckold husband.

Twenty-four seconds after hitting the pillow, two lithe, extremely wakeful creatures came and bounced on the bed.

"What the fu—"

"Morning, girls," said Francesca brightly, cutting me off.

"What bloody time is it?" I squinted at my watch.

"Well done, you two," said Francesca, inexplicably.

"Well done? Well done for what? It's still dark outside."

"For waiting until seven."

"Seven!"

"We've been up since six, we waited and waited—"

"Poppy nearly came in."

"Did not."

"Did."

"DID NOT!"

"Don't shout, Poppy."

"And she spilled the cornflakes."

"Didn't!"

"Don't tell tales, Katie," said Francesca patiently.

I fell back on the pillow and groaned. Since when had their voices got so unbearably squeaky?

"Welcome to my world," whispered Francesca, peeling the duvet off her and stepping back into the clothes she'd removed only a few hours earlier. "Right, everybody, what are we up to today?"

"BALLET!" shouted Poppy.

"OK, ballet kit, in the airing cupboard."

"Gym," said Katie.

"Borrow one of Poppy's shirts, I haven't had time to clean yours."

"Nooooo," shouted Poppy.

"It's too small. I look like a boy in it," Katie complained.

"You don't."

"I do."

"I have to take something for 'show and tell.' Something I cooked," said Poppy. Cooked? She's only five. Francesca swore quietly, but recovered quickly.

"Right, cupcakes it is."

The two girls started jumping up and down and shouting very loudly, "CUPCAKES! CUPCAKES! CUPCAKES! CUPCAKES! CUPCAKES!"

I thought the pair of them would make extremely effective tools in Guantanamo Bay. I tried to smile.

"Don't worry," said Francesca. "They go very well with strong black, heavily laced coffee." It was rather like waking up after a beer-goggled one-night stand—a very *When Harry Met Sally* moment—I lay there wondering how long I could bear it before being able to leave without causing offence.

princess and the pea

By the time I got home I felt pure love and gratitude for the solitude my little flat offered me. I closed the door behind me. It was all getting a bit much, even for me: Claudia and Al sacrificing their health to have a child, Francesca admitting to an affair, Helen stuck in a ruinous marriage, and little Cora, lying on a sofa, ill, at home alone because her mother couldn't climb out of the rut she'd got herself into. Don't get me wrong, I think I'm a good person to have around in a crisis—but this was one crisis too many. This was one crisis too real. What had Fran said? The appeal of fantasy was that no one got hurt. She was right. Discussing Helen leaving Neil was almost entertainment to me because I didn't like Neil, but it would rock my world if Fran and Nick split up—they were my family; it would be like my parents getting divorced. They were the rock I had always clung to. I depended on their solidarity. More so now, since my parents weren't as active as they used to be, and as much as I wanted to overlook Dad's age and Mum's condition, there would come a time . . . I banished the thought. I hated thinking like that.

I went to the kitchen and got to work making a real cappuccino. I have these wonderful big soup-bowl coffee cups I bought during one of several weekends in Paris with Helen. Thanks to her dad, we had the run of a hotel suite whenever he was in Europe doing business. We were once picked up by Sylvester Stallone's entourage in the Bain Douche, a famous nightclub, and whisked off back to the Ritz in a limo. Anyway, that's another story . . . Unfortunately, the problem with my French coffee cups is that the contents get too cold too quickly so I had to buy a microwave to reheat them. Benefit of microwave is it makes proper foam for the top of the cappuccino. I'm now quite a pro. I sprinkled chocolate on the top, slid open the glass window and stepped out on to the balcony. I call it a balcony, but it's more of a shelf. Still, it's wide enough for a couple of fake French café chairs from Homebase, and a wobbly table.

I sat and soaked up the sun. Was it always like this, or was it just that I was around more? Sometimes work got so busy I wouldn't see Fran, Helen or Billy for months. We'd speak on the phone every so often, and, hangover permitting, I would drop by on the weekends, but it probably wasn't as often as I thought it was. In fact, thinking about it, there had been times recently when I wouldn't see my friends more than once every couple of months. I was busy. It was easier to go out with work mates—they were in situ, their lives more in keeping with mine, and they didn't have to book babysitters. Had these feelings of discontent been under my nose all along? My finger itched to call Ben. I missed talking to him. Every day I was aware of the lack of contact between us. It was the only sign that confirmed to me that not all of this was in my head. Ben. Ben. Ben. How was I going to cure myself of Ben once and for all? Was I like Francesca? Mistaken? Or was it real? I stared out over the river. If it felt real, how was anyone ever supposed to know for sure? Later, after finally getting around to tidying the flat, I sat at my desk, went through my post and checked my emails. There was one from Claudia. I have to admit it, I opened it up reluctantly. There is only so much gloom and doom a girl can take in a day.

*   *   *

Darling Tessa

What an amazing place Singapore is. The swimming pool is on the roof of the hotel which is forty-seven floors high. Pretty cool. I wanted to let you know that I am feeling so much better. In fact, almost as soon as the wheels left the ground, my spirits improved. Al took my hand and squeezed it until the seat-belt sign came off and I thought, How lucky I am, how incredibly lucky I am. It makes a nice change. We've been having fun. We've been getting pissed. (Me, pissed—when did you last see that?) We discovered a great bar and I have to admit, I've developed something of a margarita habit. On the rocks. With salt. Mostly I just like the way that sounds. Anyway, we've been dancing. Every day I go to the hotel gym, which is like something out of a science fiction film, have massages in my room and incredible acupuncture. I feel so much stronger. I've made a decision about what we're going to do. I am not going to put Al or myself through it again. It's not just the terrible disappointment when it doesn't work, I've begun to think about what it would be like if it did work. My Down's stats don't look great because of my age, my cervix has had so much invasive treatment they'd want to staple me up to prevent me going into spontaneous labor again, basically I'm tired of feeling like a lab rabbit and have realized how much I have forgotten what it feels like to be a person. Am I mistaken, didn't I used to be quite fun?

I know how worried about me you were, and I don't want you to worry any more. I'm actually crying now, which I haven't done for days, but only because I'm so grateful to have had you as a friend, and so happy to put this behind me. Please just imagine the scene: I am surrounded by immaculately dressed, conscientious Japanese businessmen (are there any other kind?) who are all typing away furiously in the business center and I have wandered in from the pool in the floaty kaftan you gave me, to send you this email. The air-con is ferocious so not only am I sobbing, my nipples are picking up satellite signals. Yes, people are now starting to leave . . . I ought to go before they call security. Oh dear, I've made a wet bikini mark on the seat.

Luckily Al is a bit of a golden boy at the moment and the hotel group has asked him whether he'd like to do a tour of all their possible sites in the Far East. One is a proposed tree-top hotel in the jungle in Vietnam. You can only get there by elephant!!! We might stay a while, maybe even find China Beach again. It is v exciting but it does mean we won't be back as soon as we'd thought. Apart from missing you guys, I think that is no bad thing.

I love you and miss you, and if you fancy meeting me in Vietnam for old times' sake, get on a plane. I'll keep you posted of the dates. In the meantime, take care of you, find a job before you start going mad and lose confidence (trust me, I know, it doesn't take long) and stay away from trouble. And don't pretend you don't know what I'm talking about. Love to all. Claud xx

PS We had sex for fun the other night for the first time in years and it was great!!!

OK, so it wasn't all bad. If Claudia could put those years of peeing on sticks behind her before summoning her husband to the marital bed, then wasn't anything possible? No more IVF. I knew Al would be pleased about her decision and I'm sure Claudia would continue to be as brave as she had been since this wretched business began. When people asked her, as they often did, when was she going to have kids, could she now look those people in the eye and say, "We can't have children," rather than her tried and tested, knee them in the bollocks answer, "We're trying, but we haven't been blessed yet." Less thoughtful people would say, "Sounds fun," or, "How long have you been trying?" More sensitive people would respond with a "Good luck," or, "Poor you . . ." Actually, more sensitive people wouldn't ask in the first place. Would she miss the whisper of hope that every procedure gave her? What would fill her daydreams if there was no imaginary child? Could she really give it up? I reread her email. Maybe, maybe not, but I had to hand it to her for trying.

James called later in the afternoon to say he'd booked a table at a restaurant, gave me the address and the time and then offered to pick me up. Since the restaurant was next to a bar I knew, I said I'd meet him at the bar. I'd been inspired by Claudia's email and had developed a bit of a craving for a margarita myself. The exchange of this information took no more than a minute so I was pleasantly surprised when I finally ended the call and saw that I'd been on the phone for forty-five minutes. What on earth had we talked about for forty-five minutes? I already couldn't recall. I wrote back to Claudia, answered some boring emails and discovered another headhunting company wanted to see me. After setting up the interview, I watered my plants, had a long shower and did my nails. I put my iPod onto its speakers, set it to shuffle and leapt around the room to Eminem and then sang loudly along with the three tenors to Bizet's *The Pearl Fishers* while my nails dried. I felt light inside. Buoyant. It took a while for me to put a finger on it. Carefree. I felt carefree. Which was odd, considering the events of the past few days.

I was just about to sit down to the task of blow-drying my hair, when the phone rang.

"Hello?"

"Hi, Tess."

Ben. I swallowed. Damn, bugger, balls, bollocks, hooray. "Hi," I said.

"You answered your home phone."

I'd been doing that recently. I must be better. Even though I changed my number, I had stopped answering the phone. I had changed my mobile too. I only ever gave people my email address now. If my old boss ever did contact me, I had to notify the police immediately, but that would already be too late; I never wanted him to cross my defense line again. Police or no police.

"You disappeared the other night. It wasn't nearly so much fun after you left."

I had seen Ben doing dirty dancing with his wife, so I knew that wasn't true.

"Helen needed to be taken home."

"Yeah, Fran said she'd drunk a skinful. I didn't think she drank."

"She doesn't. That was the problem." That and her shit of a coke-snorting husband. Normally I would have told Ben all about it, which was horribly indiscreet of me, but back then I thought we had no secrets. Turns out, all we have are secrets.

"I was just wondering whether you'd heard from Claudia."

"Got an email today, actually."

"Everything OK with them?"

"Better than. Claudia sounds great."

"Thank God."

"Why?"

"I just got a strange email from Al, that's all."

"What did it say?"

"'All good here, how goes it with you?'"

"That was it?"

"Yes."

And therein lies the difference between men and women. I get a fifty-line email from Claudia, Ben gets eight words from Al, effectively saying the same thing, but meaning so much less. I was glad I wasn't a boy. Boys are weird.

"Well, Claudia put it a bit better than that, but yes, I think all is very good with them. She sounds like a different person, and that's in an email."

"Are they coming back?"

"Not yet. And they're not going to do IVF again, either."

"What a relief."

Relief? I wondered. Relief in the sense of someone being very ill, for a very long time, and eventually dying. It wasn't really a relief. It was a gut-wrenching tragedy. But sometimes no life is better than that life. And in Claudia's case, no life was better than some life at any cost.

If only I was a fairy godmother, I thought in that moment, if only I could wave a magic wand and give Claudia her baby, ease Francesca's guilt and worry, rescue Helen and give Billy back her strength. I could not magic my friends' ills away, but what I could do was break my own spell.

"How are you, Tess? It feels like I haven't seen you for ages."

I wonder why. "I've been busy."

"What about tonight? You up for a pint or two?"

"Actually I've . . ." Say it. Go on—say it. Why didn't I want to say it? What was I afraid of? That it would put Ben off me? He was married! Wave that magic wand, Tessa. Now, before it was too late.

"I'm meeting up with that bunch of reprobates, you know, the journalists. They love you, please come."

I wondered whether Ben sensed I was none too keen to be alone with him. I guessed he was just trying to get things back to normal. Trouble was, normal had been killing me.

"Actually, I've got a date."

Silence.

"Ben?"

"Sorry, lost you for a second. A date? Great. Anyone I know?"

I felt really awkward, but forged ahead nonetheless. I wanted us to be the friends we were supposed to be.

"You met him the other night."

"Not that old bloke?"

"He's not old."

"He's got grey hair."

"Salt-and-pepper. And it's very sexy." I found it easier to defend James than I'd thought.

"Him, sexy?"

"Well, you're not the one who's supposed to find him sexy."

"He's not your type, Tess." This had to stop. Ben had to know I was serious.

"What is my type?" It was a gauntlet. I threw it down.

"Younger," said Ben, sidestepping.

"Younger blokes think women of my age are scary."

"You're not scary."

"No, I'm fabulous. But they can't seem to see it."

"That's my girl."

I'm not your girl, Ben. "It was your wife who gave him my number," I said, throwing down another one. "Didn't she mention it to you?"

"That's not a very Sasha thing to do."

"Perhaps she thinks he is my type." Or at least someone other than her husband should be my type. I agreed with her. I needed to take a page out of Claudia's book. It was time to move on. It was all very well lecturing Helen about coming out from under Neil's shadow, Billy from Christoph's, but it was high time I did that myself. "I like him. We've had lunch. I find him incredibly easy to talk to. And he likes me, I can tell."

"Of course he likes you, Tessa. There aren't many women like you."

"Well, thank you. I'll let you know how it goes."

"What did you say his name was?"

"James Kent."

"James Kent." He said it again. "I'm sure I've met him before."

"Yeah, the other night."

"No, before then, maybe work . . . I'll remember eventually."

I didn't want Ben to know James Kent. I think I wanted this one all for myself. "Look, I've got to go, you're jeopardizing my date."

"Me?"

"Yeah—my hair is frizzing up while we speak."

"When is he allowed to know that he is in fact dating Chewbacca?"

"Ha, ha. Get off my line."

"If it's boring, call me, we'll be in the Eagle."

"Eight inebriated male journalists and you, no thanks." Actually, that sounded like fun.

That was good. That was better. Claudia would have been proud of me. Was James Kent the reason I was feeling like this? I thought about it as I watched my reflection doing my hair. Instead of having a clothes crisis, I put on my good jeans, a Matthew Williamson top and my favorite, most beloved cowboy boots. They came in and out of fashion, but I didn't care, and since men rarely noticed what went on below the empire line, I didn't think causing myself pain by tottering around on heels was worth it. He'd already seen a large portion of the Tessa King spectrum. Drunk and disheveled at the nightclub. Scrubbed up to the nines at the launch. Untarnished by make-up and in old comfy clothes at lunch, and he'd still asked me out for dinner. So perhaps? Was it possible? Could it be? Was James Kent genuinely interested in me as a person? Wonders would never cease. Unless, unless . . . I dismissed the thought. He was a good guy, I could tell, but the thought came again: unless he was just going through the motions until he saw the last on the Tessa King spectrum. Naked. No. I would not be plagued by negative thoughts. I would not self-sabotage. I would not drag my previous bad experiences with me. New person. New experience. Just thinking about how he was with Cora encouraged me. I felt very good about this one. I checked over my reflection once more before leaving the flat. I may have been wrong about men before, but I was pretty confident that I wasn't wrong about this one. Even so, I reiterated my autumnal resolution: James Kent would not see me naked. Not tonight, anyway. I really should have known myself better by then.

He was at the bar. Not at a table. At the bar. Had I told him I liked drinking at bars or was this just another happy coincidence? He stood up and pulled out a stool. We quickly fell into an easy banter which didn't normally come until I was halfway down a second cocktail. We sat there for twenty minutes before I even ordered mine. A margarita, with salt, on the rocks. I raised a glass and asked James to toast my good friend Claudia. Bless him, he didn't even raise an eyebrow. We didn't talk about anything that mind-blowing, and nothing we said was really that funny, but I was fascinated by everything he said, he hung off my every word and we laughed a great deal.

Ben could not have been further from my mind as we walked the short distance to the restaurant, except that I was thinking about how far from my mind he was. I have no memory of what we ate except that it was delicious, there was masses of it and yet we still found space to share two puddings and drink aged Armagnac. That was probably when my resolutions started to slip. I heard myself say something about the waiters clearing up around us, one more drink and Blakes Hotel. Blakes Hotel! The only thing I knew about Blakes Hotel was that you didn't go there for one drink. It wasn't even that

I was pissed and not thinking straight. I just didn't want the evening to end because the end meant going home alone and I didn't want this good feeling to pass. It had been a while.

Blakes is a very sophisticated small London hotel in South Kensington. The outside brickwork is black, the interior always dimly lit, and it has a small, hidden away bar in the basement which is so dark you can barely see the faces of the other clientele. Which is no bad thing, since there were a lot of uncles and nieces huddled over glasses of champagne. It oozed sexual tension and illicit intentions. It spoke to me. We ordered a couple of whisky sours and continued chatting. When we asked for another round the barman told us it was last orders. Mistaking us for guests, he said we could, however, order anything from our room. Our room. Our room. I rolled the words over in my mind. They sounded tempting. I looked at James, James looked at me. We both started to smirk, then giggle.

"What do you think?" he asked.

"I think that is a terrible idea."

"Me too," he agreed, smiling.

"Let's do it."

Man, he was good.

It was all very silly and I'm sure the night staff had seen it a million times before. Couple come up from the bar a little more ragged than when they'd gone down, approach the discreet, setback reception area, and enquire after a room. Naturally, there was only one room left, and it was a cripplingly expensive suite. Quite a good scam, really. As one of my aunts once said of such hotels, "For that sort of money I'd have to lie awake all night, staring at the ceiling with matchsticks in my eyes." Well, I didn't exactly stare at the ceiling, and I wasn't always lying, but I was awake. I think I could safely say, in fiscal terms, I got my money's worth. Or James did, since he was paying. But at that point, as he handed over a credit card, we were ostensibly getting a room in order just to have another drink. Right. We were shown down a narrow corridor, out into an immaculate, yew-strewn courtyard, over flagstones to a wide, white door.

If I hadn't known before that I was going to end up naked, despite all my promises to myself, I knew then. It was the most beautiful bedroom I had ever seen. Fairy tales aren't usually very sexy—the ones I read to Cora always lean towards the righteous—but this was a perfect mix of pure fantasy and impure thoughts. *The Princess and the Pea* meets *9½ Weeks*, *Alice in Wonderland* meets *Emmanuelle*, all in snowy white. The bed was huge. The ceilings were high. Even the floorboards were white.

"The White Room," said the porter.

"Champagne, I think," said James. And that, I suppose, was that. It was a very sedate seduction. The champagne arrived, so we cracked it open, ran a bath, filled it with Anouska Hempel's signature grapefruit bubble bath, and both got in. We refilled our glasses and the hot water a couple of times. It was really fun. But the real action was getting dry.

Usually having sex with someone for the first time is embarrassing. Unless, of course, the dreaded drink has stripped you of all inhibitions, in which case, the embarrassment is reserved for the morning. I wasn't embarrassed with James. Since I'd already taken my clothes off and climbed into the bath before we'd even kissed, getting naked was no longer an issue. We first kissed sitting knees to knees in the bath. There wasn't enough room for the kiss to lead to anything else, not even a big, fat, deep kiss. So until the water got cold for the last time, and my skin wrinkled, we just talked and let our lips touch from time to time. After that there was some lovely rolling about, quite a lot of lying and looking at each other, unend-

ing chat, and then more rolling about. Things didn't get really serious until about five in the morning, by which point we were both
completely relaxed. Or exhausted; they feel about the same. It was
definitely getting light when we finally fell into a deep and dreamy
sleep.

played

I was woken up by a kiss. James was smiling over me, which was nice. But he was dressed, which wasn't so nice. I propped myself up on one elbow.

"Morning, gorgeous," he said.

I screwed up my face. Morning—yes. Gorgeous—I very much doubted it.

"I have to go, I've got a meeting I can't miss."

"OK." I sat up. "I'll get up."

"No, don't. Sleep. I would if I could. Order some breakfast when you wake up."

That sounded nice. It seemed sacrilege to leave such a place before time was up.

"Listen, I've had a crazy idea," said James.

"I like your crazy ideas."

"I've got this morning meeting, then a lunch. As long as I can get out of something this afternoon, I could be free again from about four." I waited. "What would you say to holing up here until then and being really decadent and staying another night?"

My lips spread into a wide smile before I had time to be cool.

"Is that a yes?"

"You bet."

"OK. I'll see you later." He kissed me hard on the lips and then groaned. "God, I wish I didn't have to go."

I was quite glad. I needed to clean my teeth, I was desperate to go to the loo, and the truth was, I had terrible wind. I may have felt extraordinarily at ease with this man, but there were limits.

The second sleep I had was luxurious. As was the second bath, though not quite as enjoyable. My limbs felt like I'd been to the gym. I know, it was very Harlequin, but my lips felt bruised. James sent me a text saying, "can't concentrate!" I read it many times. Two words. I was being pathetic.

I decided that I would really go for it so, with every intention of paying for the "extras" myself, I summoned a masseuse to the room and had a ninety-minute massage, I ate lobster and drank fine white wine, then I had a facial. I even sent the concierge out to get me ridiculous glossy magazines that I never normally read and sent my crumpled, smoky clothes to the ridiculously expensive express laundry. Everything was ridiculously expensive. My peppermint tea with one small piece of shortbread cost a fiver. What did I care? This was the sort of thing I never, ever did. I created a whole world inside the White Room, was on first name terms with the staff, and counted down the hours until four. It wasn't hard. I almost wished I had more time.

Then my phone rang. Why, oh why, did I pick it up? I believed I had been cured. I believed James Kent had cured me. And so I picked up a call from one of my oldest friends in the world.

"Hey, Ben, how are you?"

"Good. You sound like you're in a good mood."

"I am. What can I do for you?"

"How was your date?"

"Really fun, thanks."

There was a pause from Ben. It confused me. Why was he silent? Did he disapprove?

"You didn't sleep with him, did you?"

Was he jealous?

"No," I lied.

"Thank God for that."

He was jealous!

"What's going on, Ben?" I asked, trying to keep the excitement out of my voice. Damn this man.

"I remembered where I'd met him. The reason why I couldn't remember was because I hadn't met him exactly, I'd met his wife."

"What?"

"We were at a City lunch, I was with Sasha. She's a cool lady, actually. We were talking, then he came up and they left."

"That doesn't mean anything. Did she say they were married? When was this, anyway?"

"Not long enough ago to get a divorce."

I was panicking now. "But did she say they were married?"

"No, but her name was Barbara Kent and his name is James Kent, right?"

"Brother and sister," I argued. There was no way James was married. No way. No one can act that well. Can they?

"With two kids at Francis Holland, whom they were late picking up?"

"What?"

"The one in Baker Street."

"What?"

I was playing dumb, but I knew exactly what Ben was saying. Baker Street. I rewound to our lunch. What time was it when he jumped into the cab? It was when I'd mentioned the pavement being awash with school kids. Baker Street. He'd gone to pick up his daughters.

"I remember it perfectly. We were talking about the school because Sasha's nieces go there."

"Do they?"

"You know they do."

My heart was beating far too fast. The lobster was repeating on me. I thought I might be going into anaphylactic shock.

"I'm mortified I didn't recognize him the other night but we were so pissed. They're married and they have two daughters, Lainy and Martha Kent. Sorry, hon, I wanted to warn you before you did something stupid."

"What, like kiss a married man? I've already done that!"

"Oh Tess—"

"I didn't mean him!" I swore extremely loudly, put the phone down and burst into tears. I clutched my head in my hands. I couldn't take much more of this. When was this going to end? Even when the opposite sex were playing by the rules it was hard, but this, this was too much. *Let's make a pact now, no rehashing of past love lives* . . . The little-known Burmese restaurant chosen because *you never see anyone you know* . . . Even Blakes, it felt like it was my idea, it felt like I was the one making all the suggestions, but I was played. I was played good and proper. I very much doubted he was coming back at four. And even if he did, the next day would have been the last. Or was he going to tell me about his wife and daughters when I was too weak to resist? Was he going to turn me into the other woman and lie to us all? Why did men do things like this? What was the point? I wasn't thinking straight. I was all over the place. Married with two kids. Married with two kids. It went round and round in my head. I was full of fury. And then I did something I will always regret. I ordered a £200 bottle of wine, watched calmly as the sommelier theatrically opened it in front of me, then got dressed in my beautifully pressed clothes, stole a dressing gown and, with the bottle and a glass swinging from my hand, left the hotel not really knowing whether I was furious with James, Ben or myself.

At ten past four my phone rang. James left a message. "You are coming back, aren't you?"

Then another.

"Pick up the phone, Tessa, this is very weird."

Then another.

"If this is a joke, I don't like it."

Then another.

"I'm checking out. I've seen the bill. What the fuck is going on?"

Eventually I switched off my phone. He didn't deserve a response.

I walked through the enviable houses of Kensington until I reached Holland Park. I deliberately found myself a bench in a place that would hurt the most. Overlooking the playground. From the swings and sandpit the nannies and mothers eyed me warily. I didn't blame them. If they stared at me, I stared right back. They always looked away first.

I sat like an old wino in designer clothes and a dressing gown and drank my vengeful bottle of wine. I was being mad, I knew it, but I didn't care. I started to think, as the alcohol warmed my stomach, that it had cost more than money, it had cost my sanity. James Kent was married with two kids. I had been fooled. Even if there was the remotest possibility that he had recently separated from his wife, Ben was right, he couldn't be divorced by now. I could almost, almost understand why he hadn't bothered mentioning an ex-wife; it could be construed as too much excess baggage, especially since it was recent, but this was too recent. This was rebound with possible reconciliation. And that did not put me in a good position because I already knew that I liked him more than anyone else I'd met in a long time. Failing to mention two flesh and blood children, however, was something else entirely. That was a big black mark. It was mean. It was disrespectful. It was a terrible thing for a father to do. It was the sort of thing Christoph or Neil would do and as far as I was concerned there was not a worse type of man than them.

Wide, flat leaves fell intermittently from the plane trees around me. The day darkened. Was it that time of year already? Halloween was around the corner. Then Bonfire Night. Fireworks. Sparklers. And then, oh God, it was too awful to think of. My birthday, swiftly followed by Christmas and New Year—the triple-headed assault course I tripped up on every year when I was forced to accept that another year had passed and nothing had changed.

When there was more wine in my body than in the bottle my self-pitying, angry thoughts turned to the inevitable. I was not cured. I was worse than ever. Ben was who I wanted. Ben was who I fell back to when all else failed. Ben. He wouldn't do this to me. Whatever else the difficulties were, and yes, that included being married to someone else, he did love me. Even if he wasn't in love with me, which he obviously wasn't since he had married someone else, he did love me. That meant he wouldn't hurt me, or lie to me, or cheat on me, or lead me up garden paths, or strip me of another layer of dignity, or make it impossible for me to love someone else. I lowered the glass from my lips. Actually, he did do that.

People stared, I didn't really care. I got very cold. I took it as another sign of old age. When I was younger I would skip around London in barely any clothes at all, and don't remember ever feeling the cold. Now, however, I harped on about the cold weather like an old woman. I was an old woman. A lonely, sad old woman. How the hell had this happened to me?

I watched the kids squabble over their position on the slide. I watched expressionless women push swings like robots. I watched kids fall and cry and run to their mothers and nannies. I watched the endless blowing of noses. I heard the endless "why?"s I saw women yawn and sigh and respond over and over again to the same hop, skip or jump. Every few moments someone yelled. Somewhere at some time a tantrum was unfolding before my eyes. I saw one boy hit his mother. I saw one woman pretend she had not been reduced to tears by her charge. But my pity was reserved solely for myself for I would have given my left leg to be any goddamn one of them. I got colder and colder as I watched until eventually I couldn't feel the cold any more. The bottle was empty, the park was dark and all the children had gone home to be warmed up in bubble baths, read stories to and be tucked in.

I stood up before I was politely, but firmly, asked to move on and took myself home. I tried a bubble bath. I tried reading. I tried tucking myself in and falling asleep. It didn't work. In the end I took a sleeping pill. With vodka. I didn't think I was being overdramatic, I just wanted my brain to stop and couldn't be bothered to go and get any water.

When I woke up the next morning, I took another one. Honestly, I had no idea how strong they were.

It was the sound of the buzzer that finally pulled me out of my heavy, dreamless sleep. I was completely disorientated. It was dark outside. The buzzing continued. I hit my alarm clock and fell back to sleep. Had I been in less of a stupor I would have remembered that my alarm clock bleeps, not buzzes.

Someone was shaking me. It was really annoying. I tried to turn over. A man's voice was talking loudly into my ear. Hadn't I put the "Do not disturb" sign on? I didn't want any more disgusting airplane food.

"Mizz King, Mizz King. Wake up, Mizz King."

"Leave me alone," I said, though later Roman told me all I had actually managed to do was drool. That was when he saw the pills and the empty tumbler by my bed which one sniff confirmed was not water. He panicked and started shaking me. What woke me up in the end was the shaking. He wanted to call a doctor; I told him he was being ridiculous. Well, I tried to tell him, but my God, my head felt heavy. I just wanted to close my eyes again. It was very embarrassing, or would have been, had I been more with it. I forced myself to sit up because Roman was about to call 999, and I really didn't want him to do that. I explained again slowly that I had simply taken a sleeping pill because I hadn't been able to get to sleep.

"Not sleeping pill," said Roman, holding up the empty bottle. Funny that, I could have sworn I'd had two in there. "Horse tranquillizer."

"What?" I took the bottle. "How do you know?"

"I read. Where did you get these from?" I frowned at him. Who are you, my father? Perhaps I had got too friendly with my doorman? The truth was, someone at work—a bit of a party boy himself, now I come to think of it—had given me the pills ages ago. I was paranoid about my ex-boss getting into the flat. Every noise made me sit bolt upright and I hadn't slept for weeks. I was a mess. He was trying to help but in the end I never took them because I was too terrified that if I did I wouldn't hear my ex-boss break into the flat and he'd murder me in my sleep. During that whole period of my life I'd never actually resorted to these, but now . . . I looked at the empty bottle of pills again. Were things really worse? Roman brought me a cup of coffee. I took it from him without asking why he was giving it to me. I was being very slow.

"What time is it?"

"Eleven-thirty."

I slumped back against the pillow. "What are you waking me up for? I need more sleep."

"You've been sleeping since Wednesday night. You came back blue."

I vaguely remembered seeing Roman behind the desk when I finally walked in through the door. I didn't stop and exchange pleasantries with him as I usually did. I grant I may have looked a bit of a state, what with an empty bottle of wine still in my hand and a toweling robe over my clothes. But then again, nothing he hadn't seen before. I frowned at him crossly.

"So?"

"It's Friday morning."

"Hmm . . ." I felt my eyes closing again. Those pills were good.

"Did you hear me?" Roman took the cup from me before I spilt it. "It's Friday morning—not Thursday."

I rubbed my eyes. "What?"

"You've been up here for thirty-six hours. There is a woman trying to get hold of you."

"Someone's looking for me?"

"I tried knocking, I buzzed, we've rung and rung, I got worried . . ."

"Who?" Had James come to tell me that Ben had got it wrong, he didn't have children, there was no wife. Or that there were all those things but he couldn't live without me, and he was leaving them. Or was it B—

"Billy. You must call her, it is urgent."

I groaned. "I'll call her back later—"

"She is in the hospital."

Billy was in hospital? My brain started moving. Billy was in hospital? Moving faster. Billy didn't go to hospital. Bam—I was awake. The most effective smelling salts invented. Unless—

"Cora," I said, leaping out of bed. My legs gave way under me. I fell. What the hell had I taken? Roman helped me to a chair and brought me clothes as I drank his coffee and listened to the answerphone.

8:30 a.m. "Tessa, are you there? Your phone's switched off. Pick up."

8:45 a.m. "I have a huge favor to ask you. Cora isn't well and Magda can't sit for her, she's got exams this whole week. Please, please could you come over . . . I guess you're in the shower. Call me when you're out." I turned my mobile phone on, it immediately started to bleep. I had six missed calls. Five from Billy. One from Ben.

8:50 a.m. "Don't worry, the Calpol is working and she says she's feeling better. She's going to school. Call me, anyway, at work."

11:28 a.m. "Tessa, slight panic. Cora's in the sickroom with quite a high fever—any chance you could be fairy godmother? I'm the only one at work, Sue's on holiday. Sorry to ask. If you can't, don't worry, I'll sort something out. Is your mobile broken?"

3:02 p.m. "I'm at Chelsea and Westminster. Cora is very ill. Please call me."

3:44 p.m. "Where are you?!"

5:02 p.m. "Will you come? Whenever you get this message, just come . . ."

7:59 p.m. "They've done a lumbar puncture and they're taking her to intensive care. Tessa, they think it's meningitis . . . Oh my God, where are you? They say I should prepare myself for the worst . . ."

8:03 p.m. Dialing tone. *The worst . . . ?*

8:22 p.m. Dialing tone. *The worst . . . ?*

*   *   *

I didn't hear how many more times Billy had tried to call only to get the answering machine, because, half-dressed, I threw myself out of the chair and ran unsteadily to the door, leaving Roman in the middle of my bedroom looking bewildered.

He followed me into the corridor. "Mizz King, you should take it easy."

"Don't you understand?" I shouted. "They need me."

I saw him shaking his head as the lift doors closed. On Vauxhall Bridge Road I hailed a taxi. Sitting in the back of it anxiety, lethargy and disbelief overwhelmed me. Had I really slept through an entire day? I tapped on the driver's partition.

"Could you turn that up, please?" I asked.

According to BBC Five Live, it was true. It was Friday. The midday news. A scandal had erupted in government, according to the presenter, following "yesterday's revelations" . . . I had slept through a scandal. I had lost a day of my life. I hadn't been there when Billy and Cora needed me. I didn't know very much about meningitis except it killed children unless caught in time. *Any chance you could be fairy godmother?* No. I'd been too busy wallowing in self-pity. I shifted uncomfortably in the back of the taxi recalling how I'd sat on a park bench, in front of children, and swigged wine from a bottle. I recoiled at the thought of myself stumbling into my building wearing the dressing gown I'd stolen. What sort of crazy behavior was that? I remembered taking the first pill because I desperately wanted to stop thinking about Ben and James, Sebastian, my ex-boss and all the other pitiful excuses of relationships that I've had. Obviously I didn't realize how inebriated I was or I would never, ever have taken the pills with . . . I stared out of the window as the Embankment shot passed. I could still taste the bitter residue the pills had left at the back of my throat, and the sting of vodka as I gulped them down. I tried Billy's number again.

It was still switched off. I stared out at the cloudless, blue sky and imagined the worst.

I paid the driver and, still uncertain on my legs, climbed out of the taxi. I felt stupidly weak as I half jogged, half walked through the massive revolving doors of Chelsea and Westminster Hospital. The man behind the crescent reception desk took one look at me, excused himself from the person he was talking to and offered me his assistance. He rapidly explained where I would find the children's ward, and told me I would be directed to the children's intensive care unit from there. I ran the length of the hospital to the correct bank of lifts and pressed the button. I was tapping my foot nervously; I looked up at the illuminated numbers to track the painfully slow journey of the lift coming down and saw a small cloud pass over the glass atrium of the hospital. Was I hallucinating or did that cloud look like an—

No, you can't have her back, I thought, shaking my head at the sky. Do you hear me? My heart was pounding in my chest so furiously I couldn't quite catch my breath. The lift doors finally opened. I stared into the empty lift and was frozen to the spot. Go on, I told myself, but my feet refused to move. Go on! I stood resolutely still. The lift doors started to close again; only when they were halfway across did I put my hand out to stop them. Get in the fucking lift, I told myself. My head was full of vile thoughts; funerals, coffins, eulogies, sympathy . . . I was losing my goddamn marbles. Why didn't I want to reach Cora's floor? Because of what I would have to face? Or what I would have to face up to? *The world is full of trickery*, but none more damaging than how we trick ourselves. I pressed the button for her floor.

If Cora was all right I would lock my thoughts of Ben away for ever. If Cora was all right, I would cease with these foolish dreams. If

Cora was all right, I would be all right. Please, God, listen to me and look after all those I love. I felt the hydraulics hiss into action, up I went, one floor, two, three. Finally the lift doors opened. A haggard, grey-haired, shriveled woman was standing right in front of me. She burst into tears the moment she saw my face. It was Billy.

cry wolf

"She's going to be OK," sobbed Billy.

I managed to stop my legs from buckling.

"What?"

"She's going to be fine."

I stepped out of the lift, my heart still pounding in my chest. "Are you sure?" I asked.

"Sure." Billy hugged me. "It's not meningitis, it's all right, Tessa. It's not meningitis."

I still wasn't quite with her. I wasn't even sure it was really Billy. It sounded like her, but she looked so different. "Your message said . . ."

"I was going mad, she was so ill. My God, her temperature was so high and she was totally unresponsive. I thought I was looking at a corpse, I swear, I've never been so terrified in my life and they were doing all these tests to find out what it was. I was panicking . . ." We hugged again. "They did a lumbar puncture, to rule out the worst. All I heard was meningitis . . . They were worried, Tessa, I was so frightened. I'm sorry, I thought I called you back."

"Doesn't matter, is she OK now?"

"She's not well, but it's not meningitis. I mean, it's still serious, just not like that."

"What is it?"

"Pneumococcal pneumonia, common in children who've been ventilated at birth. That's why she was so unresponsive, it was her chest, poor thing. It's really weak and they say she'll need physio on it, but fucking hell, physio I'll take, physio I'll take any day . . ."

I put my arm around Billy's shoulders as we walked in no particular direction. I felt her lengthy exhalation. "I've never been so frightened in my life," she said, leaning against me.

You and me both, I thought.

"I'm so relieved, I can't tell you," said Billy.

I watched one foot move in front of the other. Relieved? I was obviously in too much shock to feel the relief quite yet. Although my heart beat had slowed, I still felt winded.

"I'm sorry I didn't call you back," said Billy.

So was I. I'd made a pact with God. Shut up, Tessa.

"Where've you been? Your phone's been switched off for days. I called your building and left a message with your security guy."

It wasn't the time to share my last forty-eight hours with Billy. "There was a problem with my SIM card," I replied.

"I rang the flat—"

"I'm sorry you couldn't get hold of me. Tell me what happened. From the beginning."

"I was about to go and get something to eat, I haven't eaten since yesterday. Do you have time?"

"Of course, but what about Cora?"

"She's sleeping. She's fine."

"You sure?"

"Honestly, Tessa, she's all right now, they've got it under control." We turned round and walked back to the lifts. "I wouldn't be leaving her if she wasn't. A quick bite to eat and I'll go back."

We summoned the lift again and went downstairs. The atrium

was filled with bright sunlight; we walked through the hospital and out into the stunning blue day. I looked up; the wisp of cloud had vanished. I shook my head quietly to myself. What had I thought I'd seen? Cora's soul? An angel? Her angel? Myself dressed in black, standing at a lectern, a coffin below me, a crowd out front? *Do not distress yourself with dark imaginings* . . . What the hell was wrong with me? I must have sighed more loudly than I'd realized.

"She's going to be all right," said Billy, taking my arm and leading me across the pedestrian crossing. I nodded. I didn't trust myself to speak.

We found Bella Pasta. It was bustling with lunchtime trade, but Billy seemed reassured by the noise and haste. We weren't the only ones who'd escaped the hospital for some better quality sustenance: the restaurant was full of the walking wounded. There was a kid in a sling. A woman in a cast. A man on crutches. Each patient had at least two people with them. Mothers, fathers, grannies, friends. Billy had me. Better late than never, I guess. She told me about her hectic morning, bustling Cora off to school against her better judgment but with no alternative; the call from the school, the race to the hospital, Cora blacking out, her temperature rising, the lumbar puncture . . . I listened intently. So intently I almost drowned out my own thoughts. Almost, but not quite. The plate of pasta that was put down in front of me seemed to empty before I'd lifted the fork. I was hungry. I would be. The last thing I had eaten was lobster in the White Room in Blakes Hotel, I realized. How much had that cost, I wondered? It depended on the daily market price but I hadn't stuck around to check the bill. I ordered a side salad, which wasn't enough so I ordered pudding too. I needed refueling. I needed my head examined. I'd made a bargain with God, and he'd come up with the goods. Now I had to tread carefully.

". . . would you mind doing that?"

I looked at Billy.

"Please?" she asked.

"Um, you know I'd do anything for you."

"Thank you." She passed me a piece of paper with a couple of numbers on it. There was a name above it.

"Oh no, Billy—"

"You just said you would."

"I didn't think you meant call Christoph now," I replied bluffing. I couldn't tell her I hadn't been listening. "I thought you meant, you know, about court, about the money. Why would I call him about Cora?"

"Please, Tessa. He has a right to know."

"That's questionable. What do you think he's going to do about it? Come flying in on the private jet he says he doesn't use?"

"You said you'd do anything for me. What was that—some throw-away line?"

"No." Yes. "No. I would, I just don't think you should phone him."

"He has a right to know that his daughter is sick."

"But she's going to be fine, you said so yourself."

"She still needs him. Please, Tessa," her voice was wobbling.

"You do it," I insisted.

"He doesn't answer my calls."

"He will if you tell him that Cora is ill."

She shook her head.

"Well, he sure as hell won't listen to me then," I said. "He never liked me."

"But he'll believe you."

I was getting frustrated. Now wasn't the time for this. Damn Christoph, and all like him. "What's not to believe? That his daughter got pneumonia because he is a tight-fisted lying bastard?"

"Come on, Tessa, it wasn't his fault she got ill. Please, just call him and tell him what's happened."

"Oh, really? So it isn't his fault that you can't stay home and look after Cora when she's sick. It's not his fault that she doesn't get better care. It's not his fault that you can't afford a nanny to look after her when you are at work? It's not his fault that you never turn on the bloody central heating . . ."

"Tessa, look at me. I haven't slept, I'm wrung out, now is not the time for this."

"You're right. You should go home, have a rest, and then decide whether you want me to make this call. You're not thinking rationally."

"Thank you for that," said Billy, stiffly, "but I'm not leaving Cora."

"I'll stay with her. You should get some sleep. You're no help to Cora in this state."

Billy glared at me, then methodically placed her fork and spoon across her plate.

"I mean, honestly, Billy, when are you going to see this for what it is?"

"Tessa . . ." warned Billy. But I wasn't to be warned.

"She doesn't need him, Billy. She needs you, not some mythical figure you call her father. She doesn't know him, she doesn't think about him, I don't think she even cares about him. It's you. You're projecting all of this on to poor Cora's head."

Billy started fussing with the empty plates, then she waved at the waitress. I could see she was biting back the tears.

"I'm sorry, Billy, but I have enough information on Christoph to make sure you get plenty of money."

She reached for the bill.

I tried to take it from her. "It's OK, I'll pay for it," I said.

"No thanks," said Billy. "I can cover this."

"For God's sake, let me pay."

"No!" shouted Billy. "Stop shoving cash in my hand. I can pay for my own lunch!"

"What the hell are you getting cross with me for?"

"Leave me alone, Tessa. Please."

"I'm trying to help you."

Billy looked at me. "No, you're not. You are not helping me at all. What you are doing is what you always bloody do. If anyone is using Cora, it's you! Somehow you manage to turn this into your own little drama, with you at the center of everything, telling us how to live our lives when you can't fucking well live your own! So, please, just leave me alone."

"What are you talking about? You just asked me to call Christoph."

"I know. It was a mistake."

I was momentarily wrong-footed. "You don't want me to call any more?"

Billy looked at me for a moment. "Can't you see what you're doing?"

"What are you talking about?"

"Come on, Tessa. I know I may be treading water waiting for the impossible to happen—"

"Christoph to grow a heart."

Billy ignored me. "But you are just treading water."

"Me?"

"Yes. You. Whoever you are."

"Now you're being ridiculous . . ."

"You can dish it out, but you can't take it."

That was probably true. I didn't have siblings so I had never learned to be teased. Or share. I wasn't very good at sharing. I was generous. I gave a lot of things, but I didn't share my things. Thinking about it, I was quite particular about that. Maybe I didn't want to share my life. Maybe that was the problem. My moment of clarity was short-lived.

"The Tessa King I know has got lost in some parallel universe where God knows what is happening, while you just fill the gap in her absence."

I shook my head with a laugh. "I think you've just described yourself perfectly."

"You're right. I'm stuck on Christoph, I wish to bloody hell I wasn't, but it was at least real, what we had was real, we had a child together. Do you have any idea how that feels? I love her so much it hurts me," she jabbed at her stomach. "I thought the last forty-eight hours were going to kill me—you want that, you really ready for that?"

"I . . ." I tried to fish a response from the sea of words that engulfed my brain, but nothing I liked hooked on, so I threw them back in.

"We were together for eight years, Tessa—"

"Off and on."

"Fuck it, there's no point talking to you—" I watched her count out enough cash to leave for lunch. I wanted to take that back immediately and apologize, but the words were strangling me. Billy threw her purse back in her bag, took her coat off the back of the chair and put it on. Don't go, I wanted to plead. This was all going wrong. This wasn't how it was supposed to be. I was the rock. I was the lynchpin, the fulcrum, the dependable one. They needed me.

"What about Cora?"

Billy didn't even bother looking at me. "What about her?"

"Can't I see her?"

"You know what? No. Go home, go back to doing whatever you were doing when I did need you."

Now who was being overdramatic? "I'm sorry I wasn't around when you needed me. There is a reason, Billy," I said, suggestively, "but I didn't want to bother you with it." I was relieved because I knew I had my pills and vodka "get out of jail" card. Billy stared at me, then sighed heavily. But she didn't bite. So I went on.

"And I'm sorry I won't call Christoph, but—"

Something in her snapped. "Fucking hell, Tessa," she shook her head. "You don't listen, do you?" Billy grabbed her bag. "I've got to go. Thanks for coming."

"Billy?"

"Bye." I watched her leave the restaurant then sat back down. I ordered a coffee. I shrugged apologetically at the waitress. Billy was stressed. Billy was tired. Billy was in denial. Poor Billy. I looked at the telephone numbers still in my hand. OK, I'd do it. For Billy. Pulling out my phone, I dialed Christoph's number.

I knew where Christoph was, I'd spent the previous week spying on him. He was building a second yacht for Sheikh Ahmed in Dubai, estimated to cost a staggering £13.5 m, of which Christoph would get a 20 percent commission. That didn't factor in the backhanders and tickles that he would receive from every fixture and fitting manufacturer in the boat-building business. Nor did it factor in the first boat he'd built, the one that cost a measly £5 m. The one he'd been photographed standing on, alongside his wealthy client, for *Ahlan!*— Dubai's version of *Hello!* He was ludicrous, and Billy was ludicrous to carry a torch for him.

There was no answer, or he was ducking the call, so I called the other number. His London home. "Hello?"

"Is that Mrs. Tarrenot?" I asked.

"Yes," came a wary reply.

"It's Tessa King. I'm Cora's godmother."

"Oh, hello. Christoph isn't here at the moment, can I take a message?"

"I'm in the hospital. Cora is ill."

"Again?"

"What do you mean again?"

"Um, well—"

I cut her off. "Cora has pneumonia. They thought it was meningitis."

Christoph's second wife didn't respond.

"Hello? Are you there?"

"Is she going to be all right?"

"Yes . . ." I meant to sound certain, but this woman wasn't being very nice and I felt my voice crack. "I'm sorry . . . Obviously Christoph needs to . . ." My voice cracked again. My jaw ached with the stress of trying to hold off the tears and get the words out. "It's been a bit stressful," I managed. I couldn't tell her I was crying because I'd just had an argument with my friend.

"It's all right. I'm sorry. Tell me what you want me to do."

I pulled myself together. "Can you give me the number of where he is?"

She paused again.

"Trust me, if it was my choice, I wouldn't be calling him."

"It's just that—oh, it doesn't matter."

"What?"

"Well, Billy has done this before."

"Done what?"

"Told us—my husband—that Cora was ill."

"She is ill quite a lot," I said, exasperated.

"Not as ill as Billy led us—Christoph—to believe."

"I don't know what you're talking about. I'm at the hospital, Cora has pneumonia and for a little while they thought it was very serious. Billy just thought he should know." Christ, I'm not surprised Billy didn't want to make this call.

"OK. Sorry. He's in Dubai, staying somewhere called the Burj Al Arab. I don't have the number because he always calls me. But that's where he is."

"Thank you."

"He won't come home, she's cried wolf too many times," said Christoph's wife before I could end the call. "To be honest, he wouldn't come back for his own daughters."

I didn't correct her Freudian slip. I didn't remind her that Cora was his own daughter. I didn't ask what she meant by cried wolf. *He'll believe you.*

International Directories put me through to the hotel. I didn't know much about Dubai's landmark hotel, except what I had learned going through back copies of *Ahlan!* I knew that it cost $1,000 a night. I also knew that some people called it the Cockroach—because from a certain angle it looks like the filthy beetle—though the name better suited a large proportion of the guests inside. A perfect place for a bug like Christoph to dwell.

"Burj Al Arab."

"Mr. Tarrenot, please." I waited to be put through.

"Hello?" came the familiar voice.

"Christoph, it's Tessa. I just called to tell you that Cora is in hospital with pneumonia." There were no tears this time. My voice was steady.

"How did you get this number?"

"She is on the mend though, thanks for asking."

"Is this for real?"

"Course it's for real."

"Is she stable?"

"Yes," I replied, knowing exactly what was coming next. God, how I would love to get this man in court. It was worth considering changing fields for.

"I can't come back."

"I wasn't asking you to, Christoph. I was simply informing you that your daughter has been ill. Your wife has the details. Goodbye."

I absolutely loathed that man.

I shouldn't have challenged Billy. It was my mistake. Not hers. I didn't understand why she had wanted me to call Christoph, now I understood. I still didn't think she needed to, but perhaps I was wrong about that. He was Cora's father, however poorly he did that job— even I knew he had rights. I shouldn't have pushed Billy while she was tired. She may have been behaving irrationally, but it was to be expected. I didn't want her sitting up in the hospital worrying about our argument, on top of everything else she had to worry about. I walked to a coffee shop and ordered Billy a latte to go. I pocketed some brown sugar and a twig to stir it in with, and returned to the hospital with my peace offering. This was the grown-up thing to do. I pressed the buzzer of the children's ward.

"I'm here to see Billy Tarrenot, she's with her daughter, Cora."

"Can I have your name? Oh, sorry, I've just been told, she's . . ." There was a muffled pause. "She's not here."

"Oh. Can I come in and see Cora?"

"Are you family?"

"Excuse me?"

"Are you family?"

I waited too long before replying. "I'm her godmother."

"Sorry," said the nurse over the intercom. "Hospital policy. Only family allowed in."

The speaker clicked. I was alone in the corridor. Only family allowed in. If I wasn't allowed to see Cora, who was allowed to come and see me?

I walked slowly back to the King's Road and caught the number 11 bus back to Victoria. Normally I would have been on the phone to Ben in a second, gabbling madly into the phone for the length of the journey, telling him about our argument. Almost every word. That way I'd have been able to stop any possibility of reflection and I would have let him make me feel better before I'd had time to work out why I really felt bad. I wondered, as I watched the high street shops judder past me, how long I'd been using him as a crutch. Ben would have told me not to worry; Ben would have reassured me that we always lash out at the person we love the most; that I was family, absolutely. He might have gently teased me that perhaps my timing was a little off, and I would have taken that tease on the chin and felt magnanimous about it. I stared at couples on the pavement below. But what he'd really have been doing was lying to me and I would have chosen to believe all those well-intentioned lies. I stared at my phone. I missed him. I missed that layer of protection he offered me. I put my phone away and stepped off the bus. I couldn't call him, it was out of the question, I'd made a pact with God—but I felt desolate because I realized that there wasn't anyone else in the world I ever wanted to talk to as much. I didn't trust myself to go home.

I cut through the back of Victoria and instead of crossing the motorway that separated me from the river and home, I turned left and made the short walk to Tate Britain. I climbed the wide stone steps to the museum and walked in. As soon as you are through the doors, the air changes. It is softer. The building has the ability to wrap itself around you, making you feel safe. All the animosity of the street is left outside, for everyone in there has come for the same reason. To

be humbled by art. I walked through the reverential hush to the
Turner exhibition and stared up at his mammoth paintings. I felt the
rain in his paintings splatter my face. I heard the whisper of shingle
on his beaches. I felt the rush of speed. The echo of silence. I got lost
there for a blissful couple of hours. It wasn't as good as a chat to Ben,
but it was close. And certainly a damn site healthier.

By the time I left the museum it was dark. I was feeling much calmer.
I had climbed out of my funk unaided. People were hurrying home.
Stressed, tired people, working all hours to educate their kids, rushing home to put them to bed, trying to cram in a day's worth of
parenting into an over-wrought hour. I ambled along the pavement,
enjoying, for once, my leisurely pace. Maybe I was being selfish, but
was that bad? I had to admit to myself that, arguments aside, today
had been a good day. Cora didn't have meningitis. We got lucky.
But what about the others? The people whose tests didn't come back
negative. What about the mothers of those children? The ones who
would not be leaving hospital. The whole children thing was a mine-
field, and that was after you'd managed to survive conception and
pregnancy.

I walked past my local pub. On impulse, I ducked in through the
corner door. It's an old-fashioned free house, no big football screen,
no computer games, just a small telly behind the bar, good beer with
strange names, Heineken on tap and packets of prawn cocktail crisps
(a weakness of mine). I ordered a half from Kenny, the landlord. Yes,
he knows me by name. Last time I'd been in was when I'd discovered my ex-boss had been institutionalized by his wife. It wasn't so
much a celebration as a punctuation. But tonight wasn't going to be
one of those nights; it wasn't even six, so just a quick half, no more
and maybe a bottle to take home for later . . . Order a curry . . . Have
an early night. Cora was going to be fine. Billy and I would sort out

our little mess. And as for Ben, well, we would have to be fine. I relied too heavily on his friendship not to make it better between us. I had made a pact with God to put away my foolish thoughts and get back on track; He, in turn, had looked after the ones I love. So Ben and I would go back to being friends as we always had, and all would be well. It was a fantasy of my own making, my own perpetuating and only I could end it. Billy was right in a way—by imagining a parallel universe I'd made living in the real one seem unsatisfactory. But honestly, what was so wrong with my life? I hadn't had to give up the notion of having children, but having them didn't feel quite so vital to me at that moment. *The universe is unfolding as it should.* I would take a leaf out of Helen's book. I would put my life in the hands of fate for a while and see where that took me. Beyond the pub, that is.

baby tinnitus

I was sitting at the bar, happy in familiar surroundings, exchanging pleasantries with a couple of the regulars when the Channel 5 news came on. Kirsty Young was mouthing words at me that I couldn't hear. Television is strangely mesmerizing, even with the sound off. I took a long, grateful sip. A tag line appeared at the bottom of the screen. "Comic killed," it said. I took another. The lager was good. Cold and wet and immediately hit the spot. A face flashed up. A face I knew.

"Kenny," I said, frowning as the face faded away, "can you turn that up, please?"

Kirsty, was suddenly replaced by a clip from a sitcom. The landlord picked up the remote control and pressed a button. The glass of beer hovered somewhere near my mouth. There was Neil, delivering some slapstick line; I heard the canned laughter, but I had no idea what the cans were laughing about. I shook my head rapidly, and looked again. Kirsty was back, speaking in her low, dour Scottish accent, eyeballing me from behind her glass plate. Eyeballing *me*.

"That was Neil Williams, appearing in the hit Channel 4 show, *Value Added*. He was declared dead today following a road accident outside Bristol in the early hours of this morning."

I jumped as though I'd been burned. My glass slipped through my fingers and fell to the floor. The glass bounced, the beer leapt up like a Las Vegas fountain and for a split second was suspended midair, then it fell back to the floor, covering me, the stool and the hideous carpet.

"Shit, sorry," I said, bending down too quickly, and beginning to feel queasy.

"Don't worry, I'll get it."

I leaned against the bar. I didn't feel too good. "I know him," I said, in disbelief. "I know him," I said again. "I've got to call Helen."

The pub was filling up but I couldn't wait. I looked for my phone in my bag; I couldn't see it. I searched my pockets. Was Neil really dead? Surely not. I felt something vibrate in my pocket. It was in the pocket I had just looked in. I answered the call.

"Helen?"

"Tessa King?"

"Yes."

"As a close friend of the deceased, would you care to comment on allegations that this was a drunk-driving incident?"

"Who is this?"

"I'm calling from the *Express*—"

I pressed "end," then stared at my phone. I looked at Kenny. "Who the fuck was that? How did they get my number?"

He shrugged. I rang Helen's mobile. It was switched off. She was probably being hounded by the press. I called her home. The answerphone picked it up.

"Helen, don't worry, I'm on my way." Maybe she was in Bristol. Maybe she'd gone to identify the body. Drunk-driving? Early hours of the morning? There was no allegedly about it. Damn it, he'd gone and fucking got himself killed. I reached for Kenny's remote and flicked through the news channels. Sky. CNN. It wasn't being covered. I looked at Kenny again. "Who's got the twins?" He replied by passing me another drink. Vodka and tonic.

"Thank you," I said, gratefully. I had to do something I never thought I would: I called Marguerite for help. It wasn't hard to get the paper's number. I was put through to her assistant. "I need to speak to Marguerite now," I said, knocking back the vodka.

"I'm afraid she isn't taking calls at present."

"I know, I've been hounded by the press too. Tell her it's Tessa. Tessa King. I just need to know where Helen is."

The woman didn't answer me.

"I'm not some mad woman, I promise. Helen is a friend, I'm the twins' godmother. I just found out about Neil. Please help me."

There was another lengthy pause. "Hang on." I started tapping the bar with my nails until Kenny looked at me, so I started pacing a very small area instead. Come on. Come on. The line crackled. I should be at home.

"I'm putting you through to Marguerite. I'll text you her number, in case there is a problem."

"Thank you, thank you, thank you . . ." I managed to get my coat back on.

"Tessa, are you there?"

"Marguerite, sorry to bother you. I just want to know where Helen is, there's no answer at home . . ." I waited. Marguerite didn't say anything.

"Marguerite? Are you there?"

"Yes . . ."

"What's wrong?"

"Tessa, about Helen . . ."

"Is she with you?" No answer. Unless you call a sigh an answer. The woman was infuriating. Did I have to beg? "Marguerite, someone should be with her."

"Tessa . . ."

"Yes!"

"God, Tessa, Helen was in the car."

"What?" No. Helen, in Bristol, in the early hours of the morning. She didn't do press junkets. She didn't leave the twins. "Is she all right?"

I will remember this moment for as long as I live. A woman came to the bar in a sorry state and asked for a cider and black. She was wearing fake fur and fake pearls. Kenny knew her by name too.

"I'm sorry, Tessa," said Marguerite. "She was killed outright."

I staggered backwards and landed against the stool. Marguerite wasn't making sense.

"Neil's been killed," I said.

"I know. Helen was with him."

I looked down. The swirling pattern of red and purple started to rotate beneath my feet.

"You all right, lass?"

"That bastard killed her," I said.

"No, Tessa. It was an accident."

"Fucking drug-addict, piss-head bastard killed her."

"Tessa, no, stop it, please . . ." Was Marguerite crying?

"How can you defend him?"

"I'm not. Oh my God, Tessa, I don't know how it happened. Helen was driving. Helen was driving the car."

Where was all that noise coming from?

"What?"

"They came off the road at ninety miles an hour and hit a tree. She was killed outright; Neil was thrown from the car, but died in hospital from massive internal injuries."

I looked up at Kenny, he was undulating too.

"It was a terrible accident."

There was an excruciating pain in my chest. I'd been tricked. God was a two-faced, lying b—

"Timbeeeer," yelled a voice from somewhere. The next thing I knew I was staring at Kenny's shoes.

*   *   *

I was out for seven and a half minutes. The motorcycle paramedic reached the pub within six. If I had been having a heart attack, the man would have saved my life, but he couldn't fix me because I wasn't having a heart attack. I was having a panic attack. Apparently, they feel much the same—agony, but quick. Because of my mild hyperglycemia, I experienced a brief blackout. The paramedic advised against alcohol for a few days. I didn't tell him that I would ignore his advice as soon as he was out of the building. Helen was dead. Every time I thought that, my chest tightened again. It was agreed that I shouldn't walk home although it was literally over the road, but it was a fast main road, where the speed camera flashed as regularly as the paparazzi, and they didn't trust me. So Kenny went out to flag me down a cab. The paramedic left, someone passed me a brandy. I knocked it back. Helen was dead. Squeeze.

"Cab's outside," said Kenny.

"I'm sorry," I said, as he took my arm.

"You take it easy now, girl," he said. "Can't go on like this."

"Helen is dead," I said.

He simply nodded and closed the door behind me. Three pounds later, I got out. Roman buzzed me in before I had to start fishing around for my keys. I looked at him. I could see the concern in his eyes. I felt a fool. A bloody fool. I walked over to his desk.

"I'm so sorry," I said. "For worrying you."

"Are you feeling OK now?" he asked.

How could I tell him? How could I ask for more sympathy, more attention? I couldn't. I too had cried wolf many times before. I nodded. "Thank you," I said, and walked to the lift. The doors opened with a ping. The hollow, lonely tune to my homecoming. I wanted Ben more than I ever thought possible. The deal was off.

*   *   *

The inside of my flat was dark. The string of lights that edged Battersea Park glowed across the river. It was a high tide. High and choppy. The barges battered one another. The water pummeled the foundations of the bridge. Clouds had descended from on high to soak up the spit and dribble of Londoners on the move. And Helen was dead. I didn't care what Marguerite said. As far as I was concerned, she'd been killed by her husband. As good as killed by her husband. I turned on the television and watched the flat fill with its flickering blue, electric light. I'd missed the six o'clock news. I'd wait for Channel 4. In the half-light, I located the holdall that held my life in photographic form. I picked up a handful of packets. Somewhere in there was Helen as I'd known her. Alive. Free. Young. I went to the kitchen to get a drink. There, on the fridge, attached by a cowboy magnet, was the thank-you note she'd sent me for the twins' christening present. I stared at her handwriting, but what I heard was her voice. It was so clear, as clear as if she were standing next to me: *Whatever you do, don't let my mother get her hands on my boys* . . . I took the note off the fridge.

My darling Tessa,

What a hit you were, as always. I absolutely adore the hip flasks you gave them . . . *Whatever you do, don't let my mother get her hands on my boys* . . . And the quote from the "Desiderata" you had engraved on them nearly finished me off. I'm sorry I didn't say goodbye, I hit a hormonal wall, I guess, but thank you for all your support, as always. *Whatever you do, don't let my mother get her hands on my boys* . . . I know that the boys will be in safe hands with you and Claudia as godmothers and guardians. I trust your judgment more than my own, so I know that you will be a great godmother and will always know what to do, whatever the circumstances.

I love you, as always, and remember—the universe is unfolding as it should, even if you think it isn't.

Helen xx.

PS *Whatever you do, don't let my mother get her hands on my boys* . . .

There was no ink on the page after her kisses, but there may as well have been. I called Marguerite back. Holding the phone to my ear, I put my head on my knees and listened to the ringing.

"Tessa? Are you all right? Some man said you'd fainted."

"I'm all right. Well, I'm not all right, obviously."

There was an awkward silence.

"There was nothing about Helen in the news," I said, finally speaking.

"Not yet. I have some clout, but not as much as I need."

"I don't understand."

"I'm afraid Helen might have been drinking."

"Helen? She never . . ." Well, once, at Neil's launch, but . . .

"I'm afraid she did."

"She didn't."

"So, you didn't get the crazed, ranting calls in the middle of the night?"

I opened my mouth to reply, but couldn't think of what to say. Helen and Marguerite's relationship had always been destructive.

"That was just reserved for me. I see."

"I never saw her drink," I insisted.

"Well, anyway, they'd been at a party, not her favorite environment, so I thought it best to keep the attention away from Helen; she never liked it."

"No, she didn't." Though you love it.

There was another silence.

"Anyone else hurt?" I asked.

"Thankfully, no. The police told me it was an empty road. There were no brake marks, or evidence that she lost control of the car. They think she probably fell asleep at the wheel and the car simply drifted off the road."

"So they don't think it was drink-related?"

"No. But they don't know my . . ." Marguerite cleared her throat. "Didn't, um . . . What do you want, Tessa?"

To talk to someone who knew Helen long into the night until my heart caught up with what my head was being told. To make good my promise to your daughter, although, as ever, at the time I hadn't known what I was promising. "I was wondering where the twins are."

"I have them."

"And where are you?"

"At their house."

Promise me.

"I'm coming over."

Promise me, Tessa.

"I am about to take them home to mine."

I peeled myself off my floor. "Don't go anywhere, Marguerite."

"The press is camped outside."

"Please. For Helen, don't go anywhere."

"What are you talking about?"

"I'm coming over."

"I think there has been enough drama for one day, Tessa, don't you?"

"I mean it, Marguerite."

"I'm taking the nanny, they'll be perfectly well looked after. I'm not proposing to do it on my own."

"I don't care if you have an army of nannies, stay there."

"Tessa, these are my grandchildren. I can take them wherever I like."

"I am their guardian. You'll stay where you are."

My strong words belied the state I was in. I ended the call and slumped back down on the floor. Helen was dead. Neil was dead. The twins were mine.

I didn't have to call Ben, he called me. He was the first of many calls that peppered that night and the following days. But Ben was the first. Of course. Death put silly stolen kisses into perspective. Death put arguments in perspective. Death put everything into perspective.

"Where are you? Shall I come over?" asked Ben without introducing himself, or saying hello.

"I'm in a cab, going to Helen's house. Marguerite is with the twins and all I know is that Helen would not want that."

"You're going to take the twins?"

"No. God, no. I'm just going to make sure someone is there representing Helen." Representing Helen. I shuddered.

"Are you all right?"

"I just can't believe it. How did you find out?"

"A hack called me, he knew I knew them both."

"Someone from the press called me," I said, suddenly remembering the random call.

"People are sniffing for a story," said Ben.

"There isn't one, is there?"

"No. Neil was paralytic, but I doubt Helen would have let him drive."

"She didn't," I said sadly. "But she should never have been driving at that time of night." I remembered Helen literally dropping off to sleep on the sofa mid-sentence. It made me feel sick. She should have been at home, tucked up in bed, planning her divorce, not partying with him. It didn't make sense. "I don't even know what she was doing there. Bristol, of all places." We talked round in circles until the taxi pulled up outside the cream-colored house. Marguerite was right: the press was hovering.

"Listen," I said. "I've got to go."

"Good luck, darling. If you need support, you know where I am."

I thanked him, paid and got out of the cab. I pushed my way through to the gate and pressed the buzzer. I knew the security code into the front porch, but didn't dare use it in case someone saw the numbers. Cameras were flashing, but they quickly lost interest when they realized I wasn't anyone important. I couldn't understand why they were there. It must have been a quiet day in the newsroom.

Marguerite let me in, but not until she'd let me sweat for a minute or two. All the time I had known Helen I had known that, given the chance to be kind or mean, Marguerite was mean. It was in her DNA, she didn't know how to be any other way. I wasn't sure she even knew she was doing it. As I stood on the doorstep waiting to be let in, I squeezed and released my fists like a boxer preparing for a fight. I knew I had one on my hands; I didn't know that in that brief thirty minutes, Marguerite had already taken the first punch.

A bewildered-looking woman opened the door and showed me through to the drawing room with the large cream sofas. It was there that Neil had held one of the twins high over his head, high on drugs, shaking him in time to the music. It was there that I had sat, having put Helen to bed, and poured myself a large whisky. It was there that I had thrown myself once again into the middle of someone else's drama and only seen the episode I had wanted to see. Had Helen had any intention of leaving Neil? Or had she gone to Bristol to patch things up again?

Marguerite sat as still as stone; she looked as immaculate as ever but I couldn't help noticing the empty brandy glass and the rapid pulse in her neck. I wanted to go over and hug her, but she wasn't that sort of woman, we didn't have that sort of relationship. I stood uncomfortably.

"I'm so sorry for your loss, Marguerite," I said.

"Thank you," she replied.

I tried to think of something else to say, but my words deserted me. Marguerite was looking at me with disapproval. I glanced at my own reflection in the large gilded mirror that hung over the fireplace. I had dressed in a mad panic. I had dressed a lifetime ago, preparing myself for the worst before dashing to hospital, not knowing whether I was going to make it in time to see Cora alive.

I thought going back to being just friends with Ben was enough to meet my part of the bargain I'd made, but it clearly wasn't—not by God's standards, not by Marguerite's and not by my own. Because here I was, in those same clothes, standing in the house that Helen would never come home to, trying to come to terms with her horrific, sudden death.

"I'm sorry," I said, self-consciously pulling my jersey sleeve up my arm. "I dressed in a hurry."

"Weren't you in a pub?"

I frowned. How could I explain the inexplicable? "Can I get you something? Water, a drink—"

"Another brandy, please." She held out her glass. Her short, dark red nails brushed over my skin. As a child, Helen had been beaten with a hairbrush by those same hands. I snatched the glass away. No wonder Helen never wanted her children being brought up by this woman. "Help yourself," she said. I did. I carried the refilled glass back to her. She took it without thanking me. This was not a time for small talk or manners.

"How did you find out?" I asked after another lengthy silence.

"Bristol police called me in the middle of the night. I didn't answer it at first, but Helen never rang more than twice, so in the end I picked it up." She swirled the brandy around the bulbous glass bowl. "I wish I hadn't."

"Did you have to go and . . ." I faltered.

"I will tomorrow. A name can't be released to the press if it hasn't been officially identified," said Marguerite, sounding a trifle victorious.

"So it might not be her!" I exclaimed, suddenly excited.

"It was her."

I wasn't listening. Neil liked picking up girls, it could have been any of his floozies. Maybe Helen had left him, maybe she'd set up home in the Mandarin Oriental.

"I'm sorry, Tessa, but wishful thinking isn't going to get you out of this one. It was Helen driving the car."

"I hate to tell you this, now of all times, but Neil often went off with other women. She was thinking of leaving him because of it."

"She was never going to leave him over a couple of minor indiscretions. Honestly, you'd have thought I'd taught her nothing."

"I don't understand," I said, perplexed.

"Please will you stop pacing." I hadn't realized I had been. I stood still. "Anyway, I know it was Helen, because she rang me before she got into the car."

There was still a possibility that Marguerite was mistaken. "What did she say?"

Marguerite looked at me, then shook her head a fraction. "Nothing."

"She rang you at two in the morning and said nothing?"

Marguerite paused again. "Yes."

"Had she been drinking?"

"Tessa, do you mind? I'm not feeling up to an inquisition right now."

"Sorry, I just thought—"

"I know. That's you to a T. Underneath it all, you've always been a very positive person. I hoped it would rub off on my daughter. I don't think it did." Marguerite looked at me again. "She wasn't a very happy woman, was she?"

I shook my head. Marguerite downed the rest of her drink and put it on the coffee table next to a pile of *Hello!* magazines.

"The twins will fare better. I'll see to that."

Ah . . . So the easy bit was over. The ceasefire, what little there had been of it, had ended. I braced myself for battle.

"Where are the twins?" I asked, taking a seat opposite her.

She looked me over. "Upstairs, of course. Sleeping."

"Do you think they know?"

"Don't be ridiculous, Tessa. They're babies."

I sighed. She was right. They'd never know. "Poor little things, life without a mother to care for them . . ."

"The nanny seems very competent. She specializes in twins and has been very eager not to alter their routine."

I decided she was missing my point on purpose, but I refrained from saying anything. I was going to try and keep things amicable. Trouble was, Marguerite and I didn't do amicable very well.

"Rose telephoned," said Marguerite, not bothering to wait for my reply.

I looked up. At last, someone I could genuinely commiserate with. Rose loved Helen, had cared for her since she was a child; she'd come, she'd come back.

"I told her she was no longer required since I'm fairly sure she has no intention of coming to live with me. She hated me the day I moved to Hong Kong and she's hated me ever since. She spoilt my husband and Helen rotten. Well, I'm sorry, but indentured servitude wasn't my style."

I opened my mouth to protest.

Marguerite held up her hand. "Please keep those thoughts to yourself and try and remember that my daughter died last night."

That's all I was thinking about. "Marguerite, about the twins?"

"Yes, Tessa." It was clear to me that she'd simply been waiting while I plucked up the courage to have the conversation. My stalling, my pretence at sympathetic chat, had just given her the opportunity to see how scared I was.

"Helen left me in charge of deciding what should be done in the event that she and Neil died. I never thought I would have to have this conversation with you, I never thought in a million years . . ." I couldn't go on. I paused, breathing deeply. "I don't believe this is happening."

"You want the twins," said Marguerite, putting me out of my misery, and adding to it at the same time. "My daughter has just been stolen from me, and you want to steal the twins, too?"

Stolen? Steal? I wasn't stealing anything.

"No, Tessa. Family is family."

Since when did family mean so much to you? I thought. She could con everyone else, but she couldn't con me. Forget trying to keep this amicable. I stood up. Even if she stood too, I had height on my side. "I think you're forgetting who you're talking to. Your relationship with Helen has always been strained. So don't 'family' me."

"Or what? What are you going to do?"

That, I didn't know. "Come on, Marguerite, let's not do this. We both loved Helen, we both love the boys. Let's do this together."

"You are not getting my grandsons, Tessa, and that's that."

I opened my mouth, but Marguerite went on.

"I mean, look at you—hardly the model parent, are you?" she said, eyeing me with obvious disapproval. "My daughter is not yet dead for one day and you're already planning how to get custody of her children."

"I don't want custody of them. I wish this wasn't happening."

"Oh, you just don't want me to have them."

Whatever you do, don't let my mother get her hands on my boys. "It's complicated. We've got to be adult about this. Helen had wishes, wishes I intend to see she gets."

"I've called the lawyer. You being the twins' guardian is just a whimsical thing that Helen did to tie you to her. But it doesn't stand up to very much. It isn't statutory law. The courts deal with everything on a case-by-case basis. Really it is up to Helen's trustees to decide where the boys should go and I've already spoken to them. I am their next of kin, whether you like it or not. Bad luck, you don't get an instant family."

"What the hell are you talking about? Helen died in a car crash. I only found out a couple of hours ago." I ran my hands through my hair. "I'm still trying to get my head around that!"

"Lie to yourself, Tessa, all you like, but it doesn't wash with me."

"Lie to myself about what, exactly?"

"You want the boys for yourself. This is nothing to do with Helen's wishes."

"What?"

"You want the twins. It's a perfect solution to your life, isn't it? Can't get the man, but you can get the babies, who happen to come with a considerable amount of money."

I didn't want to be in the same room as Helen's mother, but temporarily found that I lacked the strength to stand. She'd sucked the last of my courage from me. I landed in the oversized cushion and felt myself sink slowly into the sofa. That was when I noticed the same silver-framed photo of Neil and Helen's wedding day that I had seen Neil use to chop out lines of cocaine on. My beautiful friend, who'd swung from a hammock on a Vietnamese beach, was dead. The man standing next to her in the photograph had killed her, I didn't care

what the police report said; I didn't care if she had fallen asleep at
the wheel, she wouldn't have been exhausted if it hadn't been for
him, so whatever the outcome, he killed her. He killed my friend,
but long before she'd met him, the woman sitting opposite me, had
been bleeding her dry. I wanted to cry but I would not. For Helen's
sake, I would not. I knew what Helen wanted better than anyone. I
knew she wouldn't want her mother taking care of her kids. No way.
Whatever Marguerite threatened me with, I would fight her to the
bitter end. I would use any means I had to ensure that Helen's wishes
were met.

I lifted my chin from my chest. "Apart from the christening, when
did you last come over to the house to see the boys?"

"That is irrelevant."

"When were you last invited to?"

"Tessa—"

"You only live round the corner, you must have popped in all the
time."

"I work, remember."

"What about the weekends—did you look after them and let
Helen have a few minutes to herself?"

"Helen had her own nanny living here, as well as one for the
boys. I didn't think she needed my help."

"OK, when did you just pop over for a visit? When did you and
she last have a nice mother-daughter lunch? And her last exeat from
school doesn't count!"

Marguerite simply stared back at me.

"Where did she want to be buried?"

"I presume where she was married."

"Wrong. She wanted to be cremated. She wanted her ashes to be
scattered on a beach in Vietnam. China Beach, to be exact. It spoke
to her roots. What was her favorite piece of writing?"

Marguerite raised her chin slightly.

"'Desiderata.' Where were the twins conceived?"

I watched with satisfaction as Marguerite shifted uncomfortably.

"What song did she play loudly on the stereo every time you invented a new way to hurt her?"

Marguerite stood up. Her Nicole Fahri suit hung off her slim frame. "Yes, yes, I'm sure she confided all those things to you. No doubt trying to impress you. But then you know that; that's why you liked her, isn't it, Tessa? Because she relied on you so much. How very life-affirming it must be, to be so pivotal to others." Marguerite turned the clasp of her large Mulberry handbag with a click and looked at me. "Doesn't leave you with very much, though, when they move on, does it?"

I let a little sarcastic laugh fall from my lips while simultaneously erasing Marguerite's words from my mind. "If finding fault with me provides you with comfort at this difficult time"—I spread my arms wide as an offering—"then I am glad." I straightened up. Two could play at this game. "But let's get one thing straight: I didn't fuck up your daughter. The damage was done long before we ever met."

Marguerite leaned closer towards me. "And don't you just love a pet project."

I opened my mouth to retaliate, but Marguerite held up her manicured hand. "I'm going to let this pass, on the understanding that you may be suffering from some kind of shock. But mark my words, Tessa King, you're not going to win this one. You think I'm the only one they'll turn the microscope on? Do you? You think you are so fit to be a parent? A girl who can't even keep a job down without creating some kind of sexual scandal? How many other marriages have you wrecked, I wonder? I shouldn't think it would be hard to find out. What will the courts think of all those men, coming and going in the night? The booze. The parties. Not a great deal." She looked me up and down with disdain. "You can't even look after yourself."

I wanted to rise up out of the sofa and hit her, but it would only serve her more. She could say what she liked. It was her way. But finally this wasn't about me; it was about Helen. She couldn't defend herself when she was alive, but I was going to make damn sure she was defended now.

"I'm going to go now," said Marguerite. "I will let you ponder upon my words, and when you've come to your senses, you can call me. Failing that, my lawyer will contact you as he will Neil's family."

"Neil's family?"

"Yes, Tessa."

"What do they want?"

"I've no idea. Until the police told me, I wasn't even sure that his parents were alive. But they are, so even if they weren't particularly important to Neil himself, I will see that their wishes are considered. There's a brother, too. A builder in Norfolk, I gather."

"And what about your daughter's wishes. Are you even going to ask me what they were?"

"Tessa, you have always been very loyal to Helen and whatever you may think, I appreciate that. But you have to realize that Helen said one thing to you, another to me, and probably something entirely different to her husband. You couldn't possibly know her wishes."

"Why's that?" I asked belligerently.

"Because she didn't know them herself. I may not be the perfect mother, but I did try to instill some sense of purpose in my daughter, but she refused to learn. I would have been happy for her to just be a mother and wife, if she'd been happy. But she wasn't. She liked to blame me for everything, but you don't get to gad around for thirty-five years and then suddenly ask to be taken seriously."

I was emotionally exhausted. It made me less cautious. "I think she just wanted to be loved. By you, if you want the truth."

"The truth, Tessa? You have that unique ability to see the truth, do you? Tessa King—the Oracle?"

"Didn't take a genius to work it out."

"Oh, Tessa, when are you going to learn that there are no simple answers in this life. I loved her, she knew that, but she drove me mad." Her voice cracked a little, but she quickly composed herself. "She did nothing with the gifts she was born with. Was I wrong to expect more from her? Does that make me so terrible? I have no doubt your parents ask just as much from you, probably more."

"My parents didn't get divorced."

Marguerite shook her head at me. "That barely deserves a response, but yes, I made a mistake marrying Helen's father. Our cultures were too different. Should I have stayed and lived a half-life? Would that have made me a better mother? Living to a fraction of my capacity?"

I couldn't answer. I didn't want Marguerite becoming too human.

"Don't look for simple answers, there aren't any." She rose out of the chair, and stood in front of me. "The trustees have frozen funds for the time being, just to make sure nothing untoward goes on. Since you're determined to make sure the twins stay here, then you'll have to stay here too. Keep the nanny if you wish, but she is a hundred pounds a day, so you may want to reconsider. You know where I am."

Marguerite collected her hat and coat from the banister. I heard her heels clip the marble floor.

"Do you care at all that your daughter is dead?" I shouted from the sofa.

The heels stopped. Only for a fraction. Then I heard the door slam. That was her answer. The flashing lights of the cameras firing off sparked through the muslin drape. The grieving mother. Poor,

poor Helen, to have been born into her care when there were so many others who could have done a better job. I climbed the stairs and crept into the twins' room. I lay on the floor between their cots, stared at the luminous galaxy on the ceiling and listened to their snuffling, grunting baby breathing.

All you'd have to do is find them a happy home, Helen had said.

That was it, then. I had to find my godsons a happy home. Easy. Who was I trying to kid? If the last few weeks had taught me anything, it was that happy homes were hard to find. Life on the other side of the fence wasn't as blissful as I'd thought.

I woke up in the middle of the night with a sore neck. It took me a moment to figure out where I was. The luminous stars had faded, I was in pitch-black. I couldn't hear anything. I felt the carpet I was lying on, then found Peter Rabbit. I sat up in the dark. I was in the nursery, so why couldn't I hear anything? I crawled towards the bar of pale light under the door and eased myself up. I found the light and slowly switched on the dimmer. Two babies lay, spreadeagled in their sleeping bags, in the middle of their enormous cots. I'd never known babies lie so still. I crept over and placed my hand on Tommy's chest. I felt nothing through the quilted blue gingham. I pressed slightly harder. Suddenly he flinched. It startled me. His arms and legs shot up. He grunted, then his limbs lowered slowly back down again, and he resumed his restful sleep. My watch said 4:02. So I was right, it hadn't been the twins keeping Helen up all night.

I crept back out of the bedroom, left the door ajar and went downstairs to the spare room I'd slept in on Saturday night. I couldn't really sleep. I kept hearing the twins crying out, so I'd climb back up the stairs, peer into the cots, only to see two babies sound asleep. My ears were playing tricks on me. Fran told me she still occasionally hears a baby crying in the house. Two nights sleeping in the same house as the twins and I already had baby tinnitus. Eventually, the nanny came out of her room, closed the twins' door and told me to stop worrying. Poor woman looked terrified. I didn't blame her.

Of course, it was really my brain that was keeping me awake. Memories kept coming back to me. Memories of Helen, happy and carefree. Of the ridiculous things she made me do. Dangerous and wild at times. We hitchhiked to Oxford once, gatecrashed an Oxford University May ball and ended up jumping on the bouncy castle with the band. A totally unheard of Jamiroquai. She took me to Cuba for a week when I was broke and another badly chosen boy had let me down. It was Helen who'd told me I picked badly on purpose. I didn't believe her, but she'd been right all along. She'd never forgotten what I had told her floating down the Mekong River. She alone had tried to pull me out of my "comfort circle," as she called it. Nick and Fran, Ben and Sasha, Claudia and Al, and I would go with her— Cuba, Las Vegas, skiing, hiking, yoga retreats were all her doing, but I always returned to my friends. To Ben. And then she met Neil and, bit by bit, the Helen I knew began to change. All this time I'd been worried about Helen selling herself short, becoming invisible, but the person who'd really been living a half-life was me.

At seven the twins woke up. A blessed relief, I was going mad lying there. I got dressed and went up to the nursery. I leaned over each cot and smiled down. I got two gummy grins back. Was it my imagination, or were these kids getting more attractive? I was halfway through changing Bobby, when the nanny came in.

"I can do that," she said.

"Don't worry, nearly done."

I explained to her who I was and apologized for creeping around the house.

"So, if you are the twins' guardian, does that mean I'm working for you or their grandmother?"

"Everything is a bit up in the air at the moment," I replied, "but you'll be paid."

She looked back at the babies, satisfied that she'd be looked after at least. "Poor little things," she said.

I brushed a tear away. I didn't want the boys seeing any sad faces. I didn't want them to be disorientated, or hurt. I wanted them to think nothing was wrong. Trouble was, Helen fed them herself, so that was going to be hard.

"I'll need your help feeding them."

"Sure," she said. She went over to the cupboard and took out two cartons of readymade milk.

"Shouldn't we use the breast milk? Won't it be less stressful for them?"

"What breast milk?"

I pointed to the cupboard. "There is a freezer behind there, packed full of the stuff." She looked confused.

I understood her confusion. "It's a clever design," I said, hoping to reassure her.

"I know there is a fridge there, but there's no breast milk in it."

There was, she'd been looking in the wrong place. I'd seen it myself. I'd used it. Well, I hadn't, because it had curdled, but that was my fault. I'd heated it up wrong. "You do this," I said. "I'll find it."

The nanny took over changing Bobby and I opened the freezer door. It was empty except for some ice-cube trays. I closed the door again. That was weird. I opened it a second time, just to make sure. Then I looked in the fridge. That was empty too. Where had all the milk gone? There had been row upon row of it. We could have fed the boys on Helen's milk for a month. I didn't understand.

"Mrs. Williams told me to use these." She showed me the cartons before deftly decanting them into waiting bottles. "It is expensive doing it this way, but they have benefits. The twins aren't used to warm milk, which makes feeding in a hurry much easier."

"Isn't breast milk warm?"

"Yes."

"They didn't have to get used to the difference?"

"Difference between what?"

"Breast milk and that—" I pointed at the cartons. I was beginning to recognize the expression on her face. Was I losing my grip on reality?

"Wasn't Helen feeding them herself?"

"No."

That didn't make sense either, though I had told her myself to quit.

"I think she stopped breastfeeding some time ago, but I don't know the details. I was going to talk to Mrs. Williams when she returned. I don't think this brand of milk suits Tommy. He drinks more but is then very sick, which is why he weighs considerably less than his brother. I would like to try him on a formula for hungrier babies; it should keep him happier for longer. If that doesn't work, we could try goat's milk."

"How long have you been working here?" I asked.

"Since Monday night. It took me a couple of days to figure out what was wrong with Tommy."

"And everything was OK?"

She didn't answer.

"You can tell me, what harm can it do now? I know Neil wasn't very easy. I was here Monday morning myself. There was a bit of a scene."

"I don't think the problem was with Mr. Williams."

"Oh."

"Really, I don't know the details. Personally, I didn't notice anything."

"Anything about what?"

"Well, um, they did warn me that Mrs. Williams had a small problem—"

"She didn't go by that name. She was called Helen Zhao, OK?" The woman nodded. "And for your information, it was Mr. Williams who had the problem, not Helen, I assure you."

She held up her hands. "Sadly, I didn't get to know them. I really wouldn't like to say."

I was perplexed, but since she'd been around for such a short time, I didn't continue the conversation. Instead, I quietly fed my orphaned godson and saw Helen in his eyes for the first time. I put Tommy over my shoulder to wind him and was rewarded with a waterfall of puke down my back. I gave him back to the far more competent nanny.

"Get the new milk," I said bossily, and left the nursery. Had that been my first parental decision?

I stood in Helen's bedroom and looked around at the immaculate dressing table, the silk cushions and vast bedspread. I opened the closet; there was row upon row of designer outfits, all the "must-have" pieces, accessories, handbags and shoes. I ran my fingers along them. I wanted to find her smell, something I could hold on to, but everything was clean and in bags. There was no trace of her at all. I thought about my friend. She was lying in a bag too. The Helen I'd known was gone. Long gone. I stared into the vast wardrobe.

"What's going on, Helen?" I asked her clothes. Strangely enough, it was her clothes that gave me my first answer. I was covered in puke. I felt strange wearing her clothes, but I needed something to borrow while I put my stuff through the washing machine. Helen was much smaller than me, but there were some items of hers that I did suit, and had always coveted. Her vast collection of Maharishi trousers, for example. I found a pair and put them on. Then I saw the jumper she'd been wearing that day in the kitchen when I'd come over to visit. It was only a few weeks ago, but my God, it seemed like years. The jumper was folded on the top shelf. I heard her voice again. *Consider it yours.* Here was a piece of Helen I could keep. As I pulled it down, a large plastic see-through ziplock bag fell on my head. I picked it up. It was from the Portland Hospital. It had a medicine helpline number on it and Helen's name and her room number at the private hospital. I glanced at the contents. Inside were flattened packs of some hefty-looking medication. Codrydamol. Dicloflenac. Zanax. Diazapam. Vicadin. Volderol. They were all empty. Helen had had a long and complicated Caesarean and her scar had got infected. I remembered visiting her in the hospital and she was panicking then about taking medication and breastfeeding but the maternity staff had reassured her that it would be fine. Some even recommended she wash them down with a nice red wine. I looked briefly at the packets. From the amount in the bag, it looked like she'd been taking them for some time. I threw the ziplock bag in the bin, pulled the jumper on, and went downstairs.

I looked at my watch: 7:53. Far too early to call anyone without kids. I dialed Francesca's number.

"Hello?"

It was Nick. "You're back. It's me, Tessa."

"Oh my God, Tessa, are you OK?"

"Not really. Do you know—"

"About Neil, yes."

"Oh Nick, there's worse, more . . ."

"We know. Ben called everyone. He said you were off to get the twins, is that true?" I imagined the jungle drums had been beating fairly loudly between my friends. Did they feel, as Marguerite felt, that I was off to claim my instant family? Just add death.

"It's not like that. Helen didn't want her mum to have the kids. I don't know what's going to happen."

"It's a big responsibility."

"I haven't even spoken to the solicitor yet. I'm just trying to do what Helen asked me to do."

There was a pause from Nick.

"You still there?" I asked.

"Yes, of course. Just, oh, I don't know, be careful."

"I know how to handle Marguerite," I said, full of bravado I didn't feel.

"Just, well, be careful you don't get so involved you can't get un-involved."

I didn't like where this conversation was going. "Is Fran there?"

"Just getting everyone up. Caspar's home."

I didn't have the energy to think about Caspar right then.

"I think I see a glimmer of improvement," said Nick.

"Well, he's always loved your mum and dad," I said, forcing a response.

"True. Maybe seeing things through the eyes of someone he respects so much has helped." Meaning he didn't respect me? Now I definitely didn't like where this conversation was going.

"Well, anyway—"

"Sorry, now's not the time to talk about that. Is there anything we can do for you?"

Lay off me?

"No, thanks. And don't worry about getting Fran, I'll call her later."

"It's no problem."

"Actually, the twins need—"

"I understand. I'll tell her to call you."

I put the phone down and stared out across the empty kitchen. The twins didn't need anything, the nanny had everything beautifully under control. I really hadn't charged over to Helen's house to claim her children as my own. I really, really hadn't. Who wanted that kind of responsibility suddenly foisted on them? It wasn't going to improve my chances of finding a pod partner and, anyway, I didn't have the room. I was doing this for Helen. Surely my friends knew that.

I paced the house, feeling at odds with myself until I could call Helen's solicitor. It was nice to talk to someone who had clearly cared for Helen, and was in as much shock as I was. We could have talked for hours, but I needed some vital information. So he went over the rules of guardianship with me. He had taken care of Helen's legal affairs since her father had died and had power of attorney over Helen's affairs. More importantly than that, I quickly learned that he did not care for Marguerite. If this did turn into all-out war, I was fairly sure this man would be my ally. Ally? The word triggered a memory. A recent conversation: *You remember my solicitor, he makes a pretty good ally. He's good at dealing with Marguerite too.* It sent a shiver through me.

"For now, the twins are in your hands," said the solicitor, rounding up. "The money is in the control of the trustees; whatever is decided should be by mutual consent, and then the courts won't have to get involved. Are you thinking of taking them?"

I sat at Helen's desk and stared out of the bay window on the raised ground floor. "I don't know what to think yet," I said truthfully. "Helen wanted me to find them a happy home and I don't really have a home as such to offer them."

"Well, they sort of come with their own home, so that shouldn't matter."

I didn't think Helen was thinking bricks and mortar, but I took his words on board anyway. My mobile phone started vibrating on the leather desk. I glanced at it. It was Billy's number. I swore silently. "Do you mind hanging on for one second?" I said to the solicitor.

"Not at all."

I held the phone in one hand and picked up my mobile with the other.

"Billy, hi, everything all right?"

"Fine, I just wanted to say . . . God, I'm so sorry about Helen and—"

"I know, I know." I felt my voice cracking. It hurt my throat. "I'd really like to talk to you, but . . . I'm so sorry about—"

"Shh, doesn't matter."

"I'm just on the other line so can I—"

"Course, any time. And Tessa, you know I—"

"I know. Me too. Thanks for calling."

"Don't worry about us. You and me, I mean. We're fine. Call me later." I clutched the phone before placing it back on the desk. With monumental effort I brought the other phone back up to my ear.

"Sorry about that," I said. "Where were we?"

"Marguerite."

I sighed. "All I know is what Helen told me, and that was if anything ever happened to her, she didn't want her mother bringing up her children." I thought about what Marguerite had said to me. About the different sides of Helen. About the fact that she was one person to me, another to her mother. That she'd only been trying to impress me. Was that true, or was Marguerite just trying to manipulate me? "I believed her when she said it, but, oh, I don't know, maybe she was being overdramatic?"

"Possibly. But that was my understanding of the situation when we last spoke."

"It was?"

"She made it very clear."

I was relieved, for a moment. Until another thought struck me. "When was that?"

"A couple of months ago when she came in to amend her will—"

"What for?"

"Nothing sinister, the twins had been born, her will needed to reflect that. While we were at it, she made a few changes. I suggest we all meet up after the funeral and then we can decide what we are going to do."

"The funeral," I said, aghast. "I hadn't thought about that."

"I'm afraid Marguerite does have jurisdiction over that. My understanding is that Marguerite wants to arrange a burial at St. John's, followed by a wake at her house."

"Helen wanted to be cremated," I said.

"Are you sure?"

I'd like my ashes to be scattered on China Beach. What had I told her? That China Beach would probably resemble the Gold Coast by the time she and I popped our clogs, so she'd said any beach would do.

"Yes, I've told Marguerite already," I replied.

"Well, you'd better tell her again. She is already making plans for when the police release the body. You've got a bit of time because of the coroner's report."

"Coroner's report?"

"It's normal practice."

"She won't have to be—" I couldn't finish the sentence.

"They will take a toxicity reading of the blood, just to rule out drunk-driving. It's all for insurance purposes. Nothing sinister."

"She didn't drink," I said. "Neil, Neil was the boozer."

"I know, but they have to be able to rule the cause of death as accidental."

"Of course, it was accidental! You think a woman drives herself and her husband into a tree at ninety miles an hour without braking on purpose?"

As soon as the words were out there, Helen's voice came ringing in my ears. And then they kept coming, more and more of Helen's well-chosen words.

Whatever you do, don't let my mother get her hands on my boys . . .

All you'd have to do was find them a happy home . . .

I have a very understanding doctor . . .

I can't afford to get divorced . . .

Neil has to be dealt with and I am going to deal with him . . .

Deal with him . . .

Deal with him . . .

I ran upstairs to Helen's bedroom and retrieved the bag of pills from the bin. I pulled each one out, searching for dates. They had been represcribed over and over and over again. Long after the scar had healed and the pain had gone, Helen had been mixing what looked to me like a terrifying amount of medication. I sat down on the bed and stared through the open doors of her wardrobe. The jumper had sat proudly in the middle of the shelf. *Consider it yours.* Consider it yours? Why had she left me these to find? Why? I looked back at the empty boxes of pills. This? This was the universe unfolding as it should?

hook, line and sinker

It is the strangest things that get you in the end. For me, it was an innocent-looking yellow plastic nappy bin. The nanny had taken the boys out for an afternoon walk and I was left alone in Helen's great big house with nothing to do but think about what was happening to her broken shell a hundred miles away down the M4. I was mute. I was on standby. I had gone into sleep mode. Everything felt very removed. So I went upstairs to the nursery to find something to do. That was when I saw the nappy bin. I knew it was full because I'd struggled with it earlier. The nanny had tried to teach me how to work it. You had to twist something and push something else and hopefully the bin swallowed the nappy whole with all its odorous outpourings. How difficult could emptying a nappy bin be? I prised the yellow plastic lid off and was hit by the smell. It was supposed to work like a manual compressor, so why could I see the stained, wet nappies bursting out of the top? I tried to do the twist thing, but I just managed to loosen the bag, so I gave it a good yank instead. It held steadfast for a second then ripped. I stumbled backwards, spilling filthy old, throat-clenching sodden nappies all over the floor. It wasn't the stinking mess that made me cry. It was the two empty miniature vodka bottles buried in among it.

I turned the cute-looking bottles around in my hand and experienced a very vivid memory. I was a few days off being sixteen when my parents and I went on a rare family holiday. On the plane the air hostess had offered me a drink. Boldly I'd asked for a vodka and tonic. Dad didn't bat an eyelid. I felt like such a grown-up. She passed me this beautiful miniature of Smirnoff and a small can. In the end I drank the tonic alone. I couldn't bring myself to ruin such a perfect-looking object. It is still at my parents' house with an assortment of oddities from my life that I keep in a box; I never felt desperate enough to crack open its tiny red-foil lid. I'd been pretending to be a grown-up then, and I was still doing it now.

Stepping over the nappies, I pulled open the wardrobe doors. Everything was folded and ironed in stacks. Bibs. Muslins. Babygros. T-shirts. I ran my hand under and over all the piles, trying to find a hard object in among all this fairy-smelling softness. Once I felt something and retreated my hand rapidly. It took a few moments to find the courage to look again. Here I was, standing in a nursery, asking questions that I didn't want to know the answers to. Wasn't that the story of my life? I pulled out a clear plastic box. There were two pacifiers inside. I doubted I'd be so lucky again. I knew what two empty bottles of vodka meant. It meant there were more. Sure enough, inside a box holding an unused baby bath, I found several others. I started pulling out the contents of the cupboard and throwing them on the floor. In among all the baby paraphernalia, more and more vodka bottles were hidden. I threw them on to the Beatrix Potter characters until I was surrounded by dirty nappies and dirty secrets.

I was still in tears, sitting amid the detritus of Helen's miserable secret life, when the door to the nursery opened.

"Get out!" I screamed, leaping towards the door and slamming it back in the nanny's face. I would not have this information spread-

ing like wildfire through her chattering community. I would protect
Helen now, since I'd so palpably failed to do so while she'd been
alive.

"Please, just leave me alone. Take the twins downstairs . . ."

"Tessa?" It was a woman's voice. "It's Rose. I've come back."

I was leaning against the door, trying to barricade myself in with
the evidence. "Rose?" I turned and reached for the door handle. She
stood there in her hat and coat, with the same suitcase still in her
hand. "Rose," I lamented. She dropped the case and held open her
arms. I fell into them and together we sobbed. The tears kept coming
and coming.

Just as suddenly I stopped crying because somewhere part of me
couldn't accept what was happening. It was too far-fetched. Too sur-
real. Other people died in car crashes. Other children got ill, became
drug addicts, forced their parents apart. Other people fell in love with
the wrong man and wasted their lives endlessly drawn like a moth to
a flame. Not me. I was a lawyer. I wore sensible shoes from Monday
to Friday. I had dark-colored suits in my wardrobe. I thought I was
in control. I thought I had my say in the future. Wrong, Tessa. The
future toyed with us, it was up to us to try to enjoy the game. But
not everyone liked the game, or they weren't given the tools to play.
I held out my palm to Rose and showed her the perfect little bottle
I had been squeezing. It looked so sweet, so harmless. Drink me, it
said. If it had been full, I would have.

I registered no surprise on Rose's face as she reached down to
pick up the scattered remnants of Helen's hidden existence.

"You knew about the drinking?"

Rose glanced at me before placing the empties in a sickly sweet
scented nappy sack.

"I suspected. She always denied."

"And the pills?"

"They were for pain at first. After the Caesarean. But she became dependent on them quickly."

"But she was feeding the boys herself?" It was this that had quieted my suspicious heart. Helen was obsessed with breastfeeding her babies. She had fed them for five months. I didn't believe she'd ingest all those pills and carry on feeding her children. But I had only learnt about the vodka habit.

"She wasn't," said Rose.

"But I saw her . . ." Hadn't I? I thought about this for a minute. No, I hadn't. I'd seen her try to. I'd seen the babies fuss. I'd heard her talk about it. About the need to feed them alone, in the quiet, because they were easily distracted. I thought she was just being a weirdo new mother. There were plenty of them about.

I wiped a streak of snot down my sleeve. "What about all the milk in the freezer?"

"She put formula in bags."

That definitely sounded bonkers.

"If they ever went out as a family, she would take the bags with her, pretending she'd expressed it. She said she didn't like feeding in public. Neil didn't like it either. He said it was common."

I remembered my disastrous attempts in Starbucks with the curdled milk and the way the boys had happily sucked away at formula. I remembered too the way she'd latched herself on to that spooky little machine that had tugged at her breasts until they'd bled. Why would she do such a thing when she'd known there was no milk? I told Rose.

"She did a lot of strange things when she'd eaten too many pills."

I couldn't quite absorb what Rose was telling me. "She was pretending to breastfeed the whole time?"

Rose nodded sadly.

"Did she know you knew?"

"Yes."

"And you didn't tell her she was being mad?"

"She was afraid of Neil. I believed her fear."

I recalled the deranged conversation I'd had with Helen that same Sunday. "Did he hit her?"

"I never saw, if he did. No bruises."

This was getting more and more complicated as the hours went by.

"But he was a bully," said Rose. "I'm afraid I never liked him, God rest his soul."

"Nor me, Rose. Nor me."

"I suppose Marguerite will get the children."

I took Rose's arm. "Not if I have anything to do with it."

"But, Tessa, she is their grandmother."

"I know. Do you remember what she was like when Helen was little?"

Rose lowered her eyes to the floor. I don't know what slide show went through her mind, but she looked pained.

"Helen didn't want her to have the boys," I stated.

"I understand," said Rose, "but she is so"—Rose searched for a word that didn't cross the boundary—"strong."

"Let me worry about that. But I'd like your help with the boys."

"Of course. Where are they?"

"Out with a temporary nanny, but I'll send her home if you'll stay. They don't really know her, they don't know me . . ." I knew it wasn't a question of money. "Will you stay?"

"I should have stayed with Helen." She looked pained again. "There were a lot of things I should have done." Finally she looked me in the eye. "I will stay with the boys."

"Thank you, Rose. And please, don't feel bad, you didn't know this was going to happen."

Rose sat down in the blue gingham nursing chair. As she rocked gently back and forth, I was reminded of her age and all she'd given up to care for a child that was not her own. She stared out of the window. "I didn't know what was going to happen. But I knew something." She turned back to me, a look of steel in her eyes. Did Rose suspect what I suspected? Did she, like me, think Helen had masterminded this fatal solution?

"Something like a car crash?"

"No, not that."

So it was just me, then.

"I feared she would hurt herself."

I stared at her hard, trying to understand her. Trying to understand. I had to know. "But not Neil as well . . ."

Rose did not answer at once. Then she shook her head. "I couldn't see how."

"But now you can?"

Rose handed the miniature bottle back to me. "I think we both can now, can't we?"

Yes, we could, but the clarity was hurting my eyes.

"No one must know," I said to Rose, firmly.

"No one will."

We cleared up the rest of the mess together, lost in our own private thoughts. I heard the nanny call up from the hallway to let me know she'd safely returned. I liked the woman, I thought she was good with the boys. Clear and uncomplicated. In other circumstances I would have hired her permanently, but now I wanted her out of the house, and fast. It wasn't that Rose was back. It wasn't even that her services came at a considerable price. It was because I feared there were more secrets lurking within the house, and I didn't want anyone but myself or Rose to find them.

*   *   *

Two days passed. I meant to go home and change, but the house was like a hotel, it had everything I needed, so I stayed with Rose and waited for news. I knew what the coroner's report was going to say: Helen was driving while under the influence of alcohol and medication. I'd caught one story on Sky News. Neil and Helen had been at some party in Bristol. There was footage of Neil leaving the party, clearly inebriated. Rumors of a marital argument were circulating. Oddly, Helen looked completely composed, but her composure no longer convinced me. There was an almighty chemical balancing act taking place in her blood stream. The newsreaders talked about the twins; how they were only six months old. They were talking tragic accident.

I hadn't heard another allegation of drunk-driving since that first odd phone call in the hospital and what Marguerite had told me. That would all change when the coroner's report came out. It wouldn't take long before something was leaked to the press. Marguerite was right, she wasn't powerful enough to prevent that. Helen hadn't been famous, but she was too beautiful to ignore. Who better to make an example of for those silent, long-suffering mothers than Helen? If a rich, well-married mother of two can crack, then maybe they weren't doing so badly after all.

On the third morning, while I toyed with breakfast, my mobile rang. It was Ben. He asked whether I wanted him to come over as he had every day since Helen had died. This time I said yes. After Helen, the person I'd been thinking about most was Ben. Life had to be grabbed. Things had to change. And if I didn't grab and change things now, then maybe I never would and losing Helen would have taught me nothing. I had been warned, but Cora hadn't been enough. It had taken a death to shake me out of my stupor; I was going to make damn sure I didn't betray her memory by pissing away whatever time

I had left. The girl in the hammock was not going to die, I would take her with me, wherever I went and in whatever I did. I had emailed Al and Claudia, but they were on an elephant somewhere in the jungle, rediscovering the bare necessities of life—each other. It had taken a death for them, too, I should have seen it sooner. How foolish I had been to think that I lacked love in my life. My life was full of it, with all the risks involved. The pain I'd been feeling since Helen's death was proof of one thing: I was alive. I was alive.

Half an hour later, Ben was on Helen's door step. I had the twins ready. He helped me lift the enormous and now very heavy pram down the steps. Then he hugged me tightly.

"Everyone is in shock," he said.

"It's unbelievable, isn't it?"

"Completely . . ."

We stared at each other. I looked away first. "I thought we could take them to the park, if that's OK with you. I could do with some fresh air."

"Whatever you want. I've managed to sneak a couple of hours, told work I was pitching a new account," he said. "But I can come back after work too. Sasha will understand."

"Thanks, Ben."

He put his arm around me and kissed my head. "Got hold of Claudia and Al?" he asked.

"Not yet. I can't bear the thought of a funeral without them."

"You'll have me. Don't you worry about that."

"I can't believe she's dead," I said, more to myself than to Ben.

"I know."

He stroked my hair.

"I keep expecting her to walk through the door."

"It's such a shock. One minute we're all at a party together, the next . . ." Ben sighed. "They had the twins, Neil's career was just beginning to take off; it's too unbearably tragic."

Neil had his career. And all the added perks. I could not bring myself to mourn his death. I leaned my head against Ben's chest. I wanted to tell him about the real tragedy that this "accident" had exposed, but I couldn't.

"It doesn't make sense," he said. "These things never do."

It made horrible sense to me.

"When I first heard, I thought the twins were with them, you said she never left them."

I'd been thinking about that too. "I told her it was time to get out of the baby bubble."

He pushed me away and held me in front of him. "Don't you dare, Tessa. This is no one's fault." He knew me too well. "It was an accident. A terrible accident."

"I don't know, Ben."

"Of course it was. Tessa, stop it. Come on, let's go for that walk."

He let go of me to push the pram out on to the pavement. I immediately missed the physical contact. We walked out to Holland Park Avenue, up the hill and through the innocuous white stone wall of Holland Park. Within a few meters of leaving the gate behind us we were in a woodland labyrinth, surrounded by precocious squirrels and fat pigeons. A world away. This was the kind of setting I needed. It was time.

"Ben, you know what happened the other day, I need to talk to you about it."

He stopped.

"Keep walking," I said. "Or I may not get this out."

"Get what out?"

"Keep walking!" I insisted. We started moving again, slowly. "I've been trying to tell myself we had an excuse—"

"We did," said Ben, interrupting. "Our oldest friends had lost yet another baby; for a split second it was all about the four of us. It was late, we were emotional—"

"That's the thing, Ben, it wasn't about Al and Claudia. Not for me."

"What?"

"It was about us."

I put my hand to my chest to reassure it. I asked it not to panic. I asked it to continue calmly rising and falling, so that I could get the words out. "I adore you, Ben. OK?" I shrugged. The single biggest confession of my life was no confession at all. "I always have."

"Me too."

"I know. But I adore you too much."

Ben stopped walking again and looked at me strangely. "What are you saying?"

What was I saying? I was trying to say those three little words, but I couldn't. "I'm saying that I value your friendship above all others, but the thing is, you're married, which is great. For you. But it doesn't work so well for me. I compare everyone to you and no one comes close. How could they? Our foundations are so deep and I don't have to wash the skid marks out of your boxers."

"Excuse me?"

"Never mind, I know what I mean. The thing is," I said, forging ahead, "I have to move on to a new plot, find someone to make some new foundations with. Or maybe not, maybe I won't find anyone. But I can't go on like this. I mustn't." I kicked at some freshly fallen leaves. There. I'd said it.

Ben took my hand. "Are you saying what I think you're saying?"

"If you think I'm saying that I want to move house, no." Big, deep breath. "But if you think I'm saying that I have imagined a life with you in another role, then yes."

"But not a priest or an electrician, or a bus driv—"

"No. None of those." It was all right to make light of this, but only if it was me, and only if it wasn't too light.

There was a lengthy pause after that.

"I didn't know."

I found that hard to believe, but men are wired up differently, so anything was possible. "For a long time I didn't know myself. Or I pretended not to, I can't really remember. It's all been going on for such a long time, through most of which I've been having fun."

"A lot of fun," reiterated Ben. "You've never been anything but fun."

"Have no fear, I shall be again." I managed a smile. "But somewhere along the line I got tired of doing it all by myself. I got tired of being strong; of paying all the bills; of having to make all my own plans; of working; of living in London; of going on dates that came to nothing. I got tired of it all. I guess you became an easy option." I looked at him. My breath left me. Damn those eyes. I had to see this through to the end. "Which was madness. Because you are not the easy option."

"Is that why you took those pills?" asked Ben.

"How the hell do you know about that?"

"I have my sources."

I frowned.

Ben shrugged. "You put the phone down on me then disappeared off the face of the earth. I didn't know what was going on. Eventually I went round to your flat. You weren't there, but Roman told me what had happened."

"He shouldn't have done that."

"He was worried too."

"I had no idea how strong they were."

"Maybe. But I would be worried if you took junior aspirin if it was with vodka."

"A foolish oversight."

"Do you promise me?"

"I promise."

"It's just that everyone I know who's got into trouble with pills, took them with vodka."

I thought about those innocuous miniatures strewn over Beatrix Potter characters, the bag of pills. Motherhood had not brought Helen the peace she craved. It was not the solution. If anything, having the twins had compounded all of Helen's insecurities and sent her spiraling out of control. I wanted so much for Helen's death to be an accident because then I could stop imagining Helen going into the nursery for the last time and kissing her children goodbye, knowing she was never going to see them again. I didn't want to think that my friend had sunk so low that she thought killing herself and her husband was the answer. "Ben, I haven't been having the best of times recently, but I promise you, it wasn't even an accident, it was nothing."

He looked even more concerned now. "What do you mean, haven't been having the best of times?"

"I've been wasting so much time peering over the fence at you lot, wondering how the hell I can get over, that I've forgotten how to enjoy it over on my side. Life is pretty good over here; it has many, many advantages."

"That's what I've been telling you," said Ben. "We're the ones who are jealous of you, didn't you know that?"

I shook my head. I didn't believe him, of course. It was one of those perfect lies that Ben told me all the time to make me feel better about myself. Lies that a few days earlier I would have chosen to believe. But things were different now. A seismic shift had taken place. Helen's death had altered everything. I couldn't pretend to myself, or anyone else, that my view on life hadn't changed—suddenly, dramatically, changed for ever.

"Everything looks different from where I'm standing now and

that is because of Helen. My only regret is that I didn't see it sooner." I looked at Ben. "I honestly feel I've got her in here, a piece of her." A pretty big piece, since there weren't a lot of people to share her memory with. "Ben, she had so much potential." I felt the tears again—was it possible there were still more? "I don't want to be like that . . ."

"You're not."

I rubbed my face with the palms of my hands.

"One of the headhunters I called to arrange an interview with asked me whether I would be interested in a posting abroad."

"What did you say?"

"It doesn't matter now. It was this week, I missed it."

"Tessa, you should have gone."

"I couldn't. Until I know what's happening with the twins, I can't leave them."

"They're not your sole responsibility," said Ben.

"They are for the moment," I insisted. "Until something better comes along."

We walked along in silence for a while. "You'll rearrange the interview though, right? You know what the job market is like, the longer you stay out, the harder it is to get back in."

I must do that, I reminded myself. I nodded then fussed with the blanket covering the sleeping babies.

"So what did you say about moving abroad?"

I'd said no, of course. But I wasn't so sure. I looked at Ben. I was free to go anywhere in the world. I looked back at the twins. Then again, maybe I wasn't. "I said I'd think about it. Forty is not as far off as I'd like. I've been doing the same thing for nearly twenty years. Twenty years, Ben! Where did that time go?"

"I don't know, Tessa, but I tell you one thing, it wouldn't have been nearly as much fun without you."

There was that word again: fun . . . "Thank you," I said. "But I don't think you really understand what I've been saying."

"I do."

"No, you don't."

"I do, Tessa."

"You don't. I'm not here just for you to have fun with!"

"But I don't have fun with anyone else."

"Yes, you do! You have fun with Sasha." I stressed her name. If I didn't get this point across we were back to the beginning and God might think I'd ducked again and kill off my mother. "I'm the one who doesn't have fun with anyone else, because I haven't got an anyone else."

"We have a nice time, sure, but it isn't fun, fun, fun. It's talking about whether to have chicken or steak for dinner. It's about whether to take the promotion or move to Germany. It's life stuff. It isn't fun. You, on the other hand, have fun with everyone. Everyone adores you. Everyone who meets you adores you. You have more fun than anyone I know."

"I'm not going to argue about who has more fun with whom. It's ridiculous. All I'm saying . . ."

"Yes?"

"All I'm saying is . . ."

"Yes?"

"What I'm trying to say is . . ."

"What?"

"I wish we'd stayed in that passageway."

In Ben and Tessa speak, you can't get more clearer than that.

"Oh," he said.

Oh, indeed.

*　　　*　　　*

I don't know what I'd been expecting from this monumental revelation, but "Oh," followed by a swift departure through the woods, wasn't it. He had the decency to look at his watch first, then gawp at the time, and make the old excuse about a forgotten meeting. Before hugging me and telling me that I was the most precious thing to him, before hurrying off down one of Holland Park's many paths. But that was basically it. "Oh." Followed by a swift departure. I had imagined so many variations, over so many years—how was it possible that I hadn't imagined that one? Surely the possibilities were finite. Surely I'd covered all angles. But no: "Oh" it was. "Oh," indeed. I sat on a hard bench in the Zen garden and watched koi fish blow kisses at me. I concentrated on them for a minute or two, until the numbness I was feeling faded.

Now, of course, the truth was all too apparent. "Oh" was the only ending to this. What on earth was he going to say? Sorry? That was too patronizing. Me too, let's get married? No, because he was married to an amazing woman whom he adored. Me too, let's have an affair? No, because he was an amazing man married to an amazing woman whom he adored. The reality was that "Oh" was the only answer. I hadn't been dealing in reality, though; I'd been playing make-believe. The game had gone on for so long that I had lost my grip on reality. I will forever be sorry that Helen had to die in order for me to realize that I'd been sleepwalking through life. When the twins started to stir, I stood up and began pushing them home. Feeding time at the zoo came round quickly. I increased my pace.

When I got home, I mean Helen's home, I recognized the shabby brown Volvo parked opposite. It was incongruous among the Cayennes and Range Rovers. There wasn't anyone in the world I was happier to see, except Helen, of course.

"Fran!"

"The housekeeper said you'd be back at 2:30, and you're bang on."

"Amazing how quickly you get into a routine," I replied, smiling down at the twins.

Francesca got out of the car and looked into the pram. "Wow, you forget how small they can be."

"How dare you . . . These boys are enormous."

Francesca looked at me, then hugged me. "You all right?"

My friend was dead, Cora was in hospital with pneumonia, Billy and I had fought and I'd just ended a twenty-year imaginary relationship. I rocked my hand back and forth. I was doing so-so. I waited for the lump to let go of my throat.

"How's Caspar?"

"He's OK for the moment. He wanted to come and see you, actually, make sure you're holding up."

"Tell him I am. Just. I spoke to Nick, that feels like a long time ago. I'd only just heard." I tried to clear my head of the memory. "How is he, you haven't . . ."

"Said anything?" Francesca shook her head. "No, but he's getting a bit freaked out by all the love notes I keep leaving him."

I managed a weak smile. "And the girls?"

We walked back to her car to place the ticket on the dashboard. "Katie wanted a pair of knickers with cherries on the front. One had a bite out of it. She's still not speaking to me." She shook her head. "If I'd known what I was letting myself in for . . ." She shook her head again. "Just as you get over one hurdle, another looms in front of you." Francesca had been trying to cheer me up and for a moment it had worked, but for some reason I found that last scenario really disturbing. Maybe that was her point. We ambled back to the house.

"You heard about Cora?" I asked.

"Poor Billy. I just popped by the hospital with some more expertly made cupcakes. She rang and told us what had happened."

"I was an arsehole."

"Huh?"

"We had a fight. She didn't tell you?"

"No. She just told me about the nightmare with Cora."

I stared into the pram. Two moon faces peered back at me. I had a very new, very real litmus paper for life. Gone were the days of creating storms in teacups. Gone were the days of making mountains out of molehills. Amazing how unimportant many things had now become. "I went over there and like an idiot got all heavy about Christoph."

"Probably not the best timing."

"You think?" I started humping the pram up the steps.

"Do you want help?"

"Actually, I'm getting the hang of this monstrous thing."

"So what happened with Billy?"

I gave her the quick version, without the usual Tessa King revisionism. I unbuckled the babies, handed Tommy over to Francesca and followed her downstairs with Bobby.

"I promise you, she didn't mention it. In fact, she's concerned about you, as we all are. She knows about Helen and Neil, obviously. So please don't worry about a silly argument." She looked down at Tommy. "What's happened kind of puts everything into perspective."

She was right about that.

We stowed the twins safely in their matching bouncy chairs, ready for take-off. Thankfully, I was no longer confounded by the NASA-style harnesses you had to strap them in and out of twenty times a day. Next job was to make their bottles. Seven scoops in seven fluid ounces. Repeat. Quick shake, repeat, and hey presto—meal for two.

"How are these little ones?" asked Francesca, playing with them while I stood behind the vast stainless-steel kitchen island.

"They're getting a bit fussy, actually. I think they know Helen isn't coming back. It breaks my heart just to think about it. Tommy is much happier now on goat's milk, though, he's not been sick since, but he's more needy. He likes to be cuddled all the time. And Bobby just keeps looking around like he's lost something. You know when you go into a room to get something, then forget what it is, so you look around trying to remember what it is you've forgotten? That's exactly the expression on Bobby's face. And it's weird, because sometimes he looks just like Helen. Helen without the skin coloring. They're actually very cute, you've never felt anything so soft as their ridiculous cheeks."

Francesca looked at me strangely.

"What?"

"Listen to you."

I felt foolish. It must have registered on my face.

"No. It's nice. Just, maybe you should be careful."

"Of what?"

"Falling too much in love."

"With the twins? That's not going to happen. Between you and me," I said lowering my voice, "I never even liked them."

"That was then."

I handed a bottle to Francesca, and we sat on the sofa with one baby each. "Rose does this most of the time, but I don't want her getting too tired, she must be in her fifties by now."

"Where is Rose?"

"We have a little system going. She does the mornings, I do the afternoons and then she comes back to help me with bath-time. It's working pretty well." I glanced at my watch, I never knew what it was going to say. I seemed to have lost my sense of time and place.

Sometimes hours flashed by in minutes with the twins, other times they ticked past excruciatingly slowly. "We make a right pair, she and I."

"Tessa . . ."

I stared down at Bobby. His big eyes looked up at me. I smiled at him as he sucked hungrily. "I like being here, Fran. The twins keep me busy. This terrible, terrible thing has happened, but bang on eleven o'clock those boys need feeding. You've got no choice but to go on. It's a blessed relief. I hate it when they go to bed. Too much thinking time. Except there's washing to do and bottles to sterilize and sheets to change. I'm sort of hoping that if I keep on going through the motions, eventually the motions will feel real again." They were being fussy, they didn't like being put down, they needed to know I was close by. Me. Not Rose. Me. They smiled at me whenever I looked their way. I couldn't get enough of those wide, wet, gummy mouths grinning at me, so I looked their way a lot. They were terrible time-wasters. Francesca was right, of course, I'd fallen—hook, line and sinker. It had taken three days. Sasha had been right too. Being a parent didn't have to begin with birth.

"I think Tommy is getting teeth," I said, apropos of nothing. "Two, right at the bottom."

"Tessa, what's going to happen to the twins, where are they going to go?"

A happy home.

"I don't know. Helen left it up to me to decide."

"You need to make that decision then. They can't stay in limbo."

Why not? I was rather liking this limbo. Nothing hurt as much when I was with them. "No decisions will be made until after the funeral."

"On Thursday, right? The 28th."

"I don't know. Marguerite is organizing it."

"It is. I read the announcement in the paper. Don't worry, we'll be there."

"What announcement?"

"*The Times.* Yesterday. Both of them are being buried up the hill at St. John's."

I swore, then apologized to the twins, who looked at me quizzically. "The body hasn't even been released yet," I whispered.

"I'm pretty sure that's what it said." She lifted Tommy over her shoulder to wind him.

"Actually, he's better if you just sit him on your knee and lean him forward," I said. Francesca smiled at me. "Marguerite wants the boys, of course; she's already staked a claim. Whatever I decide, there will be a fight because they aren't going to that witch. She hasn't even had the decency to tell me about the funeral, which, by the way, Helen didn't want, and to be buried with him . . ." I growled. Bobby's face creased in concern. "Sorry, hon, shh, not you . . ."

"You know what I think?"

That I'd make a perfect mother? I looked at Francesca expectantly.

"I think that you should consider Claudia and Al. Claudia is their godmother too, isn't she? They've been trying to have a family for years, they're set up for it. They have a lovely house and Claudia would be a spectacular mother, and Al, well, you can't fault Al. They want children, and those babies need parents. They'd make such a happy family."

All you'd have to do was find them a happy home.

She said home, not family.

"Claudia seems to have moved on from that . . ." I wasn't convincing myself and, by the look on Francesca's face, I wasn't convincing her either. Nine years of trying for children could not compete with a couple of weeks in a Singapore spa, however good the salt scrub was.

"Just think about it. If you are going to have a battle with Helen's mother then you will need to present her with a realistic alternative."

Meaning I'm not a realistic alternative?

Meaning "Oh."

I felt tears welling up again.

"I'm sorry," said Francesca, "I didn't come over here to make you cry." It wasn't her. It was everything. She took my hand. "You're obviously doing a grand job here, but, darling, do you really want to take this on permanently?"

I shrugged.

"Are you sure that's what the twins need?"

I tried to tell her that I hadn't been thinking I would take them, but it would have been a lie. Why shouldn't I look after them? We'd make an odd family, but I knew now that odd families worked just as well, if not better. I couldn't think of anything to say.

Francesca went on. "After all they've been through, what they're going to need is some serious stability. Tessa, this is a very big decision and, you're going to hate me for this, but you have a tendency to be a bit whimsical when it comes to commitment."

But I'd changed, couldn't she see I'd changed?

"And don't you have your own life to sort out? Like going back to work?"

I sighed. Going back to work didn't seem like such an appealing prospect at that moment. I was getting used to having other things fill my day. I kissed Bobby on his round, fat cheek and he giggled. "No one knows what's going to happen," I said. That was true, at least.

Francesca didn't stay for very long after that. I was quite relieved after she left; I felt her beady eye on me every time I did anything for the boys. Rose was much less judgmental. I stopped cleaning the bottle and leaned against the sink. What was I doing? What on earth was I doing? I had to get out of there. I had to have time to think, away from all these distractions.

As soon as Rose walked back through the door I told her I had to get home. She assured me she could handle putting the boys to bed on her own that evening. She'd done it every weekend since they'd been born, they would be in good hands. I'd been at Helen's for four days. I'd locked myself away for four days. I needed to go home. I needed some space. I needed to regroup and get some perspective. I needed time to think about what Francesca had said: if I was to fight Marguerite successfully, I needed a plausible alternative. I would love those boys until my dying day, but was that enough for a court of law? If I wasn't good enough in the eyes of my friends, would I be good enough in the eyes of the law? Was anyone?

Another memory came back to me. This time it was my own voice. *He has a problem with drugs, and a problem with booze. What court in the land would give a parent like that the twins?* Well, I didn't have a problem with drugs and drink, but I wasn't squeaky-clean either. As for Helen . . . My words must have felt like daggers in her side. I'd only wanted to reassure her.

I put the key in my own front door for the first time in an age, closed it behind me and threw myself down on the sofa. I stared up at the ceiling. Had my reassuring words pushed her over the edge? Was this my doing? *What court in the land would give a parent like that the twins?* None, she'd replied. I could not imagine how desperate and alone she must have felt at that point. It was me . . . I had pushed her over the edge. I had to think very carefully about what I did next.

A couple of hours later I called the solicitor. "It's Tessa King," I said to the receptionist. I waited for the call to be put through.

"Hi, Tessa, I was just leaving," said Helen's solicitor.

Where'd the day gone? I'd been up since dawn. "Apparently there was an announcement in the paper about a funeral. Do you know anything about this?"

"Yes."

"I don't understand. What about the post mortem?"

"It was all done yesterday. I think Marguerite put some pressure on them to move quickly, but it was just routine."

"What did they find?"

"Nothing."

"Nothing?"

"No. What were you expecting them to find?"

"It makes no sense," I said, not answering his question.

"No, it doesn't. What they're saying, though no one will know for sure, is that she fell asleep at the wheel. Neil was drunk, but everyone knew that, so Helen would have had to drive. It was a long way home, no one to chat to, sadly it happens all the time. The insurance will be paid out."

"Insurance?"

"Helen's life insurance. The boys aren't going to have to worry about money."

"The boys were never going to have to worry about money."

"Helen had funds, yes, but everything is wrapped up in Hong Kong businesses. She had capital. Not cash."

I didn't really care about the details. "So she hadn't been drinking, or . . ." What was I going to say?

"It was an accident, Tessa. Nothing more. At least the boys will be OK. Neil didn't have any money. If it had been drunk-driving, the insurance company wouldn't have paid out."

I was stunned. I'd been so sure. The pills, the bottles . . . Had she stopped? Was she sober? Had she really fallen asleep at the wheel and driven into a tree, or had she, in a moment of madness, driven into a tree? Worse still, had she been in control enough to sober up in order to be able to drive into a tree? This had to stop. I was sending myself mad. I would never know the answer, and perhaps it was better not to.

"What about the funeral?"

"I'm sorry. Marguerite got her way, as expected."

Yeah, this had Marguerite written all over it.

"Have you decided what you're going to do about the twins?"

"I'm working on it," I said.

"Well, now you know how quickly Marguerite can move, you ought to hurry up."

"It's all right for her, I've been changing nappies for days. My hands have gone all scaly from the amount of Carex I've washed in . . ."

Why was I telling this man about my hands? Bloody Marguerite was more conniving than I thought. Of course she'd been happy to leave the twins with me, she'd known full well I wouldn't have a moment to myself.

"Knowing Marguerite, she'll make her move as soon as the funeral is over," said the solicitor.

"The 28th," I said. "When is that?" I couldn't remember what month it was. I glanced out of the window, across to Battersea Park; the leaves were turning golden brown. It was nearly the end of October. In two short months my life had been shaken like a snow globe and the flakes were far from settled. No wonder I didn't know what day of the week it was.

"Three days," said the solicitor.

Three days. I had three days to find a happy home.

It was pointless, I knew, but I fired off another email into outer space in the hope that Al and Claudia would pick up my distress signals. I couldn't fight this battle without troops, but my troops were gadding about on an elephant somewhere, finally having fun. Was it fair of me to summon them home? No. But I needed them. They were the only ones who could back me up. It was six in the evening but the conversation with the solicitor had finished me off. I went to my bedroom, lay on the bed and fell fast asleep.

I awoke from a nightmare, sweating, fully clothed and completely disorientated, to the sound of my doorbell buzzing. My arm was numb from sleeping on it. My watch had left an imprint on my face. It was dark outside. The doorbell buzzed again, followed by a knock. I couldn't think of one good reason why someone would be knocking at my door at two o'clock in the morning. Not one. I sat up and put my feet on the ground. The knocking came again. Firm and insistent. Phone calls in the middle of the night are bad enough, but messages delivered face to face are far worse. I only knew one person who was in a situation that might require such a message. Something had gone wrong with Cora. I could not push myself off the bed. I couldn't take any more. I peeled my eyepatch off my face.

Knock, knock, knock. Buzzzzzzzzzzzzzzzzz.

"Coming," I whispered. "I'm coming."

Knock, knock, knock. Buzzzzzzzzzzzzzzzzz.

I stood up and walked into the living room.

Knock, knock, knock. Buzzzzzzzzzzzzzzzzz.

Not Cora. Please, God, anything but Cora. Anything but Cora.

I reached the door and opened it.

It was Ben.

"Ben?"

"I have to tell you something."

So, they'd sent Ben to soften the blow. That made sense. I braced for impact.

"You may have wished you'd never left the passageway, but I never did," he said.

"What?"

"I thought I had. But I hadn't. I've been waiting there for years, I didn't even know it."

This wasn't about Cora. This was about—

"Us," said Ben, finishing my thoughts for me. "I'm here about us. You and me. Tess, my darling, ridiculous, wonderful Tess, don't you understand? It's you I love. You."

I stared at him.

"Aren't you going to say anything?"

I held open the door. No. Yes. "You'd better come in."

We stood in my flat, lit only by the lights along the river, looking at one another. He glowed a strange murky color and the pattern of raindrops on the glass made his skin look blistered. I'd never seen a man look so beautiful.

"I don't understand."

"What's there not to understand?" said Ben. "We've been bloody idiots."

"You said 'Oh.'"

"Well, obviously I said 'Oh,' I was in shock. I had no idea you felt that way. I had no idea I felt that way; I've lived with it for so long."

"With what?"

"Being in love with you."

I put my hands to my face. "I don't believe this," I said.

He took a step towards me. "Believe it. Helen's accident made me see it too. I love you." He took my hand and led me to the sofa. This was my dream come true and I was scared to death. "What about Sasha?"

"I'll tell her. I fell in love with you when I was fifteen years old. But we were friends, I never thought it could last."

"Me too, I thought we'd split up and wouldn't be a group any more; I didn't think it was worth it."

"But it has lasted, hasn't it? You still make me laugh, you've never annoyed me, you're more gorgeous than you were back then, you understand me like no one else, you're my best friend, I'm never bored in your company, when odd things happen I call you first, when sad things happen I call you first, when funny things happen I call you first. I'd tell Sasha when I got home, if I remembered, but I always called you first."

"Me too," I said again. "The hardest thing about the last few weeks was not being able to speak to you."

"Exactly. I've been in a bloody grump and I didn't even know why. It's because we weren't talking. I didn't realize why until that moment in the park. And then I realized just how pivotal you are in my life. Don't get me wrong, I've been happy with Sasha and I do love her, I do, but the person who makes me feel really great is you."

Sasha. Sasha. This was bad for Sasha. I grimaced. "Where does she think you are?"

"She's in Germany, but I would have told her. I nearly rang her, but this is not the sort of thing you tell your wife over the phone in the middle of the night. Maybe we should tell her together."

"God, no."

"She should have someone to love her wholly. Not partially, as I've been doing."

"You really love me? Seriously?"

He grinned. "Absolutely. And I want everyone to know."

"She's going to hate us."

"This has only just happened to me. I can look her in the eye and tell her I have not, and I would not, cheat on her. I've thought about it, as you know, but I've never acted on it. It even makes sense to me now why I sometimes had a wandering eye. I didn't love Sasha enough, but I didn't realize. She deserves better and she'll find someone like that." He clicked his fingers.

"Probably. She's an amazing woman."

"I think she'll be fine."

"Really?"

"Really?"

"I can't look her in the eye and tell her this just happened to me. I was happy for you both, I was, but I was jealous."

"I probably would have been too. I hated James Kent, married or not. But you didn't meet anyone, so I've never had to live without you. You've always been there. I didn't mind the flings, because I always knew they weren't going anywhere. You made that abundantly clear, so I guess I've always thought of you as mine anyway, not consciously, you understand, but . . ." He took my face in his hands. "I just love you," he laughed. "I know this is the worst possible time in the world to be ecstatic; Cora is ill and Helen . . ." He couldn't finish his sentence. Nor could I. "But, I am." He laughed again. I started laughing too. "It's ridiculous. I had to come and tell you. I was lying in bed, unable to sleep, thinking, I love her. I love her. I love Tessa King." He pulled me towards him and kissed me gently on the lips, then sat back. "And I do."

I smiled again. "Do you have any idea how long I've been imagining this?"

"Tell me."

"First I thought you'd follow me to Vietnam."

"I was in traction, you fool, but I thought about it."

"Why didn't you say anything when we got back?"

"You went weird on me," said Ben.

"You went weird on me!"

"I thought it was all in my head."

"I thought it was all in mine," I said.

Ben kissed me on the forehead.

I frowned. "You let me go off to university without so much—"

"Tessa, all you talked about was how excited you were, what fun you were going to have."

"I was trying to tell you that it was OK that you didn't like me that way, I'd get over it."

"God, women are strange—why didn't you just tell me?"

"Why didn't you ask?"

"I did. You left the passageway. Not me. Next time I saw you was in the hospital, pretending nothing had happened."

"You were with Mary."

"I could hardly throw her out of the hospital room, and anyway, you weren't giving me cause to and frankly I wanted someone to keep me company. You buggered off to Vietnam, remember?"

"I missed you so much; I banged on to Helen all about it."

"Helen?"

"Yes. She's the only one who knew, who's ever known."

"God, we've been idiots," he said again, reaching out for my hand. "And the sooner we put that right the better."

"What are we going to do?"

We? We? I'd never been a we before.

"Get married and have a host of children, obviously."

"I didn't think you wanted children."

"But you do. So bring it on. I don't care. It'll be fun. Let's just have lots and lots of fun together."

"Nothing happens between us, until Sasha knows."

"Nothing. I've waited twenty years to get you into bed, I think I can wait another day."

"Day?"

"Sasha is home tomorrow."

I thought I heard a faint pop. Was it my imagination or did our bubble just burst?

"Tomorrow? Wow."

"What are we waiting for? Helen and Neil were wiped out in a car crash. I mean, what the fuck are we waiting for?"

Neil and Helen. Bobby and Tommy. Ben and Tessa. Ben and Tessa plus Bobby and Tommy. Equals. Happy. Family.

speak your truth

We woke later that morning on my bed, fully clothed, spooned together. It was the best night's sleep I'd had in days. My back was pressed against Ben's wide, warm torso, my legs were imprinted alongside his. My eyes opened and I stared out at a whole new world. Ben loved me. Wanted to marry me. Wanted to have children with me. Ben wanted to tell Sasha. Today. I tensed.

"What's up, beautiful?"

I eased myself over to face him. "About telling Sasha?"

"Hmm?"

"Please don't do it today."

Ben propped himself up on his elbow. "Why not?"

"I know this may sound very selfish, but I've got to sort the twins out, and there's the bloody funeral, which Helen didn't even want, she wanted to be scattered on a beach. Cora's still in hospital . . ."

He stroked my hair. "I get it. Too much going on for our bombshell."

"Sort of."

"Your friends want you to be happy."

"I know that, but there's a difference between being happy and dancing on someone's grave."

"No cold feet, Tessa King. You're the bloody queen of cold feet."

"No cold feet. God, no. I don't want to offend anyone more than we have to, that's all."

"I don't think we'll offend anyone."

"You underestimate how much people adore Sasha. If she takes this badly, so will they. There's no getting around it."

"I don't think she'll take it badly."

"Of course she will, Ben, she loves you."

"But she's so independent. Honestly, there've been many times when I've felt surplus to her requirements."

"Let's hope you're right. In the meantime, please, not a word until the funeral is over."

"I promise, but it's going to be hard. I feel like a teenager."

"You look like one."

"So do you."

"Liar," I said.

"It's true. You're divine." He ran the back of his hand down my cheek.

"Me? You're the one with the ridiculous eyelashes. Boys shouldn't have eyelashes like that, it's not fair."

And so it went on for another nauseating hour. Knee to knee. Nose to nose. Fingertip to fingertip. Flattering, cajoling, teasing, loving. How we didn't end up ripping off each other's clothes, I'll never know. But we didn't. I can be proud of that, at least.

Ben was right, it was near impossible to keep the jaunt out of my step. We allowed ourselves the pleasure of holding hands until the lift doors opened, and then, like any other illicit couple, our hands dropped away, and our normal roles took over. We walked to Sloane Square, talking incessantly about our imaginary future—where we'd live, when we'd get married, what my parents would say, what his mad mother would say, what Claudia and Al would say—and arrived there in a nanosecond. I let three buses go on up the King's Road without me because I didn't want to leave him. When I did finally get on one, Ben got on too. It was pathetic. I was delighted. Halfway up the road, his mobile rang. It was Sasha. I felt like I'd swallowed the bus whole.

"Hi, Sasha."

"Hello, listen, really sorry, but they want me to fly on to Düsseldorf tonight. I know I promised that I'd cut down on this—"

"Don't worry."

"Thanks, hon. Listen, call Tessa. She'll need cheering up." I grimaced. Ben shrugged.

"OK, babe."

Babe . . . I didn't like the babe much.

"I'll see you tomorrow."

Ben put the phone back in his pocket and looked at me.

"I feel sick," I said.

"That bit is going to be difficult, but once she knows, it'll be easy."

It felt worse than difficult. It felt downright treacherous.

"Look on the bright side—at least I can come over again tonight," he said.

"Not tonight. I have to go back to Helen's house."

"Really?"

No, not really, but I didn't think we'd be able to resist one another much longer. We were almost always touching. Leg, face, cheek, hand . . . But it wasn't enough. I didn't want difficult to become ugly.

"We'll speak," I said, getting ready to leave the bus.

Ben grabbed my arm. "Don't go. Can't you go to the hospital later?"

I looked at his large hand wrapped around my slim forearm. It looked so good there but I could feel the callus on the palm of his hand, just below his wedding ring, brush my soft skin.

"I have to go. I haven't had a moment to visit since our stupid argument. And I need to see Cora."

"But you said everything was OK with you and Billy."

It was. We'd been playing telephone tag since our brief conversation and the messages were kind and supportive on both sides, but that didn't mean I no longer owed her an apology. We both knew that Helen's death had kicked our fight into touch, but I wanted her to know that I didn't think I'd got away with it.

"No, Ben," I said, more emphatically. "I've got to go." I pressed the button on the pole and heard it ping up near the driver's ear.

"Can't I come with you?"

And make Billy and Cora complicit? "No," I said, kissed him on the end of his nose, and stepped off the bus.

"Hey, where am I going?" he called after me.

"Work?"

"Shit, work . . . I'd forgotten about work."

The doors closed. Daydreams are powerful things. I should know.

I walked from the King's Road to the Fulham Road, oscillating between utterly overjoyed and completely dejected. I had to steady myself as I approached the hospital. Jaunty wasn't how I should be approaching this visit. I went up in the lift. I pressed the buzzer of the ward, my speech prepared, but I didn't have to get past my name, I was buzzed in. The woman behind the reception desk smiled at me and pointed me in the right direction. I was so relieved to see Cora propped up in bed and not surrounded by tubes in intensive care, as I had imagined, that for a split second I forgot all about Helen's death and just rushed to her bedside. Billy stood up, and after letting me smother her daughter in hugs, held her arms open to me.

"I can't believe you're here. Fran told me you've been looking after the twins, is that true? Have you brought them? Are you OK?"

"I just wanted to come and say sorry," I mumbled over her shoulder. "To your face."

She looked at me then turned to Cora. "What do you say to Tessa and I going out and getting something good to eat?"

"In other words, you want to talk about things I'm not allowed to hear," said Cora.

"No," said Billy. "Well, OK, yes, but we'll get something good to eat too."

"You could stay, I can't hear anyway."

"What?" I asked.

"She can, it's just—"

"My androids," said Cora proudly.

Billy looked at me and forced a look of concern on to her face. "Cora has something wrong with her adenoids, her hearing is a bit impaired."

"From the pneumonia?"

"Actually, no; they only found out because of all the tests they were doing. It explains the head in the clouds, but not the hearing, since I'm pretty sure that's always been selective."

Cora opened her mouth in protest.

"Doughnut?" Billy asked her daughter.

Cora nodded happily.

"We'll be back in five."

As soon as we were out in the corridor Billy turned to me. "I haven't told her about Helen."

I clenched my jaw shut and nodded. The moment had passed. Cora was well, but Helen was still dead.

"I'm so sorry, Tessa."

"You have nothing to be sorry for. It was me, I don't know what I was thinking. I had no right to storm in like that."

Billy looked at me. "I know how frustrating it is when you see someone you love missing out on life."

"Especially since it is so precious," I said, agreeing with her.

"Ever since Ben called me and told me that Helen was in the crash too, I've been thinking about Christoph, me and Cora, what you said."

"Me too, and—"

"Let me finish," said Billy.

"Sorry."

"Christoph doesn't deserve her, or me, for that matter. I've embarrassed myself enough. It's over. I honestly thought I'd lose her, Tessa; she went so floppy and white, her lips were grey and everyone was running around shouting things. Look." She pointed to her long, dark hair. She didn't need to show me, I'd seen the new streaks of grey. She looked ten years older.

"I'll live with the memory of that moment for the rest of my life. I should have seen it sooner, it shouldn't have taken something like this to make me realize what was important."

I knew exactly how she felt. I took Billy's arm and squeezed it. "I think we've both been coasting a bit."

Billy looked at me. "Putting on the brakes, you mean."

I nodded, agreeing with her again. Well, I was certainly taking my hands off the brakes now.

We passed another ward. Sick children lay in rows. We averted our eyes. "I would have disemboweled myself if I'd thought it would have helped Cora," said Billy. "And the pain wouldn't have compared one iota to what I felt, still feel, still fear."

There was a bench in the corridor. We both sat down, and Billy held my hand. We sat in silence for a while, the noise of the hospital drifting past us. "Christoph doesn't love her. If he did, he'd be here. I've done some very stupid things over the last few years, but he didn't even bother to call . . . I can't believe Helen could just be killed like that. Who knows what's round the corner?"

Suddenly Billy squeezed my hand then released it. "I've made a decision," she said. "When this is all over, you have my full permission to get what we deserve from Christoph. No more. But no less." She looked at me sideways. "I'm not settling for less any more. Life is too goddamn precious."

For a moment I was torn between doing the right thing by Sasha and spilling my guts about Ben. He loved me. We were going to get married and have a host of children and none of them would ever have to worry about me again. I wasn't settling any more either. I must have smiled a fraction.

"What?" asked Billy.

"I'm just very pleased that something good has come out of Cora being unwell. You'll be rewarded, I know it."

Billy shrugged. "This isn't about meeting someone else, Tessa. I'm fine on my own, actually. I feel lucky because I have Cora and she's a very special little thing. I need to re-engage with life, not men. If I meet someone, fine. But, you know, they usually bring a fair amount of complications with them and, to be honest, I'm not actually sure it's worth it. I've always wanted to learn the piano. I think I'll start with that." She looked at me again, more closely. "What about you? Are you going to keep the twins?"

Wow, that was direct. "Um . . ."

"Being a single mother isn't easy, but you'd never regret it."

Disembowelment? Are you sure? "Right now I can't see beyond the funeral."

"Well, we'll be there for you, whatever you decide to do, OK? Me, Fran, Ben. You have a great network of friends. Use us."

A network I was about to blow apart.

"Thanks, Billy."

"You are an amazing person, I hope you know that." Billy turned her body towards me so that I couldn't look away. "That's why people flock to you."

"Thanks," I said, trying to sound humble.

"I'm ashamed about what I said to you in that restaurant because deep down I know that the last seven years wouldn't have been bearable without you." I shifted, embarrassed. Billy grabbed both my hands. "No, I mean it. You had every right to shout at me. The truth is, you've been more of a parent to Cora than Christoph ever has and I know we are lucky to have you. The twins will be lucky too."

I expected to experience a sense of victory, but I didn't. I felt ashamed. Who was this great friend, this person to whom people flocked? Not a marriage-wrecker. Not a stealer of other people's husbands. Were friendships unconditional? I wasn't sure. I think you earned them, that's why they were so valuable. I looked at my feet.

"One day you'll learn to take a compliment," said Billy, misunderstanding my awkwardness. "But for now, why don't you go and sit with your goddaughter, and I'll get the doughnuts."

"I'd like that," I said, and walked straight back into my safety zone.

Cora was lying back against the pillows, looking a little less perky, and for a moment I stopped in my tracks, but she lifted herself up when she saw me and smiled.

"How are you feeling?"

"What?"

"How are you feeling?"

Cora roared with laughter. "Got you."

"You minx."

"I'm learning sign language," said Cora.

"Really?"

"What's this?" She crossed her arms in front of her like a Russian dancer, raised the top fingers to make horns and wiggled her fingers on the bottom hand.

"Absolutely no idea," I said.

"Bullshit!"

I laughed.

"One of the nurses told me that."

I sat on Cora's bed. There were flowers all over the room, and books and teddy bears. Word had got out. Cora had been inundated with gifts. I picked up a Paddington Bear. "To Cora, with love Ben and Sasha." I put it down quickly.

"Do you want a cupcake?"

"No, thank you. You had us scared there, honey."

"Sorry."

"I'm not blaming you, bunny, but please, don't do that again."

"OK."

"How's the hearing, really?"

"If I put my hand over my good ear it sounds like I'm in the swimming pool. Now when my teacher says, 'Cora TarreNOT'—she always says the 't'—'you're not listening,' I'll have a brilliant excuse." It didn't matter what you threw at this girl. She impressed me no end. "I get tired very quickly. My chest hurts. I thought I was wide awake a minute ago, but now I'm sleepy."

"That's normal, you've still got a lot of getting better to do."

"Will you stay with me, Godmummy T?"

"Sure I will."

She pointed to her eye, then her heart, then at me.

"More sign language?"

Cora nodded. I did the same. Eye. Heart. You. I held up two fingers. Cora smiled. I pulled the thin hospital sheets up around her. "You warm enough?"

"Uh-huh."

"I'm sorry I didn't visit you earlier."

"That's OK," said Cora sleepily. "Helen was here."

I felt myself shudder. "What?"

Cora didn't answer me.

"Cora?"

Her eyes were closed. She'd fallen asleep. I kissed her softly on her forehead and left the children's ward.

I stood on the cold pavement and listened to an approaching ambulance siren. "Marguerite, it's Tessa again, please call me back."

"Boo!"

I jumped.

"Ben! What the hell are you doing here?"

"Called in sick. Couldn't stand the idea of not seeing you for three days. Let's spend this afternoon together."

"Where have you been?"

"Watching the exit from Starbucks. I nearly missed you, I thought you'd be longer."

I panicked. "Cora's sleeping."

"So, come and have lunch with me."

"Billy's around here somewhere."

"So?"

"So she might see us."

"I've come to see Cora, you happened to be here. Big deal."

I'd been playing mummies and daddies with Ben and Cora for seven years, but the game had gone sour.

"We've got to do this right, Ben."

"I know, but, God"—he squeezed my face—"I can't bear not being with you."

I pressed my hand against his, then pressed my lips against his palm. He pulled me closer and wrapped his other arm around my neck. We stood squashed against one another, me with my head in his neck, him wrapped around me. It was broad daylight, on the Fulham Road, outside a busy London hospital, yet it didn't cross my mind that anyone would see us. He kissed me on the forehead, I kissed him on the cheek. What was there to see really? We'd done this a million times before. He kissed me again, I kissed him back. He kissed me all over my face; when he took my face in his hands again and kissed me on the lips I thought I would burst. We pressed harder and harder against each other; our mouths remained closed, but the kiss intensified, nearly beyond my control. I was breathing far too hard when he pulled away.

"This is why I can't see you," I said, panting.

"It's going to kill me," said Ben.

"Three days," I told him.

"I don't think I can."

"Three days, then we tell Sasha."

"Then you're all mine."

"All yours," I said.

Ben turned away from me, then turned back. "Hell," he said, "these are going to be the longest three days of my life."

They may have been for Ben, but I swear, to me they passed in a blink of an eye. I returned to the twins and before I knew it, it was bath-time again. I stayed at Helen's house and spent three hours on the phone arguing with Marguerite about the service which she had completely hijacked. True, it was only my word that Helen wanted to be cremated, so I could almost forgive Marguerite for riding rough-shod over me, but to plan a service that in no way reflected her daughter was just plain mean. And what about Neil's family? Had Marguerite contacted them? Were they in the loop? They certainly hadn't made any effort to see the twins. Did they know Neil's marriage was tempestuous, that their daughter-in-law was addicted to pain medication and vodka? No, like most people, they probably thought Helen and Neil had it all.

The following day was busy with the boys. As was the third. Perhaps it was because I was in such denial about what was happening that the three days passed so quickly. Despite talking at length about burying my friend, I was still in denial about Helen's death. I was also in denial about the circumstances of her death. Then there was the question of having to be parted from the twins, and whether Claudia and Al really were the obvious choice to adopt them. I was in denial about that.

Sasha had called three times, leaving messages because I hadn't been able to pick up the calls. She said she was thinking about me, she asked if there was anything she could do, she told me if I wanted to rant, scream, cry or get pissed with someone, she was there for me. Each message made me feel worse. So I busied myself further still. I was blessed with great girlfriends whom I loved unequivocally, but they all fulfilled different roles in my life. Billy was whom I played mother with. Francesca was whom I moaned to. Helen had been whom I took risks with. But Sasha, Sasha was the person I sought advice from, it was she whom I gathered strength from, who made me most comfortable with the choices I'd made in my life. I admired her and was horrified that I was going to lose that. If I was half the person I hoped to be, wouldn't I choose the sisterhood over the love of my life? Yet here I was, on the cusp of losing a great friend. I was bewildered that being with Ben was going to cost me Sasha. And who knew what else? I was dreading the funeral, I was dreading the day after, I was dreading everything, so I ran around like a headless chicken for three days so I wouldn't have to think. But finally, because time stops for no man, the 28th arrived and I found myself in the utterly bizarre situation of dressing for Helen's funeral.

*   *   *

Rose knocked on my temporary bedroom door.

"Come in."

I was standing in front of a full-length mirror watching a woman of a certain age, dressed in black, stare back at me. It didn't matter how often I looked away, whenever I looked back, there she was, checking me out. I didn't recognize her, but she seemed to know me. I wanted to find an ally standing opposite me, someone who would support me over the next forty-eight hours, someone who'd confirm that I was doing the right thing—but what I saw in her eyes was disapproval. When I started to cry, it made her feel bad. I knew this because she started trying to cheer me up. She pulled funny faces, she poked out her tongue and pushed up her nose like a piggy-wig would, but it didn't work, she could not get me to smile. I'd seen the look she'd given me, it was no trick of the light. She was not impressed and I had a horrible feeling I knew why. "The twins are ready," said Rose.

Rose and I had debated what we would do about the twins and the funeral, and come to the conclusion we would take them. I was not going to miss it and I would not have asked Rose to. Neither of us wanted to go, but someone had to represent Helen in this circus.

"I can't go looking like this," I said to Rose, marching out of the guest room and into Helen's. I flung open the wardrobe door and scrawled through the clothes. I found a fur-trimmed vintage pink Vivienne Westwood coat and a magnificent Philip Treacy hat. I took off my sensible black heels and donned a pair of black patent stilettos that rose me up to an easy six foot. No one could miss me now. Then I went to the pile of photograph albums that I had taken to bed every night and pulled out all the ones I could find of Helen smiling. Lastly, I grabbed a beautifully framed photo of the twins with their mother looking relaxed and easy in one another's company. I didn't care what happened at St. John's, or what Marguerite had planned; the girl I knew would remain in front of me. I would think of her and only her, so help me God. Rose and I took one baby each and left the house.

Leaning against the railings opposite the church was a boy in an ill-fitting suit, tugging at his exposed shirtsleeve. He saw me pushing my weighty charges up the hill towards him and immediately straightened up. He looked very serious as he crossed the road towards me. My godson. Trying, I now recognized, to be as grown up as he'd ever feel.

"Hi, Tessa," said Caspar, lolloping down to greet us. "Mum and Dad are inside already. Need a hand?"

"Thanks," I said, slightly panting. Caspar got behind the huge contraption. I introduced him to Rose; he politely shook her hand before taking over pushing the twins. Today Caspar was appearing as Model Teenager. I looked at him closely; it wasn't an act I wholly believed in any more. "I wasn't expecting you here," I said.

"I've only come to nick a few fivers out of the collection plate."

My mouth dropped open.

"I'm joking. God, lighten up."

"Not a good day for jokes," I replied.

He shrugged. I took it as an apology. "I thought you might need cheering up, you always tell me it was one of the few things I do best."

"One of the many things you do, Caspar. Not few."

He squinted at me.

I nodded, encouragingly. "One of the many," I repeated. We crossed the road and stopped at the gate of the church. People were still arriving. Blacks, greys and navy blues. People stared distrustfully at my pink coat. Rose fiddled with Bobby's harness and silently passed him to me. I put him on my hip.

"I just wanted to make sure you were OK," said Caspar, tickling the baby under his chin and immediately getting a smile. "I know Helen was one of your best friends. And I know you don't like doing these things alone." He was talking like an adult, but he couldn't quite look me in the eye. It was easier to tickle Bobby under the chin. I'd been doing much the same for three days. I watched him take a deep breath and force himself to face me. "So, I'm here if you need an arm to lean on, but it looks like you've got your arms full."

I took his arm before he managed to move away. "There's always room for you, my friend."

"We are friends again, right, Tessa?"

"Right, Caspar. But there are conditions with friendships," I said. "You don't steal off a friend, you don't lie—"

"You don't look through their things."

"No, you don't and I'm very sorry about that. Let's say we're even. From now on I'll leave all the shitty stuff to your parents. They will love you no matter what; I, on the other hand, have limits."

Caspar nodded.

"But it would be nice if you could give your mum a break, eh, Caspar?"

He exhaled loudly. "All right, all right, but even you've got to admit they're a pair of do-gooders, and sometimes it just gets up my nose."

I forced my smile into a frown. "Come on, this baby is getting heavy."

Rose came and stood next to me with Tommy.

"They look like the Sopranos," said Caspar, eyeing the twins with blatant pity.

"They do not," I exclaimed, covering Bobby's ears. "They're beautiful."

Caspar just rolled his eyes at me and led me to the church.

*   *   *

It was packed. I walked in with Caspar on one side and Rose on my other. We carried our charges like armor. Every pew we walked past was full. People in somber suits craned their necks to have a look at us. At first I looked back, hoping to see a friendly face, but I didn't recognize anyone. No one I knew, anyway. There were newsreaders, journalists, comedians, television presenters—all of Marguerite's crowd. The crowd she loved, the crowd Neil aspired to, the crowd Helen never felt comfortable in. They were all there, in their funereal best. Proud in Helen's pink coat, I pushed up my chin and walked on. Caspar went and sat with his parents. When I took my place in the "family" pew, I looked down at Bobby. He was staring wide-eyed at me, his little lower lip jutting out and his brow furrowed.

"Hush, little one," I whispered. "Everything is going to be all right, I promise you." I kissed the soft folds of skin under his chin. Immediately he smiled. Children are amazing like that. Their emotions are fluid, they come and go. There is no harboring, no stagnation. That all comes later.

I opened the service sheet. After the second hymn was my bit. "Desiderata," by Max Erhmann. It was the only thing Marguerite had conceded on. She wanted me to read something from Shakespeare. I adored Helen for many reasons; her love of English literature was not one of them. An extract from a Jilly Cooper novel would have been more appropriate. But Marguerite was busy rewriting history and my input was not welcome. I only got "Desiderata" past the old witch because Helen had it framed by her dressing table. Marguerite had complained that it was too long. I told her it was either that or I said a few words myself. Funnily enough she accepted—the last thing she wanted was someone working off the script.

The music changed tempo and I knew the terrible moment had arrived. I turned in my seat. Four rows back, on the other side of the church, sat Ben and Sasha. Sasha blew me a kiss, Ben stared. I tried to smile, but I couldn't. I had no time to think because suddenly the doors were open, and there was Marguerite. Beside her was an elderly couple holding hands. They were small and wide and together. Marguerite was tall and thin and alone. Behind them were two coffins. Bobby could not see what I was seeing, but I shielded his eyes anyway, and rocked him gently side to side. His eyes started to close as if some sixth sense was telling him to vacate the premises, Tommy's too. I heard Marguerite take her place in front of us. Her heels clicked as they always had. Neil's parents didn't make a sound, but I saw Neil's mother looking towards the twins. I tried to smile, but I couldn't. Neil's mother. I hadn't thought about a mother. She looked devastated.

As the cortège passed our pew, I looked again. There may as well have been no coffin, so clearly did I see my friend lying inside. I'd been doing fairly well up until that point, but then I lost it. I didn't listen to a word the vicar said, though I'm sure it was all very sensitive; he'd christened their children so at least he had known them.

We stood and sang. I cried. Not noisily. Painfully. Rose tried to comfort me, but I was beyond comforting. I didn't want to be comforted. Bobby lay asleep in my arms, he didn't flinch when a tear landed on his cheek. I heard the door to the church open again, but didn't think to look around. I wasn't interested in latecomers. I just wanted the coffin lid to pop open and Helen to come bursting out and tell us that it had been a horrible joke. Maybe Neil was in on it too. That sort of dark humor was too avant-garde for him, but he might have been willing to try it out. Then again, maybe the joke was on him and Helen had in fact killed her husband.

"Budge up," said a voice as I felt a hand on my shoulder. *Budge up*? I looked up from under the rim of Helen's magnificent hat and saw Claudia and Al looking down at me. Claudia burst into tears as soon as our eyes met. I take it back—I thought I'd lost it earlier, but when

I saw Claudia cry, I howled. Marguerite turned in her seat to see who was making the commotion; when she saw us, her eyes narrowed. I shimmied down the well-rubbed wooden pew to make room for my friends. I couldn't understand why they had suitcases with them. There were so many questions—how, why, when, what—but the vicar cleared his throat and we settled into line. Al and Claudia, me and Rose. The forces were gathering. Claudia held out her arms to take Bobby, and silently I handed him over. Rose passed me Tommy. I guess she knew I needed something to hold on to. Each with a baby in one arm, Claudia and I held hands, turned our faces to the front and, with dry eyes now, joined the funeral.

Eventually it was my turn to stand. I handed Tommy back to Rose and took my place at the lectern. I looked at the people, then down to my paper.

Go placidly amid the noise and haste,
and remember what peace there may be in silence.
Breathe in. Breathe out.
As far as possible, without surrender,
be on good terms with all people.
I paused. Without surrender.
Speak your truth quietly and clearly;
and listen to others.
Speak your truth.

I looked at Marguerite, then back to the script. Then I looked at Claudia and Al and two orphaned boys, then I looked back at Marguerite. I could feel her fury.

"I'm sorry," I said. "I can't do this." I faced the congregation. "You've got the poem right there, you don't need me to read it to you." I looked back at the coffin. "Helen knew these words by heart." I swallowed. "She clung to them, my lovely, exotic, crazy friend, but they weren't enough. You have to be guided in this world. It's too big a place for anyone to deal with alone. She thought she was *a child of the universe*. I used to love that about her; it felt so free, so wild, but I think it cost her dearly and constricted her more than any of us will ever know."

I looked out at the sea of faces, faces I didn't know, then back at Helen's coffin. "I'm sorry that I let you down, I'm sorry that I didn't understand how hard marriage and having kids is, and I'm so sorry that I turned home because I couldn't face the traffic when I should have come to see you. We should have talked more. I wish you were here, Helen. I wish you could have seen yourself as those who loved you saw you. But you've left your mark. Everything good about you is in those boys; I can see your potential in them whenever I look at them. I promise you I'll make sure that this time they're nurtured and encouraged. And whether you like it or not, I'll tell them about all the ridiculous scrapes you got us into."

I found the strength to raise my head. "I don't think Helen is in that box. I don't think she's a child of the universe either, she's right here." I pointed at the second pew. "Grounded, at last. In Tommy and Bobby." I looked back at my piece of paper. "So, to cut to the chase:

With all its sham, drudgery, and broken dreams,
it is still a beautiful world.

I looked up and saw Ben watching me.

Be careful.

Strive to be happy.

I stepped down from the lectern, took my seat and started to shake. Claudia took my hand again, and held it until the service was over.

Thankfully, polite conversation was not required, so when we all filed out of the church and waited to be directed up to the graveyard, my proximity to Ben and Sasha was not made more uncomfortable by the obvious absence of our usual chat. I saw James Kent leave the church. I was deeply ashamed of my behavior—yes, I'd been duped, but mad psycho-bitch wasn't my style. I wanted to apologize, or at least offer to pay him back, but he never looked our way and I didn't see him again at the wake. I saw Neil's parents emerge from the church followed by a younger woman with two small girls in tow. The vicar came up behind them, looked at me, then placed his arms around them and guided them over to the other side of the church. They stood talking in a quiet huddle when Marguerite appeared and called the vicar over. It was clear from his expression that he didn't want to leave them. I watched them for a while; at one point both of the women caught my eye, but they quickly looked away. I wanted to introduce myself, but the vicar instructed those who were family and close friends to follow him for the internment. Up ahead the two coffins sat on wooden boards. Alongside them were two hillocks of AstroTurf. It was supposed to hide the sticky earth that would soon be dumped on top of them. No amount of landscape gardening could mask what was taking place.

The coffins were lowered into the gaping wound in the ground that was to be Helen and Neil's final resting place. Kindly words were spoken by the vicar, then people started to trickle off. People once again found their voices, but I couldn't move and I couldn't speak. On the other side of the graves stood Neil's elderly parents. The people who'd held him like I held Bobby now. In fact, I was holding their grandson, yet we might as well have been at different funerals for all the contact we'd had. Marguerite barely looked their way. This was all a mad scam, and now these two people were going to lie side by side, rotting away, like their marriage. I wanted to get Helen out of there. Out of the box. Out of the hole.

"Tessa?" It was Al. Tall and strong. He put his arm around my waist gently and pulled me back from the edge. He held on to me for a while, and when it was only our little group standing by the open grave, he whispered to me. "We've brought something."

I looked up. Claudia gave Tommy back to Rose. "We brought it all the way."

"I was terrified we'd get stopped in Customs."

I frowned. Al brought a jar out of his coat pocket. It was full of a whitish powder.

"What is that?" asked Ben.

"Sand," exclaimed Claudia.

"From Vietnam," said Al.

I nearly fell to my knees.

"It was the weirdest thing, Tessa. We'd been in the jungle, and the hotel guy said they'd drop us off in Hanoi as they were going off to look at a competitor's site elsewhere."

"China Beach," said Al, interrupting.

"Let me tell."

"Sorry."

"I'd just got your emails, all of them. I ran out to tell Al about Helen. He was talking to the hotel guy about China Beach. Not any old beach, China bloody Beach—I couldn't believe it. So I said, 'We're coming with you.' I figured we had enough time to collect some sand, get to Saigon, and get here."

"And we just made it."

She held up the coffee jar. "So here it is. Couldn't take the girl to the beach, so we brought the beach to the girl."

I thought I was going to cry, but I didn't, I laughed in wonderment. The noise woke up Bobby and I swear on Helen's soul, for perhaps that's what I was looking at, he laughed for the very first time, not his usual chuckle but a long, spontaneous, joy-filled, happy laugh. He set the dormant laughter off in the rest of us. As the sand ran through my hands and girl and beach were reunited, I thought yes, with all its sham and drudgery and broken dreams, it was still a beautiful world.

The last thing I placed inside the grave before turning away and leaving Helen for good, was the photograph of her with the boys. Frame and all, it went into the hole in the ground. And then we all moved away, out of the graveyard, away from the church. As the distance between ourselves and the graves increased, the atmosphere changed. We started talking again, as the group of friends we were.

"I didn't realize Helen struggled with so many things," said Francesca.

"I knew the relationship with her mother was bad, and the last time we spoke she told me things with Neil were coming to a head," said Claudia.

"When was that?" I asked.

"Just after I arrived in Singapore."

"I hate to leave her there with him," I said.

"She's not in there, Tessa. What you said in the church was right. It's the boys we've got to concentrate on now," said Claudia.

"What you said was amazing," said Francesca.

Ben threw his arm over my shoulder. "Yeah, I'm so proud of you." I stopped in my tracks, creating a pedestrian pile-up.

"We all are," said Al, ushering me on.

"Was their marriage really bad then?" asked Sasha.

I nodded. I couldn't speak to her. It was terrible. I wanted to throw Ben's arm off me.

"She told me that he'd slept with someone," said Claudia.

"I think it was more than one someone," said Ben.

There was a collective murmur of disapproval.

"I need a drink," said Al. "Look, there's a pub, let's go and drink to Helen."

It was all so sad, but the weight of Ben's arm kept distracting me. "Good idea," said Francesca. We walked towards the pedestrian crossing.

"Why didn't she leave?" asked Sasha.

"Sasha," warned Ben, turning back to his wife.

"What?"

While Ben was looking backwards, Nick came up between us and, wrapping his long arms around us both, separated us. I finally exhaled.

Francesca pushed the pub door open. "I think Ben means we should change the subject," she said and quickly looked my way.

You and me both.

"That's the trouble with infidelity, it only gets easier," said Sasha, filing in with everyone else.

"That's not necessarily true," said Francesca, bringing up the rear.

"You'd forgive Nick, would you?"

"Francesca is right. I don't think this is the time or place for this discussion, Sasha," said Ben, a trifle too firmly. He moved away from Nick and me. "I'm buying. Pints?"

We all nodded.

"If it only happened once," said Francesca, climbing on to a stool, "and it was a mistake, which he regretted, I would; I would forgive him." Francesca wasn't looking at Nick, she was looking at her feet, but I was. He was watching his wife intently.

Sasha nudged me. "Was it really like that, Tessa?"

I pretended that I was lost in thought and hadn't heard Sasha.

"What about you, Nick? she said. "Would you forgive your wife so easily?"

"Come on, Sasha, change the subject," said Ben, handing a drink to Nick.

"Ben, will you please stop jumping down my throat. You've been doing it all weekend."

"Hey, guys, not a cool time to start having a marital," said Al.

"Sorry," said Sasha.

Nick walked over to the stool Francesca was sitting on and kissed his wife's head. Then he gave her the pint that Ben had given him. "If Francesca felt the need to have an affair, it would be because I hadn't been doing my job. It would be me asking for her forgiveness, not the other way round."

"Really?" asked Ben, Sasha and Francesca in unison.

Told you so. For a second I thought I might have said that out loud. I didn't dare look at Francesca.

"Mind you"—he gave me a very distinct, although fleeting look—"I'd expect to be given another chance to make the marriage work."

"You're an idealist," said Ben. "Always have been."

Nick took the next pint Ben offered him. "Marriage doesn't work without ideals." Now Francesca and I both stared at our feet. "In fact, marriage is the most ludicrous thing, if you think about it. Which two human beings can live together happily ever after without at some point getting irritated or just bored? It's insane. It's impossible. The 'love of your life' is a notion, it doesn't actually exist. If you go on holiday with your best mates in the world, at some point everyone annoys everyone else, yet that's not supposed to apply to husbands and wives. So you have to be an idealist to be married. You have to believe the magic. If you walked into marriage with your eyes open, you'd start running in the opposite direction before you got to say 'I do,' because on paper, marriage simply doesn't make sense."

"But your marriage works," said Claudia.

"That's because I *know* I married the love of my life."

"Me too," said Al.

Ben turned back to the bar to get the last pint.

"Poor Helen," said Claudia. "I hope she didn't know about the other women."

"They always know," said Sasha.

Sasha looked at me intently then raised her glass. "To Helen," she said, and we all drank.

a mean margarita

Sham was the word. The wake reminded me of a magazine launch Helen had once taken me to. There were even some paparazzi outside. I drank far too much, far too quickly. Considering the circumstances, I thought far too much was restrained. I understood for the first time why Helen had succumbed to medication in these situations—I would have happily taken a handful of Helen's smarties myself. Inside me, my excessive emotions strained against the crush, I could feel them pressing against my sides. My soul was trying to escape, to flee. I had thought that the kernel of horror that gripped my core was for Helen, was about the funeral, but now I wasn't so sure. Funerals are strange and terrible things, but they are a punctuation of sorts. Wakes allow people to laugh again.

I was feeling worse and the drink wasn't helping. I wasn't the only one knocking back the champagne. The subdued mood in the vast marble vestibule of Marguerite's Kensington house started to rise, the decibels with it. I didn't have the stomach for laughter so excused myself from some of Helen's distant relatives and went out into the floodlit garden. I saw Nick standing under one of the many impressive mature trees.

"Hey, Nick," I said, walking over the flagstone terrace. "You OK?"

He looked at me and nodded. "You?"

I shrugged. "I guess. I'm glad Caspar came. He seems more like his old self."

"We'll see."

"I'm sorry I meddled in your family business." I seemed to be saying sorry a lot these days.

"You are family, Tessa, you're entitled to meddle."

I looked at my old friend. "Thanks, Nick, that means a lot to me."

We stood side by side, breathing in the cool evening air. Suddenly he sighed heavily. "I'm not sure you'll be thanking me again."

That sounded ominous. Was that why he looked at me in the pub? He knew about Francesca and was going to leave her? "Why won't I be thanking you?"

"Because there's something I have to say to you."

I started shaking my head before he'd even mouthed the first word.

"I was at the hospital the other day . . ."

I fell still. "The hospital?" I put my hand to my mouth. "Oh my God. Don't tell me you're ill."

He smiled sadly. "I'm fine, Tessa, you daft thing. I went to give Cora a wooden monkey puzzle."

I hit him playfully. "You scared me," I said. "Don't do that again. You're far too important to all of us. I need another drink now."

He grabbed my arm. "This is the trouble with you, you make it so hard for anyone to be cross with you because you say nice things like that, so we all end up shying away from telling you things that, frankly, you should hear."

"Like what? Actually, forget I asked."

I was hoping Nick would laugh, but he kept staring at me. I'd seen the expression before but couldn't quite place it.

"You know Billy and I are fine now, I apologized to her too."

"I know. You'd just been in when I arrived. In fact, I missed you by seconds." I looked at him then looked away. When I looked back I knew where I'd seen that expression before. On my own reflection. In the mirror in Helen's house. I felt truly sick. I closed my eyes. It made me feel worse, so I opened them again.

"What are you doing, Tessa? Anyone could have seen you two. I saw you!"

I buried my head in my hands, I couldn't speak. Everyone will be so happy for us—what had we been thinking? Happy for us? That we had annihilated a great relationship to go chasing after a teenage fantasy. I tried to meet Nick's eyes. I couldn't. Shouldn't I be able to justify myself more easily than this?

"Marriage is tough, Tessa. No marriage can survive that."

"I . . . Nothing's happened."

"And you think that makes it all right?"

"Well . . ."

"You think sex is the big thing, you think that because you and Ben haven't gone to bed with each other that you're OK? Sex is the easy bit. You can have sex with anyone. It's not ideal, I grant you, but a meaningless shag is surmountable. And yes, I mean even a fling with a bloke you may think you've fallen in love with for a moment, even that a couple can get beyond."

So he did know, and loved his wife regardless. I frowned, trying to hide my thoughts.

"Don't pretend you don't know what I'm talking about." My eyes met his. "Look, that's not important now. What's important, vital, is you think very carefully about what you're doing and what you think you're going to achieve. Ben and Sasha are good together."

We stood side by side. "Have you told Francesca you saw us?" I asked.

"Haven't you?"

I shook my head.

"Embarrassed about something?" he asked.

Mortified, but I didn't want to admit that. Ben was in love with me. We were in love with each other. Jesus, it sounded so childish.

Nick shifted his weight. "Dreams, myths, fantasies are one thing but once they're out in the open it is very hard to put them back in a box. And in this case, impossible. There is a point of no return for everyone, no matter how strong a relationship is."

Why do tears sting so much? I reached inside Helen's pink coat which I'd refused to take off, and brought out a damp, screwed-up tissue.

"Be very sure about this. Absolutely, fundamentally, categorically sure. Can you be that sure? Of course you can't. No one can. So is it really worth it?"

They burnt, not stung. I moved my head a fraction. Yes? No? I don't know?

"It has been a very, very strange time for you. I understand that," said Nick, putting his hand on my shoulder. "But you've got to think about what you're doing. Don't get me wrong, being married is wonderful and I love my wife, but it hasn't been easy. This Caspar thing has been so awful, I still don't know where he's heading; the girls are growing up way too fast, our worries for the kids seem to get bigger, the sleepless nights never end . . . That's the reality. Would I give them back? Of course not, but . . ." He put his hands together, as if begging me to listen, as if he was terrified that I wouldn't. "We started from a good place. No one got hurt when we got together. We both have our fair share of guilt, but it hasn't been hanging over our heads like the Sword of Damocles, making a difficult job impossible. I know you think you want all this, but really, Tessa, are you willing to pay such a high price?"

I couldn't answer him. My head was reeling.

"I'm so sorry to do this here, today of all days, but I'm begging you to think about it. Please. You don't need him, Tessa." He started to walk away, then turned back. "You never have." It was Helen's voice that came to me out of the darkness. *Listen to others*, she had said. *Listen to others.*

There was only one option. And that was to drink more. A lot more. I saw Rose in the cloakroom. "Where are the twins?" I asked, over-articulating. I sounded like Maggie Smith.

"With Neil's brother."

"The elusive brother."

"He seems nice," said Rose, drying her hands on the white linen towel, folding it precisely and replacing it on the countertop. "Time to go?" she asked.

"No," I said. I walked back out to the massive hall and noticed it was thinning out. People were starting to drift away. I saw Margue-rite holding court by the door. Pencil-thin in black. Her long grey hair was curled up in a chignon and held in place by a black rose. I wanted to spit. Those blood-red nails were clasped around the fist of a middle-aged man who was clearly sympathizing with her about her terrible loss. His dowdy wife stood awkwardly behind him, look-ing uncomfortable. People hovered around her like a bride on her wedding day, waiting for their moment with the star of the show.

I grabbed another glass. I was supposed to be finding Claudia and Al to talk to them about the twins but I got waylaid by a group of comedians at the bar. They were absolutely paralytic and made me feel considerably more sober than I was. Everything's relative. They had some great stories about Neil and when I forgot who they were talking about, I started to like him. Who knew he did stand-up, aged seven, at his granddad's working man's club?

Someone put their arm on mine. I was beginning to find those stilettos hard to keep steady.

"Tessa." I felt a hand snake around me. "Come and have a little leveler."

"Oh God, it's you."

Sasha gave me a stern look. Shit, I had said that aloud. "I'm not going to start lecturing you, honey, you get as pissed as you like. I'm with you all the way. We all are. Just didn't want you falling over unless it was among friends. Come on, we found the drinks cabinet. Claudia's been making mean margaritas."

"I love you," I said to Sasha. God knows where it came from.

She drew me closer. "Yes, Tessa."

Claudia was doing some kind of hooly-hooly dance. Ben and Al were in hysterics. They were the only people left in Marguerite's well-staged drawing room. I noticed a few photos of Helen that I recognized from the house in Notting Hill Gate, but was too pissed and too riveted by Claudia's party piece to register my anger. But it was all there, bubbling away under the surface, waiting for one drink that would compound all the others. Unbeknown to me, it was the one Sasha handed me. A mean margarita.

"On the rocks," shouted Claudia.

"Hello, you," Ben whispered into my ear.

"What about the salt?" I said, moving away from him.

"We've made a bit of a mess with the salt," said Al, laughing. He'd written "I love you" in it. Claudia had returned the compliment by writing "Soppy git." I picked up the salt cellar. I had a message of my own. I. Hate. Marguer—

"Tessa!"

"Oops." I smiled at Marguerite and wiped the salt away, spilling it all over the carpet.

"Where are my grandsons?"

"I saw them with Neil's brother and sister-in-law," said Sasha. "They've got two adorable girls."

"Could someone get Tessa a glass of water, please?" said Marguerite, staring at me.

I was about to retaliate when Ben stepped up beside me. "Lay off her," he said.

"Ben," warned Sasha, touching her husband lightly on the arm.

"She's been looking after those boys single-handed," said Ben, continuing his protest. Marguerite dismissed him as though he were a boy. "It's what Tessa wanted. To have them all to herself. I see you managed to get Rose back, so you haven't really been doing it on your own, have you? Not as easy as it looks, is it?" I squinted at Marguerite. Was it me, or was she swaying slightly? Al and Claudia came up on either side of me. Sasha went to Ben. "Don't make this worse," said Sasha quietly, but she was drunk too, so it wasn't that quiet. Ben shrugged her off. It was a bit more than a shrug, actually; I didn't see it myself, but Al did a quick U-turn to put a restraining arm around Ben.

"And how are you planning on getting them home tonight? Drive? Taxi? Or will the hired help be doing it for you again?" asked Marguerite.

I wanted to point out that I'd only be copying her approach to parenting if I did, but a petulant retort was just playing into her hands. I was pissed, of course, so petulant retorts were the only things coming to mind. I tried to focus. "Actually, I thought," I started slowly, "that you'd have . . . that they might stay here. I assumed you'd have most of the kit here." I was warming to my theme. "What did they do when they stayed before?"

"Helen didn't bring them to stay here," said Marguerite.

"Oh, silly me, I thought you were used to having them to stay. My mistake. Don't worry, we'll push them home in their pram."

"It's freezing out there, Tessa, what on earth are you thinking?"

"We came prepared, Marguerite. Helen's house isn't far." Rose had pushed the twins there. We would push them back.

"You're not taking them anywhere in your state."

"My friends will help me."

She looked at my friends with unveiled contempt. "I think it would be better if they stayed with me."

"Hey, we're not so bad," said Ben. He was saying far too much for my liking. Every syllable that came out of his mouth ricocheted through my conscience. I was glad that I'd seen Nick and Francesca sneak out of the door with Caspar. But that still left Sasha, whom I caught looking at me every time I looked at her.

"We'll order Rose a taxi," said Al. The problem-solver, even when pissed and jet-lagged. It was quite annoying, actually. I looked back at him, about to tell him so, but nearly fell over. I fixed my concentration on my leg muscles until the leg righted itself.

"And who will take care of her?" said Marguerite, watching me.

"I will take care of myself, thank you." I replied faster than Ben could, who, I saw, was readying himself to answer. Unfortunately, replying that fast also meant loudly and not very clearly.

"You're incapable of looking after yourself, Tessa. You can't even speak, let alone stand up straight."

I laughed heartily. "Well, thank you for a simply lovely evening. Remind me, what was it in aid of?"

"How dare you—"

"Excuse me."

We all turned. The young woman from the church stood in the doorway of the drawing room. She was holding Bobby. There was a man standing next to her who looked weirdly like Neil. He held Tommy. It freaked me out to see Neil holding his son. I shook my head and tried to sober up.

The man spoke first. "We've got to catch the last train to Norwich."

"It's been lovely to see the boys. I can't believe how much they've grown in a month."

"Yes, well, babies do that," said Marguerite, practically snatching Bobby from her.

"Say goodbye to Granny," I said, coming in to reclaim Bobby. I've no idea where the coffee table came from. It hadn't been there before. I tripped, fell into Marguerite and watched in dreadful slow motion as Bobby toppled out of her arms. He fell face-down on the sofa. Thank God it was the squishy kind. Thank God it was there. Marguerite and I were too shocked to move. The woman scooped him up, expertly checked him over, calmed him down and made him smile.

"No harm done," she said, looking at me.

How many times did I need warning? Another few centimeters and Bobby would have landed on an unforgiving floor and he wouldn't be smiling at me now, oblivious to the harm both Marguerite and I were capable of causing him. No harm done? I looked at Sasha. Who was I kidding?

"Look at you," said Marguerite, recovering faster than me. "Think about it, Tessa. What have you really got to offer them? I can do this." I was in shock, I just kept seeing Bobby fall, over and over. Marguerite went in for the kill. "You think you can be a single mother of two? Do you? You can't look after yourself."

"She doesn't have to," said Ben.

Oh God, no. Not here. Not now.

"You're all going to muck in, are you?" asked Marguerite in a sneer.

Sasha looked from me to Ben. "It's been a tough day. Let's go home. Before we all start saying things we'll regret."

Why we didn't listen to her, I'll never know.

"We'd really like to see the boys again," said the woman who'd tried to assuage my guilt.

"I'm sorry, we haven't met," I said, turning to her.

"I'm Lauren Williams. I'm married to Neil's brother, Daniel." She nodded to her husband standing next to her.

"I dropped our daughter once," said Daniel, looking down at Tommy. "She was fine—it took me weeks to recover."

I was concentrating furiously, trying to make a good impression. Rose came in; no one stopped her when she silently took the boys away. Not even Marguerite. "I'm sorry we finally get to meet in these circumstances," I said. "It must be very hard for you."

"It's my mum and dad who are finding it hardest. I know they'd love to see the twins from time to time too, if that's all right."

"Danny, our train—"

"Can I give you our number? Helen brought them up to visit a few times. Well, we'd really like to, um . . ." He looked at Marguerite nervously.

"Dan—"

"We've got a spare room. And the girls adore them. I built them this great den under the willow and, well . . ."

Lauren gently took her husband's arm. "Come on, my love." I was staring at them. By the willow. In Norwich. "Helen loved you both," I blurted out. "She told me all about you."

They looked relieved.

"I think your wife wants to leave," said Marguerite. "You know where I am now."

"Marguerite," I said, my alcoholic fury rising again. "You are not getting the twins."

"And nor are you. You can't do this alone, I should know, god-damnit!"

"She's not going to do it alone," said Ben, stepping away from Sasha again.

We were all so pissed.

"What are you talking about?" asked Marguerite.

"Now is not the time, Ben," I said, trying to sound matronly. In charge.

"Marguerite should know, this affects her."

"Ben!"

"Please, Ben, listen to Tessa," said Sasha. My heart cracked at the sound of her voice. Nick was right. I could feel the precipice beneath my toes. *They always know.* We were going to fall and take everyone with us.

Ben looked at me. "Tessa has decided—"

"To give the twins to Claudia and Al," I said, turning to them with a false smile.

"What!"

"You're joking, right?"

"Really?"

"Oh."

Al.

Claudia.

Sasha.

Daniel, Neil's brother. The one I knew I'd like. And did. The one who lived in Norwich with a weeping willow in his garden.

Ben didn't say anything, he left the room.

Marguerite scanned what was left of our little group. "You'll be hearing from me," she said. "Make no mistake about that." Then she walked out of the room too.

"What the fuck were you thinking, Tessa?" said Al. "After everything we've been through! You didn't think it worth mentioning before?"

"We knew this was going to happen, we talked about it on the plane. I had braced myself for it," said Claudia. "But not from you, Tessa."

"Yeah, give the babies to the poor infertile couple. Perfect fucking solution, Tessa."

"I mean, we want to be involved in their lives, we do, but after everything we've been through, it's over for us. We've made a choice, the hardest choice there is to make, but we've made it."

I so desperately wanted to retract my words. Tell them I'd only done it to shut Ben up. But I couldn't. Sasha was still there. Still watching my every move.

"The very least you could have done was tell us, rather than drop it on us like that."

"I'm sorry," I muttered.

Claudia started collecting her things. I was so sad. Only a few minutes ago she'd been doing the hooly-hooly and now she'd go home and question all her decisions because I'd been too much of a coward to face up to what I'd done. Claudia looked at me. "I thought you of all people understood."

"I do," I pleaded. "I'm sorry. As soon as I saw you I realized it was a bad idea, but in your absence, well, people kept mentioning it and I just thought . . ." I fell into the sofa. "I'm a fucking idiot."

Claudia looked down at me. "I have Al. Loving anything else right now feels too dangerous, impossible. Do you understand?"

"I'm sorry, it was a bad idea," I said again.

"Fucking bad idea," said Al. "Come on, Claud, let's get out of here."

But Claudia held back. "It's not that I wouldn't, but I'm spent. I can't live like that any more." Tears welled up in her eyes. "I couldn't be a relaxed mother and I wouldn't do Helen justice. I'm sorry."

"We've talked about this, my love," said Al, putting his arm around his wife. "We're off on a different adventure."

She nodded but still looked so pained. I felt terrible. She wouldn't wait for the journey home, she already doubted herself. Yet I knew better than most that they'd made a good decision. Now I had to face up to my own.

"I didn't mean it," I said.

"Easy to say now," said Al.

"No, really. I didn't mean it. The truth is I didn't want you to take them. I've grown rather attached to them myself, but Marguerite was on at me, she thinks she should have the twins and obviously thinks I'd be hopeless. Oh God, I'm sorry, I really am."

Claudia looked from me to Al, but he was not moved.

"So why did you say it?" asked Al, furiously.

I glanced at Sasha, then back to Al. "I panicked. I just panicked." I put my head in my hands. It was throbbing angrily.

Claudia crouched down in front of me. "What is it, Tessa? What's going on?"

I peered at her through my fingers. I didn't dare look over to Sasha. I stared hard at my friend Claudia, taking in her features. Her dark bob, her wide eyes, her small, round head. Help me, I pleaded silently. Help me, I don't know what I'm doing. Suddenly she moved up on to the sofa next to me and took my hand in hers.

"I think that you've been carrying a lot, on your own; we should have been here earlier," she said.

I wanted to kiss her feet.

"Come on, Al. Think of the pressure she's been under," she said. "Marguerite was being a bit out of order. Everyone knows she's a battleaxe."

He wouldn't even look at me. "I'd like to go now," he said.

"Al, I'm sorry—"

"Not now, Tessa." He was clearly still struggling to contain his anger. He ran his hand over his head. "We'll talk about this tomorrow. When everyone has sobered up."

Claudia squeezed my hand and I watched them go.

"We better go too," said Daniel.

"We'll never make the train now," said his wife.

"It's OK, we'll find a hotel near King's Cross."

"I'm terribly sorry about all that," I said.

"Emotions are running high, it's understandable," said Helen's sister-in-law. "We're all anxious about the twins," she said.

"You don't have to go to a hotel. There is plenty of room at Helen and Neil's house."

"We've got the girls," said Lauren.

"And my parents."

"Thanks, but don't worry."

"Please, Helen would want you to stay. I know she would."

There was a pause. Why would they want to stay with me after that little debacle? I was about to give them an out when I was surprised by the warm smile that crossed Neil's brother's face.

"Well, if you're sure?" he said.

"Absolutely. You're staying with us."

"We'll go and tell the others." I watched them leave too. Finally, I turned around. Sasha stood facing me.

"I think I'd like to go home now," said Sasha.

If this was going to be done, it had to be done now. How many times had I asked this question? Hundreds. I would never be able to ask it again.

"Do you mind if I borrow your husband?" I forced lightheartedness into my voice. Sasha drained her drink, then placed the empty glass on the bar. She turned to me.

"Will you give him back?" she asked quietly.

"Don't I always?"

The look Sasha gave me was impenetrable, she gave nothing away. Eventually she nodded, more to herself than to me. Then she, too, left the room.

*　　*　　*

Much later, after several cups of tea and beans on toast in the kitchen of the house in Notting Hill Gate getting to know Helen's in-laws, I sat on the teak bench in the garden and stared up at the indigo sky. Ben came out and wrapped a jacket around my shoulders.

"They're very nice people," said Ben. "He looks so like Neil, but he's so different, it's weird."

I didn't reply.

"And what gorgeous kids," he said.

I agreed with him, but again, I didn't reply.

Ben took my hand. "Sorry I nearly dumped us in it earlier."

I held his hand for a moment, then retrieved my own. "That's OK. I think Al and Claudia will forgive me eventually."

"You're mad at me, aren't you?"

"No. We'd all drunk far, far too much. Funerals kind of do that."

"It was that bitch Marguerite, she just pissed me off."

"There is so much front with her," I said. "No one really has that much front. I think in a weird way, she thinks that if she can get the twins, she'll be able to make it up to Helen. That's what I'd like to think, anyway."

Ben sat down next to me. I leaned against him, tired and fighting off a hangover.

"I love you, you know, Tessa," he said.

"I know."

We held hands and sat in silence for a little while. My dreams had been filled with moments like this. I couldn't believe what I was about to do.

"Ben?"

"Uh-huh?"

"You and me."

"Yes, my love."

"It's not going to happen."

"What?" He turned suddenly, facing me. "Come on, Tess, today was bad, I grant you, but think about the circumstances. You were right, we've got to wait until all this is over."

"No, Ben. Today would have been as good as any, if it was the right thing to do."

He grabbed my hands. "You adore Sasha, she was in your face; of course you're going to get freaked out. Don't do this, Tess. We've finally got it together." I slid my hands out from under his and placed them on top.

"Exactly. Finally. This is our teenage nonsense. I've been waiting twenty years to be told what I already knew. I wanted you. You wanted me. We had our chance and we fucked it up, Ben, way back then. But that isn't Sasha's fault."

"But I'm not in love with her, I'm in love with you," he pleaded.

I worked very hard at keeping my voice steady. "Today. A week ago you weren't."

"I was, I just didn't know it."

"I don't think it works like that. I think you're going through a bad patch with your wife. It happens. It's cyclical. The trick is to work it out. She said she'd been traveling too much. You resent it so I bet you're not very nice to her when she comes home, which means she travels more. You've just drifted apart. You need to go on holiday, get back in the groove." I tried to tell him about the corridor thing, but I didn't do it as well as Francesca.

"Please don't tell me how to patch things up with my wife. I want to be with you." He sounded petulant.

"Because I'm fun."

He stroked his hand over my cheek. "No. You're perfect."

"Of course I bloody am." I was like Caspar. Ben was my hero, so for him I was always on best behavior. "I'm single. I get dressed up.

I'm out on the razz. I don't have to be at my desk at six a.m. I'm not covered in baby puke. I have lie-ins. When I'm in a filthy mood, I stay in. When I have my period, I go to bed. You never see me when I've picked all my spots."

"You don't have spots."

I tried to inject some humor into the conversation. Relieve the tension. "That's it then, you clearly don't know me at all."

"OK, so sometimes you have spots, I don't care. I love you." It got harder then, because he sounded like Ben, my Ben, and he sounded like he believed every word. All I had to do was choose to believe them too, just as I'd been doing for years and hey presto, I'd have everything I'd ever wanted. I turned away from him instead.

"I'm sorry."

"I don't believe you." Ben pulled me back. "What did Sasha say to you?"

"Nothing. You've been together for seven years. I don't know, maybe there's something in this seven-year-itch thing."

"It's eight years," said Ben.

"Even more reason to try and salvage it. Eight really good years, Ben—I know, because I've been there with you. Sasha is stronger than me, she's more reliable, she's smarter; more than all of that, she actually makes you be a better person than you are on your own."

"Thanks!"

"Well, isn't that what it's all about? We're just kids in a passageway. You think kids in a passageway have what it takes to survive the odds?"

"Yes."

"What happens when you realize I'm not perfect?"

"That won't happen."

"Of course it will. God, Ben, let's not piss about here. Marriage is tough for anyone. If it weren't, we wouldn't be sitting here now."

"You're just getting cold feet, as usual. You never see anything through—"

"I thought you said I was perfect."

"You are, please don't do this."

"You're just being belligerent now. You don't want to listen to me because you know what I'm saying is right."

Ben was shaking his head. "I don't believe this is happening."

"My dad says you should always go with your gut reaction. When I told you, you said 'Oh.' Then you went home and thought about all the little things that annoyed you about Sasha, which I'm sure are plentiful, and many of which she deserves, and I bet there are just as many things that you do that piss her off. Then you thought about all the things that don't piss you off about me, and you thought, I must love her too. Nice, easy solution. You said it: I make you feel great. I worship the ground you walk on, naturally I make you feel great."

"Sasha doesn't make me feel great."

"Because she asks more of you. You're the man you are because of her. You feel great about yourself. Sasha did that."

I could feel Ben's resistance to the idea that we'd got it wrong start to slip away. But he was still fighting.

"Our marriage won't survive," he said.

"Maybe not, but you should take Nick's advice and give it a bit of attention before you make that decision. I was speaking to a divorce lawyer the other day; he said that divorce rates are much higher among second marriages. Why? Because the couples find themselves back in the same place, with the same problems. Many even go back to their first partners. It would be really sad if you and Sasha didn't make it, but either way, it can have nothing to do with me. I won't be waiting for you, Ben. This isn't a trick, some strange test I've set you, I'm done. It's over. I'm sorry."

Ben looked at me. He hadn't changed since we were kids. It was true, I did worship the ground he walked on, but, like him with me, I never got to see the shoddy bits. When he sulked. Went out and got so pissed with his mates that he couldn't get himself home. Since I was getting pissed with him, I thought it was funny. I wouldn't think it was so funny if I was the one waiting at home. Leaving the lights on all the time. Never emptying the rubbish. All the stupid little things that annoy one person about another, they'd all pile up, eventually And that was before something really challenging happened, like infertility, illness, truancy, infidelity, death . . . the list was endless.

"You promised no cold feet. You started all of this," he said.

"I'm sorry," I said again. "But Ben, we've both been peddling the myth, leaning on each other, using the other like polyfiller. The only person who doesn't think Sasha is fun, is you. You've got to appreciate what you've got. We both must." If I didn't learn to love what I had, how could I move on? Nick had been right on so many levels. I wanted to have a family, and while that might never change, what had changed was that I no longer wanted it at any cost. And this; this was far, far too high a price to pay. I stood up. "It's time to go home, Ben."

"I'm going to sit here for a bit."

"OK. But Ben, when you go home, please be nice to Sasha. Whatever is going on between you two is one thing, but this bit, us, isn't her fault. Let her be the amazing woman she is."

He nodded.

"It's not my place to tell you what to do, but I strongly advise you to never tell her any of this. Ever."

He sighed deeply. "What about us?"

I shrugged. I hoped that we could go on being friends but in a different way from before. Better. Because we'd no longer be one another's safety net. The walk would be much more terrifying without him, but at least I'd be doing it on my own. The rewards would be mine to keep.

"Can I kiss you goodnight?" asked Ben.

It took a long time for me to reply. Finally I came up with the only answer there was. "Kiss your wife instead," I said, squeezed his shoulder and walked back into the house.

Epilogue

possibly ever after . . .

I only took Cora to Regent's Park because of the elephant. I was afraid of ruining Cora's day when we were told that the elephant had been sent elsewhere, but Cora was pleased. She didn't think London was big enough for an elephant to live in. Instead, we walked up the hill to the playground. It was too cold to sit on the bench with the other parents, so I climbed the rope wall, walked the rickety bridge, squeezed my adult bottom down the child-sized slide and generally made an ass of myself. Cora tried to escape me by making some friends, as she tended to do wherever she went, but I followed them inside the Wendy house. There we spent a happy half-hour sitting on cold, damp sand making endless birthday cakes.

"That's probably how the elephant felt," said Cora.

"I sincerely hope I'm not the elephant in this little scenario."

Cora and the two girls she'd befriended giggled.

"Cheeky monkey. Right," I said, trying to stand, "this elephant needs a coffee. My bottom has gone all itchy from the wet sand."

The girls giggled again. It was easy to make children laugh. You just had to say bottom a lot. Grown-ups aren't supposed to do that. I started to wrench myself out of the corner of the Wendy house, but it seemed to have shrunk since I'd squeezed myself in.

"Pineapple-juice man," said Cora, glancing out of the window.

"What?"

"It's the pineapple-juice man."

I glanced too. Oh my God. James Kent was walking towards the sandpit. I ducked, lost my balance and fell into a heap.

"Hide me, hide me," I whispered desperately. "Get down."

The girls immediately looked out of the window.

"Everyone, shh!" I whispered.

"Daddy!" yelled one of the girls.

Oh no, this could not be happening. James Kent was going to stick his head through a Wendy house and think that mad-psycho bitch had abducted his children. There was nowhere to hide, but I still tried.

"Hey, girls."

"Daddy, Daddy, Daddy!"

He was crouching outside the little house. I could see his feet, but he couldn't see in. I might just make it.

"We've made cakes. This is Cora, can she come to our house to play?"

"Cora?"

Then again, I might not.

"Hello, pineapple-juice man."

"Hello, Cora."

"How do you know my daddy?"

"We went to a party together," said Cora. "You got me pineapple juice."

"Yes, I did. How are you?"

"Deaf in one ear."

"Oh, I'm sorry about that."

"Actually, it's quite useful. We live on a noisy street and now I sleep on my left side and I don't hear the cars any more. But we're moving soon to a bigger house with a garden."

I was pressed against the wall.

"Godmummy T thinks I only pretend to be deaf when it suits me and that I can hear perfectly well whenever she's whispering about grown-up things that I'm not allowed to hear." There was an almighty pause. Cora looked at me, I pleaded with my eyes. "Don't you, Godmummy T?"

I closed my eyes in shame. James Kent got on to his hands and knees and peered in. He saw me cowering in the corner. I'd never been so embarrassed in all my life.

"Hi," I said.

"Hello," he said tersely, then stood up. I stared at his feet. "Come on, girls, we ought to go."

"No, no, no," cried the three girls.

"Please can we stay a bit longer? Please?"

"Ten minutes," said one of his daughters.

"Five," said James, and walked away.

I owed it to myself to clamber out of the Wendy house and explain my behavior to him, but I really didn't want to. However unfaithful he'd been, I didn't want anyone walking around with such a hideously low opinion of me. I crawled out of the house, stretched myself back into human form and walked towards the bench he was sitting on.

"I owe you some money," I said.

"Yes, you do."

His tone slightly changed my consolatory mood. "I should have explained in person that I didn't sleep with married men. I can write you a check. Joint account is it?"

"What?"

"Where is your wife?"

"My ex-wife is at home. Her home."

"Ex?"

"You thought I was married?"

"You are."

"I was. We separated four years ago."

"Four years? Are you sure?"

That came out worse than intended. He stood up and thrust his hands deep in his pockets. "Don't worry about the money. Frankly, I've tried to forget the whole sorry thing. Have a nice day."

He couldn't wait to get away from me. "Clearly I behaved badly. I'm sorry. I found out you were married and had two kids, I was . . ." Upset. Disappointed. Staggered because nothing in his behavior had hinted that he was that type and yet I didn't even bother to offer him the courtesy of an explanation. "Whatever, I shouldn't have behaved like that."

"No, you shouldn't have."

"Well, you should have told me about your daughters. A fairly big detail to leave out, don't you think?"

"You'd have run a mile. The mention of kids and you started to shudder."

"That's not true."

"'Kids, who'd have them,' I think is what you said."

"I wasn't being serious. You got that one wrong."

"Well, I wasn't married, so I guess we're even."

"Let me pay you back," I pleaded.

"Don't worry about it," said James, dismissively.

"Please?"

"No, it's fine. Honestly." He moved back towards the Wendy house. "Five minutes are up. Come on, kids, let's go home." They emerged, pink from the cold, and started to run rings around us.

"Lainy and Martha, right?" I said, trying desperately to end this on a happy note.

James nodded.

"Beautiful girls," I said.

James wasn't taken in by my pathetic attempts to suck up to him. "It's all right, Tessa. I understand now. I'm glad I ran into you, the whole thing had slightly freaked me out, but now we can forget about it."

"I thought you were married with kids. I'm sorry I didn't just stay around and ask you."

"Me too," he said.

I felt the atmosphere soften.

"Can we have our raisins now?" asked one of James's daughters. James brought the boxes out of his pocket.

"Can we share them with Cora?"

"Of course you can," said James. He was too polite to say no.

"I saw you at the funeral," I said.

"I was very sorry about your friend; you did her proud though, I thought."

I brightened. Two months on and I still wasn't sure about my ad-libbing at the funeral.

"Thank you."

"Where are the twins, by the way?"

"With Neil's parents this weekend."

"How are you coping with them? Must be hard on your own."

"Me? Oh no, they don't live with me. They're being adopted by Neil's brother. Lovely family. He's a builder, he's building an incredible extension to their house, it's like kiddy heaven there. I go up quite a bit. They're crawling now." I felt the familiar swell of pride when I thought about the twins, coupled with the familiar sting of tears when I thought about them without their mother—or rather, their mother without those little boys.

"I heard you were their guardian."

I looked at James again. "You checking up on me?" I asked, an itsy-witsy, teeny-weeny bit flirtatiously.

"No," he lied. He scuffed the ground with his shoe. "Though I did hear you'd got yourself a new job."

I smiled. "So you have been checking up on me?"

Cora and James's daughters had wolfed down the raisins and it was obvious to both James and me, though not to them, that they were cold and hungry.

"Come on, Cora, we'd better go. You need refueling."

"Us too," said James.

"Can we play again?" asked Cora.

There was a slightly awkward pause.

"Well, we're here every other weekend," said James.

Every other weekend. He really was divorced.

"Can we, Godmummy T? Can we come back?"

"Yeah," chorused the girls. "Daddy never talks to anyone in the park normally, so we're never allowed to stay and play."

He grabbed his daughters playfully around their middles and tickled them until they screamed. "Oh yeah, you two have a terrible life, no fun." They giggled again. "No toys, no treats." They laughed through their half-hearted protests. "No trips to the playground." Finally he put them down and held them to him, then he looked at me. "What do you think?"

"I'm sure we can, I'll check with Billy."

"Well, we'll be here anyway, so if you can make it then . . ." What? What was he going to say? I suppose I'll talk to you, if I have to . . . "Great," he said.

"Great," I repeated.

We all ambled towards the playground gate. I looked up at him once; he looked quickly away. We said goodbye.

"I am sorry," I said again.

"Let's forget it."

I thought about myself sitting in the park, near a playground like this one, wearing a stolen dressing gown and knocking back the wine.

"You must have thought I was an absolute nutter," I said.

"Still do," he said. But this time there was a faint smile on his lips.

We walked away in the opposite direction.

"He's nice," said Cora.

"You think?"

"For an old man."

I ruffled Cora's hair. She was getting to the age when that was beginning to really annoy her.

"Should we come back to play with them, then?" I asked her.

"Maybe," said Cora. Maybe was right. Moments later my phone rang. I didn't recognize the number. I turned back to where James and his children had gone. Could it be . . . ?

"Hello?"

"Is that Tessa King?"

Not James then. "Yes?"

"You probably don't remember me, my name's Sebastian."

"Sebastian?"

"We met at Samira's curry night."

You've got to be kidding. We did a little more than meet. "I remember." I think I started blushing.

"I know it's been a while"—nearly six months and you didn't call me once—"but, well, here's the thing, I've been invited to this amazing party in a derelict castle in Wales."

I watched James help his daughters on to their bikes then turned away. "That's nice for you," I said coolly.

"It's organized by this mad friend of mine with unlimited funds who's decided no one throws proper parties any more."

"I agree with him."

"He's hired professional cocktail makers, tequila girls, there'll be fireworks and a great band. The setting is incredible."

And Sebastian wanted to take me? I was mildly interested but not naive. "What's the catch?"

"Not a catch as such, but there is a criteria I was hoping you could help me with."

"Go on . . ."

"I'm not on loud speaker or anything am I?"

I laughed, nervously. "No."

"Well," he hesitated.

I may as well admit it. I was curious.

"You have to bring along a one-night stand."

Cora was busy picking a weed. "Kinky," I said, quietly.

"Obviously there were many options . . ."

"Obviously . . ." I said, smiling despite myself.

"But it had to be a great shag and no nutters, which kind of narrowed down the list to, well," he paused, "you. What do you think?"

I turned 180 degrees to look back down the hill. James Kent was looking our way. I took a few steps backwards, watching him watching me. What did I think? What do I think? I think that life has to be lived and while maybe meeting James Kent again in two weeks' time was an appealing thought, I wasn't going to idle in neutral waiting, dreaming up scenes that would never happen. I'd done too much of that. In the meantime, a night in a derelict castle in Wales sounded like an adventure. A little bit daring. Helen would have approved. All my friends would. Except maybe Ben. But I wasn't his unofficial mistress any more and how I lived my life no longer fell under his jurisdiction. I was as young today as I'd ever be, I was healthy as far as I knew and blissfully unattached. Those three things were worth celebrating.

"I think it sounds fun, morally dubious, but fun."

"Is that a yes?"

I raised an arm and waved at James. He waved back. This time with a broader smile across his face.

"It's a maybe," I said.

"Fair enough. The party is in three weeks. And Tessa, I'd rather not take anyone else."

Three weeks. A lot could happen in three weeks. I might be longing for a wild night in Wales. I glanced at the swings. Then, again . . .

"Sebastian, can I let you know?"

"Sure, whenever you can."

I replaced the phone in my bag and turned away, humming quietly to myself. There was nothing wrong with hedging my bets, was there? After all, anything is possible. That's the beauty of life. Cora returned to my side.

"Godmummy T?"

"Yes, sweetheart?"

"What does kinky mean?"

Ah . . . For a moment I panicked. I didn't know the answer. But then it came to me. "I don't know, darling," I said, taking Cora's hand. "Let's ask your mummy when we get home."

Acknowledgments

If this book is about anything, it is about the fact that no one knows what lies around the corner. I had written four crime novels and was struggling to find a good idea for the fifth. Then I met a girl called Catherine Gosling at a hen night and everything changed. She said she had an idea for a book about a woman, like her, with far too many godchildren, but no children of her own. We had a booze-fuelled, over-excited conversation about it between stripping, playing with sex toys and drinking far too much. I have had those kinds of evenings before (with less stripping); I meet a lot of people who have an idea for a book, and in the cold light of day wake up and realize that it was all a bad idea. Not in this case. The idea stuck and soon characters were beginning to form in my head. So, to Catherine Gosling, my fellow hen and much-loved godmother, I salute you. The birth of *The Godmother* is thanks to you.

Second thanks, then, must go to Felicity Gillespie for getting married. Because without her taking that mighty leap of faith, I wouldn't have found myself stripping in the first place. She also proved herself a great editor yet again. I'm sorry I've been so hopelessly occupied recently.

Third, but really first, I personally owe a vast amount to Eugenie Furniss at the William Morris Agency for getting the best out of me, guiding me and introducing me to certain people who shall remain nameless. All I had to say was, "You know that expression, three times the bridesmaid, never the bride? Well, this is three times the godmother, never the—" That was it. She clicked her fingers, ordered another glass of white wine, and took it from there. I wrote it but she knew who'd publish it best of all. And so to Harrie Evans and her team at Headline. What can I say but thank you, thank you, thank you. I know how hard publishing is, but you make it look easy and far too much fun. And then to Dorian Karchmar in the New York office who took this book to a whole new level, thanks to you and everyone at HarperCollins USA.

This has been both the toughest and easiest book to write. Tough because of things conspiring to stop me from writing but easy because it was like a protracted conversation with any one of my girlfriends. So to them and my sisters, I raise a glass. Thank you all, you know who you are. To David Bolton and Electra May for keeping me upright. To Anne Lewthwaite Haribin for keeping me sane. To Carmen Gloria, Vivi, Taffy, Andrea, Mickey, Amelia and Katie for giving me extra hours when I needed them most.

My love and thanks to Adam for his years of support. I know you think all my books should be dedicated to you; what I hope you know is that, deep down, they are. I love you.

TURN THE PAGE

FOR A PEEK AT

CARRIE ADAMS'

NEXT NOVEL,

THE STEPMOTHER

1

Crunchy Nut

I was surrounded by laughter but, for once, couldn't even pretend to join in. I wanted to place one of my daughters on my lap and hug her tightly, but I had taught myself not to do that. At eight, even my youngest considered herself too old for such public displays of affection. On our own at home was fine, but that wasn't when I needed her protection. I felt a hand land on my shoulder, and I automatically formed a smile as I turned.

"Thank you so much for everything you've done," said the woman looking down at me.

"I'm happy to help," I replied.

"Everyone tells me you've been amazing."

My eight-year-old beamed. If her headmistress said I was amazing, I must be doing something right.

"I am so looking forward to this," the imposing woman said as she took her seat. The nerves tightened. My nine-year-old, sitting on the other side of me, had not noticed the giant presence of her principal because she was too busy craning her neck to search the back of the room. Ever since we'd sat down, she'd been keeping a vigilant eye on the entrance. I eased her shoulders round to face the stage. "He'll be here," I said, glancing at the empty seat. "Don't worry."

"I'm not worried," she said, immediately turning back.

The lights dimmed and an awed murmur rose up from the assorted parents, siblings and extras, and dissolved into hush. Four worried conker-colored eyes sought mine in the gloom of the darkened assembly hall.

"He'll be here," I said again, taking their hands, and as the first note drifted up from the piano, he was.

"Daddy!" squeaked the girls, as they bounced off their chairs.

Jimmy eased his way along the narrow aisle with such charm that no one other than me seemed to mind. He even stopped to kiss a particularly good friend of ours, and shook some of the other dads' hands. "Sit down," I mouthed at him.

He leant over and kissed me, then both of the girls. "Sorry," he said. "Meeting went on."

I put my fingers to my lips and pointed towards the stage. The thick green velvet curtains were being drawn back to expose the mean streets of Hell's Kitchen, New York, where girls dressed as boys clicked and hissed and spat at one another, marking out the infamous territories between the Jets and the Sharks.

Then the aggression left the stage and there was our eldest daughter. She peered out at us through an invisible mirror, examining her reflection as intensely as everyone else was now examining her. Was it my imagination or did a collective gasp ripple through the audience? She looked phenomenally beautiful. Older and more self-possessed than her fourteen years—how was it possible that we had a fourteen-year-old child? I stared at Amber, moving around the stage as easily as liquid, my brain leaping ahead to her next line before she'd finished delivering the one she was on. I was impressed, mesmerized and terrified in equal measures. As for Amber, I could tell by the hem of her dress that she was as steady as a rock.

She looked beautiful. Did I say that already? Her dark red hair was pulled off her face with a white ribbon, her long, slender body still startling inside the neat, sensible dress of a good Catholic. She had skin the color of milk, but when she opened her mouth to sing, the London girls' school faded away and we fell into the world of a Puerto Rican on the eve of her first dance.

Jimmy reached over our nine-year-old and gazed into my eyes. He squeezed my hand hard, but then our middle daughter took ownership of her father and placed his hand firmly in her lap. I looked down at mine and watched as the warmth slowly left my skin and my fingers returned to their perpetual cold.

At the interval Jimmy and I were thickly showered with compliments by our parental alumni, some genuine, some tinged with green and some downright barbed. Why is it that I always remember the barbed ones?

"You must be so proud. When Talullah won her scholarship I made sure she stayed grounded by insisting she made her bed every day. It worked a treat, you should do with Amber so it doesn't all go to her head."

"She already makes her bed," I replied, confused.

"Oh," said the woman, equally confused.

We stood awkwardly until another "compliment" cut through the air like a missile.

"Wonderful, isn't she? You'll have a job on your hands keeping Amber's feet on the ground now," said a starched woman, whom I had tried hard to avoid. "It was quite a big decision to pick a girl from year nine. She's quite brilliant, absolutely the right choice, but I think there were some rather put-out mothers in the year above."

I opened my mouth to respond, but Jimmy got there first. "Thanks for the tips, ladies. We'll watch our backs." They tittered. Jimmy grabbed my elbow. "Let's go to the bar," he said.

"You'd better check for poison."

"Why me?" he asked.

"Do you want to sew on the nametags?"

"Can't you get iron-on ones, these days?"

"Yes. But answer me one question. What is an iron?"

The lines on Jimmy's face deepened in mock concentration. "You win. I drink first."

There were more "helpful" comments as we pushed our way through the crowd, but fortunately, since I have amassed a staggering eighteen daughter-years at this school, I know who and where my friends are. Manning the bar. Womanning the bar, I should say, because women dominate my life.

I left Jimmy happily surrounded by some, walked to the sheeted trestle table and picked up a handful of crisps. "Hey, Carmen," I said, to one of my favorite fellow maternal inmates.

She was pouring a concoction of cheap red wine into disposable cups. As she refilled one she mouthed, "My God, Bea, she's fucking brilliant."

This, I knew, was a genuine compliment. "One mother told me no one liked a show-off."

Carmen's jaw dropped. She reached below the table and handed me a bottle of decent white. "You'll need this, then."

I poured generously into a plastic cup, and handed it back. "She went on to reassure me that of course Amber wasn't like that."

"And so screamed a silent *yet*," said Carmen.

"Exactly."

"Shark-infested waters."

"And that's the ones who like me."

"Sweetheart, you sewed eight hundred school scrunchies by hand. No one likes you."

I raised my plastic cup to her. "Ah, but Lulu got a star in her reading test so it was worth the bleeding fingers."

"Why do you think I'm behind the bar?"

We smiled conspiratorially at one another.

"Enjoy," she said. "It's Sancerre."

"In which case you're forgiven your evil tongue."

Carmen emptied a party-size packet of ready-salted crisps into the bowl in front of me with a wink, then rushed to the other end of the bar to open several more long-life orange-juice cartons.

I helped myself to some more crisps and studied the field. The cheap wine and the accomplished show were working their magic on the throng. These were paying punters and they wanted their money's worth. Laughter moved through the air like ripples on a pond in the rain. I stood at the end of the bar and watched it. Occasionally I saw my younger two dart between adults, followed by a growing crowd of children. Amber's star status was trickling down to them. Be careful, I thought, experiencing the familiar knot of anxiety I feel for all my daughters. Star status can vanish just as quickly.

An arm slipped round my shoulders. Jimmy stood, as usual, nine inches above me. He smiled at me and his arm dropped away. He took a quick sip of my wine. "That's unusually good for this sort of thing," he said, and had another.

"Carmen's behind the bar."

His forehead creased as he tried to remember who she was. "Sarah's mother?"

"Daniella and Sophia's mother."

"Oh, yes, of course." He had no idea who Daniella and Sophia were. He bluffs well, though. Suddenly he smiled widely. "Isn't she doing an amazing job? I mean, we all knew she could sing, but sing and act and—my God, I feel disgustingly proud. I'm trying to be modest, but it's no use. When anyone tells me how great she is, I grin like an idiot and agree with them."

"That's no way to get yourself invited on to the playground committee."

Jimmy laughed at my joke. I was grateful. All too often I say things like that and the person I'm talking to starts grilling me about how important the playground committee is to their daughter's chance of becoming leader of the free world. Or, at least, marrying well.

"You're thinking evil thoughts again, aren't you?" said Jimmy.

"No."

"Yes, you are."

"How do you know?" I challenged, though, damn it, he was right.

"Because I know you."

He studied me with an intimacy that I no longer knew what to do with, so I covered my discomfort by grabbing another handful of crisps. "Okay, yes. I spend too much time inside this building. I've become institutionalized and, though I loathe my captors, I'm afraid to leave."

"Well, stop volunteering to make the sets, organize the fair, re-decorate the school and take netball practice. Though why anyone has to practice hopping about on one leg is beyond me."

I elbowed him. "Would you rather your daughters played rugby?"

"Yes."

"Bullshit."

"I would. Great sport."

"And you'd go to watch on the sidelines every Saturday after-noon, would you?"

Jimmy hesitated for a fraction of a second.

"Didn't think so."

"You're right, I wouldn't want to see any of our girls face down in a ruck." He shuddered.

The silence thickened between us. I reached for more crisps, but the bowl was empty. Jimmy pretended to scan the room for fa-miliar faces. I knew what we were both thinking. That it would be different if we'd had a boy. Everything would be different if we'd had a boy. Where were some of those "helplful" comments when you needed them?

"You've been mouthing all the words," said Jimmy, with a smile that I knew was forced.

That's the trouble with having spent the better part of your life with another person. You do know them. Sometimes, I think, too well. But I took the baton gladly. Tonight was a night to enjoy. "I wasn't, was I?"

"All the way through the first half you mouthed the words—and not just Amber's, everyone's." Now he was genuinely laughing at me.

"Oh, God," I moaned.

"Complete with intonation and expression."

"Why didn't you tell me?"

"You looked too sweet. But don't worry. Any sign you're about to stand up and prompt her, I'll bind and gag you." He then proceeded to take the piss about all the other times that binding and gagging me might have been an appropriate course of action until I was laughing, despite my attempts not to. That's the problem with Jimmy. He's always made me laugh. Except for the times when he's made me cry.

The bell rang and everyone filtered back to their seats in a neat, orderly fashion. What is it about being back on school premises, even though it's more than a quarter of a century since you last wore a uniform, that makes you feel like a schoolgirl all over again? I walk through the corridors of my daughters' school consumed by irrational thoughts of popularity and bad hair. Outside the gates I feel competent, capable, efficient and together. Inside, I feel small, fat and unworthy. And it's not that I'm reliving my own terrible schooldays, because I loved school. It's that I'm reliving my future . . . without the potential. And it scares the bejesus out of me.

I shook my head as I took my seat. This was Amber's night. Not mine. And certainly not a night for my maudlin thoughts. I may not have a great deal of potential these days, but my daughters have it by the bucketload and that's enough. It had to be.

The second half was even better than the first. Amber's performance seemed to grow with the story. I watched as my slip of a girl went from naïve to womanly to wordly as the songs spilled out of her. All of the girls performed with a gravitas that reminded me how easy it was to underestimate them. Amber wept over the bleeding body of her beloved Tony—a big-boned girl called Sammy—then stood back and sang as if her heart were breaking while we watched Tony's limp body carried out of the assembly hall by Jets and Sharks alike. Jimmy and I cried. But we cried separately. We did not hold hands.

The applause was thunderous. Everyone stood. I clapped and cried and laughed simultaneously as the cast took their bows. The girls in the audience stamped their feet, and with a surplus of energy, I did the same, which made me laugh and cry again, because I'd forgotten how much fun stamping your feet could be.

Amber stood, holding Sammy's hand, and smiled. Everyone had been impressive, but our eldest daughter had stolen the show. I don't know why that should have surprised me. She always had.

Jimmy grabbed me and the girls into a huge bear-hug and my ugly thoughts were forced aside.

Carmen tracked me down and passed me a white plastic cup with another fabulous long wink. I sipped and was startled to feel the sting of tiny bubbles bursting on my lips. I pointed at her. "You're a bloody marvel," I said, as she raised her own cup in a toast.

Suddenly a burst of applause rippled through the crowd, and people parted to let Amber and Sammy parade through like royalty. Careful, honey, I thought, careful. I scanned the room like a secret agent for the subversive enemy fire I knew was out there.

Jimmy squeezed my hand, leant down and spoke softly into my neck. "Give her tonight. We'll recalibrate tomorrow . . ." Then he did something he doesn't often do any more. He kissed my head. As I felt the hairs on my scalp settle back into place my single thought was this: Me, Jimmy. It'll be me. I'll be the one doing the recalibrating. On my own.

Amber saw us and let go of her co-star's hand, smiling at every compliment—"wonderful, brilliant, stunning"—and shaking every outstretched hand. She floated over to us.

Jimmy lifted her clean off the ground, threw her up and caught her. All eyes were on them, the women's on Jimmy, the men's, I'm ashamed to say, on Amber. No one looked at me like that any more.

Eventually Amber saw me, grinned, and put a wet kiss on my cheek. "I did it!" she shrieked.

"You did more than that, sweetheart. You were brilliant. I'm so proud of you."

"Thanks, Mum," she said, and glanced around for the next compliment. She didn't have to wait long. She blew me a wide-eyed, got-to-go kiss and allowed herself to be dragged away by a friend, whose father put his hand round her waist—slightly lower than her waist, actually.

With every compliment I imagined her puffing up like a hot-air balloon. Rather than happily watching her sail up, up and away, I found myself clinging to imaginary anchor ropes, fighting to keep her feet on the ground. "Exceptional," "phenomenal," "genius." Genius? Too much hot air was dangerous. Explosive. My knuckles were white. I stretched my fingers, half expecting to see rope burns crossing my palm.

I retreated to my safety zone. The women at the bar. Women I would be friends with irrespective of the accident of birth. Don't misunderstand me, I like most of the women at this school—that's three classes of thirty mothers—but there's a big difference between like and like-minded.

Angie slapped me on the back.

"What are you all laughing about?" I asked.

"Don't. It's too painful," she said. She had one girl at the school and three boys elsewhere.

"What?"

"Last week's save-the-animal day." She grimaced. "I forgot. Poor Ella was the only one in uniform. She screamed blue murder when she realized she wasn't an endangered animal."

"I don't know. Regent's Gate School girls are a pretty rare breed," I said, "especially the non-Russian-speaking ones."

Carmen had left her post behind the bar. She prodded me.

"Careful," I said, pulling my jumper down. "You'll lose your hand."

"Don't be silly," said Angie.

"I not only took mine to school the day after term finished," said Theresa, a GP who ran her own practice, "I brought them back a day early. My therapist would say I'm subconsciously afraid of being left alone with my children. He'd be right." Everyone laughed.

I racked my brain for a story of my own hopelessness, but couldn't come up with one. You know what? It embarrassed me. Angie and Theresa worked full-time, as I used to, and Carmen still worked part-time. Sometimes it ran smoothly, sometimes it didn't. But now I had nothing other than my children to think about so they went to school with their ballet kit, clean and ironed, their homework done, a fresh healthy snack in their bags every day without fail.

"Therapist?" I asked, wanting to change the subject.

"Fantasy therapist, along with the fantasy Pilates classes, fantasy diet and fantasy lie-ins. He's quite dishy, puts his hand on my fevered brow and tells me I'm doing brilliantly."

"You *are* doing brilliantly," I said.

She shrugged. "I know, but sometimes it would be nice to be told."

"I'll drink to that," said Carmen. The women raised their plastic cups.

Then Carmen gave her perfect, sexy smile and a second later I felt hands on my shoulders. I know that Jimmy's one of the favorite dads, boasting a near full head of hair, a sense of humor and an innate ability to talk to women. In a popularity contest with me, he'd win hands down. Years ago I trained myself not to mind.

"Ready to go?" he said.

"You've got the girls?" I asked, surprised.

"No."

I imagine only the other women heard my short sigh while I silently listed the irritations Jimmy's "no" had created. But female subtext to men's ears is like a dog whistle to any human's: they simply don't hear it. "I'll get them," I said. I'll be the bad guy. Years ago I would have sent Jimmy, but experience had taught me that he would come back empty-handed. He couldn't force his will on his eldest daughter because, where she was concerned, his only will *was* hers. I left him with my friends and sought out my shining star first.

Amber was holding court but I could tell she was tired. Over-tired, in fact, and that meant dangerous. Highs like that come at a hefty cost. I held back, forming a quick strategy. Finally I came up with something I thought had a chance of success. "Amber, darling, Dad's offering to take us to Nando's on the way home and pick something up."

"Nando's! Yum, I'm starving," said her friend Emily.

"Lucky you! We're never allowed to go there," said a girl I didn't know.

"What I wouldn't do for a plate of chips now!" said a third.

I smiled. I get a big kick out of the ravenous appetite of the prepubescent girl. I savor it, actually. I have friends with older daughters and I know it won't be long before the Special K diet worms its way into my child's consciousness.

Amber stood up. "Sorry, guys, gotta go."

"You coming tomorrow night?" Emily asked me.

"I'm coming every night. We've got the grannies and the aunts tomorrow too."

"Mayhem," said Amber, dramatically.

Here we go, I thought, taking her arm gently.

I managed to scoop up the other two on the way and the person it was hardest to prise out of the assembly hall was Jimmy. He left behind a horseshoe of crestfallen women when Maddy pulled him away from his adoring audience. Amber and Jimmy are more alike than I ever realized. Charmers. It makes them attractive to be around, but the trouble with charmers is that they need an audience. Always.

I climbed into the driver's seat, Jimmy next to me and the girls in the back. It was a cold night, and I put on the heater. Winter was stubbornly refusing to move aside for spring. I knew people were desperate for the clocks to go forward, for the season to change, but the cold early evenings suited my life. It was easier to be a hermit in the dark. I had whispered the plan and, having slipped Jimmy thirty quid because he'd spent his last cash getting a cab to the school, drove us to the fast-food place. "Anything for you?" he asked, leaning back through the open door.

"No, thanks. I'm not hungry."

A little later I let us into our small house in Kentish Town and the girls ran ahead to fight over the bucket of cholesterol now sitting in the middle of the pine kitchen table. Jimmy went to the fridge, got himself a beer, found an open bottle of wine and poured me a generous glass. The five of us sat round dissecting the performance again, as we had in the car, while the kids dipped chips into an assortment of glutinous sauces. As usual, Jimmy had ordered too much, and after a ten-minute eating frenzy, the girls pushed themselves away from the table and groaned.

"Bedtime, you lot," I said.

For once no one protested. Even Amber stood up without a fuss. "I need to rest for tomorrow. Do you mind if I don't help clear up?" she said.

Cunning . . . I thought. I'd happily throw the rest of the congealing food and paper trays away if it meant no bedtime tantrums. "Go on up. I'll put this away."

"I'm too tired to walk upstairs," said Maddy, knowing full well how her father would respond. Dutifully he picked her up, and then Lulu was begging to be carried too. But Jimmy wasn't as young as he once was—they'd have to take it in turn. It seemed like yesterday he could carry all three.

"Daddy will carry you to bed tomorrow," I said, sensing a storm brewing.

Jimmy gave me a look. I had to concentrate on stopping my jaw clamping. I knew what that look meant: he wouldn't be around tomorrow night to put them to bed. He was going to be "busy" again. I implored him not to say anything. They were too tired, and news that Daddy wouldn't be home again guaranteed a meltdown. Instead I picked up Lulu and carried her up to the room she and Maddy shared, then went downstairs to throw away the leftovers. Well, tidy up, anyway. I found it difficult to throw food away. It seemed such a waste.

"Mum! Can you bring some loo paper?" yelled Lulu.

I swallowed a cold chip. "Coming," I mumbled.

I could hear Amber singing in the bathroom as she reluctantly took off her stage makeup. I was relieved to see her emerge barefaced and swamped by Snoopy pajamas. I hugged my eldest child. "I'm so proud of you, Amber. You put so much work into that show and it paid off. I don't think even you thought you were going to be *that* good. Did you?"

"But Mummy, when the lights came up I forgot about me and became her. It was like I'd gone through the looking-glass. It wasn't until I saw you guys that I remembered who I was. It was weird."

"You were Maria absolutely. Even I forgot it was you at times," I said, stroking her hair. "But as brilliant as she was, I'm very glad I have my beautiful Amber back."

"I'm pooped," she said, flopping into her bed and reaching for a tendril of hair, which she curled round a finger and held to her face. She's been using her hair as a security blanket since the first tufts appeared behind an ear. So much easier than Lulu's rabbit, which I've lived in fear of losing for nearly a decade now. I didn't make that mistake a third time. Maddy had a muslin to cuddle up to and I used to buy them by the sackload.

"Love you, Mum."

"I love you, my amazing girl. I'll come and give you a kiss after I've settled the other two." She waved her hair-ringed fingers at me. It was these gestures, not her perfect pitch, that made me love my daughter.

Jimmy sat on the floor cross-legged between the two single beds and read from a book he'd picked off the shelf. It didn't matter that it was babyish, it didn't matter that they didn't like the story, it didn't matter that they were virtually asleep: their eyes and ears were on their father, drinking him in. My heart constricted and I retreated to the corridor. By the time I'd picked up the discarded clothes, screwed the cap on to the toothpaste, flushed the loo, put out clean uniforms for the following day, checked all three book-bags, hung up the wet laundry, disposed of the empty Nando's bucket and sorted out breakfast, the house was quiet. I went back upstairs to kiss my sleeping children, then joined Jimmy at the kitchen table. He opened the box of Crunchy Nut Corn Flakes and grabbed a handful. A few spilled out and more dropped from his hand as he threw them into his mouth.

"Sorry about tomorrow night. It'll be a late one," he said, crunching. I stared at the cereal scattered over my recently cleaned table. "I had to juggle some things to get to the play, and they've been moved to tomorrow." He put the packet back in its place but without folding down the plastic innards or the top of the box.

"It's okay," I said, itching to close it, but resisting, because I knew it would be seen as an act of aggression.

"God, she was brilliant, wasn't she?" said Jimmy.

I tore my eyes away from the bloody cereal and forced myself to remember the show. The smile returned to my lips. "Yes, she was."

"I hope they're making a movie. Lucy's coming tomorrow, right? She's got one of those digital recorders. Shall I ask her?"

I had already called Jimmy's wonderfully left-field sister and asked her. "She's bringing it."

"Perfect. That's the sort of thing we need to save up for Amber's twenty-first."

"Or her wedding," I replied. We caught one another's eye, then looked away.

"Right," said Jimmy, standing up. "I'd better be going."

I glanced at my watch. "Gosh," I said, faking a yawn, "how did it get so late?"

"Bea, I'm sorry I can't collect Lulu and Maddy tomorrow."

"It's all right. I'll sort something out. Maybe they'd like to come and see the show again."

"I would."

"Really? Do you want me to get you an extra ticket? The last night is Friday."

"Friday, Friday . . . Yes. I can come on Friday. I could take the girls afterwards for the night. Make it up to them for missing my night tomorrow, give you a break."

"Well . . ."

"Have a think, let me know. I won't make any plans."

Nor would I, since it was never going to happen. "OK. Thanks."

He gave me a brief hug. "Night, Bea."

"Night."

I heard the front door close, and as the latch clicked into place, my spine collapsed and I folded with exhaustion over the kitchen table. For a moment everything went blank. When my eyes opened again, my vision was filled with the Kellogg's cockerel. I reached for the packet, picked it up and scanned the enticing health figures. "Fortified, my arse," I said to the cockerel. "If you were fortified, I should have the strength of ten men by now." Then, as if the spirit of that damn bird had possessed me, I emptied a small hill into Lulu's bowl. By leaning back in my chair I could open the fridge, yank out the milk, pour and replace it so quickly that it was almost as if it hadn't happened.

I walked through to the front room and switched on the telly, put my feet on the table, and spooned sweet, crunchy mouthfuls of honey-coated happiness into my mouth. Hell, everyone needs a love interest. I placed the empty bowl on my chest and gazed, weary eyed, at the telly.

"I really should go to bed," I said to myself, picking up the remote and flicking through a couple of channels. I had stopped paying for cable as part of my new economy drive and didn't miss it. The kids had incredible ways of downloading all the latest series from America, and knowing I did a lot of "baby-sitting," my friends and family were generous with their boxed sets. Anyway, there was always a *CSI* on Channel Five at about this time of night.

Sure enough there was Grissom, his head in a jar of cock-roaches, and some fancy film-work to east my whirring brain.

"Five minutes," I said to myself. "Then bed."

I woke with a start and stared at the luminous green numbers on the video recorder: 12:56. I lumbered up from the gap between the sofa cushions and rubbed my eyes. I ran my dry tongue over my dry lips and knew, as clearly as if I were my old granddad, that I'd been snoring open-mouthed for a while now.

I stood up, stepped on something hard, and heard the clatter of cutlery on china. I'd upturned my cereal bowl. For once I was grateful that I had the bad habit of drinking every last drop of sweet milk at the end.

Sliding the bowl with my foot under the sofa, I reached for the light switch and forced my way up to bed. I put my clothes on the small armchair in the corner of my room, in reverse order to how I would be putting them back on in an unbearably short time.

Less than three minutes later, I was in bed with the lights off, perched precariously close to sleep but not quite stepping over the precipice. Why was I always so cold?

I curled up into a ball and tried to get warm, but all I managed to do was surround myself with a sea of cold. It was too cold to stretch my legs out, and too uncomfortable to stay trussed up like a chicken. Thinking about chickens made me think about my arch enemy, the cockerel, which made me think about my stomach, which made me fling myself into another position with such forceful loathing, that I sat up and turned on the light. I picked up the novel lying by my bed and started to read. I read and read and read until the words swarmed before my eyes and it was dawn.

Carrie Adams

CARRIE ADAMS is the author of the upcoming novel *The Stepmother*. She lives in London with her husband and three children.